D1034100

English Fiction Since 1984

Also by Brian Finney

SINCE HOW IT IS: A Study of Samuel Beckett's Later Fiction

CHRISTOPHER ISHERWOOD: A Critical Biography

THE INNER I: British Literary Autobiography of the Twentieth Century

D. H. LAWRENCE: SONS AND LOVERS: A Critical Study

English Fiction Since 1984
Narrating a Nation

Brian Finney
Associate Professor of English Literature,
California State University, Long Beach

© Brian Finney 2006

All rights reserved. No reproduction, copy or transmission of this publication may be made without written permission.

No paragraph of this publication may be reproduced, copied or transmitted save with written permission or in accordance with the provisions of the Copyright, Designs and Patents Act 1988, or under the terms of any licence permitting limited copying issued by the Copyright Licensing Agency, 90 Tottenham Court Road, London W1T 4LP.

Any person who does any unauthorised act in relation to this publication may be liable to criminal prosecution and civil claims for damages.

The author has asserted his right to be identified as the author of this work in accordance with the Copyright, Designs and Patents Act 1988.

First published 2006 by
PALGRAVE MACMILLAN
Houndmills, Basingstoke, Hampshire RG21 6XS and
175 Fifth Avenue, New York, N.Y. 10010
Companies and representatives throughout the world

PALGRAVE MACMILLAN is the global academic imprint of the Palgrave Macmillan division of St. Martin's Press, LLC and of Palgrave Macmillan Ltd. Macmillan® is a registered trademark in the United States, United Kingdom and other countries. Palgrave is a registered trademark in the European Union and other countries.

ISBN-13: 978–0–230–00855–7   hardback
ISBN-10: 0–230–00855–0   hardback

This book is printed on paper suitable for recycling and made from fully managed and sustained forest sources.

A catalogue record for this book is available from the British Library.

Library of Congress Cataloging-in-Publication Data

Finney, Brian.
    English fiction since 1984: narrating a nation/Brian Finney.
        p.cm.
    ISBN 0–230–00855–0 (cloth)
        1. English fiction–20th century–History and criticism. 2. English fiction–21st century–History and criticism. 3. History in literature. 4. Identity (Philosophical concept) in literature. 5. National characteristics in literature. I. Title.

PR881. F56 2006
823'.91409358–dc22

                                                        2006046070

10   9   8   7   6   5   4   3   2   1
15   14 13 12 11 10 09 08 07 06

Transferred to Digital Printing 2007

Contents

Acknowledgements

I want to thank Michael North, Department of English, UCLA, who has offered me valuable criticism and suggestions for improving earlier drafts of this book. Without him this would have been a less thorough and self-critical book.

I also want to thank Jacky Lavin, my wife, who encouraged me to write the book even when she knew that this would turn me into a semi-recluse for the duration of the writing.

Introduction

The primary purpose of this book is to analyze in depth one key novel written by each of eleven English writers who are representative of a new form of fiction writing that has come to dominate the two decades since 1984. The eleven novels on which this book focuses have been selected both for their intrinsic importance and to form part of an argument concerning the representation of history and identity in English fiction. The argument has been subdivided into three sections each of which addresses from a different angle the question how English fiction of this period has reconfigured the ways in which subjectivity is formed and represented within the recent history of modernity. Some of the novels could have been interpreted in a different section of the book, so that their position in it represents a compromise between the need for a fair representation of this group of writers and the demands of the book's argument. A secondary aim is to provide students and teachers of contemporary English fiction with a detailed critical analysis of eleven representative and significant novels of this period which might form the core of any course they might want to undertake under this rubric. Each of the chapters refers to much of the relevant criticism of the novel to date. The work of the generation of novelists treated here constitutes an exciting departure from most of the fiction published in England since the Second World War. It is both more innovative in its methods of narration and more ambitious and wide ranging in the material it takes for its subject. It offers thoughtful and complex fictional responses to a period of profound change in everything from international power relations and the spread of global capitalism to England's sense of national identity and the conception of subjectivity in a poststructuralist climate.

Even before the revolutionary upheavals to world order that have occurred since 1984, the Stalinist purges (1932–38), the Nazi Holocaust (1941–45), and the use of nuclear weapons to end the Second World War (1945) dramatically altered everyone's perception of the kind of civilization which they had inherited in the second half of the century. The Cold War ensured that nobody could ignore the possibility of nuclear devastation that

1

threatened to bring modernity to a premature end. As Martin Amis put it, "in one minute we turned paradise into a toilet" ("The Wit" 102). The post-war generation found itself in a unique situation. We have, Angela Carter wrote in 1983, "learned to live with the unthinkable and to think it" (*Shaking* 51). During the period of time covered by this book equally dramatic changes occurred, in particular the end of the Cold War (though not of the threat of nuclear devastation) with the breakup of the USSR (1989), leaving the United States as the only superpower headed since 2000 by an aggressively neo-imperialist administration under President George W. Bush. Far from learning from the horrors of the Nazi Holocaust, the world witnessed, and in some cases stood by while witnessing, ethnic cleansings, as their perpetrators euphemistically called genocide, in Cambodia (1975–79), Rwanda (1994), Croatia, Bosnia and Kosovo (1991–99) and Sudan (2004–present). The end of the Cold War was quickly succeeded by the Gulf War (1991), the terrorist bombing of the World Trade Center in New York (September 11, 2000), and the United States and Britain's invasion of Afghanistan (2001) and Iraq (2003). The West now found itself pitted against an invisible enemy, Islamic terrorism, which has rapidly transformed the nature of the experience of modernity in the new century, as the bombings in Madrid (2004) and London (2005) demonstrated. Rushdie observed that the attack on the World Trade Center was intended "to shape our own imaginings of the future." Its message was "that the modern world itself was the enemy, and would be destroyed" (*Step* 375). Late modernity seems unavoidably tied to a sense of apocalypse.

What this new generation of English writers have in common has less to do with a similar aesthetic than with a shared response to the changing world of the closing years of the millennium. They offer a bewildering variety of narrative modes, voices and tones. But all of them place their narratives within a context, not of one class on a small island, but of a world which is threatened by the very success of the project of modernity, a world which is so thoroughly interconnected that it is no longer possible to treat any part of it as unaffected by everything else in it. This partly explains why these narrations of a nation often see questions of identity within a much wider context than that of English or British society. These novelists are very conscious of the difference between their work and that of their immediate predecessors which seemed to them an inadequate response to the modern world they grew up in. "In its current form," Martin Amis said in 1990, "the typical English novel is 225 sanitized pages about the middle classes" ("Down London's Mean Streets" 35). Ian McEwan similarly claimed that English writing in the late 1960s "was either very tiny, self-contained, or it wore an ironic sneer which allowed it no real moments of awe or silence" ("Ian McEwan's War Zone" 181). Like Martin Amis, he looked abroad, especially to American novelists like Saul Bellow and Philip Roth, for his inspiration. Most of the earlier postwar English writers lacked what Salman

Rushdie sees as a defining characteristic of the best of this later generation of novelists, "the courage or even the energy to bite off a big chunk of the universe and chew it over" (*Step* 35). Seen from the perspective of 1980, the English novel was being widely written off as "cosily provincial" (Bigsby 137), "local, quaint, and self-consciously xenophobic" (Bowers 150).

This was also the view of Bill Buford, the editor of *Granta*, a new literary magazine launched in 1979. The editorial in the first issue, which introduced English readers to an exciting sample of new American fiction writers of the time, blamed British publishers most for the fact that "British fiction of the fifties, sixties, and even most of the seventies variously appears as a monotonously protracted, realistically rendered monologue. It lacks excitement, wants drive, provides comforts not challenges." ("Introduction" 3). However by its third issue the following year Buford detected a new kind of writing in Britain: "which, freed from the middle-class monologue, is experimentation in the real sense, exploiting traditions and not being wasted by them . . . The fiction of today is . . . testimony to an invasion of outsiders, using a language much larger than the culture" ("Introduction" 16). This new English fiction (not all by outsiders) of the 1980s and beyond has come to be seen as constituting a renaissance in the English novel, "re-establishing itself as the pre-eminent literary form by the turn of the twenty-first century" (Morrison 4). Naming fellow writers Timothy Mo, Martin Amis, Ian McEwan, Julian Barnes, and Angela Carter, Rushdie claimed in 1989 that what distinguished this "very un-English" new literary generation was that its "horizons are broader, its experience of life is perhaps not so relentlessly white middle class. The world of the book is bigger than it has been" ("Salman Rushdie Interviewed" 18). Kazuo Ishiguro in interview expressed a similar definition of what differentiated his and his generation's work: "I'm interested in writing things that will be of interest to people in . . . a hundred years' time, and to people in different cultures" ("Rooted" 153). These English novelists no longer exclusively address an insular English middle class readership. Viewing England (frequently cosmopolitan London) as a microcosm, they write to the world about the world in general. In Rushdie's 2005 novel, *Shalimar the Clown*, the character India reflects, "Everywhere was now part of everywhere else. Russia, America, London, Kashmir. Our lives, our stories, flowed into one another's, were no longer our own, individual, discrete" (37).

This widening of the English novel's frame of reference is partly the consequence of a parallel widening that characterized British society over this period. By the 1980s the nation had shed most of its colonial possessions and most of its pretensions as an imperial power. The Suez Crisis of 1956 had decisively demonstrated to the country its new diminished status in world affairs. The 1973 Oil Crisis brought home Britain's dependence on other countries, including its own ex-colonies, for its economic survival. Britain had to enter into partnerships with the United States and with the

European Common Market (which it joined in 1974) to promote its national interests. The nation acknowledged through its policies and attitudes that it was now part of the new global economy, and that London was a multi-cultural and international capital, not the center of a shrinking and out-dated empire. Just as former colonized peoples were colonizing the imperial center in increasing numbers in the postwar years, immigrating from the Caribbean, the Indian Subcontinent and parts of Africa, so, according to Rushdie, "the peoples that were once colonized by the language [were] now rapidly remaking it, domesticating it" (*Imaginary Homelands* 64). Bruce King claims that "the new immigrants made English literature international in other ways than it had been during the Empire" (1), transforming a near-homogenous white England into what Linton Kwesi Johnson calls "Inglan," and London into the "Ellowen Deeowen" of *The Satanic Verses*.

Margaret Thatcher and her Conservative administrations from 1979–90 were most directly responsible for much of the transformation that overtook Britain in the 1980s. Stuart Hall wrote one of the most penetrating analyses of the ideology of "Thatcherism" in an essay, "The Toad in the Garden" (1988). In effect, he argues, she helped form a new hegemony radically different from that of older versions of conservatism which went along with the social democratic consensus that had dominated the political scene since the War. "The aim," Hall wrote, "was to reconstruct social life as a whole around a return to the old values—the philosophies of tradition, Englishness, respectability, patriarchalism, family, and the nation" ("Toad" 39). She made freedom equivalent to the free market. Privatization became a public service. She succeeded in ideologically winning over substantial sections of Labour's social base. Hall termed her new "combination of imposition of social discipline from above . . . and of populist mobilization from below" "authoritarian populism" (40–41). Countering the unpopularity of the massive unemployment its policies produced with appeals to old-fashioned patriotism (especially during the so-called Falklands War of 1982[1]), Thatcherism became popular among many of those who were most adversely affected by it. Part of Hall's explanation of this paradoxical political phenomenon was that the discourse of Thatcherism "depend[ed] on the subject addressed assuming a number of specific subject positions." So "the liberty-loving citizen is *also* the worried parent, the respectable housewife, the careful manager of the household budget, the solid English citizen 'proud to be British . . . .'" ("Toad" 49). Julian Barnes observed that a fundamental mistake made by her opponents was that what she had done could and would eventually be undone. "Now, post-Thatcher," he wrote in 1993, "the pendulum continues to swing, but inside a clock that has been rehung on the wall at a completely different angle" (*Letters* 220).

Many of the novelists on whom this book focuses blamed Mrs Thatcher at the time for the uncaring society that they claimed she brought about by turning her back on the Keynesian consensus-based society on which Britain had modeled itself since World War II. For Rushdie her premiership was a "catastrophe" ("Keeping Up" 29). For Ian McEwan, "England under Mrs Thatcher" left him "with a nasty taste" (Haffenden 187). Martin Amis wrote of "the boutique squalor of Thatcher's England (or its southeastern quadrant)" (*War* 19). Kureishi thought that her "pre-war Methodist prig-gishness" was responsible for the repudiation of the sixties' pleasure-seeking ethos he found so liberating and for "the resurrection of control" in the country (*My Beautiful Laundrette* 116). But, as Stuart Hall astutely observed in "The Meaning of New Times" (1989), Thatcherism was simply a manifesta-tion of a much larger global hegemony, of "social, economic, political and cultural changes of a deeper kind taking place in western capitalist societies" ("Meaning" 223). Hall and others came to call the new social and discursive formation affecting not just Thatcher's Britain but Reagan's United States and elsewhere "New Times." This formation was given various labels, none of which comprehended every aspect of the momentous changes that went to constitute these New Times, labels like post-Fordism, post-industrialism, and post-modernism. What is common to all such historical terms is the preface "post-" (as it is in post-humanism, post-colonialism, post-structural-ism and post-Marxism), which suggests that they all represent the final decades of the twentieth century as a period clearly demarcated from, and defined in contrast to, the past. At the least this period is seen as a dramat-ic new phase in the ongoing project of modernity. Hall insists that "Marx was one of the earliest people to grasp the revolutionary connection between capitalism and modernity" ("Meaning" 228–29). Capitalism, Marx wrote in the *Communist Manifesto*, entails the "constant revolutionizing of production, uninterrupted disturbance of all social relations, everlasting uncertainty and agitation," which serves equally as a definition of moder-nity (229). Situated in its midst, Hall calls this new phase of modernity "a permanently Transitional Age" ("Meaning" 232).

Like most of the novelists considered in this book, I prefer to avoid exclu-sively calling this new phase of modernity postmodern because it is unsat-isfactory as a term of periodization (it fails to apply to much of contemporary culture) and it is too limiting and negative a term when used philosophically/aesthetically (many contemporary writers still subscribe to various metanarratives). As Hall insists, modernity is by its nature paradox-ical, and the paradoxes of late modernity are distinguished by being ever more extreme:

> material abundance here, producing poverty and immiseration there; greater diversity and choice—but often at the cost of commodification, fragmentation and isolation ... The rich "West"—and the famine-strick-en South. Forms of "development" which destroy faster than they create. ("Meaning" 229–30)

Whereas Lyotardian postmodernists reject the grand (or global) narratives of modernity and equate the postmodern with *petits récits*, the local and the particular, Hall claims that the "New Times have gone 'global' and 'local' at the same moment" (237).[2] Thus Rushdie, invoking Jean-François Lyotard's *The Postmodern Condition* (1979, 1984) in 1990, can champion the novel as *the* form which embraces the "rejection of totalized explanations" (*Imaginary Homelands* 422), and yet his own novel of that time, *The Satanic Verses* (1988), represents a totalized defense of his pluralist stance. It simultaneously attacks the monologic discourse of Islamic fundamentalism and of English racism while promoting its own monologic discourse concerning the superiority of plural, competing discourses within the novel, the form "which takes the 'privileged arena' of conflicting discourses *right inside our heads*" (426). Rushdie's paradoxical combination of the unitary and the plural, the local and the global, in this novel's treatment of late-twentieth-century modernity is one of its great strengths. *The Satanic Verses*, like many of the other novels considered in this book, transcends conventional definitions of the postmodern. This does not mean that the term "postmodernism" cannot be employed productively in specific cases. For instance I have used the concept of the postmodern sublime as the major theoretical perspective in the chapter on Martin Amis's *Time's Arrow*, in part because Amis himself wrote an essay expressing his admiration for Nabokov's use of the sublime.

While avoiding categorizing all the fiction of this group of writers as postmodern, I do draw on poststructuralist (including postmodern) theory throughout the book. As all of these writers grew up in an intellectual climate dominated by poststructuralist thought, it seems appropriate to draw on this body of theoretical work when interpreting their fiction. "Is Nothing Sacred?", the 1990 essay by Rushdie which I cited above, quotes not just Lyotard, but Karl Marx, Richard Rorty, and Michel Foucault. Angela Carter showed an extensive acquaintance with the work of Roland Barthes when reviewing works by him and Georges Bataille. A. S. Byatt, who spent part of her life as an English academic, writes sophisticated reviews of works by Jacques Derrida, Monique Wittig, Hayden White, Georges Bataille, and Paul Ricoeur, among others. At the same time she distances herself from literary theory even while she makes ironic use of it in a work like *Possession*: "I think many younger [writers] feel no relation at all to the world of academic criticism, which has moved far away from their concerns" (*On Histories* 6). I certainly do not, as Byatt claims of contemporary critics, "feel almost a gladiatorial antagonism to the author" (6). Nor do I identify with any particular formulation of poststructuralist theory, but use it eclectically, choosing where appropriate whatever theoretical approach best illuminates the fictional text concerned. But it can be revealing to draw on the thinking of theoretical writers who are coterminous with these novelists (who are aware of their thinking), as each draws inspiration from the other, and both help to establish a common set of responses to the contemporary world. Writers and theorists alike of this period see language not as a method of communication that reflects an empirical reality beyond it, but as one that creates subjective reality. The self or subject is no longer regarded within a poststructuralist universe as the origin and foundation of knowledge, an assumption on which humanism is founded. Rather the self is seen as constructed by language and the values already inherent in language—values that reflect the identity politics of a nation that is in the process of redefining itself.

The poststructuralist self or subject is not an autonomous, unified entity. It is a multiple construct, different selves being called into being by different discourses—discourses of nationality, class, gender, etc. One of the founders of structuralism, Claude Lévi-Strauss, like Émile Benveniste and Roman Jakobson, never felt that he was unified in a central identity: "I appear to myself as the place where something is going on, but there is no 'I', no 'me'. Each of us is a kind of crossroads where things happen," he said (Interview, CBC). John Banville, an Irish novelist who is a contemporary of this group of novelists, said something remarkably similar to an interviewer: "When I look inside myself, I don't find a John Banville. I increasingly have come to the conclusion that there is no self. There is an infinite succession of selves" (Martelle E8). Stuart Hall argues that because the new hegemonic formation of the late twentieth century has expanded the number of positionalities and identities available to ordinary people, "the individual subject has become more important." But, Hall reminds us, the modern subject is "composed of multiple 'selves' or identities in relation to the different social worlds we inhabit, something with a history, 'produced', in process" ("Meaning" 226).

This fluid sense of multiple identity, shared by most poststructuralists, surfaces in various ways in many of the novels focused on in this book. The first section of this book, History, Modernity and Metafiction, shows how some of these writers situate the subject within the discourse of history, a history which demonstrates the increasing interdependence of Britain and both the West and the global economy. This can entail, for instance, splitting the narrator/protagonist between a narrating and narrated subject each moving in opposite directions through history and from east to west, as Amis does in *Time's Arrow*, or leaving the reader in doubt whether the characters in Byatt's *Possession* possess, or are possessed by, the past in which national interests predominate. Historical memory, as the Preface to this section argues, is a vital component of identity, both that of the country and the self. The second section, National Cultures and Hybrid Narrative Modes, looks at ways in which migrant identities are either torn between two competing national cultures, or, as Rushdie puts it, "become mutants." But, he adds, "it is out of such hybridization that newness can emerge," as is the case with Saladin in *The Satanic Verses* and Changez in *The Buddha of Suburbia* (*Imaginary Homelands* 210). National and ethnic hybridity has come to characterize much of the new generation's sense of selfhood. The English—and particularly Londoners—have been compelled by changing demographics to think of themselves as heterogeneous rather than homogonous. The last section, Narrative Constructions of Identity, looks successively at the way in which gender (Carter), sexual orientation (Winterson) and class (Swift) can interpellate individuals into socially constructed positions. There is an identifiable relationship between such subject positions and the society and nation constructing those positions. Yet just as these novelists don't wholeheartedly subscribe to the poststructuralist conception of the self and insist on the possibility of individual agency, so I in my interpretations do not assume that poststructuralism's explanation of identity is infallible. It is no more than a commonly held attitude during this period in the face of the vexed question of how the self is constituted. Even Foucault, the epitome of poststructuralist thinking, was moving away from such a purely determinist understanding of subjectivity in his last two published books on the history of sexuality.

The nature of identity in a country undergoing rapid change, during a period when identities of all kinds were being radically questioned and undermined, is a topic that is of central interest to all this generation of English novelists. Thus, for instance, the problems of defining just what it meant to be English surfaces in their work at a time when loss of empire (the defining other) and devolution of England's "internal empire" (Scotland and Wales) left the English searching for a sense of specifically English identity. All the novelists considered in this book are English, although Rushdie, despite becoming a naturalized British subject, can equally be seen as international. The English used the term "British" up to the beginning of this period as a way of obscuring or evading their domination of the whole of Britain. Antony Easthope argues that national cultures are both "material in that they are produced through institutions, practices and traditions," and "are reproduced through narratives and discourses" (*Englishness* 12). Collective identity, such as national identity, he continues, involves identification with a discourse of which it is an effect. But since all discourses are constituted by rules of limit and exclusion, Easthope, quoting Slavoj Zizek, concludes, "Englishness thus becomes an 'internal limit', an unattainable point which prevents empirical Englishmen from achieving full identity-with-themselves" (22). Or as Lily reflects in Will Self's *How the Dead Live* (2000), "nowadays almost anyone is more English than the English" (94).[3]

I am not avoiding the use of the term "British" because it has become, as Phillip Tew argues, unjustly associated with "its middle-class, imperial roots," thereby leaving its user open to charges of racism and imperialism (34). True Britishness, as Tew rightly points out, has always acted as a term that is diverse "in a regional and class sense, to which progressively one can add gender and ethnicity" (34). Besides, it is extremely difficult to disentangle the two terms, "British" and "English." The latter term hardly avoids the embarrassing associations of the former with a past imperialism which turns both terms into negative definitions that invite opposition by the liberal critic. I use the term "English" not simply because all the novels I analyze in this book are about English characters (of whatever ethnic origin or class affiliation) set in English or international settings (but virtually never in Wales, Scotland, or Northern Ireland). It is also the case that their authors belong to a period of time when the fragmentation of Britain has forced those living in England (including most of these novelists) to search for an identity separate from the earlier identification with Britain as an entity. As Phillip Tew insists, "The frequent critical conflation of Englishness with Britain . . . in part is rooted in the simple demographic reality that the population of England is larger than all the other regions combined by a factor of around five times, . . . is half the land mass and certainly could be argued to be culturally dominant" (34). It would be easy to hide behind the catchall term "British." I prefer a definition that embraces all the novels I consider in this book. At the same time I recognize the number of important writers this parameter compels me to leave out of consideration, novelists like James Kelman and Irvine Welsh, writers who, as Ian Bell writes in *Peripheral Visions,* "seem to be actively contesting the status of London as the 'core' of British culture" (3). The distinction between Britain and England remains confused, as much within the novels focused on in this book as in the country at large. So the conflation of the two terms will inevitably recur in individual chapters, reinforcing the fact that the time period in which these novels were published is marked by conflicting concepts of national identity.

The problems directly associated with national identity are given prominence in the three novels analyzed in the second section of this book. But they can be discerned as unsettling any sense of self-presence in *Atonement* in the first section where the younger generation find themselves alienated from the older hierarchical notion of English society, which the mother holds so strongly that she causes her elder daughter's life to unravel. Problems of national identity are similarly responsible for the difference in A.S. Byatt's "Morpho Eugenia" between the inbred aristocratic family of the Alabasters destined for evolutionary extinction and the lower middle class William and Matilda who end up leaving a hidebound England for the Amazon. National identity is equally an issue that complicates Vince's sense of his self-worth in his dealings with Mr Hussein in *Last Orders,* and Fevvers's dealings with her American lover Walser in *Nights at the Circus.* Even where the focus appears to be concentrated on the relationship between history and contemporaneity or on the construction of individual identity, these novelists are situating their narration within the larger context of national history and national constructions of identity. Class, for instance, operates in very different ways for the English than, say, for Americans. But in every case characters are seen to be the effect of multiple identities, so that in *Last Orders* Vince's class and gender affiliations interact and compete with his xenophobic sense of national identity, just as Saladin's earlier assimilation with, and later distancing of himself from, English culture in *The Satanic Verses* is also the product of his professional identity as an actor and his family identity as a rejected husband. Peter Ackroyd has developed an entire theory about the nature of the English tradition in literature. The idea that "all the previous structures of our language lie just beneath the one we are presently using" (*Collection* 369) provides the glue which holds the three historically separate strands of *Chatterton* (or the two of *Hawksmoor*) together. So English national and cultural identity is a problematic presence that is common to most of these novels, surfacing as a major theme in some and remaining a subterranean presence in others.

The other part of my argument in this book concerns the ways in which these novelists have felt the need to seek out new and alternative forms, strategies, tones, and styles in which to narrate their experience of what I have been calling late modernity. The contradictory way in which this period is constituted has forced this generation of novelists to respond to it with equally paradoxical ways of narrating it. There is no common response among them unless it is a determination to find innovative fictional forms and narrative strategies that aesthetically correspond to the paradoxical nature of the world they are refracting in their work. However, many of them see what they are doing as some kind of reaction against fictional realism. "Realism is a footling consideration," Amis has said (Haffenden 8). Ishiguro, reacting against the common interpretation of *The Remains of the Day* as "a slice of social history," told an interviewer, "I wished to move right away from straight realism" ("Artist"). Carter insists that "there's a materiality to imaginative life"; "the story is always real as story" (Haffenden 85, 80). Winterson is contemptuous of "the mimicry of Realism." "Art is excess," she insists (*Art Objects* 72, 94). For Rushdie, as for Saleem, "[r]eality is a question of perspective; . . . or rather, it becomes clear that illusion itself *is* reality" (*Midnight's Children* 189). But what each writer means by literary realism is rarely defined and differs from one novelist to another. Following Brecht, Andrzej Gasiorek, in his book-length examination of postwar British novelists who try to reconceptualize realism, views literary realism "as a family of writings that share a certain cognitive attitude to the world, which manifests itself in a variety of forms in different historical periods" (v). "Realism," Gasiorek, insists, "cannot be aligned with any particular political position or any given set of fictional techniques" (191). All of the novelists I consider believe that they are offering a truer representation of reality by departing from what they understand to be narrative realism, by which they seem to mean mimetic artifice. But all of them share with realist writers what Gasiorek calls their "general orientation to the world: they believe it has an existence that is independent from the perceptions of the cognizing self, and that the writer's task is to explore that enormously complex world as fully as possible" (191).

This is what distinguishes the writers focused on in this book from the earlier avant-garde group of postwar English novelists who were themselves inspired by the *nouveaux roman* (new novel), the work of Alain Robbe-Grillet, Michel Butor, Nathalie Sarraute, and Claude Simon.[4] Robbe-Grillet, the leading exponent, was anti-humanist in that, as Roland Barthes wrote, he "describes objects in order to expel man from them" (*Critical Essays* 94). These French writers dispensed with psychological motivation and conventional plotting in favor of what Robbe-Grillet called "the movement of the writing" (64), turning the novel into what Butor termed "the laboratory of narrative" (Jefferson 17). Yet they saw this radical subversion of the traditional novel as a heightened form of realism. The same is true of the group of English novelists who published a similar brand of avant-garde fiction in the 1960s. The best known of these are B. S. Johnson and Christine Brooke-Rose. Frank Kermode summarizes the common element running through all Johnson's work: "Johnson's plan to revolutionize the novel came down to the use of 'devices' intended to disrupt ordinary forms of attention by involving the physical book itself, the material base of writing, in unusual ways, as if to take revenge on it for a long history of tyranny" ("Retripotent" 11). Johnson's novels employ typographical playfulness including blank pages, a hole in two pages to reveal the future text on the third one, and most notoriously in the case of his third novel, *The Unfortunates* (1969), a novel in a box, consisting of twenty seven unbound chapters of which only the first and last were identified as such at the urging of his publisher. Yet, as Dominic Head observes, beneath the physical innovation lies a personal memoir that could as easily have been narrated in a conventionally bound novel (228).

Christine Brooke-Rose is certainly more deeply radical and is steeped in poststructuralist theory. Her fifth novel, *Out* (1964) is, according to her, the only novel written directly under the influence of Robbe-Grillet and the *nouveau roman*. Looked at retrospectively, it forms the first of what she has called her successive attempts "to expand the possibilities of the novel form" (Tredell 30). Reviewers insisted on treating all her subsequent novels as English offshoots of the *nouveau roman*, despite her moving further away from it with each subsequent novel she published. But the direction she chose to move in was to "explode human discourse" (Brooke-Rose, "Ill Wit" 137). When she published *Amalgamemnon* (1984), the first of a quartet of novels which began as "an effort towards more readability" (Tredell 30), she confined her use of verbs to the future, conditional, subjunctive and imperative moods. "As a result," Richard Martin comments, "everything is talked about but nothing *can* happen" (119). The commitment of this group of avant-garde novelists to formal experimentation left them marginalized by readers, even when their intentions were to offer critiques of English society or of modernity itself. Their narrative experimentation came across as disconnected from the subject of their narration. Or, to put it another way, it is as if narrative experimentation took priority and dictated the narrative content.

John Fowles's *The French Lieutenant's Woman* (1969) may have acted as the more immediate predecessor to this later group of novelists who rose to prominence in the 1980s. He combines formal innovation with contemporary ideological interests (in, for instance, existentialism) and accessibility. Where Fowles captures the reader with the lure of sexual desire thwarted for the length of most of *The French Lieutenant's Woman,* Christine Brooke-Rose in *Between* (1968) subordinates acts of sex to a desire to have her heroine, like the Saussurean sign, define herself against her negative. So the protagonist of *Between,* a female translator who spends her time flying between conferences, is equally circumscribed by the positive and negative regulations of planes and airports (Fasten Your Seat Belts. No Smoking) and of successive lovers whose act of intercourse becomes "the confusional sliding from active to passive" (157). There is still, however, a distance between Fowles and these later writers considered in this book. Two of them who have reviewed Fowles's work distance themselves from it, both having major reservations about it. A. S. Byatt sees *The French Lieutenant's Woman* as being one of those "modern diminishing parodies" of the complexities of Victorian attitudes and beliefs and criticizes Fowles's use of an "existential moment of crisis of faith" when writing "natural histories, centring on a set of beliefs in gradual change" (*On Histories* 79). Martin Amis is more broadly dismissive. Referring disparagingly to "Fowles's considerable gifts as a middlebrow story-teller," Amis sees him as "giving people the impression that culture is what they are getting. He sweetens the pill: but the pill was saccharine all along" (*The War* 140).

So what is it that distinguishes the present group of writers from their predecessors? Put in the broadest terms, they combine a serious and complex response to the contemporary world with both a respect for the power of and desire for narratives and a realization that this late phase of modernity necessitates distinctive modes of narrating it. Like Fowles but for different reasons, they accept the fact that an omniscient narrator is an anachronism. But they do not use the fragmentation of their contemporary world to serve as an excuse to fall back on linguistic or metafictional play for its own sake. In every case the narrative strategy that each of these novelists employs represents their solution to the problem of how to narrate their response to contemporary life. Only when Martin Amis had discovered the technique of chronological inversion did he have the confidence to tell a story about the Holocaust. The how preceded and made possible the what. Narrative strategy for these writers is not a supplementary technique to be applied retrospectively to material that has an independent existence. The mode of narration enables the nature of the narrative itself. By inventing a woman with wings, Carter simultaneously entered her own world of magic realism and made it possible to embody in narrative form her unique understanding of the triumphs and excesses of twentieth-century feminism. Her feminist heroine is a narrator whose powers overwhelm not just the man she desires but the reader. A narrative about feminine subjectivity becomes also a narrative about narrativity, each being bound up with the other. The same is true of all these novels. Swift's narrative use of disrupted chronology reproduces the ways in which the past are part of and affect the present. The transition from a pseudo-realist to a surreal mode of narration in *When We Were Orphans* gives narrative substance to the protagonist's (and his world's) psychological reversion to a state of childhood fantasy which is responsible for his private tragedy and on a larger canvas for the outbreak of war. Winterson's use of an ungendered narrator enables her to construct a narrative about love and desire outside the heterosexual paradigm. So this book is equally concerned to examine on the one hand how these eleven novelists fictionally represent the contradictions of late modern life haunted by history's nightmares and by a crisis in various forms of identity, and on the other hand how these novelists have sought out narrative forms and strategies that enable them to respond to this phase of modernity appropriately, creatively, and enjoyably.

There is no conclusion to this book. Apart from Angela Carter all these writers are still publishing new and challenging work. Some, like Ian McEwan, have only recently reached their peak of achievement to date with *Atonement* (2001) and *Saturday* (2005). Jeanette Winterson has regained her readership, whom she appeared in danger of losing in mid-career, with the appearance of *The PowerBook* (2000) and *Lighthousekeeping* (2004). Julian Barnes's most recent novel, *Arthur and George* (2005), moves him closer to the genre of the kind of historical fiction associated with Peter Ackroyd, while simultaneously confronting the problematics of Englishness (the Scotsman Arthur tells the Scottish-Indian George that they are both "unofficial Englishmen" [217]). Kazuo Ishiguro has made light use of the genre of science fiction in *Never Let Me Go* (2005). The world which all these writers live in and refract in their fiction is still in a volatile and transitional state. It is too early to say whether the present ideological divide between global capitalism and Islamic fundamentalism will be responsible for the dominant hegemonic struggle in the foreseeable future, or whether the elevation of China to superpower status, or some totally unexpected development will fundamentally transform the world in the early twenty-first century. What does seem likely is that English fiction will continue to reflect global seen as national concerns (or vice versa), just as it is likely to continue to seek out new ways of narrating the bewildering nature of modernity in the new century.

Part I History, Modernity and Metafiction

Preface

Since the publication of John Fowles's *The French Lieutenant's Woman* in 1969 there has been a remarkable resurgence of the reworking of history in the contemporary English novel. Richard Lane and Philip Tew claim to identify "what might be regarded as a new phase of the historical novel" visible by 1979 (11). Many of these novels are not strictly historical novels in the traditional sense. As Margaret Scanlan points out, quoting Hans Vilmar Geppert, opposed to the traditional historical novel "there was always an 'other historical novel': skeptical, ironic, and 'discontinuous,' seeking to exploit rather than cover up the boundaries between history and fiction" (3).[1] Scanlan cites Thackeray's *Vanity Fair* (1847–48) as the first major instance in English of this alternative tradition. Steven Connor makes a similar distinction between *historical* and *historicized* fiction based on "the degree of historical self-consciousness" each implies (142). Whereas the former "enacts the possibility of a knowable and continuous history," the latter "suggests a discontinuous history, or the potential for many different, conflicting histories" (142). Novelists sharing this widespread renewed interest in history have largely adopted this alternative form of historicized fiction. Why is this so?

The concurrent change in the way historians understood the nature of historical writing may have played a part in novelists' renewed interest in the historicized novel or novel of history in the late 1970s. In *Metahistory* (1973) Hayden White drew historians' attention to the extent to which historical accounts are the products of narrative strategies. Histories, he wrote, "contain a deep structural content which is generally poetic, and specifically linguistic, in nature, and which serves as the precritically accepted paradigm of what a distinctively 'historical' explanation should be" (ix). Taking the historical events constituting the French Revolution, White showed how four different nineteenth-century historians offer four different accounts that correspond to the "mode of emplotment" each employs. Each of the four historians (Michelet, Ranke, Tocqueville, and Burckhard) "told a different *kind of story*—Romance, Comedy, Tragedy, or Satire" (*Metahistory* 143). Historical narrative, White concludes, is simply "a kind of archetype of the

17

'realistic' pole of representation," another mode of narration that is subject to the same premises and indeterminacies as fictional or imaginative forms of narrative (*Tropics* 89). "It does not matter whether the world is conceived to be real or only imagined; the manner of making sense of it is the same" (*Tropics* 98). White's (and others') focus on history as a form of narrative has encouraged "not so much the discrediting of history, as the acceleration and diversification of its modes and meanings" (Connor 163). Once the barriers separating historical from fictional narrative had been removed historians felt freer to consciously borrow from the strategies of novelists to appropriate material previously considered outside the province of history. Novelists felt equally liberated. A. S. Byatt explicitly argues that the recent trend in historiography that emphasizes our inability to know the past "is one reason why so many novelists have taken to it" (*On Histories* 11).

While making use of this new authority granted to narrative to interpret history from the underside by deconstructing traditional history's controlling myths, these recent novels of history pointedly refrain from substituting their own controlling myths. Instead they foreground the difficulties and dangers of attempting to recover the past in narrative form. Thus Peter Ackroyd says, "My own interest isn't so much in writing historical fiction as it is in writing about the nature of history as such" (Interview. *Contemporary* 3). Similarly Tom Crick, the narrator/protagonist of Graham Swift's *Waterland* (1983), melodramatically addresses his class (and readers): "I present to you History, the fabrication, the diversion, the reality-obscuring drama" (40). Specifically these novelists offer metafictional discussions of the fictional enterprise they have entered into of narrating the past. Metafictional interventions are not new to the later twentieth century. Instances of English metafiction date back to at least *Tristram Shandy* (1760) where narrative interjections provide, as Patricia Waugh writes, a "*general insight* into the very essence of narrative—its inescapable linearity, its necessary selectiveness as it translates the non-verbal into the verbal" (69). But the later twentieth-century phase of fictional writing about the past is so frequently drawn to the metafictional mode that Linda Hutcheon has characterized it as a separate genre which she calls historiographic metafiction and which she identifies as the dominant form of postmodern fiction: "its theoretical self-awareness of history and fiction as human constructs (historiographic metafiction) is made the grounds for its rethinking and reworking of the forms and contents of the past" (*A Poetics* 5). Recent English novels of history make frequent use of metafictional devices to foreground the problems involved in recovering the past, problems which are essentially narrative problems. Such fiction embodies and discusses issues involved in the narrative interaction of historiography and fiction, "issues surrounding the nature of identity and subjectivity; the question of reference and representation; the intertextual nature of the past; and the ideological implications of writing about history" (Hutcheon, *Poetics* 117).

Hutcheon's explanation of the appearance of the self-conscious novel of history belongs to a phase of poststructuralism that saw the world of referents as wholly subject to the workings of textuality. But the appearance of this form of fiction can be equally attributed to the traumatic changes that overtook Britain after World War II—the loss of empire starting with the Indian subcontinent in 1947; the accompanying loss of any pretense to superpower status (brought home humiliatingly with the Suez Crisis of 1956); the new and continuing threat of a nuclear holocaust (which came so near to reality with the Cuban Missile Crisis of 1962); the arrival of immigrants, especially from the Caribbean (starting with the *Windrush* in 1948) and Asia, confusing an imaginary sense of national identity; the abandonment of consensus politics and the conversion of Britain from a manufacturing to a service economy under Margaret Thatcher (1979–90)—to reiterate some of the more obvious changes. This rapid transformation of the old order and old way of representing that order created a demand for a reinterpretation of the past—a debunking of imperial glory, an abandonment of a dominant notion of history centered on Britain and a search for its underside, its previously buried histories (of women, of subalterns, of the working class, etc.). This demand can be evidenced equally in Foucault's theoretical insistence on freeing "the history of thought from its subjection to transcendence," that is from its defense of "the rights of continuous history" (*Archaeology* 203), and in the discontinuities of history to be found in the fictions of novelists like John Fowles, Julian Barnes, Salman Rushdie, and other writers of the novel of history. As Steven Connor has suggested, using Foucault's terms, "in the postwar period, Britain came progressively to lose its confident belief that it was the subject of its own history" (3).

All of the novels focused on in this section see the narrative recovery of the past as a necessary but problematical act. Many of these novelists focus on the marginalized and dispossessed, offering a decentered, fragmented history of the world. The need to re-evaluate those Victorian, imperial values that Mrs Thatcher still admired and wanted the country to revert to can be found in novels by Fowles, Barnes, Winterson, Byatt, and others. Some of these novelists have sought to understand the present by returning to the war. As Steven Connor paradoxically explains: "The unthinkable must first be thought in order to preserve its unthinkability, must be made actual in imagination in order to remain purely potential in fact" (201). Cornell West has suggested that all these writers belong to a new cultural politics of difference of which some of the distinctive features are "to historicize, contextualize and pluralize by highlighting the contingent, provisional, variable, tentative, shifting and changing" (19). Steven Connor believes that these novels of history make it "possible to inhabit or belong to one's present differently" (140). How? "[T]o go to the edge of oneself or one's habitual contexts may be to solidify as well as to stretch the sense of identity" (Connor 5). Like Connor, Peter Middleton and Tim Woods discern a strong connection between identity and memory (individual or collective, that is historical). In a discussion of a representative novel of history, Pat Barker's *Regeneration* (1991), they perceive a typical "belief that our integrity and authenticity as people depends upon the possession of a coherent and communicable *curriculum vitae* of genuine memories" (92). Of course memories are notoriously unreliable in recalling the facts of the past. They should rather be seen as clothing one puts on. Moreover, Middleton and Woods write, "personal identity depends upon the ability to tell a coherent narrative of one's history based on personal memory" (94).

The novels of history considered in this section offer the fictional narration of alternative forms of collective memory that produce very different notions of national identity from various "authoritative" accounts of the past. In *Chatterton* Ackroyd reveals the extent to which his modern English characters are constructed by a delusive past which is itself already a copy of an earlier past. There is no authentic national memory on which later English artists can draw for a sense of continuing identity. The fragmentation of the modern self is seen to be the product of the proliferation of competing historical memories none of which is privileged. In the same spirit the reader of McEwan's *Atonement* is faced with conflicting accounts of the past which offer alternative visions of how the war shaped the national identity of postwar English society. For a skeptical Julian Barnes "[o]ur panic and our pain are only eased by soothing fabulation; we call it history" (*A History* 240). Both Barnes in *A History of the World in 10 1/2 Chapters* and Amis in *Time's Arrow* show the way memory is responsible for the construction of modern Western identity rather than a specific national identity. But it is clear that they consider English identity to be a product of a wider construct, one that in Barnes's novel reverts to Genesis's account of the re-creation of the world and stretches to an imagined future in a dreary consumer oriented heaven, and one that in Amis's novel travels backwards from a present time without a past in the United States to the earlier defining moment of greatest horror in modern history, the Holocaust in Nazi Europe. These wider collective memories have equally helped define the national character. A.S. Byatt chooses to historicize the Victorian period held in such high esteem by Mrs Thatcher at the time Byatt's book came out. In the second of her novellas, "The Conjugial Angel," she narrates the doings of Tennyson's circle privileging the previously silenced voice and story of his sister. Like Barnes, she is choosing to reinvent a collective memory by giving voice to a neglected segment of English society. For all these novelists a historicized narrative is merely one of a wide variety of possible pasts each of which constructs present identity, whether individual or national, differently. These novels of history re-contextualize the modern, fragmented self in a more diverse and disjointed historical perspective that is given narrative life in equally new, self-reflexive, and non-continuous modes of fiction.

1
Peter Ackroyd: *Chatterton* (1987)

Peter Ackroyd is representative of a generation of English novelists whose education has familiarized them with poststructuralist literary theory. Inevitably this has affected their understanding of the nature of writing and entered their fiction—frequently in the form of increased verbal playfulness, self-consciousness and metafictional interventions. Ackroyd exemplifies this generational characteristic by publishing as his first book what he described as a "polemic" (*Notes* 9) on poststructuralist theory, *Notes for a New Culture: An Essay on Modernism* (1976). This was written while Ackroyd was spending two postgraduate years (1971–73) at Yale on a Mellon Fellowship. There he met John Ashbery and Kenneth Koch, both poets of the New York School. Ashbery had spent nine years in France and was well acquainted with contemporary currents in French thought. In the space of two years Ackroyd had absorbed contemporary French theory with as much enthusiasm as the Yale school of critics were showing at this time.

Notes for a New Culture shows Ackroyd's complete rejection of the Leavisite New Criticism he had imbibed at Cambridge as an undergraduate. Ackroyd's reaction against Leavis is typical of many of the novelists of his generation. Martin Amis claimed that Leavis "sought to reduce literature to a moral audit" (*War* 77); Angela Carter mocked him for his "'eat up your broccoli' approach to fiction" (*Shaking* 490); Ian McEwan even has a character in *Atonement*, Robbie, reject a Leavisite devotion to the study of English literature: "It was not . . . the first and last defense against a barbarian horde" (86). Ackroyd returned from America a convert to poststructuralism's elevation of language to a position of preeminence. *Notes*, he announced, "is an account of the emergence of LANGUAGE as the content of literature and as the form of knowledge" (9). Without more ado he proceeded to assign to the dust heap of history the entire humanist legacy of "modernism" which he dates from the Enlightenment: "[language's] rise has already determined a greater death: the death of Man as he finds himself in humanism and in the idea of subjectivity" (9). Ackroyd dates the first literary appearances of the new modernism to the work of De Sade, Mallarmé, and Flaubert, who he claims is "the first modern writer to detach his 'presence' from his own writings, so that language sustains itself with its own weight"—whatever that means (18). Like Nietzsche he asserts that the "world we know and recognize is simply a product of interpretation." But this "denial of meaning opens out into a new world of multiplicity and difference" (23).

Notes shows Ackroyd's early and persisting admiration for T. S. Eliot and his use of personae: "the persona takes as its mask, in fact, the inherited autonomy of language itself" (49). That inheritance, the tradition of English writing, is a topic that becomes central to Ackroyd's literary philosophy as he matures. At the same time Ackroyd parts from Eliot's modernist concept of impersonality: Eliot "constructs as an alternative [to the private voice], not an autonomy of language, but an impersonal and a-temporal voice of feeling" (51). For James Joyce, however, "the world only exists through the mediation of language" (52). What distinguishes the particular modernism of *The Waste Land* and *Ulysses* is "their creative discovery of the history of language" (54). "Once language has retrieved its history, it emerges as its only subject" (59). So "writing does not emerge from speech, or from the individual, but only from other writing" (61). Citing Barthes's belief that the "text exists in relation only to 'itself' and not to 'me'" (114), Lacan's insistence that "language both offers and denies human meaning" (139), and Derrida's assertion that in "the pure absence of meanings, language can return to a state of play" (143), Ackroyd enthusiastically concludes that "we, too, are texts to be deconstructed" (114).

In 1973 this was heady stuff, and when he published it three years later it is not surprising that Ackroyd encountered resistance from those who either did not understand or who rejected such poststructuralist thinking. Despite being savaged by critics such as Christopher Ricks in the *Times* (more for factual errors than for the substance of his argument), Ackroyd continued to develop this poststructuralist, anti-mimetic outlook in the prose fiction and biography that he went on to publish. On reissuing a revised edition of *Notes* sixteen years later (in 1993), Ackroyd wrote in the new Preface that he was convinced that the central argument was "still broadly correct." He goes on to claim that for anyone reading through his subsequent published work "the concerns, or obsessions, of *Notes for a New Culture* would be found in more elaborate form within them" (*Collection* 373). In subsequent interviews he has expressed more reservations about "the very stark dichotomies" he introduced in *Notes* (Interview with Onega 219), and said that "the novels came after a period when I disabused myself of theory" (Gibson and Wolfreys 235).

But it can equally be argued that Ackroyd has simply developed his early adoption of poststructuralist theory by giving it a more personal interpretation using his own distinctive terminology. The same year he reissued *Notes* he gave a lecture titles "The Englishness of English Literature" at Cambridge. In it he enlists the concept of "architectural historicism" in Nikolaus

Pevsner's *The Englishness of English Art* (1956) to argue that "the formal or playful use of a historical style" is "firmly at the heart of the English sensibility itself" (*Collection* 333). Ackroyd is by this time more interested in defining the essence of the English tradition in English literature. But what this Catholic tradition (as he calls it) embraces is "an older tradition of creativity which is based upon imitation"; this amounts to "the individual adaptation and reinterpretation of the best literary works in existence" (*Collection* 337). He proceeds to identify this tradition as one characterized by theatricality, playfulness, and heterogeneity. In another lecture he gave in 1999 ("All the Time in the World") he is still repeating the poststructuralist mantra which gives primacy to language within which "everybody is afloat" (*Collection* 365). He goes on to articulate a conviction that underlies all his fiction from his first novel (*The Great Fire of London*, 1982) on: "all the previous structures of our language lie just beneath the one we are presently using" (369).

Since then Ackroyd has published *London: The Biography* (2000) and *Albion: Origins of the English Imagination* (2003). Both of these books attempt to demonstrate the unchanging nature of the English genius. In Ackroyd's biography of it, London "defies chronology" and the book itself adopts a labyrinthine temporal structure to parallel his essentially anti-historical stance (*London* 2). *Albion* seeks to demonstrate the quintessential quality of English culture by revealing the presence of the same characteristics in Anglo-Saxon England as can be found in the present. The English imagination has always been a "mungrell" mixture, he writes; its history "is the history of adaptation and assimilation," absorbing waves of invasion and conquest to become Roman-Saxon-Danish-Norman-English (*Albion* 448). *Albion* is anti-historical in that, as Eagleton says of it, it summons "an England which never really existed to do battle on behalf of one which might cease to exist altogether" (*Figures* 220). The explicit evocation of this concept of a continuity of culture and its writers and artists "living for ever in the state of eternity called Albion" dates back to 1992, the year Ackroyd published *English Music* (358). But the same belief system implicitly underlies his earlier pseudo-historical fiction, especially *Hawksmoor* (1985), and *Chatterton* (1987). It is still to be found in his much later novel about Charles and Mary Lamb, *The Lambs of London* (2004) which returns to *Chatterton's* focus on plagiarism by introducing an expert forger of Shakespeare's will, William Ireland, a character likewise modeled on a historical figure, who displays his contemporaneity with Shakespeare.

Why the obsession with plagiarism? Because Ackroyd has insisted from his earliest work that true genius (especially true English genius) lies not in invention but imitation. While at Yale he wrote a play titled "No" (now lost) consisting entirely of sixty different lines by sixty different playwrights (*Collection* xvii; Ackroyd, Interview with Onega 213). In his first novel, *The Great Fire of London*, he makes a distinction between mimetic and creative imitation. The former is unachievable, the latter unavoidable. The book features the director of a film based on *Little Dorrit* who sets himself the impossible task of recreating Dickens's London using a contemporary prison for the Marshalsea Prison of Dickens's time. He ends up being burnt to death when a character who imagines herself taken over by the persona of Little Dorrit sets fire to the film set. This is the fate, Ackroyd infers, awaiting any realist artist attempting to resurrect the past untainted by the present. At the same time the past, especially the linguistic past, hovers just behind present day use of language. Ackroyd explains: "In the pre-Restoration period, the best poet was the one who used the found material and rearranged it most adeptly. Which is T. S. Eliot, which is any good writer, who takes the inheritance and changes it, just a tiny bit" ("Imagining" 110). "The history of English literature," Ackroyd has said, "is really the history of plagiarism. I discovered that when I was doing [a biography of] T.S. Eliot. He was a great plagiarist . . . I see nothing wrong with it" ("Peter Ackroyd," Interview with Smith 60).

Ackroyd's attitude to the past is paradoxical: he has, he has said, both "a reverence for . . . the past" and "a continual need to reinvent it, recreate it, almost destroy it, by making up stuff" (Gibson 245). He is simultaneously respectful and ahistorical since the past persists in the present. This is why he has repeatedly insisted that there is no difference between the biographies and the novels he writes. The only difference between the writers of the two genres, Ackroyd insists provocatively, "is that the biographer can make things up, but that a novelist is compelled to tell the truth." This is because the novelist must have an imagination powerful enough "to impress the reader with the force of reality itself" (*Collection* 367).

I want to look at the connection between literary history, intertextuality (or plagiarism, or forgery) and language in *Chatterton*, a novel which dramatizes Ackroyd's poststructuralist attitudes to language, literature and history in a more radical manner than any other of his novels to date. In a Foreword to *Thomas Chatterton and Romantic Culture* by Nick Groom (1999) Ackroyd describes Chatterton's poetic forgeries in terms that offer an insight into his own motives for continually resorting to the literature of the past to illuminate the present: "Chatterton believed that the past, and the language of the past, might be made to live again . . . By writing in the impassioned cadence and ornate vocabulary of the fifteenth century, he was able to move beyond the restricting imaginative climate into which he had been born" (*Collection* 393). Ackroyd appears to be saying that by excavating the layers of linguistic and literary past underlying the present one can renew and enrich the literary and linguistic present.

In *Chatterton*, Ackroyd uncovers two earlier strata beneath a modern day (1980s) narrative—the brief span of Chatterton's life (1752–70) and the mid-Victorian moment when Henry Wallis completed a painting of the dead Chatterton using the poet George Meredith as his model (1856). This enables him to evoke, like Groom, "a variety of literary incarnations ranging from the eighteenth-century fraudster to Romantic icon and post-modern avatar" (*Collection* 392). Chatterton's passion for the medieval past shows him to participate in "the native genius" (392) which also possesses Wallis and Charles Wychwood, the novel's modern protagonist and poet—and by implication Ackroyd himself. All are seen to belong to "the enduring consciousness of the nation" (*Collection* 393). Each of them could call himself, as Meredith does on his first appearance, a "model poet" because he is "pretending to be someone else" (2). Just as Chatterton assumes the voice of a medieval poet, so Ackroyd, having pored over Chatterton's papers in the British Museum, assumes the eighteenth-century voice and diction of Chatterton in the book. What makes it possible for Chatterton and Ackroyd (as well as other plagiarists and forgers in the novel) to successfully invoke a voice from the past is, according to Ackroyd, the fact that "the speech we use today contains or conceals previous levels of speech, from the most recent to the most ancient. They are as it were implicit in modern speech, modern writing, and it only takes a little effort to peel back the layers" ("Peter Ackroyd," Interview with McGrath 46). The modern writer's job is to give free rein to the natural play of language in all its historically layered complexity, just as the reader's role, according to Barthes, whom Ackroyd quotes approvingly, "does not consist of the subjective experience of an object . . . but rather of the relation between one text and another" (*Notes* 114). History, then, belongs to and is subject to the world of textuality. The "past and the present can effectively imbue each other" (*Collection* 368). There is no objective past to be recovered, "no truth to tell" ("Peter Ackroyd," Interview with McGrath 47), only a textual representation of it which is subject to the polysemous nature of language.

In a book which argues that every writer creates his or her own precursors, Robert Kiely observes, "One way of defining the difference between the legitimate professional historians and the new postmodern historical novelists is that the object of the former is to correct mistakes and that of the latter is to remember them" (184). In *Chatterton,* as in *Hawksmoor,* Ackroyd alters the past to suit his narrative purposes. For instance he shows Meredith, after his wife's desertion, contemplating suicide and saved by the appearance of Chatterton's ghost (70–71). In fact, as Ackroyd points out in *Albion,* it was the Victorian poet Francis Thompson who claimed that Chatterton appeared to him in a vision and dissuaded him from suicide (431). In remembering or creating mistakes made about the past these new novelists of history understand and capitalize on the fact that all historical accounts employ the same narrative strategies as novels do. As Harriet Scrope confesses in *Chatterton,* "I suppose that's the trouble with history. It's the one thing we have to make up for ourselves" (226). Narrative is subject to, among other things, pre-existing plots. Charles's friend Philip "believed that there were only a limited number of plots in the world (reality was

finite, after all) and no doubt it was inevitable that they would be reproduced in a variety of contexts" (70). The entire novel legitimizes and celebrates the role of plagiarism in historical and literary narrative.

This affects the working of temporality in Ackroyd's novels. According to
him the "English imagination . . . moves backwards as well as forwards"
(*Albion* ix). Chatterton does not so much reproduce the past in the forged
poems of Rowley as reinvent it. In *Albion* Ackroyd claims that "Chatterton
composed as many fine lines of medieval poetry as came out of the medieval
period itself" (427). In other words Chattterton's poetry was not simply an
imitation of the past; it evokes a new past in the present. Brought up in the
Age of Reason, Chatterton restored an earlier sense of mystery and wonder,
"a world of vision and dreams" (*Albion* 431). Is Chatterton collapsing time
in his forged poems? Or is he rather revealing the presence of the past in the
present? As he explains in the novel, "so the Language of ancient Dayes
awoke the Reality itself for, tho' I knew that it was I that composed these
Histories, I also knew that they were true ones" (85). Ackroyd ingeniously
justifies his obfuscation of the difference between history and poetry by
invoking the earlier use of the word "history," which, like "story," was originally "applied to an account of either imaginary events or of events supposed to be true," according to Raymond Williams's *Key Words* (146).
Ackroyd's vision is essentially atemporal; past and present interact in the
moment. Or you can say that the present consumes the past. Charles jokingly tells his son that he is "eating the past" when licking the dust from the
forged painting off his finger (15). In the same way the present-day writer
consumes the writing of his predecessors. Charles, for example, literally eats
pages of Dickens's *Great Expectations* as he finishes reading them, a trait that
Ackroyd told an interviewer was stolen from Oscar Wilde. "That was one of
his habits . . . In one of the reviews someone said it was a symbol of what I
did with my own fiction—take bits of other people's books and eat them"
("Peter Ackroyd", Interview with Smith 60).

Ackroyd has enigmatically claimed that he employs a spiral model of time
(Ackroyd, "Imagining" 105). If this is the case, he arranges his plots so as to
bring similar points on successive cycles of the spiral into conjunction,
revealing in this way the repetitions and parallels between historically separate moments of time. One obvious instance occurs in the various representations of Chatterton's death in the novel. As Greg Clingham writes of it,
"Ackroyd's narrative is self-consciously iterative; it is the most recent instance
of a series of 'historical' representations of the event, whose reality is unques-
tioned but whose meaning is narratively configured again and again in different ways" (44). The three parts into which the novel is divided also serve
to facilitate Ackroyd's palimpsest view of time. The three-part structure
brings into juxtaposition conflicting attitudes to the vexed question of
authenticity (historical and artistic). Part One entails the discovery first of the
painting of a supposedly fifty-year-old Chatterton and then of manuscripts

of his (including a poem by Blake) that Flint dates as early nineteenth century. Essentially Part One questions the authenticity (a dangerous word in Ackroyd's vocabulary) of both painting and manuscript. Part Two confirms the authenticity of Chatterton's continued forgeries of poets like Blake. Part Two is an extended meditation on the authenticity of artistic forgery, using Wallis's faked death scene of Chatterton as its principal extended (perhaps over-extended) metaphor. Part Three, half the length of the other two parts, ingeniously deconstructs the whole concept of authenticity. Harriet's response to discovering that the painting of the older Chatterton is a fake is to attempt to fake its restoration only for the painting to completely dissolve in the course of removing its anachronistic details. Similarly, after Philip has learnt that the Chatterton manuscripts are forgeries, he proceeds to start writing a book based on the imagined assumption that they are authentic. Susana Onega speculates not entirely convincingly that Philip therefore "might be the fictional author of *Chatterton*" (68). Part Three celebrates the dissolution of the distinctions between authenticity and forgery, originality and imitation, reality and its representation in art. It ends with the historical Chatterton anachronistically imitating Wallis's representation of his death down to the unlikely smile on his dead face.

In *Albion* Ackroyd suggests that there is a significant connection between forgery and the romantic movement. What he means is that the Romantics' new insistence on the private and personal experience gave new importance to the "apparent originality of expression." "As a result," Ackroyd argues, "as if they were intense shadows created by a sudden light, the dangers of plagiarism and pastiche became evident in the first generation of the romantic movement" (*Albion* 432). Where previously no writers troubled to acknowledge their frequent borrowings, now they became so aware of their indebtedness that Keats abandoned *Hyperion* because of its Miltonic echoes. It might appear anomalous that the Romantics turned Chatterton, a forger of "Rowley's" poems, into a cult figure of the neglected genius. What they did was to focus on the originality of his poetic imagination, creating the Romantic image of Wordsworth's "marvellous boy," Coleridge's "spirit blest," Keats's "child of sorrow," de Vigny's "*poète maudit*," lingering on in Oscar Wilde's "pure artist." But according to Ackroyd, there is no avoiding what Harold Bloom in *The Anxiety of Influence* terms literary "belatedness"[1]: "English art and English literature are formed out of inspired adaptation" (*Albion* xi). *Chatterton* celebrates the assimilative nature of the English imagination. Chatterton is a true genius because "he considered the past itself to be his true father" (*Albion* 426).

If Chatterton is a plagiarist he is a reverse plagiarist because he creates his own literary past in the present. Charles opens his preface to his planned book on Chatterton: "Thomas Chatterton believed that he could explain the entire material and spiritual world in terms of imitation and forgery, and so sure was he of his own genius that he allowed it to flourish under other

names" (126). How fitting that Charles's defense of plagiarism should itself
be a double act of plagiarism. In the first place, the opening half of Charles's
sentence has been lifted verbatim from the catalogue to the exhibition of Art
Brut at the art gallery where Charles's wife, Vivien (cf. Vivien Eliot), works
(cf. 109–10). In the second place, Ackroyd himself is indebted to his own
earlier novel, *The Last Testament of Oscar Wilde,* in which he has Wilde
describe Chatterton as "a strange, slight boy who was so prodigal of his
genius that he attached the names of others to it" (67). This in turn is
indebted to the real Wilde's lecture of March 1888 on Chatterton: "He had
the artist's yearning to represent and if perfect representation seemed to him
to demand forgery he needs must forge. Still this forgery came from the
desire of artistic self-effacement" (Ellmann 285). Ackroyd appears set on
overwhelming his readers in a plethora of literary borrowing or plagiarism
in which he implicitly admits his own involvement.

Ackroyd's plagiarism of his own books does not stop here. When Philip
accidentally comes across Harrison Bentley's novels in the library the first
title he reads is *The Last Testament* (a flagrant piece of self-plagiarism), a book
in which a poet's wife is discovered by his biographer to have been responsible for writing the verses produced at the end of his life that had brought
him eternal fame. This is similar in situation to the discovery within the
novel that the painter Seymour's assistant, Merk, has painted all of
Seymour's last pictures. Another of Bentley's novels is called *Stage Fire,* in
which an actor believes himself to be possessed by the spirits of Kean and
other famous performers of the past, which results in his own triumphant
career on the stage. Of course *Stage Fire* is a sly reference to Ackroyd's own
The Great Fire of London in which a character thinks she is possessed by
another character from the past. That is not to mention the remark Harriet
makes to herself when observing a blind man early in the novel: "All you
need, old man, . . . is a circle of stage fire" (30). To add to the chain of pla-
giarisms, Harriet has lifted the plots of both of Bentley's novels for two novels of her "own." Susana Onega shows how Ackroyd's allusions can continue
to be traced in the striking resemblance "between *Mean Time,* the title of the
novel written by Andrew Flint . . . and Dickens's *Hard Times*; or between the
name of Kafka's protagonist in *The Castle,* Joseph K, and that of Bentley's
protagonist [K——], or even of Harrison Bentley and William Bentley,
Galvanauska's disciple in Charles Palliser's *Betrayals* (1994), a novel that
shares interesting traits in common with *Chatterton*" (69). In this last
instance, of course, Onega is identifying an instance of reverse plagiarism.[2]
Even *Mean Time* is a pun on "meantime" which hints at the intermediary
nature of all narratives caught between their indebtedness to the past and
their becoming in turn a source of indebtedness to work in the future.

Why is it that plagiarism seems to play such an unavoidable role in literary composition? According to Ackroyd, the answer lies in the nature of
language. If Chatterton is "a thoroughly English poet," it is because "the

language of the past spoke through him" (*Albion* 428, 426). Language is an accretion, "containing within it all the potential and power of the past" (*Collection* 371). Scratch the surface of eighteenth-century English and a Chatterton will uncover the still surviving medieval strata, just as Ackroyd will uncover beneath his late-twentieth-century use of English Chatterton's eighteenth-century form of linguistic expression. Ackroyd playfully exploits this archaeological layering to show the stratas influencing one another in *both* directions. When Chatterton first discovers in the muniments room his ability to write in the style of medieval manuscripts he read there, he comments, "Schoolboy tho' I was, it was even at this time that I decided to shore up these ancient Fragments with my own Genius: thus the Living and the Dead were to be reunited." (85) Here Ackroyd employs an anachronistic reference to the fourth line from the end of *The Waste Land* ("These fragments I have shored against my ruins"). It next turns out that Chatterton's autobiographical "Account" of his life is a forgery committed by Chatterton's Bristol publisher. So the papers are a bookseller's attempt "to fake the work of a faker" (221). As if this double act of forgery were not sufficient, the reader also knows that the bookseller's faked "Account" of Chatterton's memoirs is itself faked by Ackroyd, who spent considerable time in the Manuscript Department of the British Museum reading through Chatterton's papers and other contemporary documents.[3] Seen in another light this is simply the outcome of the forces of intertextuality, a term introduced by Julia Kristeva to refer to the way "any text is the absorption and transformation of another" (*Kristeva Reader* 37).

Ackroyd's repeated use of intertextuality in *Chatterton* constitutes the literary corollary to Derrida's theory of *différance* and the "trace." In *Notes* Ackroyd singled out Derrida's definition of the "trace" to exemplify the way writing offers a world of pure signifiers disconnected from any claim to absolute meaning. Writing, Ackroyd explained (while exaggerating), "has excised the last vestiges of meaning, since its form is now that of "la signifiant de la signifiant [the signifier of the signifier]" (*Notes* 142). The written trace then is "the original absence, . . . an effect without a cause" (142). As Eagleton explains, for the words of a sentence "to compose some relatively coherent meaning at all, each one of them must, so to speak, contain the trace of the ones which have gone before, and hold itself open to the trace of those which are coming after" (*Literary Theory* 111). In *Of Grammatology* Derrida associates the way the trace deconstructs presence and meaning with Freud's use of "the arche-phenomenon of memory" to deconstruct consciousness (70). Thus the signifying chain of written historical memory can be shown to reveal the same flickering of presence and absence as Freud exposes in the working of human memory. If each signifier is incomplete, containing the traces of other signifiers that have been excluded for it to be what it is, then artistic originality is as much of a chimera as historical truth. Both are subject to the endless play of language and deferral of meaning.

Chatterton pays fictional homage to this poststructuralist world of pure *écriture*. In it imaginative writers are distinguished by their *conscious* play with a world of textuality. Historical presence and narrative meaning are subordinated to the sea of language in which they swim. In *Albion* Ackroyd is still insisting on the way the nature of language preempts any arrival at full meaning that he first expressed in *Notes*: Chatterton "invented a language with which to restore the proximity as well as the mystery of the past. Or," adds Ackroyd rhetorically, "can we say that the language invented him?" (*Albion* 429). Both authors and their writings are constructs of language. In *Chatterton* Charles quotes Montaigne's saying, "I no more make the book than the book makes me" (99). Similarly, Ackroyd has said that characters are "just words, . . . verbal representations" (Gibson 228). In Bristol Philip, Charles's friend, learns that Chatterton's physical remains cannot be located and that only the facade of his house survives. The old man who tells him this thrusts a leaflet about Chatterton into his hands with the remark, "That's all you need" (55). Chatterton lives on, but as pure writing. And as writing he lives on in the writing of his literary successors.

Later in the novel Philip experiences a moment of pure horror in the basement book stacks of the library where he works when he feels overwhelmed by the world of textuality surrounding him:

> . . . . it was now with an unexpected fearfulness that he saw how the books stretched away into the darkness. They seemed to expand as soon as they reached the shadows, creating some dark world where there was no beginning and no end, no story, no meaning. (71)

What frightens Philip is the threat that the free play of this textual world poses to his sense of identity and authenticity as a writer. As Ackroyd subsequently explained, it is "as though books themselves had some phantom reality of their own" (Gibson 232). And this reality encompasses Philip's subjectivity and thwarts his attempts at artistic originality. Unlike Harriet Scrope, who has no scruples about plagiarizing the work of others, Philip subscribes to the Romantics' myth of origins. As a result he suffers from writer's block and has abandoned a novel after some forty pages because it "seemed to him to be filled with images and phrases from the work of other writers whom he admired" (70). It takes Charles's invention of Chatterton's death for him to realize that "what Charles imagined . . . isn't an illusion. The imagination never dies" (232). Philip finally understands that because it belongs to the world of language a novel does not have to pretend to an authenticity that signification denies. He can write about how "Chatterton might have lived on," thereby giving new textual life to Chatterton's writing. What matters is not originality ("there is no real origin for anything," he states rather too categorically) but the manipulation of language. Philip concludes, "I might discover that I had a style of my own, after all" (232).

It is the manner in which a writer rearranges the writings of the past that gives his or her writings their distinctive character.

In *Notes* Ackroyd took his argument about the trace of writing one stage further. Having asserted that the trace has "excized the last vestiges of meaning," he continues: "The desire for meaning within language is precisely that quest for a lost object—in a word death" (142). Plenitude of meaning is unattainable. "Plenitude is the end (the goal)," Derrida writes in "Afterword," "but were it attained, it would be the end (death)" (129).[4] References to death proliferate throughout this book. Chatterton dies repeatedly in the course of the narrative. Or rather Chatterton's death is given textual representation again and again. The first glimpse the reader is given of the Victorian poet Meredith is of him posing as the dead Chatterton for Wallis's painting. Invited by Wallis to allow himself the luxury of death in posing for Chatterton's portrait, Meredith responds, "I can endure death. It is the representation of death I *cannot* bear" (2; cf. 138). But, as Derrida points out in "Finis," death is endlessly transmissible, not as an experience, but as a textual trace. We cannot experience our own death, only represent death as that which above all else lacks pure presence. In other words we can only textually fake death. Textual death is necessarily inauthentic. So it is fitting that Ackroyd should give ironic fictional life to the way Wallis's simulated death of Chatterton came to be accepted as the "authentic" image of the poet's death. Meredith draws the parallel between the art of Chatterton and Wallis:

> "[Chatterton] invented an entire period and made its imagination his own: no one had properly understood the medieval world until Chatterton summoned it into existence. The poet does not merely recreate or describe the world. He actually creates it. And that is why he is feared." Meredith came up to Wallis, and for the first time looked at the canvas. "And that is why," he added quietly, "this will always be remembered as the true death of Chatterton." (157)

Artistic or imaginative truth preempts historical truth. Art repeatedly irrupts into life in this book, blurring the boundaries between reality and representation. The scene of Chatterton's death is rehearsed three times in the novel. First comes the painted reconstruction of it by Wallis. Next comes Charles's death where he dies in exactly the same posture in which Wallis painted Chatterton (a painting Charles is seen to take his son to look at). Finally comes Ackroyd's own imaginative reconstruction of Chatterton's death. Between the second and third iterations of Chatterton's death, Edward, Charles's son, revisits Wallis's painting of Chatterton in the National Portrait Gallery after his father's death and is astonished to see "his father lying there" (229). Wallis's art has already been responsible for Charles adopting at death the posture of the painted Chatterton. What

Edward says about his father applies equally to Chatterton and his survival in the form of the art he created: "He would always be here, in the painting. He would never die" (230). Where history attempts to represent the pastness of the past, the new novel of history represents the way the past persists in the present. It persists in English fiction, according to Ackroyd, because of the continuity of what he calls the English imagination. Citing Touchstone's definition that "the truest poetry is the most feigning" (*As You Like It* 3.3.16), Ackroyd asks teasingly, "Is the national genius, after all, simply a collection of borrowings?" (*Albion* 147). In showing how artists like Chatterton and Wallis disappear into their own work, Ackroyd is simultaneously performing a similar disappearing act. The only subject allowed to surface in the novel is a textual construct. Even the unification of the three strands of narrative in the book is achieved by a textually contrived and wholly imaginary meeting of Chatterton, Wallis, and Charles at the end that transcends historical temporality by bringing the latter two back in time to join Chatterton at the moment of his death. Imaginary closure is achieved by purely imaginary means, means that defy any attempt to read the novel in a mode of realism. The ending celebrates the triumph of art and the autonomy of the literary work over the contingencies of life and their historical representation.

List of Books Published

Fiction

The Great Fire of London, 1982.
The Last Testament of Oscar Wilde, 1983.
Hawksmoor, 1985.
Chatterton, 1987.
First Light, 1989.
English Music, 1992.
The House of Doctor Dee, 1993.
Dan Leno and the Limehouse Golem, [aka *The Trial of Elizabeth Cree*] 1994.
Milton in America, 1996.
The Plato Papers, 1999.
The Clerkenwell Tales, 2003.
The Lambs of London, 2004.

Non-Fiction

Notes for a New Culture: An Essay on Modernism, 1976.
Dressing Up: Transvestism and Drag, the History of an Obsession, 1979.
Ezra Pound and His World, 1980.
T. S. Eliot, 1984.
Dickens: Public Life and Private Passion, 1990.
Introduction to Dickens, 1991.
Blake: A Biography, 1995.

The Life of Thomas More, 1998.
London: The Biography, 2000.
The Collection: Journalism, Reviews, Essays, Short Stories, Lectures, 2001.
The Mystery of Charles Dickens, 2002.
Albion: The Origins of the English Imagination, 2002.
Brief Lives: Turner, 2002.
Voyages through Time: Escape from Earth, 2003.
Voyages through Time: In The Beginning, 2003.
Illustrated London, 2003.
Chaucer, 2004.
Shakespeare: A Biography, 2004.
Brief Lives: Chaucer, 2004.
Voyages through Time: Cities of Blood, 2004.
Voyages through Time: Kingdom of the Dead, 2004.

Poetry

Ouch. The Curiously Strong: Vol. 4, No. 2, 1971.
London Lickpenny, 1973.
Country Life, 1978.
The Diversions of Purley and Other Poems, 1987.

2

Julian Barnes: *A History of the World in 10 1/2 Chapters* (1989)

In Julian Barnes's third novel, *Flaubert's Parrot* (1984), Braithwaite, the protagonist spends the duration of the book searching for Flaubert's parrot, an emblem for him of the authenticity of the past. But "all around is wreckage," amidst which "some delicate things have survived." Barnes instances one in particular:

> A parrot's perch catches the eye. We look for the parrot. Where is the parrot? We still hear its voice; but all we can see is a bare wooden perch. The bird has flown. (58)

Almost nothing from the past survives the destructive passage of time except for voices echoing through the ages beamed to the present through texts of various kinds. Barnes adopts a more skeptical attitude to the role that history plays in the present than does Ackroyd. Barnes shares with most modern historiographers an awareness of the way history substitutes unitary narratives for the heterogeneous realities of the past. He also shares with Walter Benjamin the rejection of an ameliorative interpretation of history. As Benjamin insisted, "The concept of progress should be grounded in the idea of catastrophe" ("N" 64). Barnes similarly writes of the "wreckage" and the "carnage" of the past (*Flaubert's Parrot* 58). Jackie Buxton has argued that Barnes is specifically indebted to Benjamin's celebrated "Theses on the Philosophy of History" for his attitude to the past. Turning to Barnes's fifth novel, *A History of the World in 10 1/2 Chapters* (1989), she writes that, like Benjamin's angel of history "who sees the past only as an accumulation of 'wreckage,' Barnes views history as 'one single catastrophe'" (60). She also points to the way Barnes echoes Benjamin's conviction that "the adherents of historicism actually empathize ... with the victor" (*Illuminations* 256). "Similarly," Buxton, writes, "Barnes enjoins us not to 'surrender' meekly to this historiographic domination in which 'the victor has the right not just to the spoils but also to the truth' (244)" (Buxton 85). That this tendency of history is still alive and kicking can be evidenced from Barnes's commentary on Margaret Thatcher's autobiography, *The Downing Street Years,* "Mrs Thatcher Remembers." Barnes writes there that Thatcher's autobiography offers a view of history calculated to act as a "justification and a continuation of her rule" (*Letters from London* 230).

Barnes also appears to agree with Benjamin's assertion in "Theses" that a "chronicler who recites events without distinguishing between major and minor ones acts in accordance with the following truth: nothing that has ever happened should be regarded as lost for history" (*Illuminations* 254). Barnes told one interviewer, "Most history slips through the net of the historian. So perhaps you can try to put together an alternative history . . . " ("The World" E-1). Barnes does just that in *A History of the World,* making no distinction between major events (like the Flood, Hitler's war against the Jews, and Chernobyl) and minor ones (like the purported seventeenth century prosecution of termites in a small French village and the fictional account of making a movie in the Venezuelan jungle). The self-evidently arbitrary nature of the selections he makes in this book serve to emphasize the necessarily arbitrary nature of all attempts at writing histories. The nearer one gets to the present the more overwhelming is the proliferation of documents and other evidence from the past. Historians' response to this predicament has been to resort to what Barnes calls fabulation, a concept first introduced in Chapter 4 of the novel, "The Survivor": "You make up a story to cover the facts you don't know or can't accept. You keep a few true facts and spin a new story round them" (109). The *Oxford English Dictionary* defines "fabulate" as both "relate as a fable or myth" and "invent, fabricate." Invoking this term allows Barnes to elide the distinction between relation and fabrication, history and story. He is as willing to invent events that represent some of the omissions from history as he is to retell other well-known historical narratives from the point of view of the losers and victims.

Barnes then is convinced like Benjamin that history is, as Benjamin put it, "one single catastrophe which keeps piling wreckage upon wreckage and hurls it at our feet" (*Illuminations* 257). In one interview Barnes compared history to a "24-wheeler that's bearing down on us all the time" (Saunders G-8; cf. *A History* 238). At the same time *A History of the World* does not show, as Jackie Buxton suggests, "a catastrophic historical decline" over the course of human history (66), or over the course of the twentieth century as the work of Martin Amis does. It opposes the Whig version of history[1] by portraying history as a catastrophe from the start. It targets the invariable way that classic historicism retrospectively recounts the conflicts and upheavals of the past as seen through the eyes of those who succeeded or benefited from the outcome. Barnes appears to concur with Benjamin's famous declaration in "Theses": "There is no document of civilization which is not at the same time a document of barbarism" (*Illuminations* 256). How, then, to avoid producing another sanitized document of barbarism? Barnes counters the grand narratives of Rankean history[2] with *petits récits,* small narrative fragments from the recorded and imagined past. These either revise by undermining the official or generally accepted accounts of history or reinsert what has been omitted by focusing on the losers and victims of past conflicts whose versions of events have been effectively repressed and silenced by authoritative historiography.

Barnes's fictional attempt to discredit official historical narratives is encapsulated in the title of this unusual work of fiction, *A History of the World in 10 1/2 Chapters*. The first half of the title self-consciously—though ironically—invokes Sir Walter Ralegh's *The History of the World* (1614), differing crucially from its ambitious predecessor in its substitution of an indefinite for a definite article. Like Ralegh's *History* it begins with Genesis. But unlike Ralegh, Barnes does not attempt an encyclopedic inclusiveness or subscribe to a providential interpretation of history. Where Ralegh's was a monumental attempt to record the history of the world starting with the Creation (it reached 130 B.C. and came to three-quarters of a million words before breaking off), Barnes's modest book runs to some 300 pages and eschews any pretence of continuity or comprehensiveness. His is merely *a* history among many possible histories of the world. The second half of the title of Barnes's book describes a work that is absurdly brief for such a subject, while its provocative inclusion of a "1/2" chapter draws attention to itself. This unnumbered half chapter, "Parenthesis," is the only section of the book to use a didactic, mildly professorial voice, with a seeming absence of irony or humor. It forms the same function that "The Preface" does in Ralegh's *History* in offering a rationale and apology for the rest of the book. Interestingly both writers see history as necessarily fragmented. Barnes's entire book can be seen largely as a series of digressions from those events normally considered central to any historical account of the world. Barnes has held this view of the past throughout his published fiction. For instance in his short story, "Tunne" (published in 1996), the ageing author, convinced that the past is unrecoverable, reflects that he "was meant to thrive on . . . the partial discovery and the resonant fragment" (*Cross Channel* 206).

Not only is *A History* discontinuous. It is achronological. The book opens with "The Stowaway," an account based on Genesis of Noah and the Flood (the biblical re-creation, if not the creation of the world) and it closes with a final chapter based on Revelations, "The Dream," that envisions a contemporary form of heaven. But between Chapter 1's origins and Chapter 10's ends, the remaining eight and a half chapters do not progress chronologically. Chapter 2, "The Visitors," stages the hijacking of a pleasure boat by modern Arab terrorists (based on the *Achillo Lauro* hijacking of 1985). Chapter 3, "The Wars of Religion," purports to transcribe sixteenth century court records of a case in the diocese of Besançon, France.[3] Chapter 4, "The Survivor," invents the journey or crazed fantasy of a woman escaping by sea from a West poisoned by radiation from the Chernobyl disaster of 1986 and is mildly futuristic. Chapter 5, "Shipwreck," is divided between a section recounting the shipwreck of the French frigate, the *Medusa*, in 1816, and a section analyzing the stages in the painting of the "Scene of Shipwreck" by Géricault three years later. Chapter 6, "The Mountain," recounts a fictional 1840 pilgrimage of an Irish woman to Mount Ararat where she dies. Chapter 7 is titled "Three Simple Stories." The first story set in 1964 concerns a survivor from the *Titanic*, the second Jonah and a sailor in 1891, both of whom were swallowed by a whale, the third the Jewish passengers aboard the *St. Louis* trying to escape from Nazi Germany in 1939. Chapter 8, "Upstream," is a story about a modern film actor on location in the Venezuelan jungle (suggestive of Robert Bolt's *The Mission*, 1986). Next comes the unnumbered half chapter, "Parenthesis," an essay about love. Chapter 9, "Project Ararat," recounts another fictitious expedition in 1977 to Mount Ararat by an astronaut in search of Noah's ark. As Kath says in "The Survivor," "I hate dates. Dates are bullies, dates are know-alls" (99). Rejecting a traditionally teleological mode of structuring its material, this book proceeds by juxtapositions, by parallels and contrasts, by connections that depend on irony or accident.

Does this mean that Barnes is offering in place of chronological sequence some alternative form of organizing the materials of history? Both Claudia Kotte and Peter Childs consider the possibility that the book might be organized on the basis of non-linear or other unconventional concepts of historiography. Childs offers a succinct and neutral summary of the various historiographical theories advanced in the book:

> It includes the theory that the past is always repeated (most clearly in "Three Simple Stories"); the belief that history is cyclical (particularly in "A Dream")' the biblical view of history (in "The Stowaway"); the concept of fate and also the Christian faith in history as providential (in "The Mountain" and "Project Ararat"); the conviction that existence on earth is governed by science, technology, and their relationship with the Gaia hypothesis (in "The Survivor" . . .); and the many arguments that history is fundamentally embroiled in the processes of evolution and the survival of the fittest (perhaps most clearly in "The Wars of Religion", but also in a story such as "The Visitors"). (82–83)

Kotte shows how each of such theories is challenged in other sections of the book. Citing, for instance, further instances of the presence of Darwinian selection in the novel (such as those who survived on the raft of the *Medusa*), she proceeds to list other incidents which challenge Darwin's theory. The woodworm on Noah's ark testifies that those animals that survived were not the fittest but those who happened to escape Noah's temper. Again, she points out, in the first of "Three Simple Stories" Lawrence Beesley, who survived the sinking of the *Titanic* by disguising himself as a woman, overtly attacks Darwin's theory: "did not the Beesley hypothesis prove that the 'fittest' were merely the most cunning?" (174). After showing similar contradictions in Barnes's use of some of the other theories listed by Childs, Kotte concludes: "Instead of assuming that events obey regularities, the author highlights ruptures, subtle contradictions and inconsistencies, differences and conflicts. He thus vehemently rejects the metaphysical concept of history as the history of a meaning or pattern which unfolds and fulfills itself" (123). While accepting her main argument I will return later to her conclusion which I believe needs qualifying.

In substituting *petits* for *grands récits* Barnes also employs a bewildering variety of narrative voices for the book's different episodes. It is as if Barnes was straining to differentiate his "historical" work from that of historians who aspire to an impersonal stance of objectivity. In his early structuralist essay, "The Discourse of History" (1967), Roland Barthes parallels the objective type of historian's concealment of himself as utterer of his own discourse to that of the so called "realist" novelist:

> On the level of discourse, objectivity - or the deficiency of signs of the utterer—thus appears as a particular form of imaginary projection, the product of what might be called the referential illusion, since in this case the historian is claiming to allow the referent to speak all on its own. This type of illusion is not exclusive to historical discourse. It would be hard to count the novelists who imagined—in the epoch of Realism - that they were "objective" because they suppressed the signs of the "I" in their discourse! (11)

As Barthes observes, we now know better than to ascribe objectivity to either type of author, because we realize that the absence of any signs pointing to the utterer merely substitutes an impersonal for a personal utterer of the discourse.

As if in reaction to this discursive camouflage so frequently deployed by traditional historians and realist novelists alike, Barnes positively flouts his proliferation of subjective narrators of both sexes. *A History* opens with the morally superior first-person voice of the woodworm for whom "man is a very unevolved species compared to the animals" (28). There is the absurdly self-important voice (first-person plural) used in the proceedings of the French medieval law courts in Chapter 3. The art historian (using "we" to lure the reader into the discourse) takes over in the second part of Chapter 5. There is the egotistical epistolary voice of the actor in Chapter 8. There are several other first-person narratives, including that of the possibly delusional Kath of Chapter 4, the eighteen-year-old prep-school master of the first of "Three Simple Stories" (Chapter 7), and the dreamer of Chapter 10. Yet in "Three Simple Stories" the second story uses the second-person and the third the third-person. Isabelle Raucq-Hoorickx concludes that "wherever narration occurs in the third person, Barnes's characters are objectivized by their respective narrators," denying for instance the Jewish refugees on the *St Louis* human empathy to evoke the way they were denied it in 1939 (51). Above all, there is the highly personal, mildly didactic voice of a narrator who seems to come close to occupying the position of the (implied) author in the half chapter, "Parenthesis." Yet Barnes has said: "All the narrators are meant to be touching in their aspirations, even if often proved to be foolish or deluded" ("A Talk" 15). Does this include the narrator of "Parenthesis"?

To further resist traditional historians' use of the referential illusion, Barnes summons up within this brief book a remarkably wide range of speech modes and different voices (those "voices echoing in the dark" [240] that constitute the history of the world). Chapter 8, for instance, consists entirely of letters sent by a second rate actor to his girl friend back home. Barnes accurately captures the clichés, lack of punctuation and poor syntax that reveal the actor's derivative mind:

> I get out your photo with the chipmunk face and kiss it. That's all that matters, you and me having babies. Let's do it, Pippa. Your mum would be pleased, wouldn't she? I said to Fish do you have kids, he said yes they're the apple of my eye. I put my arm round him and gave him a hug just like that. It's things like that that keep everything going, isn't it? (211)

Compare this to the half chapter ("Parenthesis") in which "Julian Barnes" talks in the first person about love:

> Poets seem to write more easily about love than prose writers. For a start, they own that flexible "I" (when I say "I" you will want to know within a paragraph or two whether I mean Julian Barnes or someone invented; a poet can shimmy between the two, getting credit for both deep feeling and objectivity). (225)

In drawing attention to the prose medium he is using, Barnes—unlike the actor—contrives to complicate and energize his whole discourse on the difficult subject of love. Style and authenticity are shown to be closely connected. Barnes shows an equal command of sixteenth century French legalese, nineteenth century Irish religious enthusiasm, and contemporary American (with acknowledgements to his friend Jay McInerney for technical assistance). He makes use of an equally eclectic range of narrative genres. His output to date shows him to be a master of a wide variety of genres and forms, most notably in *Flaubert's Parrot*, his literary detective novel, but also in his novel of psychotic obsession, *Before She Met Me* (1982), his political courtroom drama, *The Porcupine* (1992), his futurist farce, *England, England* (1998), and his historical novel, *Arthur and George* (2005). In the different chapters of *A History*, Barnes offers us a multiplicity of discursive genres—a fable, a political thriller, a courtroom drama, science fiction (or a psychiatric case history), a historical narrative, art criticism, epistolary fiction, an essay on love, and a dream-vision that, as one reviewer pointed out, recalls one of the most famous episodes of "The Twilight Zone" (Dirda X4).[4] In this way the novel, as Gregory Rubinson argues, "offers a wide-ranging (if necessarily uncomprehensive) survey of the different genres through which human history and experience has been recorded and passed on" ("Histories" 165). What all the modes and voices have in common is that each subjects a piece of Western history to the imperative of textual narrative. According to Barnes, "what makes each chapter work is that it has a structure and it has a narrative pulse" ("Julian Barnes" 73).

Another strategy he employs to counter and undermine the official narratives of history is to offer counter-narratives, stories of the dispossessed, the marginalized and the vanquished. The most frequently evoked *grand récit* that Barnes targets for satirical treatment and demythologizes is sacred history. Gregory Salyer claims that Barnes regards the sacred story as "the story of entitlement for the sacred ones and damnation for those deemed unholy" (224). Barnes offers versions of sacred history told by the unholy not just in the opening chapter, "The Stowaway," but in Chapter 2 ("The Visitors"), Chapter 3 ("The Wars of Religion"), the second story about Jonah in Chapter 7 and the final chapter set in heaven ("The Dream"), as well as mocking the pretensions of religious enthusiasts searching for the remains of the Ark in Chapters 6 ("The Mountain") and 9 ("Project Ararat"). Barnes admitted to one interviewer that for this book originally he "was going to write 'Geoffrey Braithwaite's Guide to the Bible.' Which would be the entire Bible, restructured for handy modern use, with the boring bits cut out, written by an agnostic skeptic rationalist" ("A Talk" 15).

Barnes says categorically that he does not subscribe to a sacred interpretation of history ("From Flaubert's Parrot" G-8). It is not surprising that he should repeatedly cite providential accounts of history as prime examples of the imposition of a privileged version of the past on the present. In the opening chapter the woodworm's portrait of Noah as an irascible, unpredictable tyrant is paralleled by his or her portrayal of the Old Testament God: "I suppose it wasn't altogether Noah's fault. I mean, that God of his was a really oppressive role model" (21). "That God of his" instantly deprives God of universality, while "role model" reduces him to the status of an unsatisfactory father figure. (Later in the book God is called a "moral bully," a "paranoid schizophrenic" and is marked down as author of the story about Jonah and the whale "for plot, motivation, suspense and characterization" [177]). Noah is held up as the first human to use God's authority to rewrite history as a justification of the survivors: "The Fall was the serpent's fault, the honest raven was a slacker and a glutton, the goat turned Noah into an alkie [alcoholic]." As the woodworm remarks sarcastically, "What a brazen attempt to shift responsibility on to the animals" (29). Here we meet the first of many instances where the victors of official history justify their stance by demonizing their opponents.

A History, then, constitutes a concerted fictional attack on traditional notions of history and of official accounts of it. One of the characteristics of such history that the novel exposes is its reliance on the art of narration. Barthes makes a similar accusation when he writes, "The historian is not so much a collector of facts as a collector and relater of signifiers; that is to say, he organizes them with the purpose of establishing positive meaning and filling the vacuum of pure, meaningless series" ("Discourse of History" 16). Barnes uses his own fictional narrative to counter history's reliance on narration. The question arises, is it possible to narrate the barbarism of the past without estheticizing and thereby undoing the purpose of that narration? Barnes's novel, as Matthew Pateman puts it, is simultaneously "worried by the brutality of specific events and by the way these events are sanitized through narrative" (45). Many reviewers of the book doubted whether it met the esthetic criteria of a novel. Writing for the *Spectator*, D.J. Taylor flatly stated, "*A History of the World in 10 1/2 Chapters* is not a novel . . . it possesses no character who rises above the level of a cipher and no plot worth speaking of" (40). Many reviewers responded similarly.[5] Barnes, however, has insisted that "the novel is a very large and generous form, and there's always been a tradition of the informal novel as well as the formal novel" ("The World" E-1). He admits that he was certainly pushing the envelope when writing *A History*, but he still considers it an example of "what happens when you bend the traditional narrative and fracture it" ("A Talk" 15). *A History* then takes the disruption of conventional narrative features such as form and narrative continuity to such an extreme that it risks accusations such as the above in its attempt to escape from the charge of beautifying history's record of barbarism.

Nevertheless, despite the book's chronological and narrative irregularities, is the reader's natural urge to make connections between these disparate segments of text, to convert this sequence of varying narratives into a larger overarching narrative, given encouragement by various connective devices in the book? Is there a shape, a beginning and end to this book? Does it qualify as what Frank Kermode has called one of those fictions "whose ends are consonant with origins, and in concord, however unexpected, with their precedents," fictions which "satisfy our needs" by giving significance to our lives, seeing that we live our whole lifetime in the midst of things (*Sense* 5, 7)? Equally does it live up to Barnes's own dictum that "art is the stuff you finally understand, and life, perhaps, is the stuff you finally can't understand" (Interview with McGrath 23)? Paradoxically, the book is equally the work of a contemporary writer who typically does not see much coherence or order in the world around him. Life is "all hazard and chaos, with occasional small pieces of progress," he told one interviewer ("From Flaubert's Parrot" 9). But that doesn't mean that art has to be equally chaotic. Writing about form in music in "The Silence," the last story in *The Lemon Table* (2004), the protagonist, a famous composer, concludes, "it is the severity of style and the profound logic that creates the inner connection between motifs" (231). So the kinds of connections and the kind of coherence found in this book simultaneously reflect this late twentieth century sense of dislocation in human life and history:

> The history of the world? Just voices echoing in the dark; images that burn for a few centuries and then fade; stories, old stories that sometimes seem to overlap; strange links, impertinent connections. (240)

That is a more accurate description of the contents and connections within this book than might be apparent.

Let us start with those strange links and impertinent connections. Chapter 1 reveals among other things that Noah and his family stayed alive for the duration of their sojourn at sea by eating to extinction a number of the species who had entered the Ark two by two. Further Noah and his family discriminated between what they called the clean and unclean species when selecting which animals to kill and cook. The next chapter describes the tourists unsuspectingly entering the cruise ship "in obedient couples." "'The animals came in two by two,' Franklin commented" (33). Sure enough, when the Arab hijackers come to start shooting two passengers an hour, they adopt a similar policy to Noah's of segregating those unclean nationalities supposedly most responsible for the Palestinians' predicament and murdering them first: "the bodies were flung over the rail in pairs" (58). While Barnes is clearly isolating some recurrent characteristics of human behavior (a proclivity for class or caste distinctions and prejudice), he is more interested in raising questions. He claims to agree with Flaubert's dictum, which Barnes paraphrased for one interviewer: "The desire to reach conclusions is a sign of human stupidity" (Interview with McGrath 23). The questions that Barnes raises in this book nevertheless show a relatedness, though one that is problematized.

The same motif —the division between the clean and the unclean—occurs in the third of the three stories comprising Chapter 7. This opens by inviting comparison with the *Achille Lauro*-type cruise ship of Chapter 2:

> At 8 PM on Saturday, 13th May 1939, the liner *St Louis* left its home port of Hamburg. It was a cruise ship, and most of the 937 passengers booked on its transatlantic voyage carried visas confirming that they were "tourists, travelling for pleasure" (181).

In fact they are anything but tourists. They are Jews fleeing from a Nazi state intent on exterminating them. They might possibly also include some of the Zionists against whom the Arabs later stage their attack in Chapter 2. Unlike that previous fictional episode involving the terrorists, this "story" is a factual account of a shameful episode dating from just prior to the outbreak of the Second World War in which many of the world's free countries, including the United States, refused to allow these political refugees to disembark for various spurious reasons. The original intention was that all the emigrants would disembark in Havana. When the Cuban authorities held out for more money than the emigrants could come up with an impasse resulted. One suggestion was that, as 250 passengers were booked for the return journey to Europe, at least the same number of Jews might be allowed to disembark. Barnes continues: "But how would you choose the 250 who were to be allowed off the Ark? Who would separate the clean from the unclean? Was it to be done by casting lots" (184)?

Those three words—"Ark," "clean," and "unclean"—carry an additional semantic burden that has been created by the earlier narrative episodes. An Ark/ship that is supposed to protect its occupants from the storms of the world turns into a prison ship for animals and humans alike, both of whom are victimized by being categorized as the other by those in control. For the reader who remembers that according to Genesis, God caused it to rain "for forty days and forty nights" (7:4), Barnes's comment in the penultimate paragraph that the 350 Jews allowed into Britain "were able to reflect that their wanderings at sea had lasted precisely forty days and forty nights" (188) resonates with irony. This biblical period of time is also precisely the duration of Moses's stay on Mount Sinai and of Jesus's stay in the wilderness. Similarly, the suggestion that the refugees might try "casting lots" reminds the reader of the biblical accounts of the casting of lots between Saul and his son Jonathan and of the Roman soldiers casting lots for the crucified Jesus's garments. What is the final effect of these intertextual references? They illustrate the fact that from the beginnings of time humans have sought to validate their own identity and status by turning on those they choose to designate the "unclean." Further, humans tend to reinforce these actions by appealing to the authority of some organized form of religion. Beneath a postmodern veil of raising questions, this accumulation of instances invites the reader to reach some provisional conclusions (I would stress the plural) concerning human nature in all these *petits récits*.

Some of these seemingly impertinent connections between chapters are predictive rather than retrospective. In Chapter 1, among the animals on the Ark who are afraid of Noah are the reindeer. But "it wasn't just fear of Noah, it was something deeper" (12). They show powers of foresight, "as if they were saying, You think this is the worst? Don't count on it" (13). What it is that so scares them is not revealed until Chapter 4. There, after a Chernobyl-type nuclear disaster, reindeer in Norway that have received a high dose of radiation are being slaughtered and fed to mink. At first the authorities plan to bury the reindeer. But that would make "it look as if there's been a problem, like something's actually gone wrong" (86). The female protagonist comments: "we've been punishing animals from the beginning, haven't we?" (87) She concludes, "Everything is connected, even the parts we don't like, especially the parts we don't like" (84). That comment equally applies to the narrative organization of this book as a whole. Noah's presumptuous use and disposal of the animals committed to his care anticipates a continuing arrogance on humans' part, the disastrous consequences of which are just as readily suppressed by the modern media as they were in the biblical account of Noah in Genesis. The reader's knowledge that such censorship on the part of the authorities is all too likely, despite the fictional nature of Chapter 4, retrospectively bestows a peculiar kind of imaginative authority on Barnes's retelling of the biblical story of Noah in which he fictionally reinscribes what he infers are the suppressed elements of the official account of the episode. His connection of the parts we don't like only adds to their credibility.

Take a different instance of Barnes's apparently insignificant yet ultimately crucial connections between his parts and chapters. Chapter 10 pictures heaven as a dreamlike state in which dreamers "get the sort of Heaven they want." The dreamer-protagonist asks his heavenly informant, "And what sort do they want on the whole?" "Well," she replies, "they want a continuation of life, that's what we find. But . . . better, needless to say" (298–99). What that turns out to be in practice is principally golf, sex, shopping, and meeting famous people (such as Noah), all of which activities reveal their underlying banality as the millennia pass by. Among the famous people is Hitler (a reference back not just to the *St Louis* but to his predecessor in prejudicial discrimination, Noah). The dreamer is naturally surprised at finding this arch-villain in heaven. What, he demands, happened to Hell? It turns out there isn't any Hell, merely a theme park filled with skeletons and devils played by out-of-work actors. As his heavenly informant explains, "that's all people want nowadays" (300). Clearly Barnes's heaven is a collective projection of the twentieth-century psyche. Only in this final chapter is the human need to separate living beings into the clean and the unclean abandoned in favor of an anodyne world where everyone is equal—and eventually equally bored by it all, so bored that they opt to die for a second time. The dreamer concludes that, "Heaven's a very good idea, it's a perfect idea you could say, but not for us. Not given the way we are" (307). The implication is that the human species is only happy when it has artificially created an unclean Other that provides it with its sense of privileged identity. A world in which no one is discriminated against is merely a dream of what we imagine we want but would actually find intolerably innocuous and tedious. Dependent on binary oppositions for our (false) sense of identity, we choose not to deconstruct them.

One critic has attempted to argue that the book has an over-arching form. María Lozano uses Derrida's model of repetition and change to suggest that, "up to chapter five we have a concentration on the isolated, enclosed situation of catastrophe and shipwreck while in the second part . . . the movement seems reversed, concentrating on the second part of Noah's story, that of arrival and rescue" (123). But neither of the two expeditions to Ararat constitute any kind of true "rescue," while the stories of the Jewish refugees on the *St Louis* or of the actor and crew on the raft repeat the "enclosed situation of catastrophe" supposed to characterize Chapters 1 to 5. There may not be a metanarrative to this book, but certain repetitive motifs are discernible. Do these recurring patterns have any referential reality? Or are they all simply products of the web of textuality, interpretation, and narration? Overtly Barnes only replies in narrative terms. If the book works for you, he has said, "then you see that it sort of thickens and deepens as it goes on, and that one chapter is set in a precise relationship to the other chapter" ("The World" E1). He is suggesting here that each chapter gains resonance by its links and parallels to previous chapters. The structural parallels are numerous. As has been noted, the opening and closing chapters offer narratives of the near-beginning and near-end of human history. Chapter 1 introduces a series of motifs that recur in subsequent chapters and carry similar associations with them. Noah's divisiveness has already been seen to echo down the ages. The motif of his drunkenness ("You could even argue, I suppose, that God drove Noah to drink" [30]) reappears in chapters recounting the wreck of the *Medusa*, the actor on location in the jungle, the monks' cultivating the vine at the monastery on Mount Ararat, and life in heaven. The Ark as a refuge-cum-prison is reincarnated in the cruise ship hijacked by terrorists and the Jewish refugees' *St. Louis*, in the *Medusa*, in the small boat in which the (possibly deranged) Kath takes off to escape the nuclear catastrophe ("The Survivor"), and in the raft that capsizes and drowns the principal actor in the jungle.

The Ark lands on Mount Ararat at the end of Chapter 1. Chapter 6 concocts a story about the journey that an Irish woman made in 1840 to Mount Ararat where she stages her own death. In Chapter 9 an ex-astronaut (reminiscent of Apollo 15's James Irwin) is convinced that God spoke to him while he was on the moon instructing him to find Noah's Ark. He mounts his expedition in 1977 and discovers the skeleton of what he at first assumes to be Noah, only for the pathologists to inform him that it belongs to a woman who died there some 150 years before—the protagonist of Chapter 6. The astronaut is himself casually mentioned by the actor in Chapter 8 as returning like him from a strange land totally transformed. The identification of the sleazy actor (who ends up—significantly drunk—writing to his ex-lover, "Listen bitch why don't you just get out of my life" 220) with the born-again astronaut provides a form of anticipatory deflation of the religious zealot's integrity. Even the half chapter in its discussion of love refers to his wife as "the centre of my world," just as the "Armenians believed that Ararat was the centre of the world" (234).

These motifs and homologous connections proliferate far beyond what has been outlined above. They suggest in narrative form a continuity beneath the bewildering variety of human activity over the ages. The extent (and culturally determined limits) of that variety is neatly summarized by the dreamer in heaven. Apart from eating, golf, sex, and shopping, he indulges in more or less all the incidents that have already been recounted in the previous nine and half chapters:

— I went on several cruises [Chapters 2 and 7];
— I learned canoeing [Chapter 8], mountaineering [Chapters 6 and 9], ballooning;
— I got into all sorts of danger and escaped [Chapters 4, 5, and 7];
— I explored the jungle [Chapter 8];
— I watched a court case (didn't agree with the verdict) [Chapter 3];
— I tried being a painter (not as bad as I thought!) and a surgeon [Chapter 5];
— I fell in love, of course, lots of times ["Parenthesis"—the half chapter];
— I pretended I was the last person on earth (and the first) [Chapters 10 and 1]. (297)

There is no master discourse. This book is titled *A History of the World*. As Merritt Moseley comments, "No claim is made that this history is the right one [. . .] there are only histories" (109). But the repetitions and intertextual allusions also assert in narrative form that certain patterns of human interaction reappear over the course of history. No matter how you tell it— and Barnes tells it in a bewildering variety of ways—history seemingly cannot help revealing certain repetitive aspects of human nature.

Perhaps the most reiterated motif is that of the woodworm related to that of the numerous reincarnations of the Ark. It is a woodworm who is revealed in the final sentence of the chapter to be the narrator of Chapter 1. He or she and six other woodworms stow away on the Ark and escape undetected after the flood has subsided. Yet the status of this woodworm is as ambiguous as that of the traditional historian who, Barthes writes, by insisting on the act of historical utterance, contrives to "'dechronologize' the 'thread' of history" ("Discourse" 10). In the final surprise paragraph of Chapter 1 of Barnes's book the woodworm speaks "with the hindsight of a few millennia" (30). This confusion between narrated and narrator's time, according to Barthes, places the historian in the same position as the maker of myth: "It is to the extent that he *knows* what has not yet been told that the historian, like the actor of myth, needs to double up the chronological unwinding of events with references to the time of his own speech" ("Discourse" 30). Thus the woodworm's atemporal status draws attention to its further use in the book as a signifier of a recurrent signified to be found in life in all its forms. The woodworm's is the voice of the outcast—excluded from God's ways and from official history. He or she is highly critical of both God and the ways of Noah and his species:

Put it this way: Noah was pretty bad, but *you should have seen the others*. It came as little surprise to us that God decided to wipe the slate clean;

the only puzzle was that he chose to preserve anything at all of this species whose creation did not reflect particularly well on its creator. (8)

Noah's carnivorous decimation of the animal population is seen as an instance of social snobbery, arrogance justified by appeal to a God suspiciously biased towards the human species that invoked (or invented?) him.

Woodworms constantly crop up throughout the rest of the book. Fittingly they are responsible in Chapter 3 for eating through a leg of the Bishop of Besançon's throne which collapses causing him to be "hurled against his will into a state of imbecility" (64).'As in Chapter 1, they are representative of those forces of nature that, excluded from human society, return to eat away at human attempts to defy the forces of time and decay. The villagers' successful prosecution of the woodworms who end up being excommunicated is ironically undercut by the conclusion in which the closing words of the *juge d'Église* have been eaten by woodworm. The facts excluded from the canon of the church are imaginatively reinserted by Barnes into its history, thereby undermining its authorized account of the past. In Chapter 8 woodworms are still the one danger to the survival of the actor–narrator's discourse (his bizarre love letters) on their journey out of the jungle; letters have to be protected from them by being placed in a plastic bag. This is typical of what Barnes refers to as his thickening effect. By this stage he has turned the insect into a potent metaphor for that which is excluded or denied by various monologic discourses. So when he comes to describe the astronaut turned religious zealot who hears God tell him to search for Noah's Ark in Chapter 9, Barnes is able to undermine the astronaut's sense of divine truth by a brief ironic reference to the woodworm: "he knew it [the Ark] couldn't have rotted or been eaten by termites, because God's command to find the Ark clearly implied that there was something left of it" (266). The astronaut shows the same blind faith in revealed truth that Noah did. He even asserts that as Noah used only gopher-wood for the Ark it was "probably resistant to both rot and termites" (266). The survival of the woodworm convincingly asserts the existence of an alternative, repressed version of events.

So many of the chapters offer versions of the Ark, boats built for human survival against the storms of God or nature and time. Yet these craft are all subject to the caprices of the woodworm eating away at them from within, or of what they come to represent in more general terms—the human and non-human, excluded forces of our world. Pleasure trips turn into nightmares. Rafts constructed to film a reenactment of a past disaster on the river repeat that disaster. Art becomes confused with reality by Indians and film crew alike, just as historical narrative becomes confused with fictional narrative by writer and readers alike. The unsinkable *Titanic* sinks and Beesley finds himself "for the second time in his life . . . leaving the *Titanic* just before it was due to go down" (175).

Barnes's two-part treatment in Chapter 5 ("Shipwreck") of the notorious shipwreck of the *Medusa* in 1816 and the subsequent painting of the survivors on the raft executed by Géricault in 1819 brings many of the themes and motifs of the book together. Occupying a central position in the book, Chapter 5 constitutes a metanarrative offering a prolonged meditation on the relationship between historical and artistic narrative. First comes his dispassionate but carefully shaped account of what happened to the 150 passengers and crew who spent fifteen days on the raft before being rescued. Based on *Narrative of a Voyage to Senegal*, a book written by two survivors (Henry Savigny and Alexander Corréard) from the raft of the *Medusa*, Barnes has, as Tomás Monterrey argues, "imposed an alternative arrangement [on the source account] to emphasize the dynamics of chaos" (420). The survivors mutiny and fight among themselves (as Noah's family did). They start eating the flesh of their dead comrades (as Noah ate his animals). Eventually the survivors are forced to make a choice between treating the fifteen healthy and twelve wounded alike, or throwing the wounded overboard to conserve the diminishing provisions. They choose the latter: "The healthy were separated from the unhealthy like the clean from the unclean" (121). We are back on Noah's Ark. The two survivors of the fifteen who were rescued and wrote *Narrative of a Voyage to Senegal* remind the reader of Noah by concluding that "the manner in which they were saved was truly miraculous, and that the finger of Heaven was conspicuous in the event" (123). But what about the 135 "unclean" who were killed or drowned before help arrived? On the one hand the "God-eyed version of what 'really' happened is a fake." But, Barnes goes on to argue, "we must still believe that objective truth is obtainable," even if only 43 percent objective truth is obtainable. The alternative is to award the victor "the right not just to the spoils but to the truth" (243–44). Even fictitious accounts of the past, such as that of Chapter 1, correct the victor's misrepresentation of history by imaginatively reinscribing the presence of the silenced opposition.

In the second section Barnes turns to the way in which Géricault chose to portray this incident. It opens: "How do you turn catastrophe into art" (125)? This is clearly the question Barnes is asking himself throughout his own attempt to turn the catastrophes of human history into meaningful, that is fictional, shape. Géricault had access to the same accounts from two of the survivors that Barnes summarized in the first section. Yet the painting shows not fifteen (as they reported) but twenty men on the raft, five of them dead. The painter has dragged five of the wounded back from the sea: "And should the dead lose their vote in the referendum over hope versus despair?" (131). Barnes wants to demonstrate the way any artist is compelled to rearrange the facts to give meaning to his narrative composition. Géricault cleans up the raft and restores the survivors to healthy muscularity. Why? In order to shift us as spectators "through currents of hope and despair, elation, panic and resignation" (137). According to Barnes Géricault

is intent on demonstrating the equality of optimistic and pessimistic interpretations of human destiny. So he chooses to depict not the moment of rescue, but the earlier moment when the survivors sight a vessel on the horizon
that fails to see them or come closer. Barnes's comment on Géricault's painting connects it to similar human responses by the occupants of Noah's ark:

[. . .] how rarely do our emotions meet the object they seem to deserve?
How hopelessly we signal; how dark the sky; how big the waves. We are
all lost at sea, washed between hope and despair, hailing something that
may never come to rescue us. (137)

Much like Beckett's reference in *Waiting for Godot* to the two thieves crucified with Christ one of whom is saved and the other damned, as many survivors hope that the boat is coming closer as conclude that it is heading
away from them. The painting invites us to read it as "an image of hope
being mocked" (132).

Barnes appears to conclude with the observation: "Catastrophe has
become art: that is, after all, what it is for" (137). Barnes is simultaneously
being ironic and yet serious here. Like Géricault, he has used all his powers
as an artist to portray history as an account not of hope alone (the narrative
of the victors) but of both hope and despair. Barnes drives home this point
by returning to the subject of Noah. Why did the artistic depiction of his Ark
on the flood waters go out of fashion in the early sixteenth century?
Michelangelo's painting of this incident on the ceiling of the Sistine Chapel
establishes a new trend by placing the Ark in the background. "What fills
the foreground are the anguished figures of those doomed antediluvians left
to perish when the chosen Noah and his family were saved" (138). By
Poussin's time "old Noah has sailed out of art history" (138). The early modern world chose to reinscribe a different story, not a conflicting one, but a
complementary one that by its emphasis on the doomed casts Noah and the
biblical story about him in a less privileged, more dubious light. History is a
construct of the present, of its emphasis and perspective.

It is surprising, then, that in his half chapter, "Parenthesis," Barnes does
not treat art as the best response to the false narratives of the past promot-
ed by religion. "Art, picking up confidence from the decline of religion,
announces its transcendence of the world [. . .] but this announcement isn't
accessible to all, or where accessible isn't always inspiring or welcome." So,
he concludes, "religion and art must yield to love" (242–43). Why love? One
reason Barnes offers is that love resists the tyranny of history which is no
more than fabulation. "Our panic and our pain are only eased by soothing
fabulation; we call it history" (240). Love can't change history, Barnes
asserts, but it can "teach us to stand up to history" (238). Love, then, represents our personal truth. But that truth bred of pure subjectivity can best be
articulated by art. And the woodworm eats away at love as much as at the

frame of Géricault's painting. So any true artist has to give a voice also to that excluded other, the woodworm in our midst. Ultimately the woodworm is a textual presence, signifying the presence of an aporia, reminding us of the many omissions made by historians in creating a textual continuum of the past.

In "Parenthesis" one notices one of those "impertinent connections" (240) that Barnes claims make up the history of the world: "Trusting virgins were told that love was [. . .] an ark on which two might escape the Flood." In Barnes's comment the irony is unmistakable: "It may be an ark, but one on which anthropophagy is rife; an ark skippered by some crazy greybeard who beats you round the head with his gopher-wood stave, and might pitch you overboard at any moment" (229). Love, the only possible resistance to the lies of history, is itself cannibalistic and highly unpredictable. Other such connections in "Parenthesis" catch the eye: love will make you unhappy, he asserts, either sooner due to incompatibility, "or unhappy later, when the woodworm has quietly been gnawing away for years and the bishop's throne collapses" (243). In the final chapter, "The Dream," the naive, typically bourgeois narrator experiences sex that casts his lifetime's relationship with his wife in the shade. And yet even this form of love palls.

Does the final chapter, then, thicken this earlier half chapter by retrospectively casting it in an ironic light that escapes notice when first reading it? Does the last chapter function as a kind of textual woodworm, undermining whatever certainties the earlier half chapter appeared to offer the reader? Is the reader being taught to live without answers, seeing that all the infallible answers offered to the narrator by his celestial informant only serve to leave him unsatisfied? Our dreams of a heaven turn out to be palliatives, something we need because, as the narrator learns, we "can't get by without the dream" (307). Past and future belong to the realm of dreams—or of the imagination, the domain of (narrative) art. In dreaming that he has just woken up, the narrator of the final chapter parallels the reader who has been induced by the power of the narrative to believe that he or she has been experiencing the fragmented actuality of human history, when all that has been shared is a dream of our past and our future. This confusion between dreaming and waking states is elaborated on at the end of "The Survivor." The reader has no way of deciding whether Kath is on an island and the men in her dreams are the dreamers or whether she is in a hospital and she herself is the dreamer.

If history is a product of collective dreaming, why shouldn't Barnes dream up his own version of the past? It is quite productive to see the chapters comprising this book as a series of images, each asking the spectator or reader to make his or her own mind up as to their relative truth-value, while each adds to, thickens or deepens our understanding of the rest. In one interview Barnes uses this analogy to justify the fictional or artistic coherence of the book as a whole. The novel is "perhaps more like a sequence of paintings on a wall," he suggests, "if you imagine a series of twelve, six on the top and six on the bottom. You can get pleasure from each in turn if you want to, but if you look at them together, then you see that they amount to one big panel" ("The World" E1). At the same time in "Parenthesis" Barnes calls those "medieval paintings which show all the stages of Christ's Passion as happening simultaneously in different parts of the picture" "a charming, impossible fake" (243).

Barnes eschews a God-eyed narrative perspective in this book. The relation between his narrative fragments is one of disjunction, ironic juxtaposition, disparity. In this way he is able to give fictional life to the barbarity of human history by restoring to the losers of history their voices and stories while avoiding estheticizing his narration of them, as Ackroyd might be accused of doing. But, like Ackroyd, he rejects the traditional assumption that "there is some special dispensation whereby the signs that constitute an historical text have reference to events in the world" (Kermode, *Genesis* 108). His book celebrates the textuality of history, the narrativity of historical narration. As Barthes writes, "in 'objective' history, the 'real' is never more than an unformulated signified, sheltering behind the apparently all-powerful referent" ("Discourse" 17). Barnes points to a signified by using as signifiers those strange links and impertinent connections that invite the reader to discover a coherent, skeptical attitude to history in the book as a whole. In reviewing this book Salman Rushdie claimed that what Barnes was attempting was "the novel as footnote to history, as subversion of the given . . . fiction as critique" (*Imaginary Homelands* 241). Seen in that light, this book can be seen to belong to the same genre as Rushdie's novels, fiction written on and about the margins of life past and present that nevertheless comes to occupy its center.

Lists of Books Published

Fiction

Metroland, 1980.
Before She Met Me, 1982.
Flaubert's Parrot, 1984.
Staring at the Sun, 1986.
A History of the World in 10 1/2 Chapters, 1989.
Talking It Over, 1991.
The Porcupine, 1992.
Cross Channel (short stories), 1996.
England, England, 1998.
Love, etc, 2000.
The Lemon Table (short stories), 2004.
Arthur & George, 2005.

Crime Novels by "Dan Kavanagh"

Duffy, 1980.
Fiddle City, 1981.
Putting the Boot In, 1985.
Going to the Dogs, 1987.

Non-Fiction

Letters from London, 1995.
Something to Declare, 2002.
The Pedant in the Kitchen, 2003.

3

Martin Amis: *Time's Arrow, or The Nature of the Offense* (1991)

Both World Wars in the twentieth century served succeeding generations as markers of a major break with the past. The time before each war was quickly mythologized as a golden age, a time of innocence irretrievably lost. The exaggerated sense of a complete rupture with previous history can be equally evidenced in D. H. Lawrence's famous declaration, "It was in 1915 the old world ended" (*Kangaroo* 240), and Martin Amis's conviction that with the 1941 German invasion of Russia "a line is crossed," a line between civilization and savagery (*Koba the Dread* 201). The historical accuracy of these assertions is less significant than the use to which they were put by postwar generations. In the case of novelists the sense of a cataclysmic break with the past frequently gave rise to an apocalyptic sense in the present; this in turn made them feel the need to seek out modes of narration that corresponded more closely to contemporary feelings of confusion and anxiety. In particular, the chronological imperative of realist narrative seemed irrelevant to a generation for whom the present was so determined and fractured by the immediate past. As Italo Calvino explained it in 1979, since "the dimension of time has been shattered" in the postwar world, novels could only represent love or thought "in fragments" in an era when time "seem[s] to have exploded" (8).

Time's Arrow (1991) confronts a question that has consumed Amis from an early stage in his writing career: is modernity leading civilization to self destruction? Amis's timeframe is much shorter than that of Barnes. His sense of the past is rooted in the second half of the twentieth century. While his main concern is about the world's development of nuclear weapons, he sees the origins of the West's drive to implode in the Holocaust (*Time's Arrow*) and the Soviet gulags (*Koba the Dread*). The Holocaust is, Amis has said, "the central event of the twentieth century" ("Unlike Father" 16). As Dermot McCarthy observes, "For Amis, his generation suffers from an event it did not experience, and will expire from one it seems powerless to prevent" (301). Whereas the emancipatory view of modernity began with the Enlightenment, philosophers since that time have continuously questioned its assumptions. Many critics contend that these questions took on a new urgency after the atrocities accompanying World War II. Jean-François Lyotard epitomizes this skepticism toward those grand narratives of modernity that he sees as responsible for those atrocities. He argues that modernity's pursuit of the universal standards governing liberal humanism has led to a lethal hostility to any deviation from or resistance to them. Lyotard proceeds to define as postmodern the large-scale postwar rejection of such metanarratives of rational progress—narratives concerned with truth, justice, and goodness. The desirability of consensus is seen by both Lyotard and Amis as responsible for the German public's support for the Nazi program of racial purification. Both writers appear to share with Eli Wiesel his conviction that "at Auschwitz not only man died, but also the idea of man"—that is, the liberal humanist idea of "man" (Rosenfeld 154).

As Lyotard wrote in *Le Différend*, Auschwitz disproves that "[e]verything real is rational, everything rational is real: 'Auschwitz' refutes speculative doctrine. The crime at least, which is real, is not rational" (179). Yet, as Zygmunt Bauman has pointed out in *Modernity and the Holocaust*, the Holocaust employed rationality to horrifying effect. Far from being "an antithesis of modern civilization and everything . . . it stands for, . . . the Holocaust could merely have uncovered another face of the same society whose other, so familiar, face we so admire" (7). *Time's Arrow* gives fictional life to the Janus-faced nature of modernity, to the fact that, as Walter Benjamin asserted in *Illuminations*, "there is no document of civilization which is not at the same time a document of barbarism" (256). In *Koba the Dread* Amis similarly identifies the Holocaust with the use of modern technology that is itself the product of rational progress: "The exceptional nature of the Nazi genocide has much to do with its 'modernity,' its industrial scale and pace" (83). The systematic extermination of six million innocent civilians, an act of the highest irrationality, relied on rational means for its implementation. This crucial event in modern history (repeated in Cambodia, the former Yugoslavia, Rwanda, and Sudan) is a paradox that invites the use of paradoxical narrative techniques on the part of a novelist attempting to evoke it.

Amis harbors an ambivalent attitude toward modernity. His novels present an apocalyptic vision of contemporary civilization, what he calls "the toiletization of the planet." His jaded view of modernity may account, he has said, for the way many of his fictional characters behave "as if they're heading towards an ending too" (Interview with Bragg). At the same time he says that he is "trying to get more truthful about what it's like to be alive now" ("Down" 35). The work of a darkly comic writer, his novels attempt to undermine as well as embody the suicidal behavior of the modern world. He sees himself as representative of the experience of growing up in a post-World War II world: "We are like no other people in history" (Interview with McGrath 194). Amis then perceives himself as modernity personified, as split between ameliorative and pessimistic versions of what it is to be modern. This two-faced vision of modernity comes to fictional life in the two incarnations through which the protagonist of *Time's Arrow* lives his life.

One can discern a further parallel between on the one hand the different perspectives of the protagonist and the narrator within the novel and on the other Lyotard's distinction between two modes of (post)modernity—the melancholic and the jubilatory. For Lyotard both modes are part of a modern esthetics of the sublime. The sublime entails a "combination of pleasure and pain, the pleasure that reason should exceed all presentation, the pain that imagination or sensibility should not be equal to the concept" (*Postmodern Condition* 81). According to Lyotard modern art seeks the experience of freedom by staging a permanent crisis in representation. If modern art is distinguished by its presentation of "the unpresentable in presentation itself" (81), what distinguishes the postmodern mode and gives it its jubilatory or pleasurable connotation is its "invention of new rules of the game" (80), of "allusions to the conceivable which cannot be presented" (81). This latter mode is arguably what the narrator of *Time's Arrow* does. Both of these two modes of modernity offer critiques of representation, of what Lyotard calls "the 'lack of reality' of reality" (*Postmodern Condition* 77). As in *Time's Arrow*, "they often exist in the same piece, are almost indistinguishable; and yet they testify to a difference (*a différend*) on which the fate of thought depends . . . between regret and assay" (80).

One could substitute "trial" or "test" for "assay," for each word accentuates the novelty and unrepeatability of such works. The point is that the first mode, like the chronological account of the life of the protagonist Odilo Unverdorben, a Nazi doctor who worked at Auschwitz, induces feelings of melancholy or regret (to understate readers' reactions to the atrocities he commits), while the second mode, like the chronologically reversed account of Unverdorben's life, leads to feelings of jubilation that the evocation of the postmodern sublime produces through its radical critique of representation. But the two modes are separated by a *différend* that Lyotard defines as "a case of conflict between (at least) two parties that cannot be equitably resolved for lack of a rule of judgment applicable to both arguments" (*The Différend* xi). This is one explanation for why Unverdorben the narrator cannot understand Unverdorben the protagonist. Amis both knows about and admires the mode of the sublime which he considers as the signature mark of Nabokov's early novels. In a 1979 essay titled "The Sublime and the Ridiculous: Nabokov's Black Farces," Amis expresses surprise that Nabokov's work has so seldom been considered in the light "of the sublime—the sublime directed at our fallen world of squalor, absurdity and talentlessness." He continues:

Sublimity replaces the ideas of motivation and plot with those of obsession and destiny. It suspends moral judgements in favour of remorselessness, a helter-skelter intensity. It does not proceed to a conclusion so much as accumulate possibilities of pain and danger. The sublime is a perverse mode, by definition. But there is art in its madness. (76)

This passage reads uncannily like a prophetic description of *Time's Arrow* in which destiny replaces conventional plot, remorselessness replaces moral judgment, and possibilities of pain and danger replace a conclusion. The novel is a perfect instance of the art underlying its perversity.

This chapter neither assumes conscious knowledge of Lyotard's theory on the part of Martin Amis, nor does it claim that Amis's novel is necessarily postmodern just because it conforms to Lyotard's definition of the postmodern within modernity.[1] But Lyotard does offer a useful definition of the way all modern art offers a perpetual critique of art's claim to representational realism, a critique which can assume its most radical form by a use of the postmodern sublime that simultaneously produces pleasure and pain in the reader. After Auschwitz and Stalinism, Lyotard insists, no one could maintain that the hopes that were bound up with modernity have been fulfilled. To write at all about the Holocaust is to risk estheticizing the unthinkable. The same danger made Theodor Adorno formulate his famous maxim that "writing poetry after Auschwitz is barbaric," though he withdrew it later (19). Further, how can something as tragic as the Holocaust be incorporated in a work of fiction by a writer who believes that in our contemporary world "tragedy and the heroic have disappeared" (Hubbard 118)? Amis instinctively resorts to narrative strategies that produce the effect of the sublime. In structuring the novel Amis employed three inter-related narrative techniques: a narrative form (temporal reversal), a narrative perspective (the splitting of protagonist and narrator) and a narrative mode (that of irony producing black humor). The narrative simultaneously embodies the pleasure of returning to a less appalling phase of modernity and the pain at the recollection of Western civilization's fall from innocence.

Amis sheds light on the form he chose for this novel when he writes that the crisis facing our prematurely aging planet "is no longer spatial. It is temporal" (*War* 33). So it is appropriate that he employs a temporal reversal in *Time's Arrow* to remind his readers of the innocent past that he considered was still inhabited by his father's generation. "For his generation you were what you were, and that was that. It made you unswervable and adamantine. My father has this quality. I don't. None of us do" (*War* 170). Simultaneously Amis accuses his father's generation of being responsible for getting it "hugely wrong" by generally endorsing the use of atomic weapons to end the war with Japan (*Einstein's Monsters* 13). Exaggerating the contrast, Amis seems to feel that his father's generation experienced a form of Edenic state that it was also responsible for losing for ever. The order in which events are narrated in the novel takes the reader from an ugly and cruel present back to a prelapsarian time when experience is exchanged for innocence. At the same time the chronological story carries us inexorably through the horrors of the concentration camps to the contaminated postlapserian world of Ronald Reagan's America. The narrative order follows the fortunes of a German doctor, Odilo Unverdorben, a Nazi who becomes active in the mass extermination that took place at Auschwitz. After escaping from the Russians who liberated the camp, he flees to Portugal where he assumes the name of Hamilton de Souza. Using false papers he emigrates to America as John Young and ends up assuming an identity as an American physician called Tod Friendly. Reminders of the chronological story repeatedly erupt into the inverted narrative, for instance in the form of Unverdorben's dreams or his wife's rejection of his Nazi beliefs. From the opening page Amis plunges the reader into an upside down world in which the beginning of life starts at its end and death turns into a second birth. In using temporal inversion, Amis is employing the postmodern sublime by his radical critique of the possibility of presenting so notorious a landmark of modernity as the Holocaust. Lyotard warns of the danger inherent in linear narrative: "Narrative organization is constitutive of diachronic time, and the time that it constitutes has the effect of 'neutralizing' an 'initial' violence" (*Heidegger* 16). Inverting narrative chronology attempts to avoid this danger.

When Lyotard asks himself how the modern artist is to "make visible that there is something which cannot be seen" he resorts to Kant's idea of "negative presentation." Kant "says of the empty 'abstraction' which the imagination experiences when in search for a presentation of the infinite (another unpresentable), this abstraction itself is like a presentation of the infinite, its 'negative presentation'" (*Postmodern Condition* 78). Lyotard specifically cites Auschwitz as an example of the "negative presentation of the indeterminate," since so much of the physical proof of its existence was erased by the Germans at the end of the War (*The Differend* 56). In the same spirit, *Time's Arrow* uses this esthetic of the sublime to present the unpresentable practices employed at Auschwitz. By reversing their temporal direction Amis can simultaneously evoke what he cannot present by invoking their negative presentation—one which culminates in a process of healing and a renewal of life. Amis acknowledges in the novel's Afterword his debt to "a certain paragraph—a famous one—by Kurt Vonnegut" (168). This refers to the Dresden firebombing passage in *Slaughterhouse Five* in which Billy Pilgrim watches backwards a late night movie of American bombers in the Second World War recovering their bombs from a German city in flames. (Compare in *Time's Arrow* the narrator's, "It just seems to me that the film is running backwards" [8].) The passage ends with Billy speculating, "Everybody turned into a baby, and all humanity, without exception, conspired biologically to produce two perfect people named Adam and Eve, he supposed" (54–55). Vonnegut's inversion of chronology offered Amis a hint for his own book length evocation of a lost Eden.

Amis first made use of the idea of narrative inversion in a short story, "Bujak and the Strong Force or God's Dice" published in 1985 and collected in *Einstein's Monsters* (1987). Basing his idea on Einstein, Bujak is "an Oscillationist, claiming that . . . the universe would expand only until unanimous gravity called it back to start again" (58). Bujak maintains that time would also be reversed causing, the narrator speculates in the last paragraph, all the events of the story to invert, concluding with Bujak "folding into" his mother's womb (59). In similar fashion the protagonist of *Time's Arrow* ends up entering his mother while she weeps and screams where he is Oedipally murdered by his father's penis at the moment of conception (164). *Time's Arrow* extends this conceit of inversion for the length of an entire book, beginning with the protagonist's death (and the narrator's birth) in America from a car accident. The book ends in 1916 in Solingen, Germany, the birthplace (and death-place) of the protagonist (but not the death-place of the narrator). Solingen is also the birthplace of Adolf Eichmann (born ten years before Unverdorben) who was responsible for overseeing the Final Solution to which the protagonist contributed (163). "Almost any deed," Amis has said, "any action, has its morality reversed, if you turn time's arrow around" (DeCurtis 147). Amis's application of this unusual form to a fictional treatment of the Holocaust involved its own "assay," its own break with all previous form.[2] Paralleling Lyotard's description of the postmodern within the modern, *Time's Arrow* "searches for new presentations, not in order to enjoy them, but in order to impart a stronger sense of the unpresentable" (*Postmodern Condition* 81). As Amis has pointed out, the effects of his inverted narrative seem "philanthropic," that is, life-giving, "if and only if, the arrow of time is reversed and that's the most fundamental law of the universe . . . that it can't be" (Reynolds and Noakes 21).[3]

In the Afterword Amis acknowledges his debt to his friend Robert Jay Lifton's *The Nazi Doctors: Medical Killing and the Psychology of Suicide* (1986). On reading this documentary account of an entire profession perversely adopting an ideology of killing as a means of healing, Amis realized that "[h]ere was a psychotically inverted world, and if you did it backward in time, it would make sense" (DeCurtis 146). How does the novel's narrative inversion give this story about the Holocaust fresh meaning? In the first place its dual reversal of chronology and causality provides an appropriate vehicle for portraying the Nazis' reversal of morality. It is no more paradoxical to represent death as birth (and vice versa) than it is for the Nazi doctors to base their practice on "a manifest absurdity—'a vision and practice of killing to heal'" (Easterbrook 57). Using a wider perspective, Daniel Oertel suggests that "*Time's Arrow's* incoherent narrative structure becomes a suitable metaphor for the incoherence of history" (132). The novel fulfils Amis's desire that history could be reversed and the atrocities of the mid-twentieth century undone. Of course he entertains this fantasy in the full knowledge that it is impossible to imagine the contemporary world without the Holocaust. As Dermot McCarthy argues "the 'terrible journey' back into WWII and the Nazi Holocaust taken by the narrator is a mirror inversion of the journey Amis sees his own generation taking *toward* nuclear holocaust" (303). Narrated in inverse order, the Holocaust is seen to be simultaneously the end product and the origin of contemporaneity. On the one hand it is seen as reverting to an archaic time in Western history: "Germans . . . have been preserved in ice from the beginning of time . . . " (131). On the other hand it is seen as progress: "But this was our mission, after all: to make Germany whole" (141). It is "a combination of the atavistic and the modern" (168). The inversion of narrative time produces what McCarthy calls a "chronillogical world" (296), which is precisely how Amis views the illogical "advance" of modern civilization after the Holocaust.

James Diedrick has suggested that the reversal of time in *Time's Arrow* offers "an audacious variation on the folk wisdom that just before death individuals see their entire lives flash before them" (133). At the same time Amis shows no desire to offer a logical rationale for his chronillogical world. To give his novel a solely rational explanation would be to return his radical experiment in narration to the fold of consensus, while "invention," Lyotard insists, "is always born of dissension" (*Postmodern Condition* xxv). Amis wants to dissent from any consensus such as that reached among Nazis regarding the superiority of the Aryan race. Amis's modern esthetic is like Lyotard's, which is "based on a never-ending critique of representation that should contribute to the preservation of heterogeneity, of optimal dissensus" (Bertens 133). Not just his argument but his entire narrative strategy stands opposed to a consensus such as the Nazis produced. In his novel, temporality, rationality, and causality are all inverted. The protagonist is characterized by his willingness to become a part of this consensus, to accept fascist ideology with what Lifton describes as its "promise of unity, oneness, fusion" (499). Even in later life the protagonist "sheds the thing he often can't seem to bear: his identity, his quiddity, lost in the crowd's promiscuity" (49).

The consequences of telling the story of Unverdorben backwards are multiple, subtle, and highly ironic. As Diedrick observes, the opening sections of the novel describing Unverdorben's (i.e. Tod Friendly's) actions as a postwar doctor in the American medical system, "eerily anticipat[e] his eventual immersion in Auschwitz and intimat[e] the terrible secret of his . . . past" (139). This is because in reverse chronology patients enter the operating room looking cured and emerge with a rusty nail that has been planted in their head by the doctor (76). From the opening pages doctors represent figures of authority "containing . . . above all power" (5). This "precognition," as Diedrick calls it, comes from the recurring dream of a figure from the "future," Uncle Pepi modeled on Dr. Josef Mengele, Auschwitz's notorious "Angel of Death." As a "biological soldier," a term first coined by the Nazis in a manual on eugenic sterilization (Lifton 30), Unverdorben joins the ranks of these doctors who "must wield the special power" (81). It is ironical, reflects the narrator, that as a doctor, "[y]ou have to harden your heart to pain and suffering" (82). But power is granted to the physician on the condition that he uses it to heal. This is part of the rationale for the Hippocratic oath a section of which is quoted early in the novel: "I will enter to help the sick, and I will abstain from all intentional wrongdoing and harm . . . " (25). In Amis's inverted time scheme the protagonist has deconstructed the oath by killing not healing, and in exercising his *power* as a doctor he reinscribes the newly inferior term (heal) within the newly superior one of killing.

Power forms one of the recurrent motifs in the novel, often becoming associated with sex. The first (i.e. last) time the protagonist has sex with Irene, the narrator says, as he "loomed above her," that he is "flooded by thoughts and feelings I've never had before. To do with power" (37). Sex makes Unverdorben feel like a lord: "you get everything on the first date . . . Instant invasion and lordship" (51). Sex is as invasive (war like) an act as surgery and becomes as perverted ("lording" over the woman) in Unverdorben's hands. Power makes those that exercise it feel like gods. Lifton describes how the "Nazis saw themselves as 'children of the gods,' empowered to destroy and kill on behalf of their higher calling" (449). Power is equated with the ultimate power over life and death that the six figures in the photograph from Unverdorben's Auschwitz period exercise over their six victims (72). Perversion of power characterizes Unverdorben's later/earlier sexual encounters with his wife, Herta, when she is "his chimpanzee required to do the housework naked, on all fours" (151). Herta is a young secretary when he meets her, and all the women he has sex with occupy subordinate social positions. Ironically sex treated as power play proves self-defeating when Unverdorben turns impotent. Is this because he has found an alternative outlet to sex for exercising his power in his role with the Waffen SS unit that was rounding up Jews in eastern Europe? He finds himself "omnipotent. Also impotent . . . powerful and powerless" (140). Amis appears to have adopted this paradoxical trait from Lifton's description of Nazi doctors who "called forth feelings of omnipotence and related sadism on the one hand, and of impotence and sometimes masochism on the other . . . " (448). Amis's inverted narrative has deconstructed Unverdorben's pursuit of power to reveal its attachment to its opposite. In adding his efforts to the consensual metanarrative of racial superiority Unverdorben has multiplied zero by zero and still got nothing, to adapt the heading of Section 6 of the novel (137).

Other critics have commented on the startling effects of the novel's inversion of chronology and causality. These effects range from the bizarre (factories and automobiles effect an environmental clean up [48]), through the perverse (Irene is blamed for her untidiness because the apartment is so much more of mess when she leaves—that is, arrives [85]), to the tragic (at Auschwitz the Nazis' purpose is to "dream a race" [120]). Amis never misses the opportunity to put the effects of reversal to use. For instance he adopts the convention of reversing the order in which dialog is given.

However, the conversations between Unverdorben and his sexual partners have an uncanny way of reading just as satisfactorily backwards as forwards, mirroring casual affairs which seem to work equally well recounted in reverse. After one such conversation the narrator comments: "I have noticed in the past, of course, that most conversations would make much better sense if you ran them backward. But with this man–woman stuff, you could run them any way you liked—and still get no further forward" (51). In *Experience* Amis asserts that "style is morality" (122). His use of inverted dialog passes judgment on the power-induced sexual encounters that Unverdorben engages in where the symmetry of the encounter reveals the outcome or termination of the affair in the opening exchange. Similarly Unverdorben's journey by ship backwards across the Atlantic from America to Europe carries an ethical charge. The narrator observes, "we leave no mark on the ocean, as if we are successfully covering our tracks" (99). This is precisely what Unverdorben was doing in real chronological time—erasing his past life. But in reality he was leaving indelible tracks in his wake that, like Yeats's rough beast, have vexed to nightmare the present age.

To effect this reversal Amis splits the narrating from the narrated subject. It appears that he found the germ of the idea for his strange narrator in Lifton's psychological concept of "'doubling': the division of the self into two functioning wholes, so that a part-self acts as an entire self" (418). At the beginning of the novel the narrator comments on his sense of estrangement from his body: "Something isn't quite working: this body I'm in won't take orders from this will of mine" (6). On the next page the narrator explains: "I have no access to his thoughts—but I'm awash with his emotions" (7). The protagonist's mind therefore directs the actions of his body as a Nazi doctor. The protagonist has had to exclude his emotions from his part-self to go through with his murderous procedures. As everyone starts to get younger, the narrator notes how "[t]hey don't find it counterintuitive, and faintly disgusting, as I do" (9). What the protagonist finds intuitive the narrator finds counterintuitive. But how could the protagonist in his chronological existence find genocide intuitive? According to Lifton, this was effected by "the transfer of conscience. The requirements of conscience were transferred to the Auschwitz self, which placed it within its own criteria for good (duty, loyalty to group, etc.), thereby freeing the original self from responsibility for actions there." This leads to a "repudiation by the original self of *anything* done by the Auschwitz self" (421, 422). That leads in turn to a split narrating subject that, unlike the reader, is disabled from being in a position to judge the narrated subject's actions with coherence. He has been deprived of life's experience, driven into a kind of limbo from which he views his alter-ego's life run in reverse with puzzlement, unable to find the key to its meaning. He can be thought of as the doctor's soul, "the soul he should have had," according to Amis (DeCurtis 146).

Most of Amis's narrators, as Amis says of Nabokov's narrators who served as partial models for his own, serve "as the malevolent force in the book." The narrator of *Time's Arrow* is the exception in being the subject of, and not the instrument for, "the spectacular humiliations that [he] is obliged to undergo" ("The Sublime" 80). Richard Menke has called the speaker of this narrative "a supremely reliable narrator: he may be relied upon to get things diametrically, and often poignantly, wrong" (960). As Amis has observed, "If the trick is to work, the unreliable narrator must in fact be very reliable indeed: reliably partial" (*Experience* 380). The narrator's partiality manifests itself in the sympathetic feelings he shows toward the disadvantaged and the marginalized in both American and German society. In the States he is affronted at the protagonist's treatment of his patients and women, while in Europe he applauds the dispersal throughout the continent of the Jews who are no longer victims of discrimination. In this sense the narrator aligns himself with Lyotard's stand against consensus in favor of heterogeneity— such as the Jewish minority in Europe. The narrator's exceptional stance then parallels Lyotard's radical esthetic of the postmodern sublime. One can only champion difference by stepping outside the rules governing the consensus—both the rules of esthetic practice (hence the inversion) and of the postwar capitalist world which the narrator is constantly condemning for its materialist and unfeeling practices. As Lyotard argues, the effect of the *différend* is to turn those outside the consensus into victims because they have no common ground on which to argue their case. This is the case with the narrator who becomes the victim of his exclusion from the master narrative that legitimated Unverdorben's conduct in Germany during the war. As McCarthy suggests, "the interrogator interrogates himself, and undergoes his own torture" (307).

McCarthy, however, pursues the metaphor too far, in my opinion, when he goes on to suggest that "Amis's narrator-as-detective discovers that he is not only the criminal he seeks but the victim as well" (307). The narrator is decidedly not the criminal that the protagonist is. The narrator can make no sense of later twentieth-century life because it offends his intuitive sense of right and wrong. Only when he returns to wartime Germany does Auschwitz "make sense" (129)—by reversing its destructive effects and turning them into an act of creation, the creation of a marginalized people. As Menke aptly puts it, the narrator "recast[s] genocide as genesis" (964). The narrator remains as ignorant of Unverdorben's criminal participation in the Holocaust as do many of those born since World War II.[4] The narrator remains a victim of an amnesia which the reader may be invited to associate with the youth of today. He is deluded, or the embodiment of a contemporary nostalgia for a reversal of the escalating horrors that constitute the history of civilization since the end of World War II.

What then are we to make of the final paragraph in which the arrow of time reverts to flying in its normal direction? Few critics have attended to this crucial turning point in the narrative. Michael Trussler claims that "ghosts can be said to spatialize time: their accusatory presence insists on infinite repetition over the irreversible loss of what we normally associate with the calendar" (28). Yet he fails to apply this insight to the predicament of the narrator at the end of the novel. Is the narrator destined to relive his life in reverse—i.e. historical—time when he will be made to experience his life in real time? Or will he become again split off from the intellectual self that cannot afford to feel the consequences of its actions? The hapless narrator represents the barren hope that we could still reverse the effects of modern history while illustrating the naivety and sheer wrong headedness that such a forgetting would involve. He embodies the inextricable combination of pleasure and pain that the postmodern sublime produces in the reader.

Significantly the reader is the absent but implied third entity in the book. Confronted with two selves, each of which is in its own form of self denial, the reader called into existence by the narrative is constantly required to supply the historical actuality that the protagonist wants to forget and the narrator misunderstands. Witness the opening dialog in the novel which offers the only instance of total speech reversal before the narrator learns to translate this back into conventional order:

"Dug. Dug," says the lady in the pharmacy.
"Dug," I join in. "Oo y'rrah?"
"Aid ut oo y'rrah?" (7)

The reader is compelled to work out the conventional order, which reads:

"How're you today?"
"Good," I join in. "How're you?"
"Good. Good," says the lady in the pharmacy.

To reach this understanding the reader must undergo three stages of comprehension. Read in reverse order the dialog appears nonsensical: the reader is presented with the unpresentable found in the mode of the postmodern sublime and experiences the pain of initial incomprehension. But before readers can reach the "translation" offered above (offering, as Lyotard suggests, pleasure which "derives from pain" [*Postmodern Condition* 77]) they must first confront the intermediate stage in which "Good" reads as "Gud" and "How're you?" as "Harr'y oo?" The full "translation" situates us in the unpleasant world of modernity. But the intermediate language suggests an interspace between the repellant modern world and the utopian world of modernity seen in reverse, an imaginary space in which we as readers find ourselves detached from the poor "translation" of the narrator while still removed like him from the hellish experience of the protagonist. The novel, in other words, instructs the implied reader in how to position him or herself in relation to both incarnations of Unverdorben. If the experienced protagonist becomes an anti-hero from whom we withdraw all sympathy, the innocent narrator proves far too naive to be trusted. Throughout the novel the narrative construction compels the reader to create meaning independently from the interpretations of events offered by either self.

Readers are made to vacillate between enjoying the conceits produced by the reversal of history and remembering with horror the actual disasters that—ironically—the narrator perceives in inverted and therefore celebratory form. An obvious instance is the narrator's reference to the Kennedy assassination, a watermark in postwar Western history, mythologized as the downfall of a modern Camelot: "JFK: flown down from Washington and flung together by the doctors' knives and the sniper's bullets and introduced onto the streets of Dallas and a hero's welcome" (81). As readers we enjoy the fantasy even as we remember (or hear of) the collective pain which swept over the world as the unfolding event was transmitted live over the airways. In Lyotardian terms, the pleasure we derive at the imagined, impossible resurrection of Kennedy "derives from the pain" we experience in recollecting the historical marker in the downward progress of recent world history. The reader is required to engage with the text in an unusually active way throughout the novel, because, as Trussler writes, "we as readers are party to, if not complicit with, a knowledge that the book desperately desires both to repress and expose" (37). At first the naivety of the narrator anaesthetizes the actions of Unverdorben, removing them from any acceptable moral context. Yet, as Amis explains, the narrator unconsciously urges readers to provide the missing dimension by showing his unease at the esthetic level: "He keeps wondering why it has to be so ugly, this essentially benevolent action" (Reynolds and Noakes 21). This entire strategy assumes a readership with a collective memory of recent Western history, and of the Holocaust in particular, one that raises important questions about the literary use of irony.

Amis's use of an irony that frequently produces humor (even if it is "disgusted laughter" that he cultivates [Trueheart B1-2]), has been attacked by some reviewers as being an inappropriate response to such a horrific event as the Holocaust. Philip Howard felt that "the ingenious form is incongruously matched with its matter, which is tragic" (14); Peter Kemp felt similarly that the reader remains "too conscious of stylistic process at the expense of human content" (7.5), and so on. But Amis maintains that the novel's irony is totally appropriate for its subject: "Nazism was a biomedical vision to excise the cancer of Jewry. To turn it into something that creates Jewry is a respectable irony" (Reynolds and Noakes 20). Irony requires a reader sufficiently alert to the stylistic use of inversion to appreciate that the fallible narrator's understanding of what his narration means is exactly opposite to the meaning (re)constructed by the reader. The last definition that the Oxford English Dictionary gives for "irony" is: "The use of language with one meaning for a privileged audience and another for those addressed or concerned."

According to Lifton, the Nazis' misuse of language "gave Nazi doctors a discourse in which killing was no longer killing" (445). In *Time's Arrow* Amis employs irony to assert an opposing ethic, undermining the way the Nazis misused language to make acceptable the business of mass murder:

> The main Ovenroom is called *Heavenblock*, its main approach road *Heavenstreet*. Chamber and Sprinkleroom are known, most mordantly, as *the central hospital.* . . When we mean *never* we say *tomorrow morning*—it's like the Spanish saying *mañana*" (124).

A further irony lies in the fact that "Sprinkleroom" is itself a euphemism, a word that attempts to sanitize the fact that gas, not water, emerged from the sprinklers. Lifton reveals how this practice of misnaming was firmly established at Auschwitz where "'Outpatient centers' were a 'place for selections'; and hospital areas, 'waiting rooms' before death" (186). The various name changes that Unverdorben undergoes further testify to the way Amis's ironic focus on language reinforces the moral stance of the narrative. If read backwards in time Tod Friendly with its associations with death (*Tod* is German for death) becomes John Young (as Jack he is a Jack of all trades and younger). John transforms into the gold-rich Hamilton de Souza, who finally assumes his German birth name of Odilo Unverdorben. His last name means "un-depraved" or "un-corrupt" in German. Thus he moves from being a figure of death to one of innocence. But of course the reader is simultaneously reversing the narrative inversion, which makes Unverdorben's journey, like the change in his ideology, one from innocence to a bearer of death. As Diedrick observes, the name Unverdorben "contains both himself and his double" (138), just as Amis's use of irony offers both a literal fantasy (of a journey to innocence) and a figurative dismissal of that fantasy (of an impossible return to the innocence of childhood or to history prior to the Holocaust). The doubling of language parallels the double time scheme and the dual codes of ethics underlying both sets of dualities.

For Amis naming, language, style cannot be separated from a writer's moral outlook. His essay on Bellow's *The Adventures of Augie March* concludes by asserting that "style is morality. Style judges . . . Things are not merely described but registered, measured and assessed for the weight with which they bear on your soul" (*War* 467). In *Time's Arrow* Hamilton, as Unverdorben calls himself in Portugal, writes some mordant lines to a twelve-year-old Rosa. "These lines of his he moodily and sometimes tearfully erases with his pen" (105). In a larger sense the benevolently inclined narrator of this inverted narration erases the entire history of the West from the 1930s to its present. The stylistic use of inversion with the irony and black humor that it produces not only overcomes the danger of automatization that attaches to the mounting accumulation of Holocaust narratives, but offers a moral standpoint from which the reader can judge what historically occurred. Amis discerns in Nabokov a "sublime" "method of moral focus." This involves a similar ethical invocation of the reader by the author's "rendering the imaginative possibilities as intensely, as open-endedly and as perilously as he can, and by letting his style prompt our choice" ("The Sublime" 82). Like Ackroyd and Barnes, Amis does not offer a totalizing panacea in place of the disasters of the past; instead he deconstructs such master narratives so as to reinforce our capacity to confront the modern world tainted by contingency, irrationality, and instability. Irony, he has written, "doesn't incite you to transform society; it strengthens you to tolerate it" ("Jane's World" 35)—by separating the reader from a society that has been permanently shaped by the trauma of the Holocaust and the specter of nuclear war.

Lyotard claims that "the little narrative [*petit récit*] remains the quintessential form of imaginative invention" (*Postmodern Condition* 60). In *The Differend* Lyotard writes that, although the Holocaust has robbed grand narratives of their legitimacy, it is still possible to legitimize small narratives: "To learn names," he writes, "is to situate them in relation to other names by means of phrases. Auschwitz is a city in southern Poland in the vicinity of which the Nazi camp administration installed an extermination camp in 1940" (44). This might seem a modest claim within the realm of philosophy. But in the world of fiction establishing connections between units of narrative associates style with ethics, legitimizing the narrative that such units construct. Amis insists that "all writing is a campaign against cliché. Not just clichés of the pen but clichés of the mind and clichés of the heart" (*War* xv). In *Time's Arrow* he wages an ironic war of words on the users of clichés (in all the above senses) who have employed grand narratives of rationality to legitimate the horrors of the Holocaust and of the blood-dimmed tide that has been loosed on the world since that crucial turning point in Western history.

Lists of Books Published

Fiction

The Rachel Papers, 1973.
Dead Babies, 1975 [aka *Dark Secrets*, 1977].
Success, 1978.
Other People: A Mystery Story, 1981.
Money: A Suicide Note, 1984.
Einstein's Monsters [short stories], 1987.
London Fields, 1989.
Time's Arrow, or The Nature of the Offense, 1991.

The Information, 1995.
Night Train, 1997.
Heavy Water and Other Stories, 1998.
Yellow Dog, 2004.
House of Meetings [two stories and a novella], 2006.

Non-Fiction

Invasion of the Space Invaders, 1982.
The Moronic Inferno and Other Visits to America, 1986.
Visiting Mrs Nabakov and Other Excursions, 1993.
Experience: A Memoir, 2000.
The War Against Cliché: Essays and Reviews 1971–2000, 2001.
Koba the Dread: Laughter and the Twenty Million, 2002.

4
A. S. Byatt: *Angels and Insects* (1992)

I

A[ntonia] S[usan] Byatt has a distinctive voice and an equally distinctive view of the role of the modern novelist. She published her first novel, *Shadow of a Sun*, in 1964. At first overshadowed by her sister Margaret Drabble, a more popular novelist, she didn't receive wide recognition until the publication of *Possession: A Romance* in 1990. By then she had produced four novels, a collection of short stories, and two works of academic criticism. Since the publication of *Possession* she has published two collections of essays, *Passions of the Mind* (1991) and *On Histories and Stories* (2000), reflecting in particular on the place of the novel and her own fiction in the modern world. To date she has published fourteen works of fiction, including the "Powerhouse" or Frederica quartet (*The Virgin in the Garden* 1978, *Still Life* 1985, *Babel Tower* 1996, and *A Whistling Woman* 2002). Between 1972 and 1983 she taught English full time at University College, University of London, and has acquired a formidable reputation as a critic with a dissenting voice in a largely poststructuralist academic environment.

From the age of ten reading became a passion for Byatt. She claims that "you actually learn a lot about life from books" (Interview with Miller). She told Clive Collins: "all through my childhood, and indeed my adolescence, what I read about was infinitely more interesting than what I was living" (182). That conviction—that the world of fiction offered more than quotidian life in the modern world—was responsible both for her taking to writing and for the form her fictional writing took. From the start her reading extended beyond the English classics and came to particularly favor Proust, Balzac, Thomas Mann, Henry James, Willa Cather, Tolstoy, and Dostoevsky (Kelly 2). She sees herself more as a European writer than an English one, despite locating much of her fiction in England (Interview with Collins 192–93; *On Histories* 1). Like Ishiguro, she believes that "the world has become so intercommunicative that ... more and more writers are aware that they will be read in several countries beside their own." (Interview with Collins 194).

Influenced by Iris Murdoch, about whom she wrote a short book in 1965 at the beginning of her career, Byatt shows a reaction against the trend in contemporary English fiction for "self-expression" (Interview with Collins 186). She cites Murdoch's belief that "a novel should have many centres of self and not just one . . . " (191). She claims not to be interested in herself: "I take myself as an example" (187). She consequently believes that the "reader is actually not related to the narrator. The reader is related to the story" (192).

Just as Amis's sense of history has been largely focused on the second half of the twentieth century, so A. S. Byatt is clearly drawn to the Victorian period and the kind of society it represented, one that she feels is more inclusive than that of today. As she told Myra Stout, "For the Victorians everything was part of one thing: science, religion, philosophy, economics, politics, women, fiction, poetry. They didn't compartmentalize—they thought BIG" ("What Possessed" 14). She has admired the writers of the Victorian age for most of her life. To date Byatt has published three works of fiction set wholly or partly in Victorian times: *Possession* (1990), *Angels and Insects* (1992) and *The Biographer's Tale* (2000). Is Byatt's fictional return to the Victorians different in kind from the nostalgia for Victorian values that appeared to have become a national obsession by the early 1980s? Should her work be linked to that of Paul Scott's *The Raj Quartet*, Richard Attenborough's film, *Gandhi*, and David Lean's film of *A Passage to India*? In 1982 Salman Rushdie cited "the huge, undiminished appetite of white Britons" for such books and films as evidence of what he calls a national "nostalgia for the Great Pink Age" of Empire (*Imaginary Homelands* 130). Britain, wrote Rushdie, was facing "a crisis of the whole culture, of the society's sense of itself" (129). This was the year of Margaret Thatcher's Falklands War, which was followed the next year by her notorious television interview with Brian Walden in which she called for a return to "the values when our country became great." "Yes," she explained, "I want to see one nation, . . . go back to Victorian times" ("The Resolute Approach"). In an essay the following year, Rushdie discerned a connection between the nostalgia for "the rise of Raj revisionism" and "the rise of conservative ideologies" such as that outlined by Mrs Thatcher (*Imaginary Homelands* 92). Are what Byatt calls her three "imitation Victorian novels" (Interview with Collins 191) belated examples of the same impulse? How significant is it that the first of these novels proved widely popular, especially after it won the Booker Prize, and that both *Possession* and *Angels and Insects* were made into films?

On the one hand Byatt clearly believes that the present is still powerfully determined by the past. In *Possession*, the two modern protagonists find themselves following patterns of behavior established by the Victorian characters they have been researching. Or, as Steven Connor puts it, as a result of the modern characters' ferocious interest in the past, "history seems to reenact itself through them" (148). Far from being escapist, retro-Victorian novels[1], according to Byatt, are "a better way of expressing a lot of energy

and vitality and life" than social realist novels set in contemporary times
(Interview with Collins 193). She believes that modern writers "are returning
to historical fiction because the idea of writing about the self is felt to be
worked out" (*On Histories* 31). On the other hand clearly all three of her retro-
Victorian works are modern evocations or interpretations of the past. Byatt
may talk about her use of ventriloquism in *Possession,* but she explains that
ventriloquism "serves to emphasise at once the presence of the past and its
distance, its difference, its death and difficult resurrection" (*On Histories* 45).
For a voracious or what she calls "greedy" reader like Byatt (*Passions* 149), the
link between past and present is a lived one: "my sense of my own identity
is bound up with the past, with what I read and with the way my ancestors,
genetic and literary, read, in the worlds in which they lived" (*On Histories* 93).
The act of the writer who re-imagines the past can be seen as an act of resurrection, the term Michelet gave to history (cf. *Passions* 32). The retro-
Victorian novelist is like Browning in his historical poems who "breathed life
into a dead corpse" (*On Histories* 45).

   For Byatt, as for all the writers considered in this section, the English past
is still part of the present state of the nation, especially for the avid reader.
Somewhat like Ackroyd, she thinks of her life "as a relatively short episode in
a long story of which it is a part," and insists that the impact of men such a
Darwin, Freud, Tennyson and even Swedenborg seem to her "more central
and urgent in this story than much of what is on television . . . or even the
day-to-day movements in Kuwait or Sarajevo" (*On Histories* 94). Accordingly
one finds in Byatt's imitation Victorian novels a complex, even a paradoxical
relationship between past and present. Thus, in *Possession,* the activities of
the contemporary scholars researching the two Victorian poets, Randolph
Ash and Christabel LaMotte, affect and alter the reader's understanding of
the meaning of their poems. As Roland, the young Ash scholar, comes to realize on rereading Ash's *The Golden Apples,* "a sense that the text has appeared
to be wholly new, never before seen, is followed, almost immediately, by the
sense that it was always there" (512). At the same time, the past appears to
determine the present in unexpected ways. In his letters Ash talks of "the
plot of fate that seemed to hold or drive the dead lovers. Roland thought . . .
that he and Maud were being driven by a plot or fate that seemed, at least
possibly, to be not their plot or fate but that of those others" (456). Byatt further complicates matters by employing a bewildering number of genres to
show how they of themselves can determine the way the past is represented
in the present. *Possession,* she writes, "plays serious games with the variety of
possible forms of narrating the past," such as detective fiction, biography, the
romance, etc. (*On Histories* 48). Each genre has a different way of interpreting
the same historical events, producing a collage of competing narratives reminiscent of Barnes's *A History of the World in 10 1/2 Chapters.*

   In Byatt's historical fiction, representations of a national past and present
interact with one another in devious and surprising ways. According to

Byatt the germ of the novel came from watching the great Coleridge scholar, Kathleen Coburn, researching him in the British Library: "And then I
thought 'Does he possess her, or does she possess him?'" (*Essays and Articles*).
"Possession" acts as a complex organizing trope for the entire novel.
Possession takes a variety of forms in the book—economic (Roland's fear of
possession by the two successive women who support him); sexual
(Christabel's and Maud's fear of being possessed by the men they fall in love
with—"You can become a property or idol" [549], but also the men's feeling
that their love for the women "was a sort of madness. A possession" [492]);
spiritualist (Mrs Lees's possession by the spirit of Christabel's lesbian lover,
Blanche Glover); materialist (Roland's and the American scholar's, Cropper's
stealing of the Victorian poets' papers—"I felt possessed," Roland tells his
fellow scholars [527]); above all literary/historical (the scholars' possession
by the two poets from the past—"I feel they have taken me over," Maud says
[548]). Ironically, the novel's last act of possession forms the conclusion to
this modern romance when "Roland finally, to use an outdated phrase,
entered and took possession" of Maud (550). The modern romance's conclusion in the actual act of sex is paradoxically made to express itself in
words appropriated from a past age.

II

Byatt has written that in *Possession* she "tried to find a narrative shape that
would explore the continuities and discontinuities between the forms of
nineteenth- and twentieth-century art and thought" (*Passions* xvii). I want
to examine the way she explores within an English social context such continuities and discontinuities in her next work of fiction, *Angels and Insects*.
The themes that are embodied in the two novellas comprising this book, like
those in *Possession*, cannot be confined to the Victorian age. Kathleen Kelly
lists concisely the concerns both novellas have in common: "A series of con-
junctions govern the structure and themes of both novellas: *Morpho Eugenia*
and *The Conjugial Angel*, insects and angels, natural society and human society, the material world and the spiritual world, lust and love, the living and
the dead, truth and deception, reality and seeming, presence and absence"
(100). Richard Todd argues that the themes that recur in both novellas
"force one to ask whether each story, taken in isolation, is quite the same as
the effect of their juxtaposition under one title" (30). I like to think of both
novellas as belonging to one another in the way, say, that a diptych of painted panels does. Byatt has provided certain textual connections that encour-
age such an integrated approach. The first novella begins and the second
novella ends with a shipwrecked man. Indeed the first shipwrecked man,
William, sails off at the end of the first novella on the *Calypso* (182), a ship
that is reported missing and was captained by Arturo, the husband of Lilias
Papagay, one of the lead characters in the second novella (193). This

retrospective information about the ship's disappearance deconstructs whatever narrative closure the first novella seemed to be given (do William and Matilda even reach the Rio Negro?); it also encourages the reader to look to the second novella for fuller closure.

In more general terms, both novellas focus on the crisis of belief that afflicted the Victorians so acutely (which, according to Sally Shuttelworth, offers a stark contrast to our postmodern "age of 'ontological doubt' without any fixed points of faith against which it may define itself" [155]). In "Morpho Eugenia" Harald Alabaster desperately attempts to reconcile Darwin's *Origin the Species* (1859) with his own theocentric belief in a benevolent Christian God. In "The Conjugial Angel" Alfred Tennyson, England's poet laureate, attempts to deal with a similar conflict between his religious belief "in the resurrection of the body" and a vision of "the earth heaped and stacked with dead things" (303) brought on by the publication of Lyell's *Principles of Geology* (1830–33). Clearly the angst Victorians like Alabaster and Tennyson experienced was different in kind from that afflicting the next century. For instance a Home Office report stated in 2004 that although 74 percent of people in England and Wales described themselves as Christians, only 7 percent of these Christians went to church. The rest see themselves as "cultural Christians" according to Nanne Stinson, director of the British Humanist Association (*BBC News*). Yet the reaction of those Victorians more open to the new ideas strikes a chord of continuity with the present. They attempted to compensate for the absence of God by making the world sacramental. William, the Darwinian scientist in "Morpho Eugenia," argues that "Mystery may be another name for God" just as it has been "another name for Matter" (70). This implies that the mystery of life has simply transferred itself from the world of the spirit to a world of matter where it continues to reside today. In Matty's fairy tale, significantly titled "THINGS ARE NOT WHAT THEY SEEM," Mistress Moufett points out a chrysalis about to hatch which contained "a yellow soup, like egg-yoke, which looks like the decay of putrefaction and is the stuff of life and rebirth" (152). In the same way, most of the characters in "The Conjugial Angel" believe that the dead form a continuity with the living, that they have an afterlife which includes, according to Swedenborg, sexual conjunction between conjugial (as he called them) angels. As Byatt explains him, "Swedenborg believed that the whole universe was one Divine Human, containing both male and female conjoined, and that heaven and hell were situated within the Divine Human" (*On Histories* 112). "Spiritualism," she writes, "was the religion of a materialist age" (*Passions* 53).

"Morpho Eugenia" constructs an elaborate parallel between the life of ants, "social insects" (12), and that of humans, the Alabaster family in particular. This might appear to suggest that the novella endorses a Darwinian determinist explanation of human life. Eugenia is likened to the Queen of the ants, although William mistakes her for a butterfly at first. ("Morpho" is a genus of nymphalid butterfly and also an epithet of Aphrodite; "Eugenia" means "aromatic tree" and "beautiful" [24], and "eugenesis" means "the production of fit and healthy offspring, esp. by deliberate outbreeding," according to the *Oxford English Dictionary*.) Like an insect William is trapped by her beauty and the aromatic "scent she spread" (61), and he ends up impregnating her repeatedly, supposedly to ensure thereby the continuity of the Alabaster species—or in effect the English aristocracy. "'You have courage, and intelligence, and kindness,' said Eugenia's father. 'All families stand in need of these qualities if they are to survive'" (65). While Eugenia lies bloated at the center of this human nest (appropriately called Bredely Hall) producing new Alabasters, the servants of the household scuttle around unseen, performing the duties of worker ants. Gradually William comes to "see his own life in terms of a diminishing analogy with the tiny creatures" (116), and talks of "his own drone-nature" (121). However, William knows that "Analogy is a slippery tool . . . Men are not ants" (116). William is repeatedly said to have "double vision" (7), finding "himself divided against himself" (65). He cannot wholeheartedly subscribe to the analogy between the human and the insect world because he can see that Harald's belief in God is based equally on a false analogy—that between paternal and divine love. "You may argue anything by analogy, Sir," he tells Harald, "and so consequently nothing" (104).

William's double vision reflects Byatt's original idea for the novella: "to interweave the images of the two communities—ants and people—so as at once to reinforce the analogy and to do the opposite—to show the insects as Other, resisting our metaphorical impositions" (*On Histories* 116–17). If Harald's stubborn refusal to accept the findings of Victorian scientists is as unsuccessful as was King Harold's resistance to William the Conqueror's invasion of England, the desire to anthropomorphize the animal world under the influence of Darwinism is made to seem equally untenable. William's principal error according to Byatt is that he "wanted to marry a butterfly and found he'd married the queen of the ants instead" ("Ant Heaps and Novelists." 1). Byatt insists that insects are "the Not-human," "the Other," and that "we ought to think about the not-human, in order to be fully human" (*On Histories* 115). When he wakes up from his sexual enslavement to Eugenia, William finds his true equal in Matilda, no insect but a Sphinx whose riddle she answers herself with an anagram that releases William from his insect-like subservience to a family that is doomed through incestuous inbreeding to Darwinian extinction. William finally renounces his desire for Morpho Eugenia, "something perfect and beautifully formed" that can "take the breath away" (24), and chooses a mate from his own class not out of an instinctual sexual drive, but because she is "full of life" (180). Yet the novella ends with the discovery of a Monarch butterfly on the ship, filling Matilda with emotion, though "whether it is more fear, or more hope" she cannot tell. "And yet it is still alive, and bright" she observes (183). Aphrodisiac butterflies and Matilda, "the Sphinx, the night-flier, who 'hath both kinds in one,' lion and woman," both participate in life now seen in post-Darwinian terms (*On Histories* 121).

"The Conjugial Angel" confronts the same dilemma facing Harald Alabaster—"the terror of being merely snuffed out, like a mere creature" as Alfred Tennyson reflects (303). Where "Morpho Eugenia" asks whether humans are no more than social insects whose being is determined by their social function and usefulness, "The Conjugial Angel" asks whether humans are distinguished from insects and animals by their ability to survive their death. What does the resurrection of the dead mean? Is it more than just the memory of them? In her researches for this novella Byatt found herself "feeling out, or understanding, the Victorian fear that we *are* our bodies," and nothing more (*On History* 108). Spiritualism and Swedenborg's journeys among the angels offered Victorians "the reassurance of the bodily identity of the departed" (*On History* 109). Byatt chose to write a novella about a Victorian English group engaged in spiritualist séances because "[s]piritualism was the religion of a material age" (*Passions* 53). Yet just as "Morpho Eugenia" insists on both continuities and discontinuities between humans and social insects, so "The Conjugial Angel" neither fully subscribes to nor totally denies the existence of a world of the spirit. In the novella Tennyson quotes Saint Paul (2 Corinthians 12:2) to express an in-between space (between physical identity and a merging with the world of the spirit) that he can occupy:

> Saint Paul had written of the man caught up to the Third Heaven, "whether in the body, I cannot tell; or whether out of the body, I cannot tell." He himself could escape from himself into a kind of waking trance, and by the strangest of methods, the steady repetition to himself of two words, his own name, until the pure concentration on his isolated self seemed paradoxically to destroy the bounds of that self, that consciousness, so that he was everything, was God, and this not a confused state, but the clearest of the clearest, the surest of the surest, the weirdest of the weirdest, utterly beyond words, where death was an almost laughable impossibility, the loss of personality (if so it was) seeming no extinction but the only true life. (307)

The second half of this passage is a word-for-word reproduction from Volume 1 of Hallam Tennyson's *Alfred Lord Tennyson: A Memoir* (1898), as Byatt acknowledges in *On Histories and Stories* (109, and note 23).

This in-between space is also occupied by some of the members of the group in this novella who resort to spiritualism to try to make contact with the dead. Lilias Papagay is typical of the ambivalent belief they display as a group in the evidence of the survival or revival of the dead elicited through a spirit medium. She reflects that "we cannot bear the . . . thought, that we become nothing, like grasshoppers and beef-cattle. So we ask them, our personal angels, for reassurance. And they come, they come to our call" (196). Lilias joins séances "not for the Hereafter," but because, like William and Matilda, "she wanted *life*," something more than the tedium of a widow's existence (196). Emily Jesse, Alfred Tennyson's sister, wants to communicate with her fiancé, Arthur Hallam, whose premature death Tennyson mourned long after she had remarried the coarser Captain Jesse. She shows the same ambivalence toward the worlds of matter and spirit in her reflections on the William Morris designed sofa in her home. It simultaneously appeals to her as a functional piece of furniture and as a depiction of "magical objects which recalled to her childhood days" when she lived in a world of fantasy and imagination. "Mr Morris's sofa acknowledged both worlds; it could be sat on, it hinted at paradise" (204–205). Byatt insists on the importance, even the mystery, of matter (70). But she is no pure materialist. She seeks to show in both novellas that English Victorians held the same ambivalent view of the relation between the worlds of matter and of the spirit, or of the imagination, as moderns (she included) do today. "The Conjugial Angel" starts: "Lilias Papagay was of imagination all compact" (187), echoing Theseus in *Midsummer Night's Dream* when he asserts that "The lunatic, the lover, and the poet / Are of imagination all compact" (5.1.7–8). Lilias, still in love with her long lost husband and seeking to make contact with him through spiritualist means, shares with Tennyson, the poet, this belief in a liminal or imaginative state of being, while being accused by Mr Hawke of being possessed by an evil spirit, which is one way of describing temporary insanity. In the world of imagination, love and poetry can be easily confused with lunacy.

However there is another area in which Victorian and modern concerns reveal both continuities and discontinuities in both novellas. How does Byatt handle questions of gender, class, and race in a book set firmly in Victorian times? None of these issues is foregrounded, but Byatt has described the triumph of William and Matilda in "Morpho Eugenia" as "a quiet image of shifting class and sexual hierarchies" (*On Histories* 81), and written that the "original impulse for *The Conjugial Angel* was . . . revisionist and feminist" (*On Histories* 104). One of the ironies implicit in the comparison of humans to insects in "Morpho Eugenia" is that in a patriarchal human society women are the ones to beautify themselves to attract men, whereas in the insect world it is the males who use brilliant colors to win the female's consent to mating. This is brought to the reader's attention early in the novella when Eugenia, on seeing the dead specimen of a Morpho Eugenia, exclaims "What a beautiful glittering white she is—" only to be corrected by her father, "No, no, that is the male" (23). When Matty remarks on this disparity between the human and insect worlds, William replies that in the "savage societies" he encountered in South America "it is the males who flaunt their beauty" (46). Byatt leaves it to her reader to make the necessary inference that in England

Victorian sexual roles are not necessarily natural, but socially constructed. As Heidi Hansson suggests, the "people are ants" metaphor both "questions the male dominated society it describes" and "questions the kind of separatist feminism that advocates single-sex communities" (462). The metaphor works to satirize simultaneously Victorian patriarchal values and the more militant versions of modern feminism.

"The Conjugial Angel" is more overtly concerned with differences between the sexes in Victorian society. There are two mediums in the novella. Byatt drew extensively on Alex Owen's study of Victorian mediums, *The Darkened Room* (1989) which she lists in her "Acknowledgements." Owen argues that spiritualism was one of the few professions open to Victorian Englishwomen offering them a source of income and self validation. Byatt ironically comments that it was also a profession "which relied heavily on what were traditionally thought of as 'feminine' qualities of passivity, receptiveness, lack of 'reason'" (*On Histories* 104). Both Emily's fiancé, Arthur, and Alfred Tennyson in conversation together make the neoplatonic assumption that "the higher Mind, Nous, immerses itself in inert Matter, Hyle, and creates life and beauty. The Nous is male and the Hyle female" (262). In labeling the female "inert Matter" the two men are already running foul of the book's identification of Matter with Mystery. Byatt has Emily overhear this exchange, outrageous to modern ears, holding a basket of books that include *Undine* (1811), a Romantic novel about a female water sprite who marries a mortal man, further undercutting the men's identification of spirit with the male. She proceeds to ask Arthur why inert matter is female and rejects all his answers as inadequate. Yet when Hallam explains his esthetic beliefs he sets feeling before thought in poetry, revealing a split between moral and esthetic values. By the use of internal contradictions of this kind Byatt deconstructs the ideology of English Victorian sexual politics without overtly intruding with a modern feminist voice. Similarly Emily ridicules Mr Hawke's exposition of Saint Paul's theological subordination of women to men in the course of which he interprets the apostle's *"For this cause ought the woman to have power on her head because of the angels"* to mean that women in the congregation ought to cover their beautiful hair "to deflect the lusts of angels" (324). Mr Hawke has just cited Swedenborg's belief that while on earth the Christian God had a human form from his human mother and an eternal form from his divine father, but that at the Crucifixion he had shed the "corrupt humanity he had from the mother, in order to experience glorification and union with the Father" (322). Here woman is not just inert matter, but deathly matter, an image that has already been reversed by the decaying remains of Arthur clinging to Sophy and endangering her life. Here again the text is made to undo these patriarchal assumptions without any intervention by the modern author. This entire gendered way of thinking is, as Byatt has written, another "example of thinking by false analogies, . . . impregnation of inert Matter by the divine

Nous, which . . . all feminists ought to deconstruct" (*On Histories* 111). The text of both novellas does just that, offering a poststructuralist response to a narrative situated firmly in the past.

Byatt touches even more lightly on the role that social class played in the Victorian period. Again she is interested in exploring continuities and discontinuities. The act of incest that lies at the heart of "Morpho Eugenia" points, as Sally Shuttleworth has observed, to "the incestuous dynamics that lay at the heart of Victorian ideologies of the family" (153). Incest is the ultimate outcome of the belief of the English ruling class in the need to preserve their bloodline untainted, or, as Harald says in a sermon on love that he preaches, to preserve "the natural ties between members of the family group," especially "the closeness of brothers and sisters" (27). That Edgar is described at one point as "an anachronism" (73) subtly indicates the fact that the English aristocracy is destined for extinction for Darwinian reasons explained within the text. Social Darwinism is simultaneously invoked to condemn the effects on humans of a newly industrialized society when a Belgian friend William meets in the tropics sees the end product of "a very high elaboration of the social instinct" (such as is found in ant colonies) as the "development of severe systems of authority" which in organized societies used "creatures pitilessly for their functional benefit" (131–32). That criticism of incipient capitalism has only become more insistent in the modern era of global capitalism to which Byatt belongs. The same friend claims that "the terrestrial Paradises towards which the social designers of human cities and communes are working so hopefully" are no different from "the cities of termites, in which fellow creatures are rationally turned to food when no longer useful" (132). This frequently iterated Victorian criticism of social engineering brought on by the Industrial Revolution repeats itself in the twentieth century, for example, in the phenomenon of utopian modernist architecture responsible for numerous "functional" tower blocks that had to be demolished as uninhabitable in the postwar period. Continuities and discontinuities.

Race and color is also given marginal treatment in "Morpho Eugenia." The novella is set at the time of the American Civil War which is alluded to when William reads to Matty and Miss Mead his account of the raid made by the red ants on the nest of the wood ants whom they captured and took back as slaves. When Miss Mead compares ant behavior to human slavery and talks approvingly of the American Unionists' battle "to secure . . . the liberation of the unfortunate slaves," Matty replies that "we [Victorians] are urged . . . to fight on the side of the slave-makers" rather than "to rescue those machine-slaves from their specialised labour" (115–16). As "much of the [Alabaster] family money came from the Lancashire cotton trade" (93), Victorian capitalism is charged with perpetuating a form of slavery long after the slave trade had been made illegal in Britain.[2] But William has already described how the Brazilian Indians practiced their own form of enslavement, complicating the issue by removing the issue of race from the argument. Yet color, if not race, is a an ongoing metaphor in this novella. At first William associates whiteness with the Alabasters (the word means white gypsum). Eugenia in particular, whose teeth are milky and whose skin is white and flawless, is constantly seen wearing white dresses. The Alabasters make William feel "sultry-skinned" by comparison (4), and he remembers being embraced in the jungle by "women with brown breasts . . . and with shameless fingers" (7). On his wedding night William is "afraid of smutching" the "cold white Eugenia, "so soft, so white, so pure" (78, 79). But the novella executes a reversal of colors after the wedding night. Matty, "a tall, dark figure, . . . her hair dark under a plain cap, her skin dusky too" gradually supercedes the endlessly fertile figure of Eugenia. Where white England had seemed a "Bower of Bliss" in Brazil (9), in England it is the dark Amazon that he sees as "the innocent, the unfallen world, the virgin forest, the wild people in the interior who are as unaware of modern ways—modern evils— as our first parents" (35). In choosing to leave the Alabaster household with Matty for the Amazon, William is turning his back on an English ruling class that is blind to its own ruthless manipulation of class and color and so destined to engineer its own natural de-selection.

III

Byatt has noted how the "renaissance of the historical novel has coincided with a complex selfconsciousness about the writing of history itself" (*On Histories* 9). Hayden White, whom she proceeds to cite, distinguished between the primary referent of historical narrative, historical events, and the secondary referent,

the plot structures of the various story types cultivated in a given culture. When the reader recognizes the story being told in a historical narrative as a specific kind of story—for example, as an epic, romance, tragedy, comedy, or farce,—he can be said to have comprehended the meaning produced by the discourse. The comprehension is nothing other than the recognition of the form of the narrative. (43)

Byatt argues that the recent trend in historiography to eschew claims to truth for historical narrative "is one reason why so many novelists have taken to it" (*On Histories* 11). At the same time, like Phineas G. Nanson, the protagonist of *The Biographer's Tale*, she finds that "the lives of the dead . . . make up the imagined worlds of the living" (*On Histories* 10). Since early childhood she has "liked very much to get into another world," the world of fiction (Interview with Collins 182). In *Possession* Roland Ash echoes Byatt's own conviction that "*the life of the past* persisting in us . . . *is the business of every thinking man and woman*" (116). Haunted by her Victorian predecessors, Byatt has consciously turned to particular narrative forms to give significance to her historical and fictitious characters from the past. She wrote "Morpho Eugenia" as "a kind of robust Gothic allegory," while she describes "The Conjugial Angel" as "a ghost story and a love story" (*On Histories* 114, 110). When one considers that the Gothic novel is a type of romance that contains elements of the supernatural, one can see how closely related "Morpho Eugenia" is to the ghost/love story comprising "The Conjugial Angel."

Byatt has written of how she described herself in her early days as "a self-conscious realist," but slowly came to see the attractions of the opposing tradition of the literary or fairy tale (*On Histories* 4). Like the ghost story, the fairy tale enabled her to renounce psychological depth in favor of "partaking in the continuity of the tales by retelling them in a new context in a way old and new." She found that she could use genre, "stories within stories . . . to make the meanings" (*On Histories* 131), and that her retellings provided the needed connection between a past and present world of the imagination. Fairy tales play a major role in "Morpho Eugenia." In the opening scene Enid, Eugenia's youngest sister, talks of the sisters' dancing all night as "like the sisters in the story"—that is Cinderella (6). William, as always "divided against himself" (65), finds himself "at once detached anthropologist and fairytale prince trapped . . . in an enchanted castle" (25). Like the Prince of Araby after seeing the beautiful Princess of China, he declares after first meeting Eugenia, "I shall die if I cannot have her" (14). William is trapped in a fairy tale world of literary fantasy. Both a great reader and a writer of scientific journals and then a book, William is torn between realist and fabulous literary traditions. His scientific writing takes him outside the self, a realist requirement Byatt imposed on her early fiction writing. But love, or rather romance, draws him in the direction of fabulation. It takes a fairy story to make him see his spell-bound state and liberate him from it. It takes a non-realist genre to get him to see the real, a fairy story about enchantment to see his own actual enchantment. It is fitting that Matty should complete the work of disenchantment by employing another linguistic form—the anagram—to make him see that the insect-like queen, Eugenia, is in fact implicated in incest with her half brother. Michael Levenson contends that Matty's imagination has its effect on William's book of natural history which, he announces, will "appeal to a wide audience, by telling truths—scientific truths—with a note of the fabulous." In complementary fashion Matty shifts under William's influence from the wholly fabulous to writing her own fables in the manner of La Fontaine, "only more *accurately*" (120). Within the narrative, then, narrative genre determines much of its outcome. "You are truly a good Fairy," William tells Matilda at the end of this Gothic romance which conforms to convention by leaving them "on the crest of a wave" (182).

Byatt uses the genre of the ghost story combined with the romance to give meaning to the interactions of her spiritualists and lovers in "The Conjugial

Angel." "I don't believe in the supernatural," Byatt has said, "but I began to see one can use it to explain human experience . . . Some things can only be approached formally, through ghost stories" ("The Magic Brew" D1). Wanting to write a historical novella in which she raises the Victorian dead and makes them speak, Byatt invokes the genre of the ghost story in which the dead are expected to speak from beyond the grave. Historical fiction can do easily what most of the characters within this historical fiction long to do—bring the dead back to life and thereby bring the past into the present. In fact the two mediums in the novella act as alter egos for Byatt who, as one reviewer wrote, "herself becomes a kind of medium—our conduit to a lost world" (Hawthorne 99). Byatt says that she "use[s] the spirit medium as a metaphor for the writer" (Interview with Collins 187). Like Henry James, she uses the genre of the ghost story to write about her own modern hauntings. Lilias and Sophy, the two mediums in "The Conjugial Angel," like William and Matilda in "Morpho Eugenia," offer respectively realist and fabulous narratives. Equally like William and Matilda, neither is wholly one or the other. Sophy and Lilias are Byatt's two most important invented characters in the novella, an internalization within the narrative of the creative impulse they share with their creator. Byatt has written that in her work "the genre of the ghost story is used as an embodiment of the relations between readers and writers, between the living words of dead men and the modern conjurers of their spirits" (*On Histories* 43). She is therefore further using the genre to point the modern readers of her narrative in the direction of the figurative while leaving them open to post-Darwinian skepticism when reading it literally.

Lilias Papagay is presented as a figure of the self-conscious narrator; she represents "the medium as artist or historian;" she stands for what Byatt terms "narrative curiosity" (*On Histories* 106). "Mrs Papagay liked stories . . . nuggets of other lifelines, other chains of cause and effect" (192). Her attempts to become a writer of fiction produced "stilted, saccharine rubbish," but her "automatic writing was different" (193). She turns to automatic writing in an attempt to contact and find out what happened to her husband, Arturo, the captain of the *Calypso*. When Lilias takes the first results of her automatic writing as "indisputable messages from Arturo" which make her conclude that "he was probably drowned" (193, 194) Byatt retrospectively creates uncertainty in the reader's mind about Lilias's powers of divination, because the accuracy of the latter "message" is disproved at the conclusion of the narrative. Lilias might lack Matilda's flights of imagination, but she has the ability to parrot (*papagayo* being the Spanish word for parrot) voices and their narratives from the spirit world. Lilias constructs for the reader an in-between world of narrative where "everyone made up everyone else, living and dead, at every turn." She cannot decide whether the constructions of narrative "could be called knowledge or lies, or both" (231). Byatt compares her to Robert Browning's Mr Sludge, the Medium (*On Histories 106*)—Byatt

quotes an extract from the poem of that name as an epigraph to *Possession*—
who is both a cheat and one of "that circle of artists who give life and form
to fictive truths" (*Passions* 53). In the final séance Lilias simultaneously recognizes the presence of unappeased and dangerous forces and knows that "it
was all a parlour game, at one level, a kind of communal story-telling" (331).
In this respect her "in-between" narratives are indistinguishable from
Tennyson's *In Memoriam* into which, he is made to reflect, "both he and
Arthur had seeped . . . , had become part of its fabric, a matter-moulded kind
of *half-life* he sometimes thought it was . . . " (311). But all such narratives are
a great deal more exciting than the "constriction and tedium" of a Victorian
English widow's life (196). Lilias is as drawn to and stimulated by the voices
of the dead as is Byatt who likewise frequently finds herself most energized
by voices from England's literary past.

"The Conjugial Angel" is not just a ghost story, but a love story. How does
the romance genre help to "[comb] the appearances of the world, and of the
particular lover's history, out of a random tangle and into a coherent plot"
(*Possession* 456)? There are a number of romantic stories interwoven in this
novella. A prime reason for holding the séances in which all the characters
participate is to reunite Alfred Tennyson's married sister, Emily Jesse, with
her prematurely dead fiancé, Arthur Hallam. Simultaneously Lilias is seeking
to speak with Arturo's spirit. Then there is the Swedenborgian Mr Hawke
courting Lilias with carnal enthusiasm. Finally there is Tennyson attempting
to resurrect his dead friend, Arthur, through the writing of *In Memoriam*.
What all these lovers of a materialist age seek is physical contact with the
departed. In the novella Tennyson expresses his preference for the term
"ghost" rather than "spirit." This is because his "imagination was stirred by
matter, by the thick solidity of the hugely redundant quantity of flesh and
earth and vegetation that either was or wasn't informed by spirit" (306). Like
William in the first novella, he sees matter as mysterious.

Ironically, flesh wins out over spirit in all three romantic sub-stories.
Sophy is finally successful in summoning up Arthur's ghostly presence, only
to be almost suffocated by his "clay-cold, airless, stinking mass, plastering
her mouth and nostrils" as "he was being unmade" (318). Simultaneously
she has a vision of the aging Tennyson seeing his future skeleton in the mirror. Both are images of the fear many thinking Victorians (such as Harald
Alabaster) shared of amounting to no more than their brief physical existence, something that has come to define modern English society. In the
final séance when Sophy acting as medium tells Emily that Arthur's spirit
has finally transmitted the message for which she has been waiting all those
years, the message being "We shall be joined and made one Angel" (328),
Emily turns from the dead to the living and tells her husband that she hopes
to be with him in the afterlife, one angel (in the Swedenborgian sense of the
word, both sexual and spiritual). Like William, she comes belatedly to a
recognition of who her true soul mate is. Her comment, "It is hard to love

the dead enough" (329), applies even to Tennyson who upstaged her with his long period of mourning that accompanied the gestation of *In Memoriam*. Part of the ambiguity that Byatt reveals in her passages of explication of the poem can be said to arise from this sentiment to which Emily gives voice in the final séance. The séance breaks up, as it is said to have done in fact, when Lilias produces with her automatic writing a series of stanzas in the meter of *In Memoriam* that are primarily fleshly and sensual, so much so that Mr Hawke denounces them as "filthy imaginings" (332). This reads like an anticipation of the effects of a modern Freudian analysis in which the censured sexual fantasies of the unconscious are brought to light. The romance genre also dictates the finale in which, not a spirit, but a flesh-and-blood Arturo reappears to take Lilias into his arms. Sophy observes that such a resurrection in the flesh occurs only "very occasionally in sober fact," but is a regular feature of stories, reinforcing the view that genre, what Hayden White calls "emplotment," is what determines the meaning of any series of events constituting a narrative.

White argues that "the testing of the systems of meaning production" were "originally elaborated in myth and refined in the alembic of the hypothetical mode of fictional articulation" (*Content* 45). White is evidently reflecting Northrop Frye's definition of myth as "the most abstract and conventionalized of all literary modes," standing at the opposite pole to literary realism (*Anatomy* 134). Byatt offers a mythic level of interpretation in both novellas. In "Morpho Eugenia" there is the obvious association between William's last name, Adamson, and Adam, both of whom take it upon themselves to name their fellow creatures. In Matty's fairy tale the Recorder of the Garden tells Seth (the Biblical Adam's son/Adamson): "Names, you know, are a way of weaving the world together, by relating the creatures to other creatures . . . " (150). Heidi Hansson even suggests that "Morpho Eugenia" "could very well be interpreted as a story about Eden and the fall" (463–64). In the same way "The Conjugial Angel" gives mythical significance to the much dwelt upon scene on the vicarage lawn when Alfred and Arthur reclined in wicker chairs and "their two hands almost touched on the turf, one stretched towards the other" (262). The next time this scene is recalled, the two friends almost touching hands are associated with both "Divine Love" and Michelangelo, offering an implicit comparison to the painter's famous fresco on the Sistine Chapel ceiling of God's hand reaching out to touch Adam's in the mythic moment of his creation (297–98). One could also cite the myth of Cupid and Psyche recounted by Miss Mead in "Morpho Eugenia" (48–50) in which William is seen to occupy a similar position to Psyche's, allowed to love Eugenia as long as he never tries to see her (for what she really is). Even the "Morpho" of the title draws attention to the way this novella is a tale of meta*morpho*sis in which Matty changes from caterpillar to butterfly as Eugenia undergoes a reverse transformation. Ovid's popular collection of myths of metamorphoses hovers over this novella.

As Christabel LaMotte writes in *Possession*, metamorphosis is *"one of the problems of our time—and all Times, rightly known"* (177).

Judith Fletcher has written an entire essay showing how Byatt has used the *Odyssey* as a narrative template for *Angels and Insects*. "Yet," she argues, "this is not straightforward imitation, for Byatt seems to have unraveled and rewoven the *Odyssey*" (217). She sees William as a shipwrecked Odysseus among the Phaeacians, Eugenia as a Calypso or Circe figure, and Matty as a female Odysseus whose narrative, "Things Are Not What They Seem," acts as "an embedded narrative which recapitulates themes of both the frame narrative, *Morpho Eugenia*, and the *Odyssey*" (222). Fletcher goes on to see "The Conjugial Angel" as a story paralleling Odysseus' return home. Like Penelope, Lilias thinks she has lost her husband at sea, is courted by a rival suitor, Mr Hawke, whom she rejects, only to recognize her true husband on his unexpected return. Fletcher quotes the Homeric simile used to describe the reunion of Odysseus and Penelope (*Odyssey* 23.232–39), commenting how much it has been admired "for the way it melds the perspectives of Penelope and Odysseus" (230–31), and compares it to Lilias and Arturo "becoming more and more completely entangled in one" (336). Frye distinguishes romantic myth from two other organizations of myths. Romantic myth shows "the tendency to suggest implicit mythical patterns in a world more closely associated with human experience" (139–40). The closer we get to pure or undisplaced myth, according to Frye, the more conscious we become of the organizing design. Fletcher contends that the "allusions to the *Odyssey* unify the bipartite structure of *Angels and Insects*," the first novella simulating the wanderings of Odysseus and the second the fixity of Penelope's domestic sphere (226). In addition the mythic element in this book partially removes both narratives from the specificity of the Victorian period and gives them an additional timeless significance that helps to turn the Victorians' crises and ideological conflicts into something that is fundamental to human thought from the beginning of time.

A further feature of both novellas is their heavy reliance on intertextuality, a feature to be found in all of Byatt's fiction. As Julia Kristeva explains the concept, which she developed from Bakhtin's notion of the dialogic[3], "any text is the absorption and transformation of another," meaning that poetic or literary language "is at least double," the transposition of one or more sign systems into another (*Kristeva Reader* 37). Intertextuality is quite different from textual influence, Kristeva insists. It generates polysemy which amounts to more than the semiotic content of either text on its own. Both Byatt's novellas originated intertextually. "Morpho Eugenia," she writes, sprung from two germs, *Middlemarch* and Maeterlinck's anthropomorphic imaging of the Ant Queen after her nuptial flight (*On Histories* 114–15). George Eliot's novel contrasts Mr Farebrother, a "clergyman and a collector of pinned dead insects" who "was of the old order," with Lydgate, "who wanted to examine living connective tissues" and "was of the new" (114).

The obvious connection is between Mr Farebrother and Harald, and between Lydgate and William, the old and the new. But intertextuality works poly-semantically. *Middlemarch*, Byatt writes, was "the result of its author's per-ception that the two stories she had embarked on were really parts of one whole" (*Passions* 199). Did Byatt likewise find that her two novellas, both exploring the meeting between the old and the new, were parts of one whole, *Angels and Insects*? Byatt has also written about the form of *Middlemarch*, how George Eliot saw it as a "natural history." She goes on to argue that "much current fiction springs out of a resistance" to the novel employing Darwinian form (*On Histories* 66). Is "Morpho Eugenia" a narra-tive of natural adaptation (on William's part) and "The Conjugial Angel" one of resistance, relying on sudden transformations at the end?

"The Conjugial Angel," Byatt informs us, "started with a footnote . . . to the *Collected Letters* of Arthur Henry Hallam, in which Fryn Tennyson Jesse, Emily Tennyson Jesse's granddaughter, tells the story of Emily's life after Arthur Hallam" (*On Histories* 104). Byatt reveals how she copied verbatim in the novella the granddaughter's account of Emily's wittily worded response to the spirit's message that she would be reunited to Arthur (cf. 329). The sense of humor and irony that a modern reader might take to be the stylis-tic signature of the modern author turns out to be historical. This is one of the principal uses to which Byatt puts intertextuality: demonstrating just how contemporary aspects of Victorian culture can be. The same is true of Chapter X in which Tennyson is given a voice. His musings on his poetic elegy for Arthur reveal the same ambivalent responses to his desire to believe and his skepticism at his belief found in the poem. That conflicting set of responses represents Byatt's desire to rescue "the complicated Victorian thinkers from modern diminishing parodies like those of Fowles and Strachey" (*On Histories* 79). So there is an anachronistic component to this intertextual chapter, an intertextual argument with certain modern texts, which serves, as Byatt says of certain contemporary historical novels, "to place the few years spanned by the book in a continuum which leads for-ward as well as back" (*On Histories* 46). *In Memoriam* is perhaps the most important intertext in the entire book, relating Tennyson's text to that of earlier ones to which it relates: "If the air was full of the ghostly voices of his ancestors, his poem let them sing out again, Dante and Theocritus, Milton and the lost Keats, whose language was their afterlife" (312). Just as Tennyson is affected by the afterlife present in the language of certain pred-ecessors, so Byatt's text incorporates the afterlife of the language used in *In Memoriam* by Tennyson, who "knew what could be done with words like 'creep' and 'prick' . . . Lovely thick words . . . Fearful and enticing" (307). Words have a life of their own, what Christabel LaMotte calls "*the* Life of Language" (*Possession* 198), that excite Byatt as they excited Tennyson. As Lilias reflects, words "were there to indicate *things*" (326). Like Byatt, Emily considers *In Memoriam* "the greatest poem" of its time (269), because it expresses "exactly the nature of her own shock and sorrow, . . . thoughts spoken and unspoken" (268).

Hilary Schor notes how in "The Conjugial Angel" "everyone gets to be an omniscient narrator; a dead character; an absent author" (244). One of the most insistent instances of intertextuality in "The Conjugial Angel" is the use of literary references by both members of the séance and—more remarkably—by the spirits they summon up. The spirit of Arthur Hallam even asks his medium, Sophy, to comfort him by reciting some of Keats's "Ode to a Nightingale," the lines of which immediately take on new meaning. "Now more than ever seems it rich to die" is the opposite sentiment to that of Arthur's spirit resisting its corporeal disintegration, while "Thou wast not born for death" echoes the only consolation Arthur can grasp—that we live on in the words written about us (292). It is no accident that Byatt took some images of the decaying Arthur from Keats's "sensuous and ghostly masterpiece, *Isabella*." She continues: "The Hallam Sophy encounters knows [*sic*] that poems are the sensuous afterlife of men" (*On Histories* 112–13). The effect on the reader of intertextual passages like that describing Sophy's communication with Arthur Hallam is spelt out in the text when she tries to define what she saw:

> Sophy herself did not feel there was a great discontinuity between the creatures and objects met in dreams, the creatures and objects glimpsed through the windows, or out over the sea-wall, the creatures and objects called up by poems and the Bible, or the creatures which came from nowhere and stayed awhile, could be described to other people, seen, smelled, heard, almost touched and tasted . . . (221).

Byatt employs ghostly intertexts to break down the barriers in her readers' minds separating the worlds of material reality, of the spirit and of the poet's (or novelist's) imagination. The numerous quotations from earlier writers that occur in the novels of both Ackroyd and Byatt suggest that we continue to be haunted by voices from the past even as we appropriate them for our own imaginative needs in the present. Haunted by Victorian English writers' words and voices, Byatt writes about Victorians haunted by the voices of their own dead who are themselves haunted by their predecessors, thereby creating a continuity between her world, the Victorian world, and earlier worlds, for the modern readers of her book. Intertexts are narratives within narratives. Haunted by the narratives of Lyell and Darwin, Victorians turned to other narratives such as Swedenborg's to restore their sense of purposefulness and form in a world threatened by random chance and formlessness. Good narratives may date but don't die.

Byatt shares with Ackroyd a belief that "the past and the present can effectively imbue each other" (*Collection* 368). When writing *Possession* Byatt has said that she literally found herself possessed as "the nineteenth-century poems that were not nineteenth-century poems wrote themselves" (*Essays and Articles*). In Byatt's world it is impossible to distinguish whether she is possessed by her Victorian subjects or they by her. That is what she seeks to make her reader feel too—that the complex past of Victorian England is still present; that we are made by the past and remake it in the present; that the voices of earlier writers still echo in our heads as we voice our thoughts today; that the past is both continuous and discontinuous with the present.

Lists of Books Published

Fiction

Shadow of a Sun, 1964.
The Game, 1967.
The Virgin in the Garden, 1978.
Still Life, 1985.
Sugar and Other Stories, 1987.
Possession: A Romance, 1990.
Angels and Insects, 1992.
The Matisse Stories, 1993.
The Djinn in the Nightingale's Eye, 1994.
Babel Tower, 1996.
Elementals: Stories of Fire and Ice, 1998.
The Biographer's Tale, 2000.
A Whistling Woman, 2002.
Little Black Book of Stories, 2003.

Non-Fiction

Degrees of Freedom: The Novels of Iris Murdoch, 1965.
Wordsworth and Coleridge in their Time, 1970.
Unruly Times: Wordsworth and Coleridge, Poetry and Life, 1989.
Passions of the Mind: Selected Writings, 1991.
Imagining Characters: Six Conversations about Women Writers [with Ignes Sôdrè]; ed. Rebecca Swift, 1995.
On Histories and Stories: Selected Essays, 2000.
Portraits in Fiction, 2001.

5
Ian McEwan: *Atonement* (2001)

Ian McEwan's early fiction was almost totally absorbed with the tortuous workings of the inner self and showed virtually no interest in the world beyond. In his first novel, *The Cement Garden* (1978), the only reference to public affairs at the time comes in a casual reference to some overflowing dustbins (caused by the dustmen's strike of 1975): "We thought there might have been a strike but we had heard nothing" (135). Otherwise the novel confines itself to an isolated house and garden and to the equally enclosed minds of the children living there after their parents' deaths. The same concentration on the inner self is true of his first two collections of short stories, *First Love, Last Rites* (1975) and In *Between the Sheets, and Other Stories* (1978), and of his second novel, *The Comfort of Strangers* (1981). All four books gave clinically detached descriptions of the sexual and social aberrations of adolescent characters whose voices offered him at the time "a certain kind of rhetorical freedom" (Adolescence and After 526). Compare this early fiction to McEwan's first two novels of the twenty first century. *Atonement* (2001) focuses on a crucial period of English history between 1935 and 1940 and ranges from an upper class household in prewar southern England to the retreat of the British army to Dunkirk and to a wartime London hospital, ending with a coda in 1999. *Saturday* (2005) is equally engaged with contemporary history, especially with the terrorist attacks of September 11, 2001 on the World Trade Center, and is confined to a single day, February 15, 2003, when a huge demonstration took place in London protesting against the imminent invasion of Saddam Hussein's Iraq.

McEwan first effected his escape from an exclusively subjective narrative perspective in his third novel, *The Child in Time* (1987) in which the lost child of the title represents an outer as well as inner world. This novel came after a gap of six years during which McEwan had turned to drama as his principal outlet. In particular *The Imitation Game* (1981), a play for television, *Or Shall We Die?* (1983), an oratorio, and *The Ploughman's Lunch* (1983), a film, reveal his awakened interest in the world of politics and social action, in the nuclear threat, environmental pollution, and the oppression of women. As he confessed to John Haffenden in 1983, "England under Mrs Thatcher leaves me with a nasty taste" (187). Once he returned to fiction in 1987, every subsequent novel has had not just a private and psychological component, but a public and historical one as well—the government commission on which Stephen sits in *The Child in Time* (1987), the Cold War in *The Innocent* (1990), the hangover of the Holocaust in the form of continuing racism and fascism, and German reunification in *Black Dogs* (1992), the conjunction of scientific, religious, psychological and literary ways of understanding human nature in *Enduring Love* (1997), and the corrupt worlds of politics, journalism and publicly commissioned art in *Amsterdam* (1998).

Born in 1948 just after the end of World War II, McEwan, like Amis, sees the war and the attacks of September 11, 2001 as natural historical markers affecting his lifetime. An older socialist historian in *The Ploughman's Lunch* says, "I can understand why people of your generation want to write about that time [World War II]. They feel betrayed. They want to know what went wrong" (27). Similarly McEwan has said that after the events of September 11, 2001 there was "the general sense of an era having finished. Everything had shifted, the whole focus of international politics" (McEwan, "Ian McEwan Still" 1)—not just politics, but a widespread feeling that, as McEwan told an audience at St. Edwards School, Oxford, "fact had overwhelmed fiction" ("Ian McEwan Hints" 3). Amis's response was equally apocalyptic: "The collateral catastrophe of September 11 is our sudden introduction to a barely recognisable planet, a planet which is not going to leave us alone" ("Window" 17). Just as in *Atonement* the outbreak of world war forecloses Robbie's and Cecilia's chances of redemption, so in *Saturday* the attacks on the World Trade Center "precipitated a global crisis that would, if we were lucky, take a hundred years to resolve."[1] "No going back . . . Now we breathe a different air" (33). Mark Lawson has written that "*Saturday* catalogues the local only in order to focus on the global" (9). The same is true of *Atonement*. But whereas *Saturday* freezes time for the length of a single historically significant day of the demonstration that epitomizes the divided loyalties of both the nation and the novel's protagonist, Perowne, *Atonement* uses a broader canvas to contrast complacent prewar English society with its shattered wartime self which continues to haunt the present of 1999.

Both *Atonement* and *Saturday* open with a description of the pleasures of everyday existence. Just as *Saturday* starts with Perowne getting out of bed and finding that "the movement is easy, and pleasurable in his limbs" (1), so *Atonement* begins with its protagonist, thirteen-year-old Briony Tallis, having read her new play to her mother who has told her it is "stupendous," "burrow[ing] in the delicious gloom of her canopy bed" and making "her heart thud with luminous yearning fantasies" (4). Yet just beneath the surface of these pleasures lurks a threat to their continuance. As McEwan observes, "anxiety runs like a fugue with our pleasure" ("Frozen Moments" 12). The threat to Perowne's pleasurable state quickly appears in the form of a plane on fire flying over London and raising fears of a repeat act of terrorism that Londoners have been told is an inevitability. The threat to Briony is both internal and external. She is a member of a privileged social class (succinctly indicated by the "canopy" over her bed) and subject to the luxury of "fantasies," flights of the imagination that isolate her from the wider social world surrounding her. Moreover, it is made clear in the opening pages that Briony's fantasies satisfy her "passion for tidiness . . . for an unruly world could be made just so" in her stories (7). This rage for order in the aspiring young writer mirrors a similar insistence on order by the ruling classes in prewar Britain.

The novel consists of three parts followed by a coda. Part 1, the longest section, focuses on the upper-middle-class Tallis family on one summer's day in 1935. Seen primarily through the eyes of Jack and Emily Tallis's youngest daughter, thirteen-year-old Briony, who is an aspiring writer, the family is waiting for the return of her oldest brother Leon and his friend, Paul Marshall and the arrival of her cousins Lola and the twins Jackson and Pierrot. Briony oversees a scene between her elder sister Cecilia and Robbie, the son of the family cleaning lady, which shows their sudden attraction to one another but which Briony makes conform to her childish idea of life as seen in fairy tales. Casting Robbie as the villain, Briony that night sees the shadow of a young man (actually Marshall) slinking away from Lola who has just been raped and allows her imagination (inflamed by the crude caricatures of children's fiction) to read into the unknown silhouette the "villainous" Robbie whom she identifies as the rapist to the police. Part 2 recounts Robbie's experiences as a soldier participating in the British forces' retreat to Dunkirk in 1940 while longing to rejoin Cecilia. Part 3 recounts Cecilia's experiences later that year as a student nurse caring for the wounded returning from Dunkirk and ends with Briony's visit to a reunited Robbie and Cecilia who make her promise to retract her evidence in a signed statement and convince her parents that her evidence had been false. A coda or epilogue headed "London, 1999" shows an elderly Briony, now a famous novelist, facing the onset of dementia. She reveals the fact that the entire novel has been her attempt to atone for her lie by rewriting the history of Robbie and Cecilia who both died in 1940 ("Who would want to believe that . . . ?" Briony the novelist asks [350]).

As Eagleton has observed, Part 1 of *Atonement* "wonderfully portrays the upper-middle-class life of a 1930's country house, a world already teetering on the brink of ruin" (2177). That impending ruin is alluded to at the start of the novel in the messy divorce in which Briony's Aunt Hermione and Uncle Cecil are involved. The imminent outbreak of world war parallels this "bitter domestic civil war" (8). Involving "dull complexity and incessant wrangling" (9), it fails to appeal to Briony's "love of order" (7). "Like rearmament and the Abyssinia question and gardening, it was simply not a subject" for her writing in Briony's immature eyes (9). At least Briony has the excuse of youthful inexperience. But the rest of the country is equally involved in turning a blind eye to the encroaching menace of fascism ("the Abyssinian question," refers to the Italian fascist dictator, Mussolini's invasion of Abyssinia in October 1935). In fact 1935, the year in which Part 1 is set, witnessed a British government ostensibly pledged to support the League of Nations' sanctions aimed at protecting Abyssinia while simultaneously planning to partition it in the Hoare-Laval plan. Similarly at this time Winston Churchill was pressing the government to step up rearmament when the official Conservative policy was the appeasement of Europe as a whole. When Briony's father, a civil servant, tells Emily, his wife, that he is kept in London working on a statement concerning rearmament, she replies, "You know, everyone's against it" (144). The Tallis family is typical of Britain's ruling class in the immediate prewar period—isolationist, blind to external threats to its continuance, unconsciously plotting its own demise. Does the family's largely absent father also indicate a similar lack of leadership in the two prime ministers of the National government in 1935, Stanley Baldwin and Neville Chamberlain? Is this particular symbolic order due to be supplanted because it has lost its *nom-du-père*?

In the course of Part 1 Cecilia becomes at least partially aware of the outmoded class system which most of the family take for granted and for which Emily acts as principal spokesperson. This new awareness first dawns when the difference in class threatens to cause a rupture between working class Robbie and her. She mistakes his removing his boots and socks before entering her house for an act of exaggerated deference, "playacting the cleaning lady's son come to the big house on an errand" (26). She has imbibed this sense of social difference from her class conscious mother, Emily. Emily resents the fact that her husband has paid for Robbie's education, an act which she characterizes as "a hobby of Jack's [. . .] which smacked of meddling to her," that is of upsetting the "natural" order of things (142). The result is Emily's encouragement of Briony in her childish lie falsely implicating Robbie which exonerates Emily's conviction that you cannot treat someone from a lower class as an equal. As Cecilia writes later to Robbie of her family's reaction to Briony's childish accusation: "I'm beginning to understand the snobbery that lay behind their stupidity. My mother never forgave you your first" (196). But tellingly Cecilia goes on in the letter to assume that Danny, the working class son of Hardman the handyman, must have been the real rapist. Here McEwan subtly suggests the invidious nature of a class system that permeates even those seeking to shed its effects and that works to protect the upper class rapist from exposure throughout his lifetime.

Marshall, the true rapist, represents the new breed of capitalist entrepreneur whose amoral pursuit of profit is underlined by his making his fortune from the war. He is equally willing to rape "[p]oor vain and vulnerable Lola" (306) as he is to take advantage of the country fighting for its survival. The rape also comes to suggest Hitler's simultaneous rape of Europe, and "the scratches on Lola's shoulder and down Marshall's face" act as remote reminders of the violence being unleashed by Hitler's blitzkrieg across the English Channel seen in gory detail in Sections 2 and 3. Lola proves Marshall's equal and accomplice by withholding her evidence that he was her rapist in return for his marrying her. But Briony pictures the marriage compact as a lifetime's entombment: "the truth that only Marshall and his bride knew at first hand was steadily being walled up within the mausoleum of their marriage" (307). When this compromised couple are raised to the peerage for the charities they have funded from Marshall's wartime profiteering, they come to stand for the ruthlessness and deceptive nature of the new postwar ruling class.

Because this is a novel and not a work of history McEwan offers these interpretations of social and political history indirectly by closely following the fortunes of the Tallises and those they interact with. Their false sense of invulnerability within the structured society to which they belong is a cause of their downfall. This conviction that they occupy a privileged position is dramatized by the privileged status Briony attaches to the constructs of her writer's imagination. By making the protagonist and narrator a writer McEwan has situated the act of artistic composition in the context of national history. Ostensibly a novel concerned with the relationships between fact and fiction, the novel's use of metafiction draws attention to the way fictional writing cannot be isolated from the wider concerns of history and politics. In the first place, when novelists force us to understand the constructed nature of their characters by commenting on their own act of creation, they invite us simultaneously to reflect on the way subjectivity is similarly constructed by ideological means in the non-fictional world we inhabit. Further, as Patricia Waugh argues, "Contemporary metafictional writing is both a response and a contribution to an even more thoroughgoing sense that reality or history are [sic] provisional: no longer a world of eternal verities but a series of constructions, artifices, impermanent structures" (7). In this sense the use of metafiction in the book serves to undermine the naturalization of social and economic inequalities that characterized English society in the 1930s.

Metafiction draws attention to the narratives we live by and their effect on our individual and collective lives. Briony's invented fictions remind the reader of the equally fallacious fictions that British citizens and the British government were making up to justify their desire for appeasement. This connection between the private and the public is also the subject of a meta-narrative commentary in *The Ploughman's Lunch* when the Lecturer wonders "to what extent individuals behave like governments, who are bound to act in the national interest which in turn is rarely separable from the government's interest, or that of the class it represents . . . " (19). A notorious instance of the nation's willed blindness to Hitler's acts of aggression in Europe is Anthony Eden's acquiescence in Germany's remilitarization of the

Rhineland in 1936 in violation of the Versailles Treaty of 1919. Would not the allies have otherwise conceded Germany control of its own territory at the conference table, reasoned the government. By convincing herself that she had seen Robbie in the impenetrable dark, Briony is telling herself a similarly deceptive story that meets her writer's need for narrative shape. The metafictional treatment of Briony's myopic formulation of her story draws attention to the constructed nature of narratives purporting to report the facts, and to the inherent contradiction in the writer's attempt to both persuade us of the particularity and yet universality of the characters and events described.

Take the way Briony the writer uses the Meissen vase to imply connections between the specific incident of its breakage and a number of wider fractures in the narrative and the society it depicts. At the most intimate level the vase suggests the fragility of Cecilia's virgin state which is about to be as abruptly ruptured by Robbie as is the vase. The vase next enters Briony's first attempt at fiction, "Two Figures by a Fountain," and becomes associated with her incorrect interpretation of the events leading to its rupture. Briony's testimony both in court and in her first narrative draft is as fragile as the mended vase, as McEwan subtly suggests when describing her initial determination of the identity of Lola's attacker: "the glazed surface of her conviction was not without its blemishes and hairline cracks" (158). Both the vase and the novel as a whole represent a fragile artifact that can easily come apart. During the war the vase is finally shattered, just as the Tallis family's way of life is shattered by historical events that cause its break up. This association between the vase and the Tallises takes one back to the first description of the vase: it was a gift awarded to Jack Tallis's brother Clem during the First World War that, despite wartime conditions, survived and was brought back to the Tallis family after his death in action. Valuable as it is, Jack Tallis wants it to be used: "If it had survived the war, the reasoning went, then it could survive the Tallises" (23). In other words the vase is a fragile object that has miraculously survived two centuries of use (as has the stratified society that the Tallises represent), that is directly identified with the family through Uncle Clem. Its fracturing and eventual destruction function as an imagistic prolepsis, anticipating that of the family and the prewar society to which it firmly belongs.

In *Atonement* the narrative forces the reader from the start to recognize that this is not simply the story of one pre-Second World War family in southern England, but a cross section of English society at that critical moment of time before the war changed everything. The first description of the Tallis's house makes clear its ugliness and relative newness—both appropriate adjectives for the English bourgeoisie of which the Tallises are representative members:

> Morning sunlight, or any light, could not conceal the ugliness of the Tallis home—barely forty years old, bright orange brick, squat, lead-paned

baronial Gothic, to be condemned one day in an article by Pevsner, or one of his team, as a tragedy of wasted chances, and by a younger writer of the modern school as "charmless to a fault" (18).

The only relics from an Adam-style house that preceded this one are an "artificial lake and island . . . and . . . a crumbling stuccoed temple" (18). The island and temple become the scene for the rape which brings this whole artificial world to an abrupt end. Marshall forces his egotistical needs on Lola just as later he forces them on the nation. Cecilia looks from their house to the view it affords, "giving an impression of timeless, unchanging calm which made her more certain than ever that she must soon be moving on" (18). That paradox is extended as the narrative unfolds to embrace every aspect of the Tallis family's existence. As one reviewer expresses the oxymoron at the center of this book, "The atmosphere is one of innocence oppressed by knowledge" (Hitchings 4). Briony teeters at the brink of adolescence, just as Lola "longed to throw off the last restraints of childhood" (306). Their growth to the more difficult world of adulthood parallels that of the nation.

The novel invites us to see these two girls as symptomatic of the state of Britain and the West at this period of history. Like these two girls, all the Tallises are expelled from the world they have constructed in their private fantasies into the unforgiving narrative of history, from narratives they concoct for their personal satisfaction to narratives concocted for them, from an imaginary state of subjective autonomy to a realization of their subjection to a symbolic order constructed by others. Briony's novel engineers the expulsion of the characters, especially her own persona, from a false Garden of Eden into the serpent filled world of modernity. How hard it was even for Cecilia and Robbie to give up the national evasion of the need to confront and repel the aggression of fascism is glimpsed in a moment in 1939 when Robbie is training for battle:

> After Munich last year, he was certain, like everyone else, there would be a war . . . But for both of them there was something fantastical about it all, remote even though likely. Surely not again, was what many people were saying. And so they continued to cling to their hopes. (195)

Part 2 (the Dunkirk segment) retrospectively casts the private family relationships of Part 1 into a quite different social and historical light. The cozy isolation typified by the Tallises' country estate could be thought to parallel Britain's deluded feeling of invulnerability under Chamberlain from Hitler's escalating aggression across the Channel. As McEwan told one interviewer, "private deceptions and national deceptions are not entirely disconnected" (Haffenden 186).

Because Briony is writing *Atonement* with hindsight she makes frequent use of what Genette terms temporal prolepsis (narrative anticipation), to anticipate this expulsion into a fallen war torn world, to show, that is, how present private actions are responsible for future public consequences. Robbie, for instance, quotes Malvolio's lines from *Twelfth Night*—"Nothing that can be can come between me and the full prospect of my hopes" (123). The quotation offers a subtle instance of prolepsis, warning the reader that Robbie is likely to prove as deluded as Malvolio proved to be. McEwan uses another quotation from Jane Austen's *Northanger Abbey* as his epigraph to warn the reader before the novel has begun of the delusions that a young girl like Briony is likely to harbor with her head stuffed full of romantic fantasies and grotesque horrors. Austen's protagonist, Catherine Moorland, who is reprimanded by Henry Tilney in the quoted extract for her naïve response to events around her, is the victim of reading fiction—the Gothic romances of her day—and failing to make a distinction between the fictive and the real. McEwan ironically has the Tallis country house renamed Tilney's Hotel as a sly tribute to this fictional precedent. McEwan sees *Northanger Abbey* as a novel "about someone's wild imagination causing havoc to people around them" (Ali 59). Tilney's reproach to Catherine ("what ideas have you been admitting?") can be applied equally fittingly to Briony whose similarly over-active imagination leads her to tell the crucial lie that acts like a bomb blowing the family apart. Brought up on a diet of stories that privilege the rulers—the princes and princesses—of a country, Briony finds it all too easy to cast working class Robbie in the role of a malevolent ogre.

McEwan's ironical use of earlier literary texts is one feature that distinguishes McEwan's citations as intertexts as opposed to sources. Both Kristeva and Jacques Derrida argue that any text seen as intertext entails productivity.[2] What they mean by that is that once a text establishes its interdependence on other texts its signification proliferates. Kristeva explains the implications of this concept when she writes that a text constitutes the "junction of several texts of which it is simultaneously the rereading, accentuation, condensation, displacement and depth" ("Problèmes" 75). *Atonement* offers particularly clear instances of what Kristeva claims are two of the ways in which a text, in relating to other texts, becomes productive of further meanings—rereading and displacement. McEwan's novel is most obviously a rereading of the mid-twentieth-century novel epitomized by Elizabeth Bowen's *The Heat of the Day* (1949), just as it is a displacement of the modernist novel, particularly as instanced in the fiction of Virginia Woolf and D. H. Lawrence. It is no coincidence that Robbie, seeking to excuse his sexually explicit note sent by mistake to Cecilia, thinks of appealing to "a passing impatience with convention" that he associates with "a memory of reading the Orioli edition of *Lady Chatterley's Lover*" which had been banned in England in 1928 (124). Like Mellors, Robbie comes from a lower class than Cecilia (cf. Lady Chatterley).

Virginia Woolf acts both as a positive and negative influence on this novel. Talking about *Atonement* McEwan states that he "was wanting to

enter into a conversation with modernism and its dereliction of duty in relation to what I have Cyril Connolly call the backbone of the plot" (Interview
with Silverblatt). Comparisons have been made between this book and
Woolf's *Between the Acts* "in which a group of well-bred characters gathers for
a family pageant against the backdrop of impending war" (Cowley 17), and
Woolf's *To the Lighthouse*, the dinner scene of which is parodied by "the
disastrous roast meat dinner fed to sweltering guests" in Part 1 (Kemp 46).
As was the case with his use of Bowen, McEwan offers his reader internal
evidence of Woolf's influence (this time deleterious) on the young Briony's
narrative style when she is pictured reading Woolf's *The Waves* between
nursing shifts. Under Woolf's modernist spell, Briony decides that characters
"were quaint devices that belonged to the nineteenth century" and that
plots "too were like rusted machinery whose wheels would no longer turn"
(265). McEwan has said that in Briony's first piece of fiction that reflects this
modernist bias, "Two Figures by a Fountain," "she is burying her conscience
beneath her stream of consciousness" (Interview with Silverblatt), indicating
how for him the ideology of modernism (especially its prioritization of stylistic innovation) has hidden moral consequences. Compare Briony's critique of her early draft of the novel: "Did she really think she could hide
behind some borrowed notions of modern writing, and drown her guilt in
a stream—three streams—of consciousness?" (302). Style, she discovers, really does have ethical implications.

Sure enough in *Atonement* there is a modulation of prose styles. In the
long Part 1 McEwan chose to write in "a slightly mannered prose, slightly
held in, a little formal, a tiny bit archaic" with which he "could evoke the
period best" (McEwan, interview with Silverblatt). In Part 2, writing about
the retreat of the British Dunkirk, he chose "to write in a choppier prose
with shorter, simpler sentences" (Ali 59), a style that is reminiscent of
Hemingway. As he explained, "on the battlefield the subordinate clause has
no place" (Interview with Silverblatt). In the final coda he employs a contemporary voice, one that is acutely self-conscious and aware of its own act
of narration. For instance: "I've always liked to make a tidy finish," says the
elderly Briony, simultaneously referring to her life and her life's work (334).
That self-conscious awareness of her own deficiencies is the product of a lifelong process of ethical as well as literary self education.

Although there is only one narrative voice that turns out to be that of
Briony, the aging novelist, McEwan employs what Gérard Genette calls
variable internal focalization in Part 1, that is, narrative where the focal
character changes (whether the narrative voice changes or not—it doesn't in
Atonement).[3] In the case of *Atonement*, the narrative is focalized first through
the eyes of Briony, then of Cecilia, then of Robbie, and so on. McEwan
employs this particular "modal determination" (Genette 188) partly to
distinguish his narrative from the classic realist novel's and "objective" history's zero focalization using an omniscient invisible narrator (Briony's lie

gained widespread credence from positioning herself as such a narrator in her fictionalized narrative of the rape). McEwan's use of this particular mode of focalization is also employed partly to demonstrate Briony's, the adult narrator's, attempt to project herself into the thoughts and feelings of her characters, a moral act which we will see is crucial to her search for forgiveness.

A further metafictional strategy that McEwan makes constant use of to draw attention to the narrativity of his own narrative is to evoke, while writing against the grain of, established literary genres. Catherine Belsey refers to Emile Benveniste's distinction between *discourse* and *histoire* in *Problems in General Linguistics*[4] to illustrate how in the *histoire* of classic realist fiction "the events seem to narrate themselves" (Benveniste 208), whereas *discourse* assumes a speaker and a hearer. Accordingly the "authority of [the classic realist novel's] impersonal narration springs from its effacement of its own status as discourse" (Belsey 72). From his earliest collections of short stories Ian McEwan has consistently drawn attention to the status of his fiction as discourse by alluding to or parodying traditional literary genres, thereby forcing the reader to take note of the presence of a self-conscious narrator. He has described each of his early stories as "a kind of pastiche of a certain style [. . .], its origins were always slightly parodic" (McEwan, "Points" 17). Similarly most of his novels, according to him, allude in some way to existing genres—*The Cement Garden* is "an urban *Lord of the Flies*" (McEwan, "Ian McEwan" 69); *The Innocent* added to and subverted the spy genre (McEwan, "Blood" 47); *The Comfort of Strangers* draws on the sinister setting of Venice established by Thomas Mann in *Death in Venice*; his play for television, *The Imitation Game*, was indebted to Virginia Woolf's *Three Guineas* (Haffenden 175); "*Amsterdam* is an Evelyn Waugh tribute novel" (McEwan "He Triumphed" E1); *Saturday* models itself on Saul Bellow's *Herzog* the protagonist of which is based on its author (McEwan "Master" 11). As for *Atonement*, it belongs to the country house novel genre, and McEwan has said that it is modeled on the work of "Elizabeth Bowen of *The Heat of the Day*, with a dash of Rosamund Lehmann of *Dusty Answer*, and, in [Briony's] first attempts, a sprinkling of Virginia Woolf" (McEwan, "Art of Fiction" 56).[5]

Narrative genre helps predetermine the reader's interpretation of a text. Interpretation opens the possibility of misinterpretation, of what Lacan terms *méconnaissance* or mis-recognition on the part of the ego, "the illusion of autonomy to which it entrusts itself" (*Écrits* 6). Briony at thirteen suffers from just such an illusion, a certainty in her own judgment that brings tragedy to some of those closest to her. As a novice writer she might even be thought of as belonging to Lacan's imaginary order. Her misinterpretation of the adult symbolic world is the product of her childhood reading habits in which she read herself as Her Majesty the Ego, to misquote Freud.[6] Her first crucial misreading is of the scene between Cecilia and Robbie at the pond. When she first observes them she decides from their formal posture that Robbie must be proposing marriage to her sister. Briony reflects: "She herself had written a tale in which a humble woodcutter saved a princess from drowning and ended by marrying her" (36). But when Cecilia jumps into the pond Briony is perplexed at this disordered narrative sequence: "the drowning scene, followed by a rescue, should have preceded the marriage proposal" (36–37). When she returns to the window after the two figures have left the scene she feels liberated from the impenetrable facts: "The truth had become as ghostly as invention" (39). She is free to interpret the scene as she pleases.

Once she opens Robbie's explicit note to Cecilia, which she is too young to process, she is forced to reconsider her interpretation of the whole scene. "With the letter," she reflects, "something elemental, brutal, perhaps even criminal had been introduced, some principle of darkness" (106–107). Like Poe's purloined letter, this letter that Briony has purloined acts as the signifier that determines her subjectivity. Just as the letter, according to Lacan, constructs the Queen's subject position in Poe's story, so Robbie's letter places Briony willy-nilly in the imaginary order. She convinces herself that Robbie is what Lola calls a "maniac" (112) and what she calls "the incarnation of evil" (108), and that her sister is threatened and in need of her help, a scenario which places the mirror image of her ego at the center of the story. So when she convinces herself that Robbie is the figure glimpsed running away from Lola in the dark, it is her novelist's need for order that clinches it: "The truth was in the symmetry [. . .] The truth instructed her eyes" (159). Fiction determines fact for her. But the subsequent acceptance by the entire Tallis family apart from Cecilia of this childish narrative of misrecognition places them in the same imaginary order. Being adults, they are more culpable than she is. But they share the national myopia, preferring to put their trust in the class that also ruled the country. Working class Robbie was damned as much by a national as by Briony's narrative. As he reflects during his fall back to Dunkirk, "A dead civilization. First his own life ruined, then everybody else's" (204).

For Briony to progress from her teenage play, "The Trials of Arabella" to *Atonement*, the final work of the 77-year-old successful novelist, she has first to abandon the fairy tale fantasies in which medical princes in disguise rescue damsels in distress and ogres threaten her princess-like sister. By the age of eighteen she is writing "Two Figures by a Fountain" in the modernist manner of Virginia Woolf, concentrating on *"the crystalline present moment"* with *"no sense of forward movement,"* as CC (Cyril Connolly) tells her (294). Ironically, in the same letter he writes her, Connolly pontificates on the foolishness of writers addressing the subject of the war. Artists *"are wise and right to ignore it and devote themselves to other subjects"* (297). In offering this advice Connolly is revealing his own implication in the national desire to avoid war at any cost. A sign of the later Briony's ethically more responsible attitude to the role of the novelist is the inclusion of Part 2 in which the description of the British Expeditionary Force's retreat from France to Dunkirk is based on solid historical research in the Imperial War Museum which significantly features in the 1999 epilogue. This change in choice of genre to one of historically based fiction indicates Briony's abandonment of the historical blindness implicit in the use of stream of consciousness found in "Two Figures by a Fountain." It is clearly endorsed in the Acknowledgements page by McEwan's own indebtedness to the staff of the Department of Documents at the Imperial War Museum for his narration of Briony's imagined narration of Robbie's participation in the rout of the British army in 1940.

What has happened in the course of Briony's long writing apprenticeship is that she has been forced to project herself into the thoughts and feelings of others. For McEwan this is a fundamentally ethical act that emerges as the core component of Briony's attempt to atone for her failure to empathize with the feelings of those closest to her in her teens. Connolly's description of "Two Figures by a Fountain" does indicate that she is already making a first attempt to project herself into the consciousness of the two characters modeled on Cecilia and Robbie: "*we have matters from the man's view, then the woman's—though we don't really learn much that is fresh*" (295). The entire work is still governed by esthetic concerns to which biographical and historical facts are subordinated. By the time Briony comes to write the last version of *Atonement* she has made herself imagine what it must have felt like to be Robbie on the retreat to Dunkirk, and to be Cecilia as a wartime student nurse by reading the history of both situations (McEwan mentions on the Acknowledgements page his indebtedness to Lucilla Andrews' *No Time for Romance: An Autobiographical Account of a Few Moments in British and Personal History* [1977]). As McEwan told an interviewer after the publication of *Saturday*, "The novel, above all forms of literature, is able to take us through the fundamental exercise of what morality is about. That is, being able to sense what it is to be someone else—that we're locked into a reciprocal manner" ("Frozen Moments" 12).

This act of empathy lies at the center of McEwan's ethics. Writing about the terrorist attacks of September 11, 2001 for the *Guardian*, McEwan observed, "If the hijackers had been able to imagine themselves into the thoughts and feelings of the passengers, they would have been unable to proceed. [. . .] Imagining what it is like to be someone other than yourself is at the core of our humanity. It is the essence of compassion, and it is the beginning of morality" ("Only Love and then Oblivion"). This belief lies at the core of all McEwan's fiction and explains its apparent amoral stance (a stance that the mature writer, Briony, comes to share once she has learnt the need to respect the autonomy of others in her work). He has said that for him novels are not about "teaching people how to live but about showing the possibility of what it is like to be someone else. [. . .] Cruelty is a failure of imagination" (McEwan, "Review" 3). It is imagination that Briony spends the rest of her professional life seeking to acquire. The novel that we read and that took her adult lifetime to complete is her attempt to imaginatively project herself into the feelings of the two characters whose lives were destroyed by her failure of imagination. Having mistakenly cast them in a story that totally misrepresented them, Briony seeks to retell their story with the compassion and understanding that she lacked as a thirteen-year-old girl. In turning "Two Figures by a Fountain" into *Atonement,* in exchanging the primacy of the authorial ego for an empathetic projection into the feelings of others, Briony is abandoning the imaginary for the symbolic order. The narrative is driven by her unconscious desire to win back the love of a sister who in fact died back in 1940. All she can do after Robbie's and Cecilia's deaths is to pursue that desire along the chain of her narrative.

The status of the coda "London, 1999" is uncertain. The novel appears to end with the end of Part 3, followed by "BT London, 1999" (330). The coda that follows is unsigned and could be taken as a diary confession. It is metafictional in that it offers an extraneous commentary on the novel proper in which it plays with the possibility of alternative endings. This concluding section of the book is both open ended and dark. In the penultimate paragraph Briony opens up the possibility of a further revision when she plays with the possibility of writing a new draft that would finally allow the two lovers to forgive her: "It's not impossible" (351). But the imminent onset of vascular dementia together with her painfully acquired honesty makes this fantasy unlikely to be realized. Then there is the shattering on the penultimate page of any suspension of disbelief that may have persisted in the reader's mind to this point of the narrative: Briony's revelation of the two lovers' deaths stands in stark contrast to the orderliness of the story Briony concocted as a child. This revelation comes in the form of a conditional proposition followed by a series of questions:

> But now I can no longer think what purpose would be served if, say, I tried to persuade my reader, by direct or indirect means, that Robbie Turner died of septicemia at Bray Dunes on 1 June 1940, or that Cecilia was killed in September of the same year by the bomb that destroyed Balham Underground station . . . Who would want to believe that, except in the service of the bleakest realism? (350).

In interview McEwan has said that Briony "cannot end a story the way events have dictated"—presumably for reasons of self esteem. Instead he "leave[s] it to the reader to decide" between ending the story at the end of Part 3 or accepting the "bleakest realism" presented in the coda of 1999. (Interview with Silverblatt).

What emerges from these competing accounts is the tremendous power of narrative. It can be equally destructive or redemptive. In *Atonement,* as in

Time's Arrow, it is both destructive and redemptive. Briony's lie destroys her family, just as the lie the nation told itself destroyed the old social order with the war. In the coda we see the Tallises' country house, once emblematic of bourgeois hegemony, converted to Tilney's Hotel complete with a golf course, benches and piped classical music. This democratization of a once elite family country residence is what the lies have brought about—a starkly different world in which upper-middle-class families like the Tallises no longer have a claim to be part of the ruling elite. Yet Briony's narrative is also redemptive to the extent that it represents her attempt to think herself imaginatively into the minds and feelings of her sister and Robbie. If she cannot bring them back to life in postwar England she can restore them to life in her novel: "As long as there is a single copy, a solitary typescript of my final draft, then my spontaneous, fortuitous sister and her medical prince survive to love" (350). Briony settles for an esthetic solution by offering the lovers, as Earl Ingersoll describes it, "an 'eternity' of youth, beauty and love in the transcendent but frozen world of Art" (254). But McEwan is careful to frame this esthetic act of atonement within the wider knowledge of what history did to the lovers. Like the society to which they belonged, they were swept away by the flood waters of the war that left in its wake the harsher if more democratic society of modern Britain. Is Briony's work of fiction an evasion or an act of atonement or both? What exactly does she mean when she says that atonement "was always an impossible task, and that was precisely the point. The attempt was all" (351)? The novel ends on a note of ambiguity. Yet an appreciation of ambiguity is just what would have prevented Briony from indicting Robbie in her first fictionalized narration of these events, just as it might have avoided taking Hitler at his word in the Munich Agreement which merely delayed a war that Britain persuaded itself was not likely to occur.

Lists of Books Published

Fiction

First Love, Last Rites [short stories], 1975.
In Between the Sheets [short stories], 1978.
The Cement Garden, 1978.
The Comfort of Strangers, 1981.
The Child in Time, 1987.
The Innocent, 1989.
Black Dogs, 1992.
Enduring Love, 1997.
Amsterdam, 1998.
Atonement, 2001.
Saturday, 2005.

Other Works

The Imitation Game [three plays for television], 1981.
Or Shall We Die? [oratorio], 1983.
The Ploughman's Lunch [screenplay], 1985.
The Daydreamer [children's book], 1994.

Part II National Cultures and Hybrid Narrative Modes

Preface

Both Englishness and English fiction have been transformed in the later twentieth century by the influx of newly decolonized peoples to Britain starting with the arrival of the *Empire Windrush* from the West Indies in 1948. The name of the ship is ironically appropriate in that it initiated a reverse form of imperialism, the colonization of the metropolitan center by the previously colonized periphery. Before the arrival of the *Windrush* Britain had been an almost homogenous white society. By 2001 the UK census showed that 4.6 million of the population was non-white and this proportion was growing. As fast as the British were withdrawing from their expanded territories in the decades following the end of World War II the native inhabitants of those territories who were automatically granted British citizenship were following their previous colonizers to the metropolitan center. As Sam Seldon and his generation of immigrants quickly realized (and described in their fiction), their presence exacerbated the crisis of identity which the end of empire produced in a nation that had developed its sense of self over the preceding centuries from its imperial mission. The loss of empire seemed to spell the loss of a national self. The British empire, Ian Baucom writes, "is the place onto which the island kingdom arrogantly displaces itself and from which a puzzled England returns as a stranger to itself" (3). That estrangement initiated a national loss of confidence epitomized by the title of Tom Nairn's seminal *The Break-Up of Britain* (1977).

Anna Marie Smith dates the rise of a new right wing populist movement to the late 1960s. This movement offered both an alternative to the political consensus that had prevailed since the end of the war and a new conception of nationalism that cut across traditional class and party lines. It found its most infamous expression in Powell's so-called "rivers of blood" speech delivered at the Birmingham Conservative Political Centre on April 20, 1968 on the eve of Parliament's debate of the Race Relations Bill 1968. This bill was intended to guarantee equal opportunity for black Britons in housing and employment. In his speech Powell claimed to be uttering the fears of reverse discrimination felt by many white Britons: "For reasons which they could not comprehend, and in pursuance of a decision by default, on which they were never consulted, they found themselves made strangers in their own country" (Powell 217). Urging "the encouragement of re-emigration," Powell in his conclusion warned: "As I look ahead, I am filled with foreboding; like the Roman, I seem to see 'the River Tiber foaming with much blood'" (219). Anna Marie Smith considers that Powell's anti-black immigration campaign, given great impetus by this speech, "brought the nation together in a particularly effective manner because it drew upon the already normalized tradition of imperial racism and put that tradition to work in re-inscribing the national boundaries" (24). By refusing to define Englishness as bound up with the Empire, Powell relieved the native English of a feeling that the loss of empire signaled a loss of national identity. As Baucom points out, Powell's speech represents Englishness as "something that exists apart from, and utterly fails to coincide with, the lost empire—uncannily figured here as an invading black body" (15).

Powell made possible a new hegemonic consensus that moved both parties to the right as well as altering their core constituencies. While repudiating Powell's overt appeal to racist sentiments, "Thatcherism," as Stuart Hall called it, represented a new "organization of consent" ("Great" 29). According to Hall the aim of Thatcherism "was to reconstruct social life as a whole around a return to the old values—the philosophies of tradition, Englishness, respectability, patriarchalism, family, and nation" ("Toad" 39). Like any hegemonic discourse, Thatcherism contrived to speak to (and interpellate) a bewildering range of subject positions—"the self-reliant ... taxpayer," "the 'concerned patriot'," "the native Briton," and so on ("Toad" 49). Its appeal to Victorian values offered a safe haven to the besieged middle classes by hiding change in continuity. Many of the writers considered in this book (almost all left inclining at this time) strongly opposed what Thatcherism represented—"nanny-Britain, straight-laced Victoria-reborn Britain, class-ridden know-your-place Britain, thin-lipped, jingoist Britain," as Salman Rushdie called it (*Imaginary Homelands* 161). But during the eleven years during which Margaret Thatcher was prime minister (1979–90) the new hegemony prevailed and enabled her to transform the fabric of British society.

Dominic Head concludes that a "corollary of the constructedness of national identity is the kind of public confusion that allows racism to thrive" (164). The Thatcher government added to a history of restrictive postwar immigration legislation by passing the British Nationality Act of 1981 which abolished the *ius soli* (right of the soil) and substituted a racialized conception of national identity solely based on "patriality." As Paul Gilroy observed in 1987, "In contemporary Britain, statements about nation are invariably also statements about race" (*There Aint* 57). Gilroy argues that Thatcherism was responsible for the redefinition of nationality based not on color but on culture, what he calls "ethnic absolutism" (59). Of course this only highlights the way in which the nation is constructed as what Benedict Anderson has called "an imagined political community," "a deep horizontal comradeship" that "is imagined because the members of even the smallest nation will never know most of their fellow members" (6–7). The Thatcher government's popular war with Argentina in 1982 over possession of the Falklands Islands/Malvinas offers an insight into the subtle workings of a nationalism that depends on a racist understanding of national identity for its appeal. Peregrine Worsthorne, a right wing journalist, made explicit the unconscious racism underlying the new patriotism of this minor military engagement: "Most Britons today identify more easily with those of the same stock 8000 miles away ... than they do with West Indian or Asian immigrants living next door" (20).

Ultimately in 1997 the Labour Party created a new hegemony under the banner of Blair's New Labour. Like all emergent discursive formations, this involved appropriating much of the previously dominant one. Appealing to notions of "stakeholding, one nation, inclusion, community," Blair argued that it was the Conservatives "who have 'nationalised the state,' becoming the party of centralised government" (x). Blair and New Labour reversed the previous Conservative governments' centralization of local government and in 1998 passed acts setting up a Scottish Parliament and Welsh Assembly. For the first time in many centuries the English were forced to face the fact that British was not synonymous with English. Previously the English, who represented four-fifths of the UK population, exercised hegemony over the rest of Britain. In effect the English had treated the rest of Britain as an inner empire that had continued to offer England some sense of national identity once the outer empire had acquired independence. Moreover Protestant England had traditionally derived part of its identity by setting itself up in opposition to Catholic Europe. The Maastricht Treaty (1991) making Britain a member of the European Union had eroded that distinction. Now, as David McCrone writes, "like the Welsh, the Scots saw in Europe a new Union to augment or even replace the older British one" (106). The English alone this time suffered a new crisis of identity. Only they had no parliament of their own. Flags of St. George appeared at any excuse, such as at international soccer matches. In *The English*, Jeremy Paxman notes that St. George's Day began to be celebrated in 1995, and on St. George's Day 1999 the *Sun* offered a four-page pullout, "100 Reasons Why It's Great to be English" (21).

Two reports throw light on the current debate over what constitutes English identity—the Parekh Report of the Runnymede Trust's Commission on the Future of Multi-Ethnic Britain (2000), and the Cantle Report commissioned by David Blunkett, then home secretary, following rioting by Asian Muslims in Oldham, Bradford, and Burnley in 2001. Both reports advocated a position somewhere between left wing separatism and right wing assimilation. The Parekh Report declared, "Britain is both a community of citizens and a community of communities, both a liberal and a multicultural society" (ix). Both reports were disturbed at the extent to which different communities chose voluntarily to segregate themselves from the rest of the nation. The Cantle report, finding that different communities lived parallel lives, insisted that it is "essential to agree some common elements of 'nationhood'" (A3). While Blunkett was recommending that members of ethnic communities in Britain all take an oath of allegiance and learn to master the English language, Hanif Kureishi was equally insistent that it "is the British, the white British, who have to learn that being British isn't what it was" (*My Beautiful* 101). Yet the real subject of these public arguments was not British but English identity, as the Parekh Report admitted: "The key issue is not fundamentally one of British identity. It is one of English identity and how previous conceptions of English identity have excluded so many people who live in and richly contribute to English society" (8). The English still appear to be inscribed by their imperial past.

Those novelists of this period who are representative of the recent ethnic transfusions into English society offer refreshingly new and complex responses to these debates about Englishness and life in contemporary England—or London, in most cases. If England has 98 percent of Britain's non-white immigrants, London has over half of them. It has become, writes John Clement Ball, "a site where formally colonized peoples could enact what is sometimes called 'imperialism in reverse': they have occupied and even reterritorialized a city that metonymically (as the 'metropolitan centre') had done the same in colonial space" (67). Novelists representing the new ethnic communities that now make up almost two-fifths of London's population began by positioning themselves as outsiders in relation to metropolitan society. But by the time Rushdie, Kureishi and their contemporaries began publishing their work they considered themselves to be as much a part of the metropolis as their white compatriots and claimed to be, or simply assumed themselves to be, giving voice to a previously near silenced segment of the nation and its capital. They lived in what Rushdie called a "city visible but unseen" (*Satanic Verses* 241). Finding overdetermined what Pierre Nora[1] calls the *lieux de memoire* (those historical landmarks, such as the Cenotaph or Lords Cricket Ground, that signify a continuity with Britain's imperial past), many South Asian novelists, as Ball remarks, represent the metropolis as unsubstantial, unreal ("A City" 67–68). For them London is no longer the center of an empire. It is a city large areas of which remain unknown to the white population. For Rushdie, cities like London present themselves as "invented spaces, artificial spaces" (*Conversations* 104). Redolent with history, London characteristically awaits the inscriptions of its latest newcomers. All three novelists considered in this section find innovative ways of constructing a portrait of modern London that is as much a narrative invention as it is a representation of a new sense of national identity.

6
Salman Rushdie: *The Satanic Verses* (1988)

The Satanic Verses, Rushdie's first novel to depict English society from an immigrant's point of view, has received a distorted reception from the moment that it was banned in India on October 5, 1988, nine days after it was first published. What has become known as the "Rushdie affair" uncannily lived out much of what happened to its two protagonists in the book, including the demonization of Rushdie and the rioting. The ensuing worldwide controversy pitted Western liberal defenders of unlimited free speech against fundamentalist Muslims demanding that the book be banned because it was blasphemous. As Andrzej Gasiorek rightly remarks, "One could hardly find a better example of Orientalism at work"—or Occidentalism, he might have added (171). One of the consequences of critics' focus on the novel's treatment of the founding of Islam and the lives of some of its more absolutist followers has been to draw disproportionate attention to its four alternating even-numbered chapters in which Gibreel dreams about the life of Muhammed (derogatively named Mahound in the novel), the Imam (modeled on then Iranian President Khamene'i), and Ayesha (modeled on Naseem Fatima), a follower of the Islamic faith who does and does not work a miracle. The framing five alternating chapters set largely in England actually amount to two and a half times the length of the four chapters dealing with Islamic matters and clearly constitute the principal matter and concerns of the book. Gayatri Spivak opened her essay on *The Satanic Verses* by declaring: "I will attempt the impossible: a reading of *The Satanic Verses* as if nothing has happened since late 1988" (*Outside* 219). I will go further. I will offer a reading of the novel largely ignoring both the dream chapters about Islam and the Rushdie affair. I refer readers to my earlier essay "Demonizing Discourse in Salman Rushdie's *The Satanic Verses*" listed in the Bibliography for a corrective to this focus. The concern of this section of my book is with national identity and hybrid narrative modes, a concern that can best be explored through the four long chapters focused on England/London and the final one located in Bombay.

From the start Rushdie has been unequivocal in identifying what he considers to be the principal thematic concern of the novel. He has stated this most fully in his 1990 essay, "In Good Faith":

> If *The Satanic Verses* is anything, it is a migrant's-eye view of the world. It is written from the very experience of uprooting, disjuncture and metamorphosis (slow or rapid, painful or pleasurable) that is the migrant condition, and from which, I believe, can be derived a metaphor for all humanity. (*Imaginary Homelands* 394)

Rushdie considers the migrant condition to be double edged, both subject to change and an agent of change: "the migrant is not simply transformed by his act [of migration]; he also transforms his new world. Migrants may well become mutants, but it is out of such hybridization that newness can emerge" (*Imaginary Homelands* 210). The novel repeatedly asks, "How does newness come into the world? How is it born? Of what fusions, translations, conjoinings is it made?" (8). The answers the narrative offers are as complex as the possibilities raised in that last sentence. The novel offers opposing and conflicting versions of the migrant condition—assimilation or nativism, plurality of identities or a return to unitary roots, transnationalism or nationalism. The two extreme forms of migrant identity are embodied in the novel's two protagonists, Saladin Chamcha, who has cultivated total assimilation into English society (or so he thinks), and Gibreel Farishta, whose nativism leads him to attempt to turn the imperial metropolis into an image of its erstwhile colony, India.

The bravura opening of the novel complicates this binary pair of opposing attitudes even before the binaries are introduced by portraying Gibreel and Saladin descending from a plane that has just been blown up by terrorists "embracing head-to-tail" (7) and becoming in the process "Gibreelsaladin Farishtachamcha" (5). Rushdie has said that for him, as for any immigrant, "[i]f you come from over there and end up over here you just have that sense of doubleness, all the time." The same even applies within a nation: "if you come from a minority community inside a majority culture, you have that sense of belonging and not belonging all at the same time" ("Salman Rushdie Talks" 59). So the book begins with an impossible descent to English earth by two contrasting Indians, one angelic, the other devilish, a distinction that Rushdie immediately confounds with the use of oxymoron and run-together words by calling it "this endless but also ending angelicdevilish fall" (5). Rushdie plunges us into the mythic world of fiction ("*it was and it was not so*" [35]) and lets us understand that this fall is meant to be understood figuratively as "the moment at which the processes of their transmutation began" (5). Where the novelists considered in the first section of this book concentrated on the transmutations effected by the impact of the past on the present (which remakes the past), those treated in this section show the transmutations that overtake both immigrant and host communities. Separate and different as the two of them wish to remain, Gibreel and Saladin are inevitably plunged by the act of migration into a mixed condition of plural identities. As Rushdie explains it, "people become combinations." Consequently purity (whether ethnic or national or moral—pure goodness or pure evil) always stands in danger of becoming contaminated: "what is supposed to be angelic quite often has disastrous results, and what is supposed to be demonic is quite often something with which one must have sympathy" (*Conversations* 84). Even in the opening pages Rekha, Gibreel's dead lover, confuses things by cursing this supposed "angel": "may your life be hell. Hell, because that's . . . where you came from, devil . . . " (8).

Another way of understanding Part I is to see the two men's fall to earth as both a reenactment of the Fall and a rebirth. The novel's opening words, repeated subsequently many times, are "To be born again . . . first you have to die" (3). Their fall is a descent down a fictive birth canal, "what appeared to be a long, vertical tunnel" (6). Saladin descends "head first, in the recommended position for babies entering the birth canal" (5). On reaching the ground Gibreel exclaims, "Born again," while Saladin, "as befitted a new-born babe, burst into foolish tears" (10). At the same time their re-creation is likened to the creation of the universe, "a big bang, followed by the falling of stars . . . a miniature echo of the birth of time" (4). Their rebirth is into a new nation and a new identity—that of migrancy. But migrants are responsible for regenerating the nation. Both protagonists, in falling, die out of their old lives, expelled from the paradisal if delusional state of national belonging, one to India the other to England. As Gibreel explains to Saladin, he half died out of his old life twice, once from illness, once from the plane, "so it adds up, it counts" (32). As for Saladin, he is possessed during his fall by a will that totally rejects his old life as a replica of the perfect Englishman, informing him "that it wanted nothing to do with his pathetic personality" (9). So their fall is equally a dying out of an earlier unthinking existence into a new fallen, confused, adult state. It is fitting that the plane they fall from is called the *Bostan*, the name of one of the two Islamic gardens of paradise, from which, like Adam and Eve, they are expelled. Migrancy, that is, also entails loss, loss "of parents, country, self," as Rushdie told John Banville ("An Interview" 34). When the plane explodes the debris falling from the sky includes, as Gillian Gane observes, "not only material fragments of the paraphernalia of air travel" (23), something that all migrants readily leave behind, but "the debris of the soul, broken memories, sloughed-off selves, severed mother-tongues . . . " (*Satanic Verses* 4–5). So to migrate is to die and suffer a loss of origins and a sense of belonging. and to be reborn into a new, strange, in-between form of existence that duplicates in adult life the migrant's childhood growth to maturity.

Inevitably the immigrant encounters prejudice. resentment. and demonization on the part of the national, especially when the immigrant is from the former British empire and the national belongs to the former imperial power now learning (or not) to live without its imperial identity. Rushdie's epigraph from Daniel Defoe's *The Political History of the Devil* (1726) exemplifies how the history attaching to the demonization of the migrant extends back to the early days of British colonialism. The epigraph reads in part:

> Satan, being thus confined to a vagabond, wandering, unsettled condition, is without any certain abode; for though he has, by consequence of his angelic nature, a kind of empire in the liquid waste or air, yet this is certainly part of his punishment, that he is . . . without any fixed place, or space, allowed him to rest the sole of his foot upon.

Rushdie prefaces his postcolonial novel with an instance of colonial discourse that reveals the fictive nature of the colonial paradigm that continues to haunt the once colonized migrants seeking to make their home in the metropolis of the former colonizer. The epigraph also acts as a reminder of the way colonialism has from the start associated the condition of migrancy with the punishment meted out to Satan (quite forgetting that Adam and Eve likewise were condemned to be driven out of Eden to wander the earth in sorrow, that in other words we all share the condition of migrancy). In finding themselves falling "out of thin air," the novel's two migrants may share the devil's predicament, but they also pass through a transformative environment, "air-space, . . . the planet-shrinker and power-vacuum, most insecure and transitory of zones, illusory, discontinuous, metamorphic, - because when you throw everything up in the air anything becomes possible -" (5). This "empire in the liquid waste," because it offers no fixed abode, can generate the big bang, creation, newness.

But what kind of newness? Martine Dutheil invokes one of Derrida's persistent theses, our inability to discover absolute origins, to argue that the newness Rushdie is associating with migrancy is never originary. According to Derrida, every beginning produces an illusory sense of limit, because the dissemination of meaning implicit in language leaks across the limit and deprives it of its originary status. In "Outwork," the preface to *Dissemination*, Derrida points to the dual and contradictory nature of any prefatory text (such as an epigraph), "the double inscription or double-jointedness of such a text: its semantic envelopment within the Book . . . and the left-overness [*restance*] of its textual exteriority" (44). Being both inside and outside the main text, an epigraph simultaneously "signals the beginning of a new narrative" and "opens a passage to the 'outside' of the novel, i.e., to the 'foreign' elements which constitute its condition of possibility" (Dutheil 56–57). Migrancy is as old as human civilization. Any newness is "a moment of cultural production divested of the compulsion to originate . . . in which newness emerges as a reinscription, a cross-inscription, a writing over"

(Baucom 215). To demonstrate his point, Dutheil cites another passage from near the end of Defoe's *History*:

> Now the injuries and injustice done to the devil in these cases are manifest; namely that they entitle the Devil to all the mischief they are pleased to do in the world . . . This is, 1, a grand cheat upon the world, and 2, a notorious slander upon the Devil. (340)

The scapegoating that Saladin (appropriately transformed into a goat) receives is no more originary than that the Devil received in earlier times. Humans have always projected their own failings onto a demonized Other.

This is what Gibreel does. A dedicated logocentrist, he insists on maintaining in watertight compartments good and evil, angel and devil, India and England, and on giving each former term absolute precedence over the latter. He projects his own schizophrenia onto the world around him: "the splitting was not in him, but in the universe" (362). A Manichaean, Gibreel believes that the universe is a battlefield between two equal and opposing forces—God's and Satan's. His binary vision insists on depriving the devil of his original status as an angel: "Iblis/Shaitan standing for the darkness, Gibreel for the light. - Out, out with these sentimentalities; *joining, locking together, love*. Seek and destroy: that was all" (364).[1] Gibreel's denial of all forms of admixture (which he identifies in this passage with "England-induced ambiguities") is directly responsible for the destruction he produces around and finally of himself. Rekha, totally out of character as Gibreel observes, cites earlier origins than those Gibreel relies on to undercut his assumption that Satan is a separate being from God (first mentioned in the Book of Chronicles in the fourth century B. C.). Reverting back four centuries she cites Amos 3: 6 where God takes responsibility for the presence of evil in the world. Rushdie shows Gibreel tussling with the origins of this confusing information. Has it (as was claimed to be the case with the Satanic verses) been implanted in him by the Devil? But what about his earlier confrontation with that "ambiguous Creature, that Upstairs-Downstairs Thing" (334), his idea of the Supreme Being, who refuses to clarify whether he is "multiform, plural" or its opposite, "pure" (329)?

When Gibreel comes to attempt to tropicalize London in an effort to confer on it all the advantages that ensue from India's climate, an act that again assumes the superiority of one binary (India) over its opposite (England), he is again undone by the language he summons to justify his unitary vision. He lists all the benefits tropicalization would bestow on London in a long paragraph, followed by a one and a half line paragraph listing the disadvantages. But among the supposed benefits, such as "[n]o more British reserve," and "[e]mergence of new social values," he includes such items as "religious fervour" and "political ferment," effects that are of dubious or no benefit. As Klaus Börner remarks of this passage, "[h]ybridity has come in

again by the back door" (160). Hybridity is a term much used and extensively defined by Homi Bhabha who has written at some length on *The
Satanic Verses*. Bhabha sees hybridity as the necessary consequence of
migrancy, what he calls an act of cultural translation. Bhabha adopts Walter
Benjamin's understanding of translation as he defines it in his 1923 essay on
"The Task of the Translator." There Benjamin discusses "that element in a
translation which goes beyond transmittal of subject matter," that in effect
"does not lend itself to translation" (*Illuminations* 75). Bhabha sees the same
effect manifested in the migrant's translation from one culture to another:
"The migrant culture of the 'in-between', the minority position, dramatizes
the activity of culture's untranslatability; and in doing so, it moves the question of culture's appropriation beyond the assimilationist's dream, or the
racist's nightmare, of a 'full transmittal of subject-matter'; and towards an
encounter with the ambivalent process of splitting and hybridity that marks
the identification with culture's difference" (*Location* 224). He claims that
the discourse of hybridity "opens up a space of negotiation" which "makes
possible the emergence of an 'interstitial' agency that refuses the binary representation of social antagonism" ("Culture's" 58). This concept allows
Bhabha to see the translated Gibreel as himself a destabilizing agent, one
whose presence "articulates the narrative of cultural difference which can
never let the national history look at itself narcissistically in the eye"
(*Location* 168). The stuttering film producer Whisky Sisodia at one point
declares, "The trouble with the Engenglish is that their hiss hiss history happened overseas, so they dodo don't know what it means" (353). Gibreel is
the embodiment of that history whose presence, as Bhabha suggests, acts as
a supplement to the national history—at once an appendage and a vital
omission.

Both Gibreel and Saladin are actors by profession. Gibreel has been the star
in numerous Indian "theologicals" (movies starring a god or gods) in which
he appeared as an avatar of the various religions' god(s). Saladin, in perfect-
ing his English accents to become a voice-over artist for television commer-
cials, parallels Gibreel. The ambivalent narrator observes, "A man who sets
out to make himself up is taking on the Creator's role, according to one way
of seeing things; he's unnatural, a blasphemer" (49). On the other hand,
"most migrants learn, and can become disguises. Our own false descriptions
to counter the falsehoods invented about us" (49). While the Indian Zeeny
Vakil mocks Saladin ("They pay you to imitate them, as long as they don't
have to look at you" [61]), the narrative adopts a more complex and tolerant
attitude to the ways in which migrants resort to acts of performance to win
recognition in the adopted country. As David Bevan observes, it is only fitting that postcolonials should take to acting, as it "sees the imperial/colonial
world of the past as a gigantic hoax" (13). Bhabha picks up Rushdie's use of
"blasphemy" in the migrant parts of the book and sees it as "a theatrical form
of the staging of cross-genre, cross-cultural identities" (*Location* 225). Secular

blasphemy reveals "the incommensurabilities involved in the process of social transformation" (*Location* 226). Both protagonists change their birth names, Gibreel Farishta from the sacrificial Ismail (the Islamic Isaac) Najmuddin, and Saladin Chamcha from the Indian Salahuddin Chamchawala. In his attempt to Anglicize his name so as to become a "goodandproper Englishman" (43), Saladin chose an abbreviation (Chamcha) that meant "sycophant," As Zeeny remarks, "You name yourself Mister Toady and you expect us not to laugh" (55).

What Saladin learns early on is that the greatest power of naming belongs to those who control the discourse—in this case the English. Those who epitomize what Althusser calls the Repressive State Apparatuses—the government of Margaret Thatcher, the immigration officers and the police—are the most conspicuous representatives of a nation afflicted by widespread xenophobia and racism. The first stage of Saladin's transformation takes the form of his metamorphosis into a goatlike devil (reminiscent of the pagan god Pan whom the Christians turned into a devil). Demonized by the racist immigration officers who react to his appearance, not his accent ("Look at yourself. You're a fucking Packy billy" [168]), he finds himself in a prison hospital where various detained immigrants have assumed the forms that their oppressors have described them as taking in their prejudiced eyes: Senegal holiday makers turned into slippery snakes, Nigerian businessmen who have grown tails, an Indian male model turned man-tiger or manticore. The manticore explains how the authorities accomplish their transformation: "They have the power of description, and we succumb to the pictures they construct" (174). Saladin's misguided attempt to assimilate with the English by parroting their accents (a key marker of class in England) comes unstuck when he finds himself confined within the shape of the devil which the English authorities have projected onto him. In quick succession he loses his wife, Pamela (his new horns are not just diabolic but those of the cuckold), his job as a voice-over actor (on the ironically titled *Aliens Show*), and his middle class home. He is forced to hole up in Brickhall (an amalgam of Brick Lane, Southall and Brixton), a heavily Asian neighborhood, with the Sufyans, a Bangladeshi family who own the Shaandaar Café and over-crowded rooms above it rented to fellow immigrants whom they exploit economically. This is where Saladin undergoes his metamorphosis while observing the inequities of immigrant life from the ground up.

The novel offers two precedents for the dual choices facing Saladin and Farishta. The first of these is the choice, posed by the Bagladeshi ex-school-master, Muhammad Sufyan, between the philosophies of change championed by Ovid and Lucretius. Ovid maintains that while the outer self can change the inner self or soul remains constant just as molten wax assumes new shapes while remaining the same piece of wax. Lucretius argues that when the self bursts its frontiers (as has happened to Gibreel and Saladin) the old self or soul dies. While initially Saladin finds neither philosophy flattering when applied to his Satanic metamorphosis, he soon opts for Lucretius—"The inconstant soul, the mutability of everything, das Ich, every last speck" (297). So he decides he "would be what he had become: loud, stenchy, hideous, outsize, grotesque, inhuman, powerful" (298). Like Gibreel he refuses at this point to accept the fact of his confused, in-between condition. Gibreel's schizophrenia takes the form of splitting himself into two entities, "one of which he sought heroically to suppress, but which he also, by characterizing it as other than himself, preserved, nourished, and secretly made strong" (351). Saladin too, in cultivating his Satanic persona, unconsciously nurtures his angelic alter-ego. Linked to this dichotomy is a second, also about the nature of change, pitting Darwin against Lamarck, the former seeing change as gradual and continuous, the latter seeing it as sudden and absolute. Saladin sides with Lucretius and Lamarck, repudiating his older assimilationist self when he becomes a living image of the ex-colonizers' grotesque fantasies.

According to Bhabha there can be no resolution between these two forms of change "because the two conditions are ambivalently enjoined in the 'survival' of migrant life" (*Location* 224). All migrants, he claims, live "in the interstices of Lucretius and Ovid, caught in-between a 'nativist', even nationalist, atavism and a postcolonial metropolitan assimilation" (224). There is an interesting passage in which the narrator, using conditional verbs throughout, speculates ("Might we not agree . . . ") that Farishta wishes to remain continuous with his past self, resisting the other self that irrupts into his dreams (cf. Ovid and Darwin), making him "good," while Saladin's willed reinvention of himself (cf. Lucretius and Lamarck) made him false and therefore "evil" (441–42). "But," the narrator next argues, "[such] distinctions, resting as they must on an idea of the self as being (ideally) homogeneous, non-hybrid, 'pure', - an utterly fantastic notion! - cannot, must not, suffice" (442). As Spivak remarks, good and evil "are no more than visual markers, inscribed on the body like special effects—a halo, a pair of horns" (*Outside* 226). The same is true of immigrants and native citizens: they all belong to an impure mix of races, cultures and moral belief systems. Harm only ensues when either (for instance Gibreel or Enoch Powell) attempts to impose its form of false purity on the other. As Rushdie told Ameena Meer, "the hybridity of the self, that's what I wanted to write about" in this novel (*Conversations* 114).

Both Gibreel and Saladin have to work through their struggles with migrant identity within the context of London, the metropolitan center of the erstwhile British empire, filled with memorials to its past power and with large enclaves of immigrant communities from the former empire. The London of the novel is simultaneously a childish fantasy, Ellowen Deeowen, onto which immigrants project their illusory ideas of "Proper London, capital of Vilayet" [Hindi for "foreign country"] (4), and a geographical reality resisting those fantasies with ghettoization and acts of racist resentment and discrimination. The London of the novel, then, is itself a mixture of the real and the fantastic, the historical and the timeless: "great, rotting, beautiful, snow-white, illuminated city, Mahagonny, Babylon, Alphaville" (4). As he wanders through London, the city sends Gibreel messages about the history of its mixed, non-originary origins: "here, it says, is where the Dutch king decided to live when he came over three centuries ago." England's modern constitution dates from 1688, the Bloodless Revolution, when Charles II was deposed and William III was brought over from Holland to replace a monarch desiring absolute powers with one subject to Parliamentary control. The message the city sends Gibreel is: "Not all migrants are powerless . . . They impose their needs on their new earth, bringing their own coherence to the new-found land, imagining it afresh" (473). The city is shaped by the visions and fantasies of immigrants. But it also offers material resistance to the dreamers that contribute to its grandeur: "Riding in the parkland . . . which he'd *civilized* - William III was thrown by his horse, fell hard to the recalcitrant ground, and broke his royal neck" (473–4). So London has always been the product of the dreams of foreigners while remaining recalcitrant (resistant) to their presence. William of Orange is to London what William the Conqueror is to England—a reminder that both are the products of successive waves of invaders from overseas who have produced the "fusions, translations, conjoinings" (8) that have given new life to the country and its capital. But "first you have to die" (3). It is no coincidence that Gibreel and Saladin fall to earth at Hastings where William the Conqueror defeated and killed Harold, king of the Anglo-Saxons, and introduced foreign customs and a foreign language to England. Migration and the newness it brings with it are constants in the history of the formation of the nation.

The London of the novel offers a concentrated image of the tensions and conflicts that the policies of the Thatcher government were producing in the country in the 1980s. London has always been a privileged center of wealth and power compared to the rest of the country. In an era of globalization what Saskia Sassen calls the "geography of centrality and marginality" is reproduced within the global city, which contains both "a disproportionate share of global corporate power" and "of the disadvantaged" (xxxiv). Peter Kalliney has written a detailed account of how one important area of the Thatcher government's policies impacted the Bengali population of Tower Hamlets, the London borough which contains the highest concentration of immigrants from the Indian subcontinent. Using legislation that bypassed local authorities, the government developed the run down Docklands into an upscale new urban community which replaced many of the previous working class inhabitants with members of what Hal Valance credits Margaret Thatcher with inventing—" a whole goddam new middle class in this country" (278). Kalliney sums up the result of these policies: "In the face of a severe housing shortage and other reductions in social services, the local white population and poor South Asians competed directly for limited resources. Before long, the immigrant population felt threatened by the actions of an unsympathetic state and the violent conduct of their white neighbors" (62). Soon the Bengali youth in the Docklands began to respond to repeated acts of racial violence by forming gangs of their own. The novel refers to this phenomenon when Mishal tells Saladin about "the white racists and black 'self-help' or vigilante posses starring in this modern *Mahabharata*, or, more accurately, *Mahavilayet*" (292). The reference to the *Mahabharata*, a Sanskrit epic dating back two millennia which recounts a great dynastic and civil war in the kingdom of Kurukshetra, suggests that such conflict is a constant throughout human history. Rushdie's neologism, *Mahavilayet* (meaning, the great epic of a foreign country), identifies that conflict as always involving ethnic difference, the clash between the dreams of the newcomers and the resistance to change of the possessors of the land.

Rushdie plunges Saladin into a city visible but unseen (the title of Part V), Brickhall, an impoverished neighborhood in which immigrants predominate. According to Rushdie, who spent 1976–83 working in race relations for the London Borough of Camden, the immigrant neighborhood "was there and nobody knew it was there" ("Salman Rushdie Talks" 68). Brickhall is representative of what Rushdie called "the new empire in Britain." In a 1982 essay with that title he claimed that "the British authorities, no longer capable of exporting governments, have chosen instead to import a new Empire, a new community of subject peoples" (*Imaginary Homelands* 130). He concludes that "Britain is now two entirely different worlds, and the one you inhabit is determined by the colour of your skin" (134). In a later interview with the London Consortium he is agreeing that by 1996 "[p]eople's eyesight has improved" ("Salman Rushdie Talks" 68). But during the 1980s Thatcherite policies and the institutional racism of the police (confirmed by the Lawrence Inquiry of 1999[2]) encouraged this form of racist myopia which contributed to the riots that erupted during that decade. Rushdie saw Thatcher's call for a return to Victorian standards as a covert form of racism. Rushdie had been particularly enraged by a speech she had made after Britain's victory against Argentina in the Falkland Islands (Las Malvinas) in which she "most plainly nailed her colours to the old colonial mast, claiming that the success in the South Atlantic proved that the British were still the people 'who had ruled a quarter of the world'" (*Imaginary Homelands* 92). Unconsciously she was betraying the fact that she did not consider immigrants like Rushdie who had come from the ruled quarter to be a true part of the national identity.

Seen from the immigrants' perspective, the riots that break out in the street (paralleling the Brixton riots of 1981) are not acts of vengeance on the country or the city. As John Clement Ball suggests, "the reclaiming of London by immigrants is all about erasing borders and renovating material reality" ("A City" 78). If riots aim at obliterating the segregation that borders impose, then they produce a highly visible example of the impurity, the mélange, which the novel constantly demonstrates is the reality of a nation as much as of national identity. It is ironic that Gibreel's blast on Azreel, his trumpet, should produce not the clarity that he desired, but the chaos and mixed messages of a riot. The riot has the same effect as the action at the Club Hot Wax. When its DJ, Pinkwalla, melts down the wax figurine of Maggie (Thatcher) in the Hot Seat (a microwave) the hard exterior corresponding to her policies—her "permawaved coiffure, her pearls, her suit of blue"—melts "from the inside out" (302), suggesting, as Steven Connor remarks, that her "resolve, clarity and unswerving self-identity, may be compounded with fluidity at their heart" (121). Ian Baucom places the riot within the historical context of earlier riots in England, all of which, he argues, aim at "restoring the nation to itself" (196). Once more the "nation" turns out to be a complex notion that authority has attempted to simplify through exclusion. He concludes that "the performative occasion of riot must be seen as writing a *certain* uncertainty onto the spaces of cultural inhabitation" (213). The same idea surfaces in the novel when a talking head on television remarks in a discussion of the riot that true outlaws are "men who stood *for* as well as *against*" (471).

Rushdie is both an initiator of, and representative of, the way most post-colonial novelists seek out new and hybrid narrative modes that correspond more naturally to the hybrid nature of their material. I have already mentioned the overall organization of the novel into alternating parts, odd numbered ones being set in present day England and Bombay, and even numbered ones describing Gibreel's dreams of an Islamic past largely set in the Middle East. At the same time Rushdie constantly draws parallels between the two sets of narratives. For instance Mohound attempts to impose his unitary vision on a city, Jahilia, that is polytheistic, just as Gibreel attempts to do with modern London. Another example is when the Imam of Part IV adopts a similarly antagonistic stance toward historical time as Margaret Thatcher does. Rushdie referred to her call for a return to Victorian values as "a heroic battle against the linear passage of Time" (*Imaginary Homelands* 92). Hal Valance makes a similar point in the novel when he refers to the new middle class she is bringing to power as "[p]eople . . . without history" (278). In the same spirit the Imam tells Gibreel that he will smash all the clocks when he comes to power in the name of God's "boundless time, that encompasses past, present and future; the timeless time, that has no need to move" (220). Time means change and newness, something which cannot occur until the old ideas (imperialism, nostalgia for past national supremacy, Islamic fundamentalism) have been allowed to die a natural death.

Not only does Rushdie establish parallels between the two sets of narratives, but also he shows a gradual breakdown of the barriers separating waking from dreaming worlds. Even before this leakage of one world into the other begins, the claims of the English sections to a status as realist representations of recognizable contemporaneity are undermined by the impossible fall to earth of the two protagonists and the transformation of Gibreel to an archangel and Saladin to a devil. Similarly the dream sections soon come to be recognized as fictional interpretations of actual historical events, as much historiographical as imaginative. As the novel advances, Rushdie carefully orchestrates the gradual leakage of Gibreel's dream world into his waking existence in London. The collapse occurs when Gibreel persuades himself that he is the Archangel Gabriel in person, "a celestial being, all radiance, effulgence" (347) and steps into the roadway to outface the traffic, only to be knocked over by Sisodia's car. On the next occasion that he mistakes the angelic persona of his dreams for his waking self he attempts to tropicalize London and ends up suffering a schizophrenic breakdown: "the real terror had crossed the broken wall, and stalked his waking hours" (366). Gibreel's schizophrenia is the medical explanation for what truly afflicts Gibreel, the alienation of the migrant subject. Rushdie has said that the "process of intermingling is what I referred to in *Midnight's Children* as leaking, in which people leak into each other; so do cultures" (*Conversations* 84). Cultural leakage forms the central thematic of *The Satanic Verses* as much as of *Midnight's Children*. But in the later book Rushdie has contrived to incorporate the process of leakage into not just the narrative material but the form into which the novel is structured.

Spivak argues that the "confident breaching of the boundaries between dream and waking" is "in the *text*—not merely in the characters" (*Outside* 226). In the first place the text is situated in a liminal region of undecidability by Rushdie's treatment of its narrator. Although one can identify moments in the text when Rushdie playfully suggests that the narrator is the devil in person (e.g. 10, 95, 137), at other moments he refuses to say whether he is "Ooparvala," "The Fellow Upstairs," or "Neechayvala," "the Guy from Underneath" (329). When Gibreel sees God (or Satan) sitting on his bed, he has an uncanny resemblance to Rushdie down to the beard, baldness and glasses (329). Subsequently the narrator, while addressing the reader, admits that he appeared in person and spoke to Gibreel: "Ooparvala or Neechayvala, he wanted to know, and I didn't enlighten him" (423). Rushdie's is a godlike narrator who refuses to intervene, refuses to "change the rules, fix the fights" (423). He also refuses to reveal whether he is "multiform, plural," or "pure, stark, extreme" (329). On his last appearance the narrator says of Gibreel, "I'm giving him no instructions" (473). Rushdie has said that "[d]ifferent voices seem to be the point of view or narrative voice at different points of the novel" ("Keeping Up" 31). The novel celebrates the plurality of voices that immigrants bring to a nation. So it is fitting that its narrator should similarly possess a confusing number of different voices.

In the same interview Rushdie goes on to call *The Satanic Verses* "a novel about metamorphosis, which should itself constantly metamorphose" (31). He has explained that a novel about transformation "should also be metaphoric in form," alternating between the surrealistic and naturalistic, the romantic and the tragic, the tragic and the farcical" (*Conversations* 102). As for tragedy, the narrator says at one point that all he can offer in place of tragedy is the echo of it, a "burlesque for our degraded, imitative times, in which clowns re-enact what was first done by heroes and kings" (424). According to Rushdie there is a connection between migrants and metaphor because migrants "had so to speak entered the condition of metaphor," and were "required to reinvent the sense of the self" in terms of metaphor (Bourne et al. 63). In their fall at the start of the novel, Gibreel and Saladin pass through "a succession of cloudforms, ceaselessly metamorphosing" (7). They too become metaphors for transformation. Saladin "was seized by the notion that he, too, had acquired the quality of cloudiness, becoming meta-morphic, hybrid" (7). Both immigrants are living metaphors, living instances of transference, the meaning of metaphor. They are transferred from one country to another, one identity to another, from one moral qual-ity to another. The survivor, Saladin, becomes neither the literal nor the fig-urative, but like a true metaphor both at once, IndianEnglish.

The language Rushdie employs reinforces this sense of mixture and fusion. For Rushdie literature is "the place where the struggle of languages can be played out," and that struggle reflects "other struggles taking place in the real world, struggles between cultures . . . " (*Imaginary Homelands* 427, 17). Words that contradict one another are fused into neologisms ("angelicdevilish," "Babylondon"). Puns (relying on literal and figurative meanings) abound—"for instance a wailing patient is referred to as "that Moana Lisa" (173), while Anahita calls her unseen homeland "Bungleditch" (267). The text is filled with allusions of all kinds—to the Qur'an, the Bible, *Othello*, Fanon, popular idols and songs, Grace Kelly and Ned Kelly, Popeye and Powell, Western and Indian classics, *The Magnificent Seven* and the *Mahabharata*—the seemingly endless list is meant to reflect the eclectic nature of today's culturally mixed archive. Phrases belonging to Gibreel's dream sequence find their way into his everyday, waking existence (*"She is the exalted bird"* [474]). Characters from different time periods and geo-graphical locations share the same name and fate often (for instance Allie Cone's first name comes close to that of Al-Lat, the pagan goddess whom Muhammad opposes, while her last name coincides with that of Cone Mountain, the novel's pseudonym for Mount Hira on which Muhammad received his first revelation). Salman, the scribe, is mischievously given the name of his author (who nearly went on to share the fate of his character). Enoch Powell's racist speech threatening rivers of blood is appropriated by the immigrant Jumpy Joshi as the title and subject for a poem in which the racial river of blood is transformed into the river of blood of humanity in all its variety: "Reclaim the metaphor, Jumpy Joshi had told himself. Turn it; make it a thing we can use" (192). All of these linguistic strategies aim at making the novel "kaleidoscopic—a formal equivalent . . . to the story in the book, which is about people changing" (Rushdie, *Conversations* 102).

The final Part IX has puzzled critics who have charged that it turns its back on the main theme concerning the experience of migration by returning both protagonists to their home city of Bombay. Referring to Saladin's reconciliation with his dying father in the finale, Gane discerns "an element of impossible wish-fulfillment in this happy ending." She agrees with Goonetilleke in arguing that Saladin in returning to his roots, "turns his back on hybridity" (36). Rushdie has explained more than once that in the ending Saladin "becomes the hero of the novel" by "facing up to love and death." In the course of "loving and allowing himself to be loved," and "looking in the face of death . . . he becomes a human being" (*Conversations* 121). But this emphasis on the personal salvation of Chamcha is said to take away the reader's attention from Chamcha's hybrid experience of being an immigrant. Or does it? How does newness come into the world in this book? Certainly not *ab ovo*. Rather, as Rushdie explains, it comes in through "[i]nfluence, the flowing of the old into the new . . . " (*Step Across* 66). This equally applies to the migrations of English eastwards and those of the Indians westwards. The return of immigrants from the old imperial center of empire to the postcolonial country places both cities, London and Bombay on a par. Bombay proves to be, like London, cosmopolitan, a center of "cultural hybridization" (*Conversations* 84). From the beginning of the novel Bombay was associated through Zeeny Vakil with "an ethic of historically validated eclecticism" (52). Further, the novel itself attempts to become the literary equivalent of the "hybridized nature of the Indian artistic tradition" of the Mughal artists (70–71).

At the same time, just as London is threatened by such champions of purity as Enoch Powell, so the India to which Saladin returns is threatened by the growing power of the Bharatiya Janata Party (BJP),[3] dedicated to the propagation of orthodox Hindu religion and opposed to the secular democracy advocated by the ruling Congress Party under Rajiv Gandhi. As one of Zeeny's fellow activists declares in the final sequence, "Secular versus religious, the light versus the dark. Better you choose which side you are on" (551). Saladin finds himself choosing the secular, the eclectic, the light which Zeeny stands for. So he is still being consistent in seeing newness as a blending of old with new, something that Gibreel cannot do and dies because of it. Besides, as Rushdie said to Ian Hamilton, "In a way, you can't go home again" ("Salman Rushdie Talks" 110). The Bombay Saladin returns to is not the Bombay of Rushdie's childhood nostalgia. It is a darker city, waiting the electoral triumphs of the BJP the year the novel was published and its eventual formation of a government in 1996. Bombay becomes even darker in *The Moor's Last Sigh* (1995) in which the narrator reflects that "what had happened was, in a way, a defeat for the pluralist philosophy on which we had all been raised" (272). Rushdie continues to write about the flowing of the old into the new and the strange hybrid territory into which this plunges those who allow themselves to die out of the old and be reborn in the new that is also continuous with the old. As Bhabha maintains, the "'newness' of migrant or minority discourse has to be discovered *in media res*," not in the old or the new, but in the liminal borderland in which these two meet and combine (*Location* 227).

Lists of Books Published

Fiction

Grimus, 1975.
Midnight's Children, 1980.
Shame, 1983.
The Satanic Verses, 1988.
Haroun and the Sea of Stories, 1990.
East, West [stories], 1994.
The Moor's Last Sigh, 1995.
The Ground Beneath Her Feet, 1999.
Fury, 2001.
Shalimar The Clown, 2005.

Non-Fiction

The Jaguar Smile: A Nicaraguan Journey, 1987.
Imaginary Homelands: Essays and Criticism 1981–1991, 1991.
Step Across This Line: Collected Nonfiction 1992–2002. 2002.

7
Hanif Kureishi: *The Buddha of Suburbia* (1990)

It can be argued that novelists like V. S. Naipaul, Salman Rushdie, and Hanif Kureishi helped change the entire debate on identity politics in England in the 1990s. But, as Bruce King suggests, Kureishi's "is a different subject matter from that of Naipaul and Rushdie," being "partly the difference between being an immigrant and being born in a country" (187). Yet all three novelists are interested in the metamorphosis that overtakes characters who meet and interact with others from different ethnic and cultural backgrounds. Kureishi's major characters are as likely to be white or of mixed ethnic origins as Asian or black, and his canvas extends beyond the minority communities in England that are becoming larger each year. Kureishi himself had a Muslim father who immigrated from India at the time of the Partition in 1947 and married an Englishwoman. Born in Bromley, Kent, a suburb of London, in 1954, Kureishi belonged to a new generation of children of immigrant/English parents. He neither grew up a Muslim nor spoke Urdu. Although light skinned, he suffered at school from a racist climate that made him try to deny his Pakistani self: "I couldn't tolerate being myself" (*My Beautiful Laundrette* 76). Yet when he visited Pakistan for the first time in 1983 he discovered that he "couldn't rightfully claim to either place"— England or Pakistan (81). His answer was to turn to writing, something his father had tried to do unsuccessfully all his life: ". . . there was writing, which was an active way of taking possession of the world. I could be omnipotent, rather than a victim" ("Something Given").

By the time he published his first and most successful novel to date, *The Buddha of Suburbia* (1990), he had already become known as a playwright and as the author of two screenplays, *My Beautiful Laundrette* (1985) and *Sammy and Rosie Get Laid* (1988). The novel is simultaneously a variation on the condition of England novel given new life in the late 1950s by writers like Sillitoe and Braine, and on the *Bildüngsroman*. Seen in the former light it offers a portrait of England in the 1970s—its liberation movements, alternative life-styles and rise of popular culture, especially music. As one reviewer wrote, Kureishi's "Seventies are what happened when the Sixties hit the suburbs" (Paton). The youthful characters in the novel enthusiastically embrace seventies' culture. Charlie turns punk ("The sixties have been given notice tonight" [131]) and changes his band's name from "Musn't Grumble" to "The Condemned." Jamila joins a commune and turns lesbian. Karim, the protagonist, takes up acting in London's radical fringe theatre. But Karim, the first-person narrator who looks back at the decade ten years later, is aware of where the seventies are going—"general drift and idleness" (*Buddha* 94). As Kenneth Kaleta points out, "Kureishi and his readers know what his characters don't: they know that the novel is gliding toward Thatcherism; that punk music would fade fast" (81). So one way in which Kureishi embodies his sense of being a split personality in the narrative is to split the vision of the seventies between a participating and a retrospectively recording and interpreting self, between an enthusiastic and bewildered youth and his later avatar who can recollect his flounderings with comic and ironic detachment.

Kureishi's use of the well-established genre of the *Bildüngsroman* is similarly ambiguous. It both evokes and yet frustrates the conventions of this genre. It charts the development of Karim Amir from the age of seventeen to his early twenties. Yet the celebrated and brilliant opening paragraph immediately undermines any expectation of teleological development. Karim says that he is "going somewhere," but his "mixture of continents and blood, of here and there, of belonging and not" should forewarn the reader that this somewhere might just as likely turn out to be unsatisfactory as fulfilling. This is an initiation story of a character whose partial ethnic origins serve to complicate his chances of normal treatment or development. Accustomed at school to being called "Shitface and Curryface" (63), Karim as protagonist is too busy seeking out alternative circles in which he can pursue the pleasure principle regardless of color or ethnicity to reach any significant state of maturity by the end of the novel. And yet the novel represents the pursuit of pleasure as itself a way of freeing the self from the constraints of a racist, materialist and tradition-bound society. Karim then is not so much developing as being developed by his hedonistic plunge into seventies subcultures. However, the narrator's vision conforms to the genre where the protagonist fails to do so. Steven Connor argues that the novel "simultaneously summons and rebuffs the *Bildüngsroman* with its typical equations between self and society, the growth of the individual and the cementing of social meaning" (94). The novel charts Karim's journey toward the disillusioning eighties when institutional racism was implicitly endorsed by the policies of the Thatcher government. How can Karim grow in unison with the cementing of a social meaning targeting him for exclusion?

Bildung translates from German as "formation" and originates in *bilodi* meaning "form" or "shape." The genre rests on the assumption that the narrative will trace the way in which the protagonist develops his or her definitive shape or identity. But this fixed concept of identity is what Kureishi sets out to demolish in the course of this counter-*Bildüngsroman*. If Karim learns anything in the course of this novel it is that seeking to fix one's sense of identity in any one position, whether that is national, ethnic, religious, or political, is self-defeating. As Shahid, the protagonist of Kureishi's next novel, *The Black Album* (1995), reflects: "How could anyone confine themselves to one system or creed? . . . There was no fixed self; surely our several selves melted and mutated daily? There had to be innumerable ways of being in the world" (285). Kureishi has taken the same position when discussing his mixed ethnic origins in an interview. Even in the separation of Asian from English identities "there's mixture." Thus to Islamic fundamentalists "mixing . . . was terrifying, just as racists finding mixing terrifying. But of course it's inevitable" ("Hanif Kureishi on London" 50). Mixing involves impurity, mélange, mutability, metamorphosis.

In *The Buddha of Suburbia* characters are either in perpetual transition (like Karim, but also at various times Haroon, Changez, Jamila, Charlie, and Eva) or at some point in their lives they settle on a fixed position that acts as a figurative or literal form of death (like Anwar, Hairy Back, and Jeannie). Bart Moore-Gilbert makes a similar division and argues that the former set of characters are portrayed sympathetically, while the latter "are antipathetic precisely because of the rigid social roles and identities within which they confine themselves and to which they expect others to conform" (128). This division is too neat in that some characters like Margaret stagnate for most of the novel and then break out by accepting their own malleability, while other characters like Haroon and Charlie embrace fluidity and change early in the novel only to become later locked in the newly adopted persona. At the two extremes are Anwar and Karim. Anwar accepts without question the role of the strict Muslim: "Like many Muslim men—beginning with the Prophet Mohammed himself, whose absolute statements, served up piping hot from God, inevitably gave rise to absolutism—Anwar thought he was right about everything" (172). Anwar's total reliance on Islam (which means "submission" in Arabic) for his sense of identity ironically throws him into a crisis of identity that leads to self-defeat. His stance as a strict Muslim demanding that his daughter marry the man of his choice is simultaneously undercut by his use of the Hindu Gandhi's strategy of passive resistance, starving himself to the point of death. Once he has won this Pyrrhic victory, he is defeated by Changez's malleable nature (the reverse of his own) and Jamila's similar use of passive resistance in not consummating the marriage. Refusing to accept his own partial responsibility for the fiasco (he did not go to India to check out his choice of son-in-law), Anwar turns his self-anger outwards onto Changez, thereby ironically engineering his own comically staged death from a sex toy. In contrast Karim solves his bouts of depression by adopting new roles and forms of identity. The self for Karim is fluid, an image to be altered at whim. In between these two are characters like Changez (whose name is almost identical to change), a character who moves from fixity to adaptability in the course of the novel and who becomes one of the most endearing figures in the process.

All the first generation Indians in the novel end up wanting to "return to an imagined India" (74), not the real one they left. Even Changez wants to return to his rights as an Indian husband. Maybe this is an unavoidable consequence for any first generation immigrant, though V.S. Naipaul's fiction denies the universality of such a position. But Karim and his generation have no country of origin beside England, even if they do inherit as part of their upbringing a second national culture. The difference is that, when Karim comes to recognize the way he has unjustly denied his Indian cultural heritage, he comes to the conclusion: "if I wanted the additional personality bonus of an Indian past, I would have to create it" (213). He has no past experience in India, only the tales his father and Indian relatives pass on to him. Whereas Haroon cannot help reverting to a form of essentialism: "I have lived in the West for most of my life, and I will die here, yet I remain to all intents and purposes an Indian man" (263). The same essentialist conviction about one's national identity can be found in some of the English characters. Jean and Ted have insisted on anglicizing Haroon's name as Harry: "It was bad enough his being an Indian in the first place, without having an awkward name too" (33). Jean in particular attempts to impose compulsory assimilation on Haroon who at first espouses it and later reverts to an essentialist notion of ethnic identity. And the likes of Hairy Back ("We don't want you blackies coming to the house" [40]) are paralleled by Anwar's Indian relatives at the wedding who shoo Hairy's daughter Helen away muttering, "Pork, pork, pork, VD, VD, white woman, white woman" (84–85).

Karim is constructed to be a fallible protagonist (rather than narrator). Karim's openness and total fluidity leaves him at the end of the novel occupying an amoral quagmire, but it also leaves him open to further movement, change, and self-improvement. The shape of the novel reflects this ambivalence. On the one hand it is divided between Part 1 ("In the Suburbs") and Part 2 ("In the City") and is structured on Karim's move from suburbs to city, but also from social fixity to limitless self exploration. On the other hand the novel is extremely episodic, transferring—seemingly arbitrarily—its focus from one character or group to another. It is held together simply by the presence of Karim and chronological progression, more in the manner of a picaresque novel than of a *Bildüngsroman*. What I mean is that many of the episodes, such as Eva's redecoration of the West Kensington flat or Changez's fatal act of self defense against Anwar, have no direct bearing on the development of Karim. They do offer contrasting modes of responding to life, but enter the narrative as witnessed by Karim rather than as directly affecting his development. The significance of their contrasting role in the narrative registers with Karim as narrator, but not with Karim the younger protagonist. So the forward movement given impetus by the two-part division of the novel is undercut by what Connor calls "the sputtering, discontinuous energy of episodic renewal" (95).

Karim's move from Bromley to West Kensington acts as a trope for a whole range of transformations, not just from fixed to fluid identity, but from colonial periphery to a partially decolonized center, from an old homogenized to a new multiple conception of Englishness, from a life style where "security and safety were the reward of dullness" to one "where life was bottomless in its temptations" (*Buddha* 8). Kureishi is very funny in his portrayal of the suburbs and their "carnival of consumerism" (65). Karim remarks that it is said of the suburbs "that when people drowned they saw not their lives but their double-glazing flashing before them" (23), which is a variant on his aphorism in "Finishing the Job," "Look into the centre of the suburban soul and you see double-glazing" (*My Beautiful Laundrette* 155). The suburbs are epitomized by Auntie Jean "who measured people only in terms of power and money" (34). For Karim the "suburbs were a leaving place, the start of life" (117), and as such are associated with the unitary family, a concept that Kureishi has said "was probably a fantasy in the first place," and that "was breaking up by the 1980s when people like Margaret Thatcher and Ronald Reagan began to proselytize it" (Yousef 13). The move of Karim, Haroon, Eva, and Charlie to central London is therefore a flight from traditional family values and their associated politics of socially determined identity (which leads to the rampant racism various characters encounter in the suburbs) to what seemed "like a house with five thousand rooms, all different," that "made you vertiginous with possibility" (126). Central London is also the location of the densest collections of immigrants which help Karim feel more a part of it.

John Clement Ball calls Kureishi's London "a cosmopolitan space not fully attached to or detached from either British nation-space or transnational world-space. It hovers interstitially between the two" (*Imagining* 227). It is simultaneously a unique cosmopolitan society, the capital of England, an international metropolis, and the center of an erstwhile empire. Among other things, Karim's move from suburbs to city center is a "move from ex-colony (country) to metropolis (city)" (Ball 232). It replicates the world at large by containing representatives of many of its peoples and, as Greater London, by replicating "within its borders the world's spatial patterning" (232) with its Anglo-Saxon center and its peripheral inner city boroughs in which are gathered ex-colonials from all over the world. Seen in this geopolitical sense, the London of the novel proves to be more complex than Karim assumes on first moving there. For instance the same urge for DIY house improvement that Karim claims characterizes the suburbs is enthusiastically pursued by Eva in her West Kensington flat. The sex and drugs that Karim says are in unlimited supply in the city were hardly absent from his life in the suburbs. And, as will be seen, the overt racism he encountered in the suburbs resurfaces in the city in a much subtler, disguised form. Yet it is a location in which the restriction and prejudices of suburban life are subordinated for most of the seventies to the uninhibited pursuit of pleasure. Sukhdev Sandhu makes an interesting case for claiming that the way Kureishi mythologizes London moves beyond the erasure of dualities advocated by Homi Bhabha in his use of terms like "hybridity" and "in-betweenness": "it involves seeing London as a generator of *aggregation*, where he can wear as many masks, create as many personae, explore as many new avenues as he wishes" (142). No longer a confusion between or mélange of binary opposites, London represents a polyhybrid state in which an infinite range of possible subject positions offer themselves.

Central London is where everyone is refashioning him/herself in the pop culture of the 1970s. As Stuart Hall observes, popular culture "is *profoundly mythic* . . . It is where we discover and play with the identifications of ourselves, where we are imagined, where we are represented . . . to ourselves for the first time" ("What is This 'Black'" 474). As in his earlier films Kureishi employs pop music as a trope for the freedom from earlier English cultural norms that still pervaded suburban life. Kureishi wrote an essay on pop, "Eight Arms to Hold You" (1991), and co-edited the *Faber Book of Pop* (1995). In the essay he argues that pop was the one area in which the conviction of most of the English that it is impossible to break through the class barrier did not hold true. He even claims that its leveling qualities and absence of ethnic separatism means that it "has spoken of ordinary experience with far more precision, real knowledge and wit than, say, British fiction of the equivalent period" (*My Beautiful Laundrette* 118). It is little surprise, then, that pop features in most of his work which equally aspires to break the barriers between classes and ethnic groupings. Even the title of *The Black Album* is borrowed from Prince's 1988 LP of that name, which is itself a riposte to the Beatles' *White Album* of 1969. Prince represents just those mercurial qualities of fluidity and transformation that Kureishi associates with contemporary English identity. As Deedee describes Prince in *The Black Album*, "He's half black and half white, half man, half woman, half size, feminine but macho, too" (34). Kureishi aspires to the same effect of *bricolage* in *The Buddha of Suburbia* as is clear from the fact that he commissioned Peter Blake (who had designed the cover for the Beatles' *Sergeant Pepper* album) to design the collage that forms the front cover of the novel.

Pop music seen as a leveler of ethnic groups and classes reached its highest point for Kureishi with the Beatles' *Sergeant Pepper's Lonely Hearts Club Band* (1967) where East meets West (as is seen in the collage on the cover of the LP). Kureishi insists that the Beatles "were at the centre of life for millions of young people in the West" (*My Beautiful Laundrette* 113). By the seventies pop music was already in decline in his opinion. But the hey day of pop music coincided with Kureishi's and Karim's adolescence, so that pop music comes to assume the significance of a climate that made possible Karim's liberation from all that the suburbs stood for in his mind. The

Beatles in particular "came to represent opportunity and possibility" (*My Beautiful Laundrette* 110). For most of the novel the protagonist sees in pop the expression of his desire for escape from hidebound customs and opinions into a world of infinite possibility. But the narrator knows that the punk movement that lifts Charlie to fame and riches is destined to be soon eclipsed. The reign of the Sex Pistols, the Clash, and the Damned (cf. Charlie's The Condemned) who were the first to market an album as "punk," was short-lived (the Sex Pistols lasted for little more than two years). Successful punk bands that began life as working class protests against their economic oppression, quickly succumbed to the lure of commercial contracts. Charlie's supposedly working class band "was a wonderful trick and disguise," a "big con trick" (154). The Condemned have a middle-class manager in the Fish and middle-class lead singer in Charlie. Karim as narrator has the same retrospective view of pop music as the narrator of *Intimacy* (1998), "I was young when the rock-n'-roll world—the apotheosis of the defiantly shallow—represented the new" (17). But for the most part the narrative foregrounds the more naïve responses of Karim as protagonist.

The exposé of punk comes near the end of the book when Karim meets up with Charlie in New York. There his protest music seems a sham: "The ferocity was already a travesty, and the music, of little distinction in itself, had lost its drama and attack when transported from England with its unemployment, strikes and class antagonism" (247). Karim concludes, "I couldn't consider Charlie a rock-star. It didn't seem of his essence, but a temporary, borrowed persona" (246). Karim appears to be forgetting his own desire for constant transformation when referring to Charlie's "essence." Maybe he is thinking of Charlie's national culture, because Charlie appears to have succumbed to the lure of international capitalism and fame, which is what New York comes to represent in this novel. Charlie's pursuit of sexual pleasure reaches an experimental extreme in the scene in which he arranges to be tortured by Frankie who is fascinated with the "deep human love of pain" (253). Promiscuous sex is one of the rewards that Karim seeks in his move to central London. In fact sex is frequently represented by Kureishi as a symbolic act through which individuals from different backgrounds and social groups can communicate. The clearest instance of this occurs in *Sammy and Rosie Get Laid* (1988) where three couples representing different generations, ethnicities, and political views are shown simultaneously having sex, a "COLLAGE OF COPULATION IMAGES" (44). Yet Charlie seems to have lost sight of the liberating aspects of sex in his masochistic search for the ultimate fuck. Karim discovers that the hedonistic pursuit of pure pleasure is not what he wants and immediately returns to London.

Apart from seeing family and friends, what Karim comes back for is the chance of playing a new role. Charlie is stuck in an assumed role that has become a fixity. Karim is ready to try out a new act even after his previous experiences have turned out to be less than wholly liberating. Acting and performance occupy a prominent position in Kureishi's work. They function as tropes for the ways in which identity is fashioned. Even the language Kureishi employs echoes the central role that performance plays in the novel. When an indignant Jean and Ted turn up at Haroon's first group session Karim likens them to "characters from an Ealing Comedy walking into an Antonioni film" (33). Later Karim refers to "the performance of conversation" (199). *The Buddha of Suburbia* opens with a conscious act of transformation on the part of Karim's father, Haroon, who turns himself into a fashionable Indian guru: "He'd spent years trying to be more of an Englishman, to be less risibly conspicuous, and now he was putting it back in spadeloads" (21). National identity is performed, not inherent, just as class is. Told by Eleanor that he has a South London street voice, Karim resolves to lose his accent (178). In New York Charlie acquires a cockney accent to promote his working class punk image (247). Personality turns out to be persona, or rather personae. Personae offer individuals freedom from the stereotypes others (or they themselves) attempt to impose on them. In his essay, "The Rainbow Sign," Kureishi objects to the way contemporary politicians projected their racist views onto immigrants whose children, for instance, it was alleged by Duncan Sandys (Secretary of State for Commonwealth Relations in the early 1960s), would feel misfits: "I wasn't a misfit . . . It was the others, they wanted misfits; they wanted you to embody within yourself their ambivalence" (*My Beautiful Laundrette* 75). Anthony Ilona claims that seen in this light the novel "can be read as a rendition of the act of self-determination through the externalization of the ambivalent discourse of national identity," and that "this process of externalization . . . is . . . the concept of performance; of 'playing not-me'" (98). The use of the concept of "self-determination," however, is problematic in relation to Kureishi's work.

The problem with acting, according to Eva, is that actors "have no personality" (206). Not that this stops her from "constructing a public personality for herself" (150). But is there a core element of any kind lurking behind the public personality that so many characters in this book assume? Playing a public role is not confined to the younger generation in this novel. It is something that the older generation is equally capable of doing. So adopting a public persona is not a phenomenon associated with adolescence and finding oneself. It is a demonstration that all forms of identity, especially national identity, are a product of performance. Even when an individual has settled on a persona that answers his or her needs, it is necessary to remember that this is not the discovery of an essential self, merely a temporary resting point. In describing one of two constituents that comprise the construction of a national identity—what he calls the "performative"—Homi Bhabha argues that "people are also the 'subjects' of a process of signification . . . through which national life is redeemed and iterated as a reproductive process" (*Location* 145).[1] At least three characters in the novel retain this purely performative response to identity (both nationalist and in a wider sense) to the end of the book—Kamir, Jamila, and Changez. Of the three, Jamila seems most certain of herself. But then she has undergone the most radical transformations, from rebellious to dutiful daughter (but not wife), from militant agitator to obedient Muslim and back, and from wife in a unitary family to lesbian in a commune. Changez undergoes his own extreme metamorphosis from traditional Muslim husband (patriarchal and helpless in the house) to becoming the adoptive father of his wife's child by another, living in a commune and acting as nurse and housekeeper.

What Karim learns through entering the world of the theatre is that the self is something we stage, that it can be changed at will, and that there is no transcendental "I," only a series of positions which we choose to occupy. But he also is made to realize that the overt racism he encountered in the suburbs is still present in a much subtler and less obvious form in the avant-garde world of London's fringe theatre. Karim's first director, Shadwell is chameleon-like.[2] When Karim first meets him at Eva's Shadwell "was being totally homosexual . . . except that even that was a pose, a ruse, a way of self-presentation" (133). Seemingly open to anything, Shadwell reveals a less flexible conception of national identity when he coaches Karim for his role as Mowgli, the "natural" Indian boy in Kipling's *The Jungle Book* that Shadwell is adapting for the stage. However radical Shadwell's staging of the book might be, his use of a children's classic of colonial discourse and his direction of Karim uncover a nostalgia for colonialism that relies on a belief in an essentialist form of identity. He forces Karim to appear on stage looking like "a turd in a bikini bottom" (146). Further he insists on Karim using an "authentic accent" (147), not his Orpington South London accent. What Shadwell means by "authentic" is a parody of Indian English, a throw back to the time of the Empire. Spivak sees Shadwell's pressure on Karim to reproduce a "real" Indian as another instance of the denial of what she calls "the productive epistemic fracture of the colonial, postcolonial, hybrid subject" ("The Burden" 149). However, it is possible that Shadwell, being so like a chameleon, is less interested in perpetuating images that figure immigrants as colonial stereotypes than in marketing the "authentic" for its exchange value in a capitalist society. Ball attempts to redeem Karim's acquiescence to playing this marginalized role by claiming that he and his father are "marketing back to the English warmed-over versions of their own popular appropriations of Indian culture" *Imagining* (133). While this may be true of Haroon, for Karim it is not his "own" but Shadwell's appropriation. However Karim does adopt a response to Shadwell's disempowering direction that Homi Bhabha calls mimicry, by which he means the reproduction of the colonizer's discourse with a difference by the colonized subject. The "*ambivalence* of mimicry (almost the same, *but not quite*) does not merely 'rupture' the discourse, but becomes transformed into an uncertainty which fixes the colonial subject as a 'partial' presence" (*Location* 86). After the initial performances Karim says, "I sent up the accent and made the audience laugh by suddenly relapsing into cockney at odd times" (158). This is not, then, the "empty and futile mimicry" that Connor alleges various characters in this novel are condemned to (97). Using a form of Brechtian alienation, Karim, by relapsing into his native cockney, makes the audience aware of the inauthenticity of the stereotypical Indian accent he has been forced to adopt.

Karim's next director, Pyke, is a more formidable figure in the avant-garde theatre whose reproduction of colonial power relations is even harder to perceive or resist. Pyke offers the most sophisticated definition of what acting out a persona involves:

> What a strange business this acting is, Pyke said; you are trying to convince people that you're someone else, that this is not-me. The way to do it is this, he said: when in character, playing not-me, you have to be yourself. To make your not-real self you have to steal from your authentic self . . . Paradox of paradoxes: to be someone else successfully you must be yourself! (219–20)

Once again, as with Eva, the narrative (with its use of indirect discourse) makes a reference to an "authentic self." While unwilling to attempt to identify what this consists of, Pyke is insistent that its primary purpose is to grant mimetic life to the roles we adopt. Export the ("authentic") working class revolt that gives punk its sense of reality, as Charlie does, to a society where the classes are not at war, and it appears lifeless, an act. Alternatively the belief in an authentic identity reveals Pyke's flawed conception of identity. Ultimately Pyke is only concerned with success, with marketing his plays to a left-liberal audience. This is why he sides with the black actress Tracey's politically skewed objections to Karim's first creation of a character modeled closely on Anwar. Tracey lumps all "black" people together in accusing Karim, "Your picture is what white people already think of us . . . Why do you hate yourself and all black people so much, Karim?" (180). In the television adaptation Karim replies that he's not black, he's beige, thereby exposing what Spivak calls the strategic essentialism adopted by Tracey and supported by Pyke. Tracey bases her argument on the fact that "we have to protect our culture at this time." Karim, who knows that his character's enforcement of an arranged marriage is based on fact, replies, "Truth has a higher value" (81). But Pyke with an eye to his radical chic audience sides with Tracey (who is adopting a diametrically opposing yet equally suspect stance to Shadwell's) and orders Karim to come up with a different Indian character.

Karim's solution is to create a character modeled on Changez while lying to him that he is not doing so. This is the first time that Karim is confronted with a moral dilemma, one which involves him in "violating self-imposed prohibitions" (186), and it is one familiar to any actor or indeed writer (like Kureishi) who follows Pyke's advice and seeks to be someone else by being himself. Kureishi makes clear that Karim, while using Changez's external circumstances, creates a character from within himself: "There were few jobs I relished as much as the invention of Changez/Tariq . . . , I uncovered notions, connections, initiatives I didn't even know were in present in my mind . . . I saw that creation was an accretive process . . . This was worth doing, this had meaning . . . " (217). Even Changez recognizes the extent to which his character is Karim's own creation: "I am glad in your part you kept it fundamentally autobiographical . . . " (231). In contrast Pyke's play, according to Karim's brother Allie, was about "whingeing lefties . . . I hate people who go on all the time about being black, and how persecuted they were at school" (267). Pyke has been exploiting liberal prejudices and producing essentialist ethnic characters just as clichéd (if more politically correct) as Shadwell had done. His politics of national identity might be the reverse of Shadwell's, but his readiness to sacrifice principles to succeed in the theatrical marketplace is identical. Karim's final acting job in the novel is to play another Indian character, the rebellious student son of an Indian shopkeeper in a television soap opera. Its producers are "boring people," but the series "would tangle with the latest contemporary issues: they mean abortions and racist attacks, the stuff that people lived through but that never got on TV" (259). Finally his acting career stands a chance of giving life to some of the elements of English culture that matter to a majority of people of all complexions and opinions.

Karim will be acting out issues not just of race but of gender ("abortions"). From the beginning the novel has resisted treating the politics of racial/national identity in isolation from the politics of class, gender, and sexual orientation. Karim, one could say, has caught up with the narrative's stance, which is also one that Kureishi has taken as a writer in general: "I think the postcolonial label has always bothered me slightly because, to me, it is a narrow term. And so much of my work is not about that and so you feel that you're being squashed into a category that you don't quite fit and you fear that there are lots of other aspects of your work which people might be ignoring" (Yousef 16). Kureishi insists, "Racism goes hand-in-hand with class inequality." He illustrates this by remarking how the English working class used the same language of abuse about Pakistanis as the English middle class used about the working class: "charges of ignorance, laziness, fecklessness, uncleanliness" (*My Beautiful Laundrette* 93). Karim himself comes from a working class neighborhood and school: "We were proud of never learning anything except the names of footballers, the personnel of rock groups and the lyrics of 'I am the Walrus'" (178). Eleanor, whose mother is a friend of the Queen Mother, introduces him to the upper middle classes with whom power resides. His confrontation with the ruling class (Pyke rules his life as an actor) jolts Karim into a realization of how wide the disparity is: "What idiots we were! How misinformed! Why didn't we understand that we were happily condemning ourselves to being nothing better than motor-mechanics?" (178). His response is to learn (like an actor) how to speak like Eleanor's middle-class circle, something which will have to be "consciously acquired" (178).

Karim describes his move from the suburbs to the city not as an escape from racism but in class terms as a "social rise" (174). Although he came from a working class suburb, Karim is more lower middle class, as he points out to Charlie who identifies with the working class punk musicians: "We're not like them. We don't hate the way they do. We've got no reason to" (132). He sees the theatre as his means of escaping from his class background, of not just learning how to lose his South London accent, but of becoming a part of middle-class culture by becoming part of a play that, as Pyke explains, is about "the only subject there is in England"—class (164). Yet by the end of the book Karim has grown disenchanted with Eleanor's rich and privileged circle. Not only do they fail to appreciate how far removed they are from the dangers and insecurities of the working poor; Karim comes to see "how much was enervated and useless in them" (225). He has also come to realize that all the left wing plays like Pyke's in such chic locations as the Royal Court Theatre and the Royal Shakespeare Company's Warehouse, plays that "took it for granted that England . . . was disintegrating into terminal class-struggle," "were science-fiction fantasies of Oxford-educated boys who never left the house" (207). Claiming to be the socially conscious segment of the bourgeoisie, these radicals turn out to be poseurs: to be middle class for this guilt-ridden radical fringe "meant you were born a criminal, having fallen at birth" (175).

The most overtly political voice in the novel is given to Terry, a member of the Communist Party. He looks forward to the revolution. For that to happen things in Britain have to get worse: "the worse they were the better they'd be in the future; they couldn't even start to get better before they'd started to go drastically downhill" (149). Kureishi's use of oxymoron reveals the illogicality of someone dedicated to the improvement of humankind spending all his time waiting for things to deteriorate. In fact Terry himself is a walking oxymoron, being a revolutionary and an actor who has obtained the role of a policeman, Sergeant Monty, in a television serial: "This proved ideologically uncomfortable, since he'd always claimed the police were the fascist instrument of class rule" (197). Ultimately Terry turns out to be as fake as Pyke (whom he regards as the class enemy). Karim comes to hate "the easy talk about Cuba and Russia and the economy, because beneath the hard structure of words was an abyss of ignorance and not-knowing" (241). Like most left wing radicals in the novel, Terry talks about a working class of which he has little first hand knowledge. Karim speculates that the working class in the housing estates he grew up among "would have laughed in Terry's face—those, that is, who wouldn't have smacked him round the ear for calling them working class in the first place" (149). All

their hatred, according to Karim, is directed not at the ruling class but at
"the people beneath them"—that is immigrants (149). When Karim, at
Terry's instigation, asks Eleanor for money for the Party, she turns him down
on the basis that they "are not a party for black people. They are an all-
honky thing" (238). This opens Karim's eyes to the fact that all left wing
political parties in England exercise a form of apartheid, that like the Labour
Party they represent "inequality and racism," as Kureishi writes in "The
Rainbow Sign" (*My Beautiful Laundrette* 97).

Kureishi uses one character or that character's stance to expose the short-
comings of another, Eleanor to expose Terry and the Party, Terry to expose
the pretensions and manipulations of Pyke. As far as Terry is concerned Pyke
is no radical but a liberal pseudo whose "only use is giving money to our
party" (197). Pyke actually reproduces the relations of inequality found in
the country at large in his relations with Karim. In Chapter 13 he manipu-
lates Karim (and Eleanor) to satisfy his desire to have sex with an exotic half-
Asian youth, after which he has no scruples about taking Eleanor as a lover
from Karim. Moore-Gilbert suggests that Pyke, like Terry, "implicitly
reduc[es] race to a secondary category in the more important dialectic of class
struggle" (140).[3] That Pyke should exert his socially superior position in the
sexual realm is indicative of the way Kureishi also involves sexual politics in
the narrative, although it doesn't play as large a role as it does in his earlier
two movies. Kureishi has talked about how for Freud "all desire is transgressive" (Yousef 21). Changez's desire for Shinko, a prostitute, is transgressive,
yet by the end Shinko has been integrated into the family and turns up with
Changez at the final dinner. In the context of the novel sex—whether heterosexual or homosexual—is largely seen to be liberating, a way of erasing
differences of class and ethnicity. Patriarchal attempts to control women's
(and gay men's) sexuality are shown in the novel (Anwar and Chavez try
unsuccessfully to control Jamila, and Haroon disapproves of Karim's gay
escapade with Charlie). Like any other area of human conduct, sex can be
used perversely as a mode of domination (Pyke) or of egotistical non-com-
munication (Charlie with Frankie). But Karim's sexual adventures with
Charlie and Helen, Terry and Eleanor offer a bridge across the divides of
color, money, and class. The novel also contains one female character, Jamila,
who is as promiscuous and bisexual as Karim but far more conscious of the
sexual politics underlying her actions. She can foresee the futility of the
group sex that Karim agrees to participate in and warns him, "You're moving
away from the real world . . . of ordinary people and the shit they have to
deal with—unemployment, bad housing, boredom" (195). After his disastrous sexual encounter with Pyke and Marlene, Karim pays tribute to Jamila's
wisdom and sense of purpose: "Her feminism, the sense of self and the fight
it engendered, the schemes and plans she had, . . . the things she had made
herself know, and all the understanding this gave, seemed to illuminate her
tonight as she went forward, an Indian woman, to live a useful life in white

England" (216). Still open to change, Jamila's combination of self-knowledge with action shows her living out her current persona to the fullest.

The novel ends appropriately on the evening of the general election of May 4, 1979 which everyone in the restaurant knows that Margaret Thatcher has won (282). Waiting to erupt are the Brixton race riots of 1981 that Rushdie fictionalizes in *The Satanic Verses* where he links them directly to Thatcherism. So the relative lack of closure Kureishi employs in this novel reflects the fact that nothing is settled, neither nationally nor personally for Karim. He is still feeling "happy and miserable at the same time" (284), showing the same fundamental split self as was apparent at the beginning. The narrator knows what the protagonist cannot yet see—that the 1970s are about to give way to a decade in which three successive Thatcher governments are destined to transform Britain—into a climate of individual enterprise but also of racism and exceptionally high unemployment (over 12 percent by 1983). The sham political stances of the likes of Pyke and Terry are about to be exposed as empty rhetoric. Eva even comes across as a seeming spokeswoman for Thatcherism when she tells the press visiting her newly transformed home, "We have to empower ourselves. Look at those people who live on sordid housing estates. They expect others—the Government—to do everything for them . . . We have to find a way to enable them to grow." But she then adds, "Individual flourishing isn't something that either socialism or conservatism caters for" (263). It takes the Buddha of Suburbia himself to suggest what is missing from both his son's and the nation's current state of being: "there has been no deepening in culture, no accumulation of wisdom, no increase in the way of the spirit. There is a body and mind, you see. Definite. We know that. But there is a soul, too" (264). Kureishi's next novel, *The Black Album*, will examine this soulless state of England in the 1980s. But this novel ends with the narrator still far in advance of the protagonist in the matter of self-knowledge.

Lists of Books Published

Fiction

The Buddha of Suburbia, 1991.
The Black Album, 1995.
Love in a Blue Time [short stories], 1997.
Intimacy, 1998.
Midnight All Day [short stories], 2000.
Gabriel's Gift, 2001.
The Body: and Seven Stories, 2003.

Original Plays and Screenplays

Borderline [play], 1981.
Birds of Passage, 1983.

My Beautiful Laundrette and the Rainbow Sign [includes essays], 1986.
Sammy and Rosie Get Laid: The Script and the Diary, 1988.
London Kills Me, 1991.
Outskirts and Other Plays, 1992.
My Son the Fanatic, 1997.
Sleep With Me, 1999.
Gabriel's Gift, 2002.
The Mother, 2003.
When the Night Begins, 2004.

Non-Fiction

Dreaming and Scheming: Reflections on Writing and Politics, 2002.
My Ear at His Heart, 2004.
The Word and the Bomb, 2005.

8

Kazuo Ishiguro: *When We Were Orphans* (2000)

Like Rushdie and Kureishi, Ishiguro is a product of and gives fictional representation to competing cultures and generations. The six novels that Ishiguro has written to date show a remarkably consistent preoccupation with the same themes. All of them focus on adult narrators who are fixated with the past, especially with the trauma of leaving behind their protected childhood. In his latest novel to date, *Never Let Me Go* (2005), Kath, the protagonist (a clone bred solely for purposes of organ donation) looks up later in life one of her guardians who helped run the humane boarding school, Hailsham, which she had attended. The guardian's justification of Hailsham's caring but deceptive regime could as easily be that of any of the parents in Ishiguro's other novels explaining to their children why they provided them with an illusory sense of invulnerability while they were young:

> You see, we were able to give you something, something which even now no one will ever take from you, and we were able to do that principally by *sheltering* you . . . Very well, sometimes that meant we kept things from you, lied to you. Yes, in many ways we *fooled* you. I suppose you could even call it that. But we sheltered you during those years, and we gave you your childhoods. (268)

Italicizing the two words, *"sheltering"* and *"fooled"* establishes by linguistic means the close association between the two concepts: no one is truly sheltered from life, as the later closure of Hailsham demonstrates. Modern life is "[m]ore scientific, efficient, yes . . . But a harsh, cruel world" (*Never* 272). The guardian goes on to say that if they had told the children what lay in store for them as adults (organ donations and "completion," that is, death) "your happiness at Hailsham would have been shattered" (268). In Ishiguro's world, an unavoidable consequence of the lies we are all told as children to ensure our happiness is that when we are expelled from the protected cocoon of childhood we experience it as a withdrawal of love. So we spend much of our adult lives attempting to prove ourselves to our parents as worthy of a restoration of their love. In *The Unconsoled* (1995) the protagonist becomes an internationally renowned concert pianist in hopes of achieving this. In *When We Were Orphans* (2000) the protagonist becomes a famous detective for the same purpose. And in *Never Let Me Go* the protagonist and her friends try to win deferrals of their organ donations by making for their guardians works of art that they imagine will bare their souls (and prove that they have them). In Ishiguro's world the lies and illusions fostered in children by parents continue to haunt and frustrate them in their adult lives.

Ishiguro's first six novels written over two and a half decades divide themselves between the initial three, *A Pale View of Hills* (1982), *An Artist of the Floating World* (1986), and *The Remains of the Day* (1989), all pursuing a supposedly realist mode of narration, and the last three which have seemingly abandoned that surface appearance of realism for what might be termed a surrealist or part-surrealist fictional mode. From his first novel on all Ishiguro's first-person narrators prove unreliable. Yet, as Joan Acocella remarks, "that is simply an advanced form of realism." The difference in the later fiction is that, unlike *Time's Arrow*, it "never points us to the reality we're supposed to read through the narrator's distortions" (95). In the last three novels to date, the line dividing the "real" from the (mis)remembered and the imagined becomes blurred or disappears altogether. The fact that the later narrators express themselves with the same restraint and seeming clarity as does Stevens, the repressed butler of his third novel, *The Remains of the Day*, merely reinforces the sense of being immersed in a delusional world that nevertheless makes perfect sense in its own terms. Both settings and characters in the later novels lose their independent existence as they are registered in the consciousness of the protagonists. In *The Unconsoled* and *When We Were Orphans* Ishiguro borrows from the dream process what he calls "appropriation": "Our view of other people is often shaped by our need to work certain things out about ourselves. We tend to appropriate other people" ("Kazuo Ishiguro Talks" 22). Not just other people but settings too are appropriated. Readers are cast adrift in cities that quickly lose their recognizable landmarks as they are distorted to suit the inner psychological needs of their narrators. This does not mean that Ishiguro's later novels have less to tell us about the world we inhabit than do the so-called realist ones. As John Carey argues, "Ishiguro's inextricable fusion of memory, imagination and dream takes us down into the labyrinth of reality which realism has simplified" (Carey 45).

At the same time any examination of narrative manipulation in his work cannot be separated from a recognition of its political and national dimensions. In *When We Were Orphans*, his fifth novel on which this chapter focuses, the settings and characters constitute departures both from narrative realism and from nationalist determination. Written for an international readership, the novel oscillates between England, the old center of empire, and Shanghai where the Occident meets the Orient, itself the product of a hegemonic Western discourse. The protagonist is as transnational as are

Gibreel and Saladin in *The Satanic Verses,* moving between center and periphery more than once in the course of the book. Childhood becomes associated with Shanghai's International Settlement where Christopher Banks, the protagonist, spends his early childhood. But the child's feeling of being protected in this privileged enclave of colonial power is exposed as an illusion when the anarchic forces of the Chinese mainland (parallel to the unconscious forces of the libido) invade this secure center and apparently abduct both parents when he is nine years old. In Ishiguro's fiction to be orphaned, to be deprived of parental security, becomes a trope for transnational identity, for being exiled from one's fatherland or motherland. And like the immigrant, the grown up child longs to win the approval of the parental imago left behind. "This desire to please the parents . . . is similar to the exile's longing to appease the sense of torment for forsaking the past and a homeland" (Luo 63). So the guilt is displaced. Eventually the protagonist comes to realize that the feared other is actually located within the self that has discursively created that other out of its own fears. Like the protagonist, the privileged West has peopled the world beyond its safe borders with monsters of its own imagination. In the course of the novel Ishiguro forces the reader to recognize that the heirs of colonialism, while attempting to foist onto the ex-colonized the stigma of eternal childishness, are in fact themselves behaving like children, having evaded maturation by projecting the unacceptable within themselves onto the subjects of their (post)colonial discourse.

Manipulating narrative conventions to break with mainstream fictional realism has political as well as aesthetic implications. The classic realist novel of the nineteenth century, as Catherine Belsey argues, "coincides chronologically with the epoch of industrial capitalism" (67). It serves to conceal from the reader the extent to which language constructs subjectivity, just as ideology conceals from capitalist and colonial subjects the ruling power's interpellation of their subjectivity. Personal and political subjection coincide repeatedly in Ishiguro's fiction, as do personal and political disintegration. In *When We Were Orphans* the protagonist's inability to counter forces of evil echoes that of democracies in the 1930s faced with the destructive forces of fascism. As Maya Jaggi suggests, "Christopher's guilt reflects that of a whole nation" (8). Equally history itself is put to figurative use in this, as in all his novels, to reveal its origins in the personal and the psychological. The adult protagonist's failed attempt to find and punish the abductors of his missing parents is reminiscent of the Western powers' failed attempt with the International Settlement to reassert parental control over an aberrant nation. Fascism, like colonialism, is the imposition of parental discipline on adults discursively constituted as children. Such a fantastic projection calls for an equally fantastic mode of narration.

When We Were Orphans opens in the more realist mode of his first three books and gradually metamorphoses into the surrealist mode of his fourth novel. The plot combines the excitement of the detective novel with the psychological interest of the first-person confessional that characterizes his earlier work. Christopher Banks, the narrator/protagonist, has spent the first ten years of his life protected from the outer world by his English parents who lived in the privileged haven of the International Settlement of Shanghai, There his best friend, Akira, is the son of Japanese neighbors. Banks occupies a bastion of the colonial center that is literally surrounded by the dangerous periphery of the Chinese mainland. When his father suddenly disappears into that peripheral area, Banks and Akira develop an elaborate compensatory game in which they impersonate the Chinese detective inspector searching for his father. Next his mother goes missing and Banks is shipped off (in about 1911) to live with his aunt in England. There he grows up determined to become a real detective in his adult life. In the 1920s he quickly becomes what his friend Sarah describes as "the most brilliant investigative mind in England" (34). But he is motivated all along by his childhood desire to clear up the baffling case of his parents' supposed abduction. To this end in 1937, after an improbably long interval, he finally returns to Shanghai which at this time is plunged in both a civil war between the Communists and the Kuomintang and the Sino-Japanese war that was a precursor to the outbreak of World War II.[1] In the Kafkaesque world of war-torn Shanghai the surreal becomes the natural mode of narration.

Just as Ryder and the city's leaders in *The Unconsoled* automatically assume that his concert will prove a turning point in the city's cultural history, so both Banks and the inhabitants of the Settlement (in his version of events) fully expect him to solve the case in no time at all. Further, as Barry Lewis points out, "Banks confuses his mission to rescue his parents with single-handedly averting the impending global catastrophe" (148–49). The absurdity of this assumption is illustrated by the farcical scene in which on his arrival Banks is greeted by a municipal official who wants to finalize arrangements for the triumphant return of Banks's parents, as if their return from captivity were a foregone conclusion. How can the mysterious, backward Orient hope to withstand the rational powers of a representative of the Occident? Later Banks is taken to a house which turns out to be his childhood home. Once again the improbable becomes the norm: the Chinese family currently living there immediately offers to move out so that he can bring his rescued parents there to live out the rest of their lives—a clear instance of wish-fulfillment on Banks's part.

His search for his parents takes him to the war zone beyond the safety of the International Settlement where he meets against all odds Akira (or does he?), now a wounded Japanese soldier, who guides him to the house where his parents were alleged to be held captive. But the house has been struck by a shell and—hardly surprisingly a quarter of a century later—his parents are not there. He doesn't learn the truth about them until finally he confronts an old friend of the family, "Uncle" Philip, now known as Yellow Snake, a

Communist double agent for Chiang Kai-shek, who would be more at home in a James Bond narrative. Philip tells him that his father ran off with a mistress and died from typhoid two years later in Singapore. Ishiguro continues to pastiche genres of popular fiction. In keeping with a Boy's Own adventure story, his mother offended an opium warlord who arranged for her to be kidnapped and kept her as his concubine. She agreed to submit to him provided he made a financial allowance for Banks until he grew up. Some 22 years later the warlord died and she disappeared in war-torn China. But in a coda Banks finally discovers her in 1953 in a Hong Kong religious institution for the mentally disturbed. She does not recognize him, but when he asks her whether she could forgive Puffin, his childhood nickname, she responds, "Did you say forgive Puffin? Whatever for?" (328). The most significant thematic departure from Ishiguro's previous fiction in this book is the tone of muted contentment in the final chapter that supercedes the angst that has driven Banks to outperform himself in his chosen profession all his adult life.

It is easy to identify in this novel those recurrent thematic motifs that have appeared in Ishiguro's previous work. Once again we are overhearing the recollections of a first person narrator. Like all his predecessors, Banks is an unreliable narrator whose memory is faulty, a fact we ascertain from his own reflections on its accuracy and from the conflicting testimony of others, such as his old school friend who remembers him as being "such an odd bird at school" (7), a very different creature from his own recollection of his regular boyish personality. As in all his earlier books, parents and children are alienated from one another, and either a parent or a child, or in Banks's case both, spend their life trying to compensate for their assumed early inadequacy and consequent loss of parent–child love. This need to put right the perceived wrongs of the past so preoccupies Ishiguro's narrators that they fail to attend to their adult emotional needs and desires. Only at the end of their lives do they recognize (or half acknowledge) the waste that their pursuit of this goal has made of their own lives. Consequently all his novels are haunted by a sense of anxiety, regret, and sadness. Another constant characteristic of Ishiguro's fiction is the way in which the carefully controlled narrative withholds more than it reveals. The narrative continually offers the reader a plurality of meanings and interpretations while remaining uncommitted. Ishiguro has said that he is primarily "interested in the way words hide meaning" (An Interview with Vorda 136).

But such an essentializing attempt to uncover the constants in Ishiguro's fiction ignores the radical differences between *When We Were Orphans* and any of the previous four books. These differences are not simply a matter of differing plots. Besides, as Ishiguro points out, he tries "to put in as little plot as possible" ("Between Two Worlds" 38). The tendency to give metaphorical significance to seemingly realist elements increases with each book. He has referred to Stevens in *The Remains of the Day* as "a good metaphor for the relationship of very ordinary, small people to power" ("Memory is" 22). Similarly he has described Ryder in *The Unconsoled* as "a metaphor for going through life without a schedule" ("Stung by Critics" 47). This tendency to give figurative significance to realist elements in his work is even more evident in *When We Were Orphans*. Take for instance the proliferation of orphans in this book. Not only is Banks orphaned at the age of ten. He later adopts Jennifer after she has been orphaned at the same age. Sarah, the only woman he cares for, lost both of her parents during her childhood. Even Mr Lin, the owner of his childhood house in Shanghai, recalls how his father adopted an orphan girl whom the son treated like his own sister. As Peter Childs observes, Banks "abandons Sarah (WO, 223), as he abandons the orphan he adopts, Jennifer (WO, 149), and as indeed he once abandoned Akira (WO, 100–4), replaying his own abandonment by both parents and his 'Uncle Philip' (WO, 122)" (126). The entire motif is given succinct expression when Banks asks Sarah whether she lost her parents long ago: "It seems like for ever," she replies. "But in another way, they're always with me" (48). The book's multiplication of orphans invites a figurative reading, forcing us to understand that to feel oneself orphaned is a common experience that happens to most children as they grow apart from their parents, just as it happens to most ex-colonials after they have gained independence from their colonial occupiers. At the same time we have thoroughly internalized the parents / colonial occupiers by the time we leave them or they us. As Freud argued, it is this internalization of the parental edict that makes possible secondary or psychological repression in adult life, a condition that Banks obviously suffers from, as do all Ishiguro's narrators and many other of his characters.[2] In the course of the novel the individual experience of the orphaned Banks is transformed by metaphorical multiplication into a collective experience. In fact Banks occupies a liminal location in the novel, as he fills the child's role as an individual, and yet is a representative of the parental colonial power as the master detective from England. Whether Ishiguro is locating the origins of the individual's neurosis in the collective mania of the age, or attributing the social malaise to the neurotic behavior of individuals like Banks, or both, remains uncertain. But the close connection between individual and collective neuroses is a given in this as in all Ishiguro's fiction.

As in his previous novels the settings also become charged with emotional and symbolic significance. In his first two novels, he has said, "I just invent a Japan which serves my needs" ("An Interview" with Mason 341). He set *The Remains of the Day* "in a mythical landscape" that "resembled the mythical version of England that is peddled in the nostalgia industry" ("Ishiguro in Toronto" 73). In *The Unconsoled* the unnamed mid-European city where the action is centered is what Ishiguro has called "a landscape of imagination [. . .] in which everything is an expression of [Ryder's] past and his fears for the future" ("Rooted" 151–52). In *When We Were Orphans* Ishiguro transports Banks from the seemingly more realistic setting of

London to the "exotic" Chinese port of Shanghai where Banks had spent the all-important years of his childhood. He has said that he constructed the novel from other books found in antiquarian bookshops ("Artist of" 9), situating his Shanghai at two removes from the real city. The International Settlement in which Banks lived is a safe enclave that the Western powers sealed off for themselves from the poverty and misery of the rest of this Chinese city. In this way, as Ishiguro has said, "the international zone becomes a metaphor for childhood" for Banks, "that he later finds is nowhere near as solid and protected as he believes" ("Memories of" 1). Part Two of the novel is largely taken up with the 29-year-old Banks's memories of the first ten years he spent in the International Settlement. What emerges is a picture of a privileged and protected childhood complete with servants, a personal amah, and devoted parents. Outside this magic enclave lay the forbidden, mysterious Chinese city which Banks once glimpsed: "I could see the huddled low rooftops across the canal, and held my breath as long as I could for fear the pestilence would come airborne across the narrow strip of water" (56). His friend Akira demonstrates the way in which those in power construct myths that reinforce their domination by demonizing the other when he makes up more gruesome stories about the Chinese city where dead bodies piled up everywhere and warlords ordered innocent bystanders to be beheaded at a whim.

This childhood fantasy of the adult outside world is so powerful that when in Part 4 the 36-year-old Banks finally returns to Shanghai he imposes his childish fantasies on the real city. At the same time the Chinese city really is undergoing bombardment and invasion by the Japanese. The adult world is as terrible and violent as the two children imagined, but in a different and perhaps more devastating way. On this occasion Banks sees the International Settlement as a place of undeserved privilege in which the Western élite view the Japanese shelling of the Chinese part of the city from their hotel as if it were just another form of entertainment. Banks slowly comes to appreciate the hypocrisy and exploitation underlying the apparent tranquility and safety of the Settlement in which he spent his childhood. This hypocrisy and exploitation is made explicit and personal in the form of the opium trade that his father's firm promotes. Ultimately the feared adult world, in the person of Wang Ku, the warlord his mother insults, erupts into Banks's sheltered existence and brings his idyllic childhood to a premature end. Banks's memories of his childhood and the International Settlement cloud his perception of the real city when he returns, undermining his principal adult skill of detecting the truth from what visual evidence is available. In the same way the older colonial powers are blinded by their past, unable to see clearly for what they are the emergent ex-colonies, preferring to continue to infantilize them.

Ishiguro has said that he believes that most writers "do write out of something that is unresolved somewhere deep down and, in fact, it's probably too late ever to resolve it" ("An Interview" with Vorda 151). Does this help to account for the strange combination of megalomania and guilt that pervades *The Unconsoled* and *When We Were Orphans*? The dream-like atmosphere into which this novel plunges us arouses just those feelings of dread and horror that Freud claims is the effect of the uncanny. Freud opens his essay, "The Uncanny," by demonstrating the paradoxical way in which the German word for "uncanny" (*unheimlich*) means both something strange and new and something familiar and old. Freud explains this paradox by arguing that "this uncanny is in reality nothing new or alien, but something which is familiar and old-established in the mind and which has become alienated from it only through the process of repression" (241). Repression is what causes the producer of the uncanny to over-accentuate the psychical reality at the expense of the material reality. In fact Freud's definition of the sources of the uncanny coincides remarkably with the fictive techniques pursued by Ishiguro. Freud argues that "an uncanny effect is often and easily produced when the distinction between imagination and reality is effaced, as when something that we have hitherto regarded as imaginary appears before us in reality, or when a symbol takes over the full functions of the thing it symbolizes" (244).

Ishiguro immerses Banks in a dreamlike world on his return to Shanghai where, Banks says, he experiences a sense of "disorientation which threatened to overwhelm me" (164). Ishiguro positions Banks midway between the real and the imaginary, so that the reader can never be sure whether an incident is located in the real (fictive) world or in Banks's (fictive) imagination. The effect of this simultaneous evocation of the homely (*heimlich*) and the alienated is that of the uncanny which pervades not just the more fantastic later portion of the novel, but in more subtle ways the earlier sections as well. For instance, the hallucinatory expectation, given expression by the members of the International Settlement, that Banks is the one who can save civilization from an encroaching evil predates his arrival in Shanghai as an adult, being voiced by Sir Cecil as early as Chapter 3 (45). In fact the novel is organized by what Freud called repetition compulsion. According to Freud the compulsion to repeat something does "arouse an uncanny feeling, which, furthermore, recalls the sense of helplessness experienced in some dream-states" ("Uncanny" 237). In the first part of the novel Banks as a child experiences a sense of extreme helplessness at his inability to recover his parents despite his impersonation of the renowned Chinese detective put onto the case. In the second half of the novel Banks experiences a repetition of that sense of helplessness when he fails again to recover his parents as a detective in his own right. Freud explains why such repetition gives rise to the effect of the uncanny in *Beyond the Pleasure Principle*, a book he worked on at the same time as he was writing "The Uncanny": "the compulsion to repeat also recalls from the past experiences which include no possibility of pleasure, and which can never, even long ago, have brought satisfaction even to instinctual impulses which have since been repressed" (21).

Freud claims that the uncanny thrives more readily in literature than in life because the author tricks us into believing in the reality of his fictive world only to introduce effects which rarely or never occur in actuality, thereby "betraying us to the superstitiousness which we have ostensibly surmounted" ("Uncanny" 250). Banks's coincidental encounter with Akira in the war zone is a perfect example of this: by the time Banks comes to doubt that the Japanese soldier is indeed Akira it is too late for the reader who has already experienced the sense of the uncanny. The point Freud is making is that the writer can manipulate our credence in his fictive world to achieve his desired effects: "He can keep us in the dark for a long time about the precise nature of the presuppositions on which the world he writes is based [. . .]" (251). This is precisely what Ishiguro does. For a long time we share Banks's obsessions and projections and do not immediately recognize the distortions and fantasies embedded in this professional detective's attempt at an objective narrative account of his life. Only when he starts to shed his illusions after Uncle Philip has revealed to him the truth about his parents' disappearances do we come to retrospectively appreciate the extent to which the author has immersed us in the uncanny by his own narrative manipulation.

Even the wounds inflicted on "Akira" and Banks come to assume figurative significance as the wounds inflicted on them by childhood. This would explain why Banks reflects so savagely on the "pompous men of the International Settlement" and on "all the prevarications they must have employed to evade their responsibilities" (258)—a fine example of displacement. Banks's entire career as an outstanding detective is just another instance of displacement which equally fails to heal the original wound. The shattering revelation of the sacrifice his mother made for him that Uncle Philip delivers in the penultimate chapter finally exposes the price paid for Banks's retention into his adult life and career of this chimera of an innocent childhood protected, like the International Settlement, from the corruption and dangers of adult life, epitomized by the Chinese city and mainland. Uncle Philip spells it out to him:

> "But now do you see how the world really is? You see what made possible your comfortable life in England? How you were able to become a celebrated detective? [. . .] Your mother, she wanted you to live in your enchanted world for ever. But it's impossible. In the end it has to shatter. It's a miracle it survived so long for you." (314–15)

Ishiguro's strategy in this book is to progressively break the reader's dependence on the conventions of traditional fictional realism. The improbable accumulation of instances of orphans detaches the reader from a realist response as effectively as does the move from a seemingly orderly London to an anarchic Shanghai under siege where the surreal activities of war merge with the surreal experiences of Banks. In point of fact Banks's unreliable memories have been distorting the narrative from the opening pages set in London. Think of his denial of being obsessed with Osbourne's "connections," or his claim in the first chapter that he and his fellow boarding schoolchildren "had all learned to get on without parents" (7). Ishiguro himself talks about *When We Were Orphans*, not in terms of surrealism but of expressionist art, "where everything is distorted to reflect the emotion of the artist who is looking at the world" ("Interview" with Richards). Banks is suffering from a common failing, according to Ishiguro, "the futile hope or wish that you can return to some point in your childhood, or your distant past, when you suppose things went wrong, when your world went askew, . . . and undo what happened" (Chartered Course" 62). Banks's illusion that he can achieve this superhuman feat becomes increasingly divorced from the reality of the situation as the novel progresses until he is brought face to face with the false image he has been treasuring of his childhood world. "In each section," Ishiguro has said, Banks's "mind has gone further away from what we call reality. When he goes back to Shanghai, we're really not quite sure if it's the real Shanghai or some mixture of memory and speculation" ("Ishiguro Takes").

Looked at structurally the book is organized into seven chronologically sequential sections of varying length. Yet the dates only refer to the time when the narrative is being written which largely coincides with the dates when Banks recalls memories from the past. As one reviewer put it, in this book "the past is alive in the present" (Sutcliffe 49). More importantly each section is structured in a non-chronological sequence that is determined expressionistically by the emotional, subjective quirks of Banks's memory. Ishiguro has said that he is "more interested in what people tell themselves happened rather than what actually happened" ("In the Land"). Ishiguro's rejection of any chronological imperative leaves him free to develop the narrative "tonally," as he puts it ("An Interview" with Mason 342), to use narrative structure to uncover the structure of the narrator's unconscious. Lacan's linguistic explanation of Freud's conception of the unconscious and its manifestation in the form of neurotic symptoms is relevant here:

> . . . if [Freud] has taught us to follow the ascending ramification of the symbolic lineage in the text of the patient's free associations, in order to map it out at the points where its verbal forms intersect with the nodal points of its structure, then it is already quite clear that the symptom resolves itself entirely in an analysis of language, because the symptom is itself structured like a language, because it is from language that speech must be delivered. (*Écrits* 59)

Banks's unconscious coincides to a great extent then not just with the unconscious of Western civilization but with the unconscious of the text. Or one could argue that the unconscious of the text is responsible for the identities assumed by Banks and the West as represented in the novel.

Part 1 focuses on Banks's first meetings with Sarah, but has flashbacks to his English schooldays and his traumatic return as a child from Shanghai. Already there appear to be discrepancies between his memories of his past and those of his old school friend, Osbourne, and those of Colonel Chamberlain who accompanied him back to England. Part 2 opens with another meeting with Sarah but then reverts to memories of an earlier period of his childhood in Shanghai spent with his parents and Akira. This crucial section establishes some of the key childhood fantasies that will come to dominate his adult life. For example the section ends with Banks's dream, continued since the age of ten, of being reunited with Akira when he returns to Shanghai, oblivious of the fact that almost twenty years have passed since he left, during which time Akira could have moved away, died, or simply changed into someone who no longer had anything in common with Banks. When Banks finally enters the war zone outside the Settlement in Part 6, he comes across a Japanese soldier whom he persuades himself must be Akira. The dialogue is carefully constructed to preserve complete ambiguity concerning the identity of the Japanese soldier. He can be seen learning his part once he realizes that his survival depends on Banks assuming that he is Akira. When the Japanese soldier is finally arrested on suspicion of giving information to the enemy, Banks is forced to recognize the possibility that his childhood fantasy overwhelmed him: "I thought he was a friend of mine from my childhood. But now, I'm not so certain. I'm beginning to see now, many things aren't as I supposed" (297). In a lesser way too Banks first ascribes a sentence to his mother when she was reproaching a company inspector, and then, after reflecting on the inappropriateness of the accusation, re-ascribes it to her when reproaching his father (63, 71, 74).

Part 3 returns to the present for the most part, but it largely concerns Banks's adoption of Jennifer, herself an orphan, which only underlines his neurotic need to compensate for his own orphaned state. Parts 4, 5 and 6 all take place during the month in 1937 that Banks spends in Shanghai ostensibly to solve the mystery of his parents' disappearance a quarter of century earlier. The increased unreliability of Banks's account of these experiences (as opposed to the experiences themselves) is indicated to the reader in the first chapter of Part 4 by an incident already mentioned—the absurd concern of Grayson, an official of the Municipal Council, to finalize arrangements for the triumphant reception of Banks's released parents at a ceremony in Jessfield Park (169). An attentive reader will remember that when Banks was describing his and Akira's childhood game of playing detectives, "our narratives would always conclude with a magnificent ceremony held in Jessfield Park" (118). The fantasies of childhood are constantly in danger of taking control of the narrative from this point until the dénouement. How much of the horror of the war-torn Chapei district of Chinese Shanghai is real and how much is it based on Banks's recollection of Akira's invented accounts of his supposed visits to the same district? How can we take literally the offer of the Chinese family occupying Banks's childhood home (which his parents did not even own) to hand it over to him now that he will need it for his parents and his old amah? Mr Lin, the Chinese head of the family, seen by the child in Banks as representative of the Orient that encircled the seemingly civilized International Settlement of his boyhood, appears to be just another outlet for voicing Banks's infantile/colonial fantasies when he says to Banks: "Of course, it is quite natural. You will wish to restore this house to just the way it was when you were a boy" (207). Equally clearly the expectations of the entire International Settlement that Banks will not just solve the mystery surrounding his parents' disappearance but will in the process restore their society to its former moral standards must be a projection of Banks. Banks, like the former colonizing nations, longs to restore the imaginary order of an imagined past on the nightmare of the present. On the other hand, don't people in imminent danger of a collapse of their civilization regularly project their needs and fantasies onto potential saviors, however unsuitable? We are in that realm Ishiguro explores repeatedly, "where," he says, " you're not quite sure what reality is" ("Ishiguro Takes").

Ishiguro has always suggested a connection in his fiction between the personal and the political—personal and political repression, personal and political disintegration. In *The Remains of the Day* Stevens's personal repression of his emotional needs mirrors the repression implicit in the most oppressive form of nationalism. As Ishiguro has pointed out, the nostalgia for Old England, for a mythical landscape that never actually existed, which is cultivated by Stevens, is also used as a tool by the political right to oppose trade unions, ban immigrants and blame the permissive sixties for ruining everything ("An Interview" with Vorda 139). In *When We Were Orphans* Banks, according to Ishiguro, "does equate his subjective world crumbling with the world around him hurtling toward the Second World War" ("Ishiguro Takes"). Most of Ishiguro's novels center on the period of Western history leading up to World War II. Ishiguro told one interviewer that he is "drawn to periods of history when the moral values in society have undergone a sudden change" ("An Interview" with Bigsby 26). What interests him is not history as such, but the way these critical periods of history expose the fault lines in human nature as instanced by his characters. Ishiguro stresses the need "to make a particular [historical] setting actually take off . . . as metaphor and parable" ("An Interview" with Vorda 140). Both setting and period are for Ishiguro primarily narrative devices rather than objective elements in his fiction. As we have seen, in *When We Were Orphans* the state of being orphaned becomes an ahistorical fact of existence. But situating Banks, his principal orphan, in the period leading up to the Second World War enlarges the metaphor. Banks's journey through the inferno of the Japanese–Chinese warfront is both a personal rite of passage and a vivid confrontation with the death and destruction produced by the imperialism of the industrial nations prior to the war. Just as Banks's protected childhood was bought at the price of his mother's servitude to a Chinese warlord, so the protected and privileged existence of the wealthy community living in the International Settlement was bought at the cost of widespread servitude to opium and poverty among the Chinese population. The novel equally shows how the same desire as that shown by Banks and Akira for ethnic and national purity has led the Japanese to invade China.

Banks, like Ishiguro, is a transnational torn between two countries and cultures. When Colonel Chamberlain reassures Banks on the boat leaving Shanghai for England that finally he is going home, Banks bursts into tears of rage: "As I saw it, I was bound for a strange land where I did not know a soul, while the city steadily receding before me contained all I knew" (30). Banks is simultaneously exiled from the safety of his childhood and from the city of his birth. What he discovers in the course of the novel is the fact that he cannot go back. No one can, as Colonel Hasegawa suggests when he quotes from a Japanese court poet: "our childhood becomes like a foreign land once we have grown" (297). He is permanently alienated from both his old and new life. Banks's mythic journey to the heart of his own repressed fantasies is homologous to Ishiguro's journey as a novelist, which he describes as *"closing in on some strange, weird territory* that for some reason obsesses me" ("An Interview" with Vorda 150). Ishiguro's compulsive return to this territory in an attempt "to write out of something that is unresolved somewhere deep down" ("An Interview" with Vorda 151) comes strangely close to Banks's obsession/compulsion.

As a child Banks, like his friend Akira, suffers from a fear that the reason his parents quarrel is that he isn't English enough. Uncle Philip comforts him by saying that because Banks has grown up in such a multiracial society he is bound to be "a bit of a mongrel" (79). But, Philip reassures him, there would be fewer nationalistic wars if everyone grew up as Banks has done: "So why not become a mongrel? It's healthy" (80). Ishiguro himself grew up a bit of a mongrel. Ishiguro "puts his ability to see England in inverted commas down to the fact that he never had an immigrant's sense of attempting to assimilate. Every year his family was planning to go back to Japan; it just never happened" (Interview with Adams 17). Ishiguro has said in a number of interviews that his bi-cultural upbringing helped him to appreciate the fact that Britain was no longer a major world power whose customs a writer could assume would be understood by readers beyond Britain. In one interview he explained how this realization inevitably involved his "moving away from realism." Because he can't use the texture of English life in addressing a wider audience, he says, "you start to create a slightly more fabulous world. You start to use the landscape that you do know in a metaphorical way" ("An Interview" with Vorda 137–38).

Ishiguro's use of Shanghai in this novel exemplifies this move away from fictional realism. He has said that he found Shanghai "a rich setting to write about the issues of multiculturalism" ("Stung by Critics" 47). Apart from his use of the International Settlement as a metaphor for childhood (already noted), he turns the larger city of Shanghai in its entirety into a metaphor for the meeting of East and West; of the barbarity of Wang Ku, the Chinese warlord, and of the barbarity of Morganbrook and Byatt, the English firm his father works for that imports opium for profit; of the civility of both Japanese and Chinese officers to Banks, and of the civility of Englishmen like Colonel Chamberlain, Mr Grayson, and even Uncle Philip to Banks, who frequently is insulting to them. In the very act of confronting each other East and West reveal their essential similarity, just as Akira and Banks share the same fear that they are responsible for the perfectly normal parental disagreements that they witness. Even this comparison of the similarity of Eastern and Western childhood experience is rendered metaphorically, by means of an image that reverberates throughout the novel. Akira quotes a Japanese monk who compared children to the twine that held the slats of a sun-blind together: "it was we children who bound not only a family, but the whole world together" (77). Next Banks uses the same image to explain to Uncle Philip his fear that if he did turn "mongrel" everything might—and he hesitates—"'Like that blind there'—I pointed—'if the twine broke. Everything might scatter'" (80). Later Banks uses the same image in a wider social context to attempt (unsuccessfully) to reassure an English police inspector who has become disillusioned by a horrific child murder:

'And those of us whose duty it is to combat evil, we are . . . how might I put it? We're like the twine that holds together the slats of a wooden blind. Should we fail to hold strong, then everything will scatter.' (144)

But, as one reviewer wrote, Banks is wrong, "for only if the strings give way can the light come in" (Carey 45). Banks is in effect urging the police inspector to play the (impossible) childish role of binding the adult community together, thereby keeping it in the dark. That double take is not some reviewer's display of his own critical dexterity. It is intrinsic to the way Ishiguro writes. Nothing of his can be read simply at face value.

That last quotation concerning the need to "combat evil" is representative of one further aspect of Ishiguro's extensive exploitation of the literary in this novel—his parodic use of the classic detective genre. This is not the first occasion on which he has parodied aspects of an old genre. Reviewing *The Remains of the Day*, Salman Rushdie called the novel "a brilliant subversion of the fictional modes from which it at first seems to descend" ("What the Butler" 53). In the case of that novel it descends from the genre of the English country house comedy made popular by P. G. Wodehouse. As Ishiguro explains, having "deliberately created a world which at first resembles that of those writers such as P. G. Wodehouse," he then starts to "undermine this myth and use it in a slightly twisted and different way" ("An Interview" with Vorda 140). Bruce King claims that all Ishiguro's novels "are imitations of stereotypes, more pastiche than realism" (167). In *When We Were Orphans* part of the time Ishiguro is parodying a genre—the detective novel—that already tends to parody itself. Just as Ryder in *The Unconsoled* deals with his parents' separation from him by what Shaffer calls "a strategy of denial, fantasy, sublimation, and later, music-making" (105), so does Banks do likewise, resorting to detection in place of music-making. Banks's rise to a position as a renowned detective can be viewed as his unconscious adult compensation for the impotence of his childhood games of detection. But Ishiguro gives this psychological interpretation a distinctly literary dimension by his parodic references to the classic detective novel featuring the likes of Sherlock Holmes (to whom Banks is jokingly compared eight pages into the book). It is fascinating to learn from Ishiguro that he excised 110 pages from the manuscript in which Banks performed as a classic literary sleuth, because "the pasteboard figures wheeled on 'simply to be suspects' in a traditional whodunnit could never co-exist with more solid characters" ("Artist of" 9). What we are left with is an old fashioned detective thrust into a modern world where evil can no longer be confined to a lone murderer uncovered by a Poirot or a Holmes.

W. H. Auden has offered one of the best diagnoses of the formula underlying classic detective fiction:

> The magic formula is an innocence which is discovered to contain guilt; then a suspicion of being the guilty one; and finally a real innocence from which the guilty other has been expelled, a cure effected, not by me or my neighbors, but by the miraculous intervention of a genius from outside who removes guilt by giving knowledge of guilt. (158)

In other words the classic detective novel creates a closed world from which evil can be separated and expelled. It represents a primitive desire for a prelapsarian world of innocence. In it evil, like the serpent, is an extraneous element that attempts to invade this paradisal state and can be defeated and ejected by the forces of righteousness. This is the ingenuous position Banks adopts throughout the larger part of the novel: "My intention was to combat evil—in particular, evil of the insidious, furtive kind" (22). Ishiguro has commented on the irony "that this genre should have flourished as a kind of therapeutic reaction to the horrors of the Great War" ("Artist of 9"). There is something essentially escapist about the entire genre and the inter-war society that made it popular. It is fitting that Banks, like the citizens of the International Settlement, should be pictured as harboring the escapist belief that a solution can be found to the complex contemporary web of evil and corruption in which they too are implicated. This fantasy in which "a greater man," an outsider, would go "to where the heart of the serpent lies and slay the thing once and for all" (144) is essentially a childhood dream still clung to in adult life. Banks's childishness, then, is exposed by Ishiguro as much through his parody of genre as through more psychologically realist means. At the same time Banks is ultimately made to face the far more complex complicity of good with evil—of his father's act of family betrayal, of the villainous warlord's honor in keeping to his bargain to provide young Banks with a generous financial allowance, of the simultaneous savagery and humanity of soldiers fighting on both sides of the Sino-Japanese war.

Banks eventually learns to recognize the childishness of his dream of cleansing the world of evil through his work as a detective. In the only case we witness, his attempt to solve the case of his disappearing parents is hopelessly misguided. It is his expectation that he can eradicate evil from his world that misleads him and makes him miss the vital clues. Or rather it is his proximity to his fictional antecedents—Holmes, Poirot, Lord Peter Wimsey—that blind him to the ubiquity of evil in the modern world he inhabits. Like Briony in *Atonement*, Banks inherits from his literary predecessors an outdated view of the separability of good from evil forces. "My great vocation got in the way of quite a lot, all in all," Banks reflects in the finale (331). The novel ends with Banks finally at peace with himself and the world, once he has abandoned the attempt to live out the fantasies of his literary predecessors which coincide with those of his childhood self. He has at last come to recognize the universality of his orphaned, transnational state, to adopt (with the reader) a metaphorical understanding of his circumstances and his world. In typically ambiguous fashion he concludes that for most of us, "our fate is to face the world as orphans, chasing through long years the shadows of vanished parents" (335–36). Whether this observation represents a deep insight into the workings of our collective psyche or a palliative for Banks's own wasted life is, as always in Ishiguro's skillfully polished work, impossible to determine. What is so satisfying about Ishiguro's fiction is the way he employs fictional means to establish connections between the personal and the social/political, and between the present and the past. It seems inevitable that he should have been drawn to non-realist modes of writing in order to establish the reality of such connections. Like Stephen Dedalus, Ishiguro remains within or behind or beyond or above his handiwork, leaving the esthetic image (as Stephen calls the work of art) to work on us principally in esthetic and figurative ways.

Lists of Books Published

Fiction

A Pale View of the Hills, 1982.
An Artist of the Floating World, 1986.
The Remains of the Day, 1989.
The Unconsoled, 1995.
When We Were Orphans, 2000.
Never Let Me Go, 2005.

Part III Narrative Constructions of Identity

Preface

All the novelists considered in this book have grown up and published work in a poststructuralist climate. As noted earlier a number of them have explicitly acknowledged this fact in their fiction or in interviews and essays. So one finds Peter Ackroyd writing a book length study on poststructuralist theory, *Notes for a New Culture*, Mimi in Rushdie's *The Satanic Verses* insisting that she is "conversant with postmodernist critiques of the West" (189), Angela Carter discussing her use of metafiction ("my fiction is very often a kind of literary criticism" [Haffenden 79]), or Martin Amis writing an essay on the sublime. A.S.Byatt, an academic for a considerable portion of her adult life, refers knowledgably in her essays to Barthes, Derrida, Foucault, Hayden White et al., while deploring their influence on literary criticism. More importantly, all these novelists in different ways adopt a poststructuralist attitude to the way they view their own and their contemporaries' writing. Byatt refers to "a new ... playfulness in writers" (*On Histories* 6). Jeanette Winterson, who claims to revert to modernism as a model, nevertheless reveals her simultaneous subscription to poststructuralism when categorically stating that "the artist does consider reality as multiple and complex" (*Art Objects* 136), and that for the writer words are not used for things, "words are things" (70). Especially relevant to the subject of this section are Martin Amis's remarks on the narrative construction of character: "I have enough of the postmodernist in me ... to want to remind the reader that it is no use getting het-up about a character, since the character is only there to serve the fiction" (Haffenden 19). In the same interview he claims that "motivation has become depleted, a shagged-out force in modern life" (5).

Amis is referring in his way to the celebrated death of the subject in post-structuralist and posthumanist thinking. Virtually all of the most prominent structuralist and poststructuralist theorists are in agreement that the transcendental subject is no longer credible once we understand the extent to which we are all constructed by language/discourse. The subject as they see it is not a free agent, but an effect of the way language/discourse functions. They prefer the word "subject" due to its two-fold meaning, its post-Enlightenment definition as transcendental agency, and its original meaning which, as Raymond Williams writes in *Keywords* (1983), had more to do with someone who is subjected to, or under, dominion or sovereignty (308).[1] So, as Louis Althusser saw it, the individual's illusory sense of freedom or agency disguises his or her determination by more powerful, external forces: "the individual *is interpellated as a (free) subject ... in order that he shall (freely) accept his subjection ...* 'all by himself'" (*Lenin* 169). Those external forces are given different definitions by different theorists—ideology by Althusser, the symbolic order by Lacan, textuality by Derrida, and discourse by Foucault. Whatever they are called these forces are necessarily partly shaped by the nation in which they operate. Individual identity is always dependent to some degree on hegemonic notions of national identity. The consequences of this approach to subjectivity are complex. For instance, identification with an individual, group, or nation is invariably incomplete, a fantasy of integration. Because the subject is constructed by language, it is subject to the forces of difference and deferral (Derrida's *différance*) by means of which language acquires meaning. This means that the subject requires its constitutive outside to differentiate itself from everything external to it. So the modern subject is necessarily split, and identification, as Freud said long ago, "is ambivalent from the start" ("Group" 134). The assumption of unity that traditionally accompanied the term identity involves a form of closure that relies upon, even if unconsciously, its other, that which it lacks.

The poststructuralist replacement of a transcendental subject by multiple subject positions constituted by linguistic/discursive forces largely ignored the obvious question of what makes up the individual who is thus multiply constructed by such external forces. For most of his life Foucault argued that the subject is an effect produced by and within various discursive formations (such as those of nation, class, race, or gender). Later in life his new emphasis on the connections between knowledge and power led him to dwell on the way in which the *body* has been regulated historically by discursive formations: "the subject who knows, the objects to be known and the modalities of knowledge must be regarded as so many effects of these fundamental implications of power-knowledge and their historical transformation" (*Discipline* 27–28). The body, like the nation, has come in this way to represent the locus of the various subjective positions constituting the individual being or nation, that which holds together the various subjective positions which otherwise rupture the unity of a subject or country. Stuart Hall argues that in the later two volumes of his (incomplete) *History of Sexuality* Foucault recognizes the flaws in his positing a "docile body" on which power operates without any "corresponding production of a response ... from the subject" ("Introduction" 12). In the first chapter of *The Use of Pleasure* Foucault proposes "to investigate how individuals were led to practice, on themselves and on others, a hermeneutics of desire" (5). In addressing for the first time what Hall calls "the existence of some interior landscape of the subject," the technologies of which "are most effectively demonstrated in the practices of self-production, in ... a kind of *performativity*" ("Introduction" 13), Foucault recognizes that the decentering of the self needs to be complemented by an account of the ways in which the subject constitutes itself. Hall proceeds to argue that after Foucault's death Judith Butler has gone on to partially develop this concept of performativity stripped of its associations with volition, choice, and intentionality. In *Bodies That Matter* she sees performativity "as that reiterative power of discourse to produce the phenomena that it regulates and constrains" (3).

Drawing on Lacan, Butler concludes that identifications (with subject positions such as heterosexuality) "belong to the imaginary" and "are never fully and finally made; they are incessantly reconstituted, and, as such, are subject to the logic of iterability" (*Bodies* 105). The relevance of these poststructuralist theories of subjectivity and identity to the world of fiction is obvious. If subjects are constituted by and within a world of language and if subjects accept imaginary positions offered them by a process of repetitive performance (meaning that our identifications with such positions have to be constantly restaged), then subjectivity itself is indebted to just those processes of textualization and dramatization that novelists employ in their writing. But obviously the poststructuralist conception of a discontinuous, fractured subject, subjected to linguistic forces beyond its control and raised to perform acts of closure that subject it to that which has been excluded, calls for a very different kind of fiction from what Catherine Belsey terms classic realist fiction of the nineteenth century. "Classic realism," she writes, "performs ... the work of ideology, not only in its representation of a world of consistent subjects who are the origin of meaning, knowledge and action, but also in offering the reader, as the position from which the text is most readily intelligible, the position of the subject as the origin both of understanding and of action in accordance with that understanding" (*Critical* 67). She goes on to suggest that classic realism "is characterized by *illusionism*, narrative which leads to *closure*, and a *hierarchy of discourses* which establishes the 'truth' of the story" (70). By contrast the fiction produced by the writers featured in this book tends to expose fiction's illusionism, resist closure and openly acknowledge, sometimes also challenge, its hierarchy of discourses.

Martin Amis's *Other People: A Mystery Story* (1981) serves as a representative example of the reaction against realism (understood differently by different writers) that all these novelists share in different ways. *Other People* opens with a confessional Prologue by the narrator. "I didn't want to have to do it to her" (9). This narrator never allows the reader to forget his controlling presence for long. Every chapter except the first and the final four has a section in which the narrator directly addresses the reader in the second person and these sections clearly claim the status of a privileged discourse. While admitting his responsibility for the sadistic treatment meted out to the female protagonist, the narrator who also participates in the narrative implicates the reader in the desire to subject the protagonist to the horrific experiences that she undergoes. In repeatedly breaking off the narrative to address the reader Amis is deliberately forcing the reader to abandon the illusion of inhabiting an alternative "real" world. Far from effacing its status as discourse, as does the classic realist novel, Amis's novel forces readers to be constantly aware of the narrative as a linguistic construct, which is just what the characters are. They are linguistic puppets that are ruthlessly manipulated by a narrator in full view of the reader. "Real people," he has said, "don't fit in fiction. They're the wrong shape" ("Martin Amis" 79). This mystery story ends so enigmatically that many reviewers declared that the mystery was unsolvable. In the Epilogue, Amis has explained, the all-powerful narrator has reverted to someone "as automaton-like as she was, and didn't realize what was going on" (Haffenden 18). He is a prisoner of his own fiction and is returned to the hellish cycle from which only a reformed protagonist can set him free. Both the narrator and the reader (who has been implicated with him) end up caught in the web of the fictional construct they have been conspiring together to weave around the hapless protagonist. This is a refusal of narrative closure with a vengeance. At the same time it allows for the possibility of assuming a different identity in the next lifetime around—itself a fictive conception. The narrator has returned to the status of pure body which can be subjected to different forms of performativity next time. The subject then is seen to be "the site of contradiction, ... perpetually in the process of construction" (Belsey 65). For Amis the free, unified, autonomous subject that realism has traditionally employed does not exist.

The same is true for most of the writers considered in this book. Rushdie constantly reminds the reader of *Shame* that he is "only telling a sort of modern fairy-tale" (68). The subjectivity of the protagonist of *Midnight's Children* is constructed by Indian history, linked to it "both literally and metaphorically, both actively and passively" (272). Here the connection between national and individual identity is central. But it remains an important factor in every novel treated here. In Ian McEwan's *Atonement* two characters, Robbie and Cecilia, turn out to be linguistic constructs of the novelist-protagonist's fantasy; their post 1940 lives prove to be doubly the invention of a novelist of English history who is herself the invention of McEwan. Angela Carter has the winged heroine of *Nights at the Circus* adopt as her slogan, "Is she fact or is she fiction?" (7). Whether fact or fiction, Fevvers is the construct of her own and others' language (part Cockney, part Oxbridge), a series of identifications with a number of possible subject positions which are mutable. Jeanette Winterson explores an even more radical subject position when she constructs a narrator stripped of gender in *Written on the Body*. This move undermines the Western discourse of heterosexuality which marginalizes any individual seeking to place him- or herself outside its parameters. The narrator of undetermined gender is wholly a construct of the novelist who has used language against itself to undermine its "normal" gendering of subjects. In *Last Orders* Graham Swift explores another common form of identification—with the subject position of class, an identification which has always especially exercised its hegemonic influence over the English and received renewed impetus under Thatcherism just when its power appeared to be receding. All the characters of this novel belong to the working class and Swift is largely constrained to use their limited vocabulary to explore their inner lives. Their use of a relatively homogenous language suggests the way they have all been interpellated in the same way by the ideology of the English class system. All three novels considered in this section explore ways in which modern, conflicted subjectivity is constructed by the forces of a nation's dominant discourses. All of them celebrate the power of language that has contributed to the construction of identity by staging consciously textual endings that resist obligatory narrative closure.

9
Angela Carter: *Nights at the Circus* (1984)

Angela Carter's most ambitious novel, *Nights at the Circus* (1984), took her almost ten years to write (Carter "Sweet" 44). It has received a lot of critical attention, the majority of it feminist. This is hardly surprising considering that the novel features as its principal protagonist a woman with wings ushering in the twentieth century. "Fevvers," we are told in the opening chapter, "has all the *éclat* of a new era about to take off" (11). Fevvers's ability to fly prefigures the new liberated woman of the twentieth century "that just now is waiting in the wings, the New Age in which no woman will be bound to the ground" (25). Carter has set the novel in 1899, the year that the British Parliament was debating a motion on Votes for Women, a fact alluded to in the novel. While many of the feminist interpreters of the book have focused on the ways in which the newly gendered subject has been formed in the course of the narrative, most have allowed their allegiance to the women's movement to simplify Carter's complex and ambivalent handling of emancipated female subjectivity. Paulina Palmer set the trend with an important essay in 1987 which argued that in *Nights at the Circus* "[a]cts of resistance against patriarchy are represented . . . A reevaluation of female experience takes place and the emergence of a female counter-culture is celebrated" (180). The same polemical approach is to be found in Julia Simon's 2004 book-length study of Carter, *Rewriting the Body*: "A powerful female subjectivity asserts itself in *Nights at the Circus*. The female body comes alive as the site of this gendered subjectivity . . . *Nights at he Circus* turns the female body into a powerful site of subversion" (151). Such broad generalizations ignore among other things the presence in the book of women like Madame Schreck and the Countess whose "powerful female subjectivity" consists of the exploitation or oppression of other women.

Carter was an unusual feminist in advance of her time. Her polemical essay on the Marquis de Sade, *The Sadeian Woman* (1979), outraged many contemporary feminists who questioned "the ethics of the connection" between feminism and Sade (Oakley). Subsequently in 1981 Andrea Dworkin dismissed Carter's book as "pseudofeminist" (84) and Susanne

Kappeler in 1986 charged Carter with validating the pornographic ("dazzled with the offer of equal opportunities") by appealing to the literary (135). Yet, as Sally Keenan observes, Carter's essay "offered a prophetic intervention into the battle that was to ensue" in the 1980s "between feminists campaigning against pornography" and those "opposed to censorship" (38). The range of the initial responses to Carter's feminist essay testify to the complexity of her response to this difficult subject area. "In the looking-glass of Sade's misanthropy," Carter writes, "women may see themselves as they have been and it is an uncomfortable sight" (*The Sadeian Woman* 36). Carter's attack on women's complicity in their oppression (embodied in Sade's Justine) and her rejection of feminists' then current idealizations of woman as mother or the maternal body elicited attacks from a variety of feminists at the time.[1] A number of feminist critics of Carter's essay on Sade show a blindness to her rhetorical tone. As Sarah Gamble suggests, such critics "either miss the irony, or see it as an inappropriate response to the subject matter" (100). This is equally true of such feminist interpretations of *Nights at the Circus* as those by Palmer and Simon. They ignore both the tone (one of playfulness, irony and exuberant excess) and the effect of the constant corrections interjected by Fevvers's cockney step-mother, Lizzie—a spokesperson for the Marxist view—of whatever Fevvers is saying or doing. At the end of the novel Fevvers, "intoxicated with vision," might claim to be "the female paradigm, no longer an imagined fiction but a plain fact" (286); but both her over-charged rhetoric and Lizzie's impatient dismissal of her utopian fantasies, warn the reader not to take Fevvers at face value. Carter critiques an exclusively feminist response with a socialist corrective, just as Kureishi critiques an exclusively ethnic response with the corrective of sexual politics.

With Carter it always seems necessary to add "but" to any generalization. Yes, she regards herself as "a rank and file socialist feminist" ("Angela Carter" 163), but she is a socialist feminist for whom the accomplishment of political goals (like "abortion law, access to further education, equal rights" and the like) makes her impatiently dismiss the 1980s "feminist preoccupation with mysticism and Mother goddesses" ("I'm a Socialist"). Yes, she is interested in the feminist debate on pornography, but she does not think that pornography is "nearly as damaging as the effects of the capitalist system" (I'm a Socialist"). Yes, as a feminist writer she sees her work as "part of the slow process of decolonialising our language," but she feels "much more in common with certain Third World writers, both female and male," than with ostensibly feminist writers in English like Marion French (*Shaking* 42). The imposition of a feminist template on Carter's novel has blinded a generation of critics to the ambiguities and complications of socialist feminism embodied in *Nights at the Circus*. Fevvers is certainly *imagined* as a prototype of the new, liberated woman of the twentieth century, but she is also constructed as a teller of tall tales who is not to be trusted. Carter is quite insistent on this aspect of her character:

> Fevvers is out to make a living. Everything she says in that direction is undercut by her mother, but the stuff she says in the beginning about being hatched from an egg, that's what she *says*. We are talking about fiction here, and I have no idea whether it's true or not. That's just what she says, a story that's being constructed . . . Part of the point of the novel is that you are kept uncertain. ("An Interview" with Katsavos 13)

Fevvers is not just a self-interested feminist, but a feminist who lacks the intellectual insights of socialism which Lizzie represents. Lizzie may start off looking like "the 'side-kick' to Fevvers," Carter has said, but "it turns out that in the end, she has actually been organizing and manipulating things behind the scenes" ("Angela Carter" 169). Near the end of the book Fevvers launches into one of her perorations (unconsciously indebted to such writers as Ibsen and Blake): "once the old world has turned on its axle so that the new dawn can dawn [the clumsy repetition draws attention to her phony rhetoric], then, ah, then! All the women will have wings, the same as I . . ." Lizzie is quick to counter this: "It's going to be more complicated than that . . . You improve your analysis, girl, and *then* we'll discuss it" (285–86). In effect Carter employs a Marxist perspective to critique a feminist one.

There is a further complication that has also received less attention than it deserves. This has to do with the way in which Carter represents the birth of this newly emancipated female subject. Fevvers is preeminently a performer who stages her liberation from the patriarchal society of the nineteenth century. Again Lizzie has to remind Fevvers to what she owes her income: "All you can do to earn your living is to make a show of yourself" (185). Fevvers escapes the nets of patriarchy by *staging* her flight above and beyond them. Fevvers is an anticipatory instance of Judith Butler's explanation of how "gender is performatively produced and compelled by the regulatory practices of gender coherence" (*Gender Trouble* 24). Butler goes on to argue that parody can reveal "the constructed status of the so-called heterosexual original" (31). In *Nights at the Circus* Carter uses parody, repetition with a difference, to reveal the way in which the traditional male construction of femininity is as much a copy as is Fevvers's parody of it. As Anne Fernihough writes, the "novel sets up expectations that the mask will eventually be stripped away to reveal a hidden self, only to show how, on the contrary, Fevvers's identity is constituted in and through performance" (94). But Fevvers's performance is not just that of an *aerealiste*. It is equally that of a narrator of her own story. The greater part of the first section, "London," consists of Fevvers (assisted by Lizzie) exercising her spell-binding powers of narration on Walser. What most feminist critics of the novel tend to marginalize is the fact that the act of narration in this novel is not merely a strategy for constructing the identity of the newly emancipated woman. The novel is as much about the power of narration itself as it is about the liberation of the new woman. Carter made this very explicit in her interview with John Haffenden in which she told him that when Fevvers at the end says "I fooled you" (294) "It's actually a statement about the nature of fiction, the nature of her narrative" (Haffenden 90). In this context Fevvers is "a really unreliable narrator" (90). Her reliability is not a matter of whether she really has wings (the narrative establishes that she does). The reliability is "a question about fiction" (90).

Carter is demonstrating how the construction of subjectivity is dependent on the construction of narrative. Subjects are narrated into being and share the ambiguous status of fictional narrative. In the first paragraph Fevvers claims, "I never docked via what you might call *the normal channels*, sir, oh, dear me, no: but just like Helen of Troy, I was *hatched*" (7). Fevvers and narration are equally parthenogenetic. Like Fevvers's aerial act which simultaneously represents her figurative performance of a new gendered position, narration depends on keeping the audience in a state of uncertainty. It is not just Fevvers who asks her audience, but Carter who asks her readers, "Is she fact or is she fiction?" (7). Carter insists that "fiction should be open-ended" ("Angela Carter" 163). To be successful fiction needs to embody uncertainty. This uncertainty principle applies equally to the status of Fevvers's flying ability, to the imagined arrival of the new woman of the new century, and to the narration itself. Walser can see why Fevvers needs to hold her audience in a state of suspended uncertainty: "For, in order to earn a living, might not a genuine bird-woman—in the implausible event that such a thing existed—have to pretend she was an artificial one?" (17). As for the figurative status of this representative of female emancipation, Julia Simon (who I claimed above appeared to be following the feminist party line) does acknowledge that the "text draws attention to the fact that it is a *fantasy of liberation*" (175). Carter and her readers in 1984 know that Fevvers's futuristic fantasies of total equality between the sexes remain only partially realized, as Lizzie forecast. Above all, the nature of narrative relies for its continued hold on keeping the reader poised in a state of suspended uncertainty.

As a narrator, Fevvers embodies this narrative uncertainty. Linden Peach remarks that Fevvers brings to mind Mendoza's proposition in *The Infernal Desire Machines of Doctor Hoffman* (1972), "If a thing were sufficiently artificial, it became absolutely equivalent to the genuine" (106; Peach 154). Fevvers is a narrative construct, linguistically produced from a conjunction of seeming contradictions, a series of oxymorons: "Cockney Venus," "Helen of the High Wire" (7), "winged barmaid" (16), "celestial housewife" (43), "the Virgin Whore" (55), "the Madonna of the Arena" (126). A bewildering fusion of the divine and the mundane, she leaves the reader guessing what her contradictory attributes will produce in any given situation. Fevvers is not just a representative of the liberated woman of the twentieth century. She is also intended "to function as the democratically elected divinity of the imminent century of the Common Man" [Carter's use of "Man" is redolent with irony] (12). Whether viewed in feminist or socialist terms, Fevvers's semi-divine status is undercut by her all too human working class characteristics, "thrown on a common wheel of coarse clay" (12). Ultimately Fevvers is a complex narrative construct, a *verbal* composite of incompatible linguistic attributes. She has "the shoulders of a voluptuous stevedore" (15), writes Carter, hilariously transferring the epithet "voluptuous" from Fevvers's shoulders to the stevedore.

Carter also uses paradox to turn Fevvers into an enigma. Despite her cockney accent, Fevvers displays an unlikely erudition that repeatedly locates her in the precarious and uncertain realms of the fictive. Fevvers has only to listen to Mr Rosencreutz's mumbo jumbo for a short time before accurately placing him in an esoteric world of pseudo theology-cum-metaphysics-cum-mysticism: "This is some kind of heretical possibly Manichean version of neo-Platonic Rosicrucianism, thinks I to myself; tread carefully, girlie! I exort myself" (77). The juxtaposition of a higher and a lower discourse ("Rosicrucianism" and "thinks I," or "girlie" and "exort") produces the comic illusion of a complex personality whose contradictory nature mirrors that of the narrative she is telling. Even the flight of this bird-woman, which has commonly been interpreted as "predominantly an image of liberation" (Palmer 199), is just as much an image of the precarious balancing act in the performance of narration. It is not a coincidence that in the introduction to *Expletives Deleted* (1992), a collection of her essays, Carter uses the image of the trapeze artist to characterize narrative: "We travel along the thread of narrative like high-wire artistes" (*Shaking* 605). Consider Fevvers's first attempt at flight from the mantelpiece in the drawing room of Ma Nelson's brothel when for the shortest moment she hovers before falling flat on her face: "and yet, sir, for however short a while, the air had risen up beneath my adolescent wings and denied to me the downward pull of the great, round world, to which, hitherto, all human things had necessarily clung" (31). That feeling of suspense, of being momentarily exempted from the laws of material existence, is the narrative effect Carter herself is attempting to achieve in this novel.

Fevvers is at once an original and a successor to a long line of intertextual predecessors. As Sally Keenan suggests, Fevvers "can be read as the image of Sade's Juliette transformed" (39). Like Juliette she is bold and transgressive, but she is humanized and does not victimize men. Carter has also said that Fevvers "is, fundamentally, the archetypal busty blonde: prototypes include Mae West, Diana Dors . . ." (Kemp, "Magical" 7). Elsewhere Carter has emphasized how "Mae West was both a fictional invention, a woman who re-invented herself . . . and also a perfectly real woman" (*Shaking* 543).

Fevvers even quotes a line of Mae West's from *I'm No Angel* (1933) when she calls the circus audience "Suckers" (180). Further, Mae West herself, writes Carter, derives from the nurse in *Romeo and Juliet* who in turn derives from Chaucer's Wife of Bath. Fevvers emerges from what Salman Rushdie has called the sea of stories. Lorna Sage has called her "an elaborate piece of revisionist mischief" (48). She is at once an original and an already established narrative type or *actant*.[2] Carter also makes intertextual connections between Fevvers's and earlier male narratives. An obvious instance is her use of the story of Leda and the Swan. A representative tale of the masculine divine impregnating a feminine mortal, this myth is reversed in *Nights at the Circus* where the god-like bird-woman ends up mounting a masculine mortal. Linda Hutcheon sees this and other parodic intertextual appropriations of *Pericles, Hamlet*, and Yeats as "ironic feminizations of traditional or canonic male representations of the so-called generic human—'Man'" (*Politics* 98). Such textual allusions also constitute additional evidence of the way subjectivity has already been linguistically constituted by Carter's literary forebears; but being a process not a product, such subjectivity is always itself subject to revision, even reversal.

According to Carter, "Fevvers starts off as a metaphor come to life - a winged spirit" (Haffenden 93). In *The Sadeian Woman* Carter identifies the origins of the metaphor in the 1949 Pauvert edition of the works of Guillaume Apollinaire: "Juliette represents the woman whose advent [Sade] anticipated, a figure of whom minds have as yet no conception, who is rising out of mankind, who will have wings and who will renew the world" (79). In an interview Carter agreed that "that was exactly how [Fevvers] started. I thought about a real woman with wings, because I thought that was a very equivocal, and rather silly thing of Apollinaire to say." Carter comments, "male intellectuals say this sort of thing . . . but I can't help feeling they're not going to like it when it happens" ("Angela Carter" 169). So Carter proceeds to literalize Apollinaire's metaphor, but, as she said in *The Sadeian Woman*, although "Juliette remains a model for women, in some ways," "she is a New Woman in the mode of irony" (79). Carter's mischievous literalization of Apollinaire's metaphor entails giving narrative reality to the way Fevvers grows and learns to use her wings, even to how her wings restrict the ways in which she can have sex. When the novel ends with Fevvers and Walser making love, she "crouched above him" (295), Carter is not just portraying the new woman in the traditionally masculine missionary position, but is demonstrating how her narrative literalization of metaphor simultaneously produces the new woman as a textual effect. Anne Fernihough comments that through Fevvers "Carter literalizes the metaphor of the performing trajectory, the lifelong impersonation, of womanhood" (89). Fevvers employs what Butler calls citational repetition, but hers is "a parodic repetition that exposes the phantasmatic effect of abiding identity as a politically tenuous construction" (*Gender Trouble* 141).

On his first appearance Walser turns out to be a different kind of narrator to Fevvers. If she is the narrator of her own fantastic story, he is the skeptical reporter, bound by "the professional necessity to see all and believe nothing" (10). A "connoisseur of the tall tale," he is questioning Fevvers "for a series of interviews tentatively entitled 'Great Humbugs of the World'" (11). As the representative of male discourse and of a materialist view of human existence, he is shown to be flawed by his failure to admit into his life the world of fantasy, dreams and invention epitomized by Fevvers, but also embodied in the life of the circus and grotesquely caricatured in the life of the Shaman. In her essays Carter makes it clear that she feels drawn to "the part of our literature, our inheritance, in which literal truth isn't important at all" (*Shaking* 32). Carter insists that "fiction can do anything it wants to do," because the "story is always real as story" (Haffenden 79, 80). For her "there's a materiality to imaginative life and imaginative experience which should be taken quite seriously" (Haffenden 85). The first stage in Walser's conversion to this view of narrative takes place when he becomes the unwilling auditor (and recorder) of Fevvers's unstoppable narration. For all his professional detachment, he quickly becomes "a prisoner of her voice . . . Her dark, rusty, dipping, swooping voice, imperious as a siren's" (43). Walser shares with other men in the novel a fascination with Fevvers's erotic winged body. He would like to inscribe his traditional male narrative of desire and domination on her female body. But what causes him to fall in love with her is as much her prowess as a narrator of her own story as it is her sexual allure. Carter is an unashamed phonocentrist who asserts, "Language exists before its own written form. The voice is the first instrument of literature; narrative precedes text" (*Shaking* 476). In the course of the novel Fevvers's oral narration assumes precedence and control over Walser the reporter—the epitome of written narration. Fevvers becomes a Scheherezade who with Lizzie's help overpowers Walser's opposition and makes him feel like "a sultan faced with not one but two Scheherezades, both intent on impacting a thousand stories into the single night" (40). As sultan Walser has lost *The Thousand and One Nights'* sultan's controlling power over Fevvers which she now exercises as she "lassooed him with her narrative and dragged him along with her" (60).

One immediate effect that Fevvers's and Lizzie's narration has on Walser is to make him feel that time stands still. Before he experiences a more radical transformation of gendered subjectivity, Walser is removed from measured time, suspended from his material existence, and drawn into an imaginative world in which the female freaks exploited in Madame Schreck's museum of monsters assume as vivid a life as those in the material world that Walser inhabits. What is the true significance of the sound of Big Ben striking midnight again and again while Fevvers and Lizzie are telling their story? In the Envoi to the novel Fevvers admits that she and Lizzie played a trick on Walser that night with the aid of Ma Nelson's clock (292). But what made Walser accept the impossible repetition of the strokes of midnight is the effect of

Fevvers's narration which cast its narrative spell on him. According to Carter, "All writers are inventing a kind of imitation time when they invent the time in which a story unfolds, and they are playing a complicated game with our time, the reader's time, the time it takes to read a story . . . A good writer can make you believe time stands still" (*Shaking* 605). What Fevvers's narration has done is to make not just Walser's but the reader's time stand still, suspend the laws of Walser's material world, and make his and our time conform to Ma Nelson's clock, for which the only permitted hour was "the dead centre of the day or night, the shadowless hour, the hour of vision and revelation, the still hour in the centre of the storm of time" (29). If, as Butler argues, "the ground of gender identity" is "a gendered corporealization of time" (*Gender Trouble* 141), then a way of escaping traditional gender identity is to enter a timeless world of "vision and revelation." Ma Nelson's realm is not just conjured up by an act of narration, but figures as a representation of the timeless fictive world created by narration. A similar effect is produced near the end of Section 3 when Fevvers and Lizzie meet Walser sporting a long beard a week after they have been parted by the train wreck (272). Lizzie's comment ("Father Time has many children") again acts metafictionally to draw the reader's attention to the way narrative can suspend clock time and with it the seeming fixity of identity.

Subjectivity is not constituted by a single performative/narrative act. Subjectivity is something continually in process. The same is true of the act of narration. Yet the spell it casts is by its nature temporary. Far from trying to conceal this feature, Carter positively revels in temporal disruptions that draw attention to the constructed nature of narrative and identity. This is an essentially metanarrative strategy that Carter cultivates. She writes, "Each time [the narrative] tips you out, you have to stand and think about it; you yourself are being rendered as discontinuous as the text" (*Shaking* 465). The text in other words positions the reader in the same precarious subject position as it does its characters whose narrative production through performance is seen to mirror the reader's. The alternation between immersion in the narrative and detachment from it is typical of the way Carter balances the claims of fact and fiction throughout the novel. The factual is invariably exposed as a flawed account of the totality of human experience. Yet once we, like Walser, have been trapped in the dark interior of a fictional world such as Ma Nelson's or Madame Schreck's, Carter lets in the light of day to reveal the cheap and sordid props that have been used to create the illusion that had us in its grip. Just before the prostitutes abandon Ma Nelson's house they open the curtains for the first time since they've been there. "The luxury of that place had been nothing but illusion, created by the candles of midnight, and, in the dawn, all was sere, worn-out decay. We saw the stains of damp and mould on ceilings and the damask walls; the gilding on the mirrors was all tarnished and a bloom of dust obscured the glass . . ." (49). The passage from which this comes does not simply constitute a symbolic representation of the passing of the Victorian age. It is also one instance of the many occasions when Carter demonstrates to her readers the power of narrative to capture us in a fictive world that simultaneously interpellates us as subjects.

It has been observed that the movement of the novel "toward increasingly foreign and remote places is accompanied by a movement away from any stable ground of reality and toward the ever more fantastic" (Michael 495). Carter has described Part 2 ("St Petersburg") as "very elaborately plotted, like a huge circus with the ring in the middle." She adds, "A circus is always a microcosm" (Haffenden 89). Many feminist critics, like Paulina Palmer, have seen the circus ring "with its hierarchy of male performers" as "an effective symbol of the patriarchal social order" at the turn of the century (198). It is equally a carnivalesque world in which the humdrum and the quotidian has been expelled and the imaginative and the fantastic is considered the norm. It reproduces the inequalities (sexual and other) of the world to which the audience belongs, but in exaggerated and grotesque form. Walser's transformation as a clown is an instance in point. Dressed in his clown's outfit, Walser "experienced the freedom that lies behind the mask, within dissimulation, the freedom to juggle with being, and indeed, with the language which is vital to our being, that lies at the heart of burlesque" (103). Notice how Carter links language to "being" or identity. In burlesquing or caricaturing the absurdities of his masculine role as a clown Walser is freed for the first time from his allegiance to the factual and material. He enters a world which can "absorb madness and slaughter into itself" (180), as can the world of fiction. Identity, he realizes, is not fixed. Walser becomes not just a performer but a narrator of identity, "your correspondent, incognito," he tells Fevvers (91). He finds himself clowning with identity and language: "Walser-the-clown, it seemed, could juggle with the dictionary with a zest that would have abashed Walser-the-foreign-correspondent" (98). Walser now recognizes the inescapable ambiguity of the language he sought to tame and confine to the factual. While he plays with language, language plays with (and signifies) him.

Walser, however, is a mere amateur in a community of professional circus performers—performers of a predetermined identity. Not only do they outperform him in their acts; they also prove superior narrators. Buffo, the chief clown, tells a story about a multiple tragedy in his family in which all those he loved were wiped out in one fell swoop; when he is forced to perform the same afternoon, his grief-stricken cry, "The sky is full of blood," only produces more gusts of laughter from the audience (121). In introducing it he says that this story is not just told about himself but "has been told of every Clown since the invention of the desolating profession" (120). He goes on to explain to his naive apprentice-clown, Walser, "This story is not precisely true but has the poetic truth of myth and so attaches itself to each and every laughter-maker" (121). Stories have their own form of truth and have the discursive power to subject future subjects to the role to which they have given narrative life. Buffo here displays a sophisticated knowledge of the nature of the narrative act in recognizing that a particular role or *actant* in a story can be filled by any number of successive characters or *acteurs*. It is also significant that the clowns' function is described in such a way that it exactly parallels that of the tellers of stories:

> . . . even if the clowns detonated the entire city . . . nothing would really change. Nothing. The exploded buildings would float up into the air insubstantial as bubbles, and gently waft to earth again on exactly the same places where they had stood before. (151)

As comic performers they seem to parallel Carter's own role as comic narrator of this book. The clown and comic writer appear to be offered the same mixed blessing: "you can do anything you like, as long as nobody takes you seriously" (152). Yet unlike the comic writer, the clowns do nothing but play at life, creating the illusion that life is nothing but play. In Section 3 the clowns stage a dance of "disintegration, disaster, chaos" (242) in the course of which they "become their true selves: that is, nothing" (Gamble 164).

Walser's assumption of a clown's mask is a stage in his re-education into the reality of a world beyond the factual and the material. In Sections 2 and 3 Fevvers undergoes her own form of re-education. Her narration in Section 1 gave vivid instances of how close she had come in the past to becoming trapped in an image of femininity constructed for or by men, by Madame Schreck or Mr Rosencreutz. In each case she falls for the lure of hard cash which men have traditionally used to buy women's acquiescence in their desires (for sexual, but also social control). At the end of Section 2 Fevvers falls for the last time for a masculine bribe—that of the diamond necklace offered by the Grand Duke. Critics such as Magali Michael see the Grand Duke's plan as a typical male attempt at "objectification," one more example of "the daily victimization of women" (502). But it is equally an attempt to freeze Fevvers in her role as freak performer, another object in the Duke's collection of exquisite miniatures. Further, he wants to "render her his plaything, . . . installing her in a miniature egg where she will become a hypodiegetic story [i.e. a story within a story] written only by him" (Malina 123). From the start of the novel Fevvers's appeal has been that of a spectacle: "Look! Hands off" (15)! She owes her independence to others' desire to look at her. Fevvers comes closest to extinction when the Grand Duke almost succeeds in fixing her for ever as part of his story, an artistic object to be gazed at by him alone. How she contrives to escape is by a double act that constitutes one of Carter's most brazen instances of narrative manipulation in the book. While she puts on a sexual performance for the Grand Duke (masturbating him), she puts on a purely fictional performance for the reader. While bringing the Duke to a sexual climax she brings her fictional life in St Petersburg to its own climax by escaping from the gilded cage in which he wishes to imprison her, which she does by jumping on to his miniature replica of the Trans-Siberian Express:

> In those few seconds of his lapse of consciousness, Fevvers ran helter-skelter down the platform, opened the door of the first-class compartment and clambered aboard. "Look what a mess he's made of your dress, the pig," said Lizzie. The weeping girl threw herself into the woman's arms . . . (192)

Before we readers have time to protest over the impossibility of such an escape (it defies all the laws of space-time), the new strand of narrative has caught us up and hurried us on into a new self-contained world of fiction that is of course just as reliant on illusion as was the last one. Fevvers has escaped the Duke's narrative plot and recovered her control over her self-narration by narrative, that is imaginative, means.

For Carter the gaze which Fevvers exploits and which almost proves her undoing represents the sado-masochistic relationship between not just masculine voyeur and feminine object but between writer and reader. The writer's attempt to control the reader's gaze is given fictional embodiment in this novel in Section 3 where Carter describes the establishment by the Countess P— of a panopticon, a prison for condemned murderesses built according to a design first outlined by Jeremy Bentham.[3] The interaction between the Countess (of whom Carter has said that she "is not really a character, she's a proposition" ["Angela Carter" 168]) and her prisoners parallels that between a writer and her readers:

> It was a *panopticon* she forced them to build, a hollow circle of cells shaped like a doughnut, the inward-facing wall of which was composed of grids of steel and, in the middle of the roofed, central courtyard, there was a round room surrounded by windows. In that room she'd sit all day and stare and stare and stare at her murderesses and they, in turn, sat all day and stared at her. (210)

Like the novelist, the Countess makes herself mistress of all she gazes at. Yet she is trapped by her own construction. She needs her gaze to be returned to reassure her of her power which involves making her captive audience think she is observing them day and night (just as the omniscient narrator deceives her readers into thinking that she is omnipresent in her fictional world). In the end the prisoners find a way of planning their escape which appropriately enough involves their writing secret notes using their own bodily fluids. Once they have escaped the Countess's controlling gaze they are free to construct their own narrative of their lives. Isn't this a metaphor for readers' freedom to impose their own interpretation (based on their own bodily experiences) on the narrative after the death of the author (as of the Countess)?

In Section 3 Fevvers suffers her greatest crisis of confidence when she finds herself no longer reflected back in Walser's gaze in her self chosen image: "Am I what I know I am? Or am I what he thinks I am?" (290). Walser, by this stage in his re-education, is totally involved in the Shaman's immersion in a world of pure fantasy. "Fevvers felt that shivering sensation which always visited her when mages, wizards, impresarios came to take away her singularity as though it were their own invention, as though they believed that she depended on their imaginations in order to be herself" (289). Fevvers overcomes this crisis of self-identity by reasserting her command over the image that she presents to her audience whose "eyes . . . told her who she was" (290). Her act of self-assertion takes the form of recommencing the oral narration (and construction) of her life. Addressing Walser, "'That's the way to start the interview!' she cried. 'Get out your pencil and we'll begin!'" (291). According to Butler, "all signification takes place within the orbit of the compulsion to repeat; 'agency,' then, is to be located within the possibility of a variation on that repetition" (*Gender Trouble* 145). Fevvers has been intent on repeating her variant construction of traditional feminine identity since the reader first encountered her. But she finally has in Walser an audience and a witness ready to record her variable repetition of her differently gendered subjectivity. He has simultaneously been transported to a newly gendered masculine position, one which will enable Fevvers to continue performing her liberated role in a heterosexual relationship that does not threaten to narrate her back into the patriarchy's definition of its constituent outside or other.

Walser has had to undergo a far more radical transformation than Fevvers to qualify as a fit partner for the newly emancipated woman of the twentieth century. The first description of Walser portrays him as "unfinished," "an *objet trouvé*, for subjectivity, *himself* he never found, since it was not his *self* which he sought" (10). Starting out as a skeptic who puts all his faith in external facts, he has to lose his protective shell and acquire an inner life, "a realm of speculation and surmise within himself that was entirely his own" (260–61). Like the reader, he has to learn to accept illusion as playing as valid a role in human life as fact. At the circus his injured arm prevents him from writing, "drawing him into an ever deeper submersion within the text" (Gamble 164). He has had to experience the death of his old skeptical, fact-bound self and a rebirth into a life in which the imagination is as real as is the life of the body. Having experienced as the "Human Chicken" at the circus the same humiliation that the Wiltshire Wonder at Madame Schreck's had (a midget served in birthday cakes), Walser becomes after the train wreck a human chicken who can only cry "cock-a-doodle-doo." Julia Simon suggests that he is made to suffer in Siberia some of the experiences of the female exhibits in Madame Schreck's museum of woman monsters: "After the train wreck Walser appears as 'Sleeping Beauty' to the lesbian escaped convicts, who wake him with a kiss" (159). He wakes up suffering from total amnesia, "the empty centre of an empty horizon" (236). His overdeveloped reason is gone, "indeed, now he is all sensibility, without a grain of sense, and sense impressions alone have the power to shock and ravish him" (236).

Walser's transformation into a fitting partner for the newly emancipated woman involves not so much his loss of gender advantage as his abandonment of a skepticism toward the life of the imagination and its realization in narrative form. Not that that life can ever supercede material existence, only coexist with it on an equal basis. When in the last section of the book he becomes the Shaman's assistant, he enters a realm in which "there existed no difference between fact and fiction; instead, a sort of magic realism" (260). Walser is literally made to enter Carter's magic realist world of fiction where the miraculous forms an accepted part of the normal. Carter shares Fevvers's distrust of the Shaman's total immersion in an inner life of fantasy and sensation, calling him a variety of the mad scientist (Haffenden 88). During his stay with the Shaman, Walser reverts to the life of "a tribal child" (266), and he is resuscitated from this child-like immersion in a life of pure sensation by Fevvers's performance which induces his awakening into a new world of love. Fevvers awakes him both to the material world and to the imaginative world of narrative. The reborn Walser has learnt to tell his own story, which ends: "And now, hatched out of the shell of unknowing by a combination of a blow on the head and a sharp spasm of erotic ecstasy, I shall have to start all over again" (294). Like Fevvers, Walser arrives *ab ovo*, hatched from the fertile brain of the narrator. The reporter of others' stories is now also the teller of his own story, narrating his identity into being. Walser narrates; therefore he is.

In celebrating its fictionality, its capacity to dazzle and deceive, the fictional text dramatizes the way identity is formed by narrative means. Fevvers's spreading laughter at the end of the novel is that of the comic narrator enjoying her narrative triumph in bringing off this book-length sleight of hand, in convincing Walser and us of Fevvers's narratively constituted identity, wings and all. Walser asks Fevvers, "why did you go to such lengths, once upon a time, to convince me you were the 'only fully-feathered intacta in the history of the world?'" (294). Fevvers, as she begins to laugh, responds, "I fooled you, then!" After her laugh has spread to infect the entire globe "as if a spontaneous response to the giant comedy that endlessly unfolded beneath it," she concludes: "It just goes to show there's nothing like confidence" (295). An alert reader will pick up on "once upon a time," "the giant comedy," and "confidence." The entire comic narrative is a gigantic confidence trick, meant to fool us as convincingly as Fevvers fooled Walser, the originally fact-laden and skeptical auditor of her narrative—as we were of Carter's. As Carter has explained, ending with Fevvers's "I really fooled you" (295) "doesn't make you realize the fictionality of what has gone before, it makes you start inventing other fictions . . .," (Haffenden 90). Just as Fevvers has reconstructed Walser's subjectivity, so Carter has reconstructed ours as implied readers of the novel. Carter insists that "reading a book is in a sense a recreation of it" (*Shaking* 33). According to Carter, Fevvers's metafictional admission that she fooled all of us, "is inviting the reader to take one further step into the fictionality of the narrative, instead of coming out of it and looking at it as though it were an artifact" (Haffenden 91). Like so many novelists focused on in this book, Carter believes that the modern novelist looks constantly for strategies "to cheat the inevitability of closure" (*Shaking* 606), The same is true of the never-ending process by which subjects narrate themselves and which only encounters closure with death.

Lists of Books Published

Fiction

Shadow Dance [aka *Honeybuzzard*], 1966.
The Magic Toyshop, 1967.
Several Perceptions, 1968.
Heroes and Villains, 1969
Love, 1971.
Fireworks: Nine Profane Pieces [short stories], 1974.
The Infernal Desire Machines of Doctor Hoffman [aka *The War of Dreams*], 1972.
The Passion of New Eve, 1977.
The Bloody Chamber and Other Stories, 1979.
Moonshadow, 1982.
Nights at the Circus, 1984.
Black Venus [aka *Saints and Strangers,* short stories], 1985.
Wise Children, 1992.
American Ghosts and Old World Wonders [short stories], 1993.
Burning Your Boats: Collected Short Stories, 1995.

Non-Fiction

The Sadeian Woman: An Exercise in Cultural History, 1979.
Expletives Deleted: Selected Writings, 1974.
Nothing Sacred: Selected Writings, 1982.
Shaking a Leg: Collected Journalism and Writings, ed. Jenny Uglow, 1997.

Plays

Come Unto These Yellow Sands: Four Radio Plays by Angela Carter, 1985.
The Curious Room: Collected Dramatic Works, 1996.

10
Jeanette Winterson: *Written on the Body* (1992)

"Everything I have written is a quest—a quest for self," Winterson wrote in the program notes to her dramatization of *The PowerBook* in 2002 ("Experiment!" 7). Every novelist considered in this book can be said to be in quest of one form of identity or another—an identity already constructed in part by the past and its recreation in the present, an identity that attaches itself to notions of nationhood, ethnicity or culture, or—as in this section—an identity determined by gender, sexual orientation, or social class. Yet gender, sexual orientation, and class are themselves partly determined by national constructions of or modifications to them. All of Winterson's nine novels to date equate the quest for self with self-narration. The self is constantly being reinvented by narrative means in her fiction. In her first novel, *Oranges Are Not the Only Fruit* (1985), when the young narrator (a preacher) is forbidden to preach the Word by the church elders she makes up her own words in the form the novel takes. In her ninth novel, *Lighthousekeeping* (2004), one of the inter-chapters reveals the continuity of this identification of subjectivity with narrativity:

Tell me a story, Pew
What story, child?
One that begins again.
That's the story of life.
But is it the story of my life?
Only if you tell it. (109)

It is by telling one's own story that we can avoid—or try to avoid—being defined by others. In a world of international capitalism and global communications telling one own story is simultaneously separating oneself from the universal, resisting one's interpellation by national and geographic forces. In *Oranges* the young female narrator's preaching of the Word becomes associated by the church elders with her love for another girl—in both activities she was perceived as having "taken on a man's world" (133).

By narrating her story (her Word) she simultaneously reclaims her right to define her own sexual subjectivity. But such sexual identity politics cannot so easily escape the patriarchal definition of women, something Fevvers found out repeatedly. As feminists were pointing out at about the same period of time, sexual difference positions the female subject within the hegemonic discourse of men. Men constitute the universal term within which only women are constructed as different. Or, as Judith Butler puts it, "only men are 'persons,' and there is no gender but the feminine" (*Gender Trouble* 19).

This realization may have driven Winterson to adopt increasingly radical measures to escape the construction of the female self by the hegemonic discourses of others. Probably her most daring narrative experiment comes with her fifth novel, *Written on the Body* (1993). A love story, this book features an unnamed, ungendered narrator who is bisexual. What happens to the quest for self when gender and what Adrienne Rich calls "compulsory heterosexuality" are removed from the narration of the self? Is Winterson implicitly evoking, as Monique Wittig does at times, some transcendental idea of a "real" individual self waiting to be released from the imprisoning discourses of gender differentiation and sexual orientation? Hardly. To cite *Lighthousekeeping* again, "There is no everything. The stories themselves make the meaning" (134). Despite her penchant for modernism, Winterson seems to adopt an essentially poststructuralist conception of the self as something that is constantly re-represented or narratively reinvented. Compare Stuart Hall's contemporary definition of identity as "always in part a narrative, always in part a kind of representation" ("Old and New" 49). Once you accept that identity is an effect of representation it offers itself to endless re-presentation. But traditional forms of narrative representation reproduce the representations of a patriarchal society by gendering the self. To release the full potential of fictional narrative to redefine the self, Winterson has totally removed all traces of gender specificity from her unnamed narrator in *Written on the Body*.

When I say "totally removed" I mean that her narrator is neither male nor female, but is deliberately given the traits of both genders at different moments in the text. Winterson herself has stated unambiguously that this is the strategy she adopted for avoiding the binaries of gender: "It doesn't matter which [sex] it is—my own feeling is that the gender of the character is both, throughout the book, and changes; sometimes it's female, sometimes it's male, and that is perfectly all right" ("No, No, Jeanette" 74). The "I" of her novel constitutes a more radical break with gendered representation than Wittig's *j/e* in *The Lesbian Body* (1973) where the *j/e* represents a sovereign lesbian subject as powerful as, and at war with, the gendered subject of heterosexual discourse. The "I" of *Written on the Body* is not a disguised lesbian as has been asserted by an astonishing number of reviewers and critics for various reasons. Winterson has been consistently quite clear about this, telling Audrey Bilger in a *Paris Review* interview, "I didn't want to pin it [the narrator's gender] down . . . So I didn't" (106). Although she is herself lesbian by choice (primarily, she tells interviewers, because hetero-sexual marriage and child raising would have interfered with her literary ambitions), she doesn't "think people's sexuality is really that fixed," and admits to having "had various boys at various times" ("Jeanette Winterson" 107). I divert into this extraneous biographical material only because the majority of the critical response to this important, innovatory novel has been shaped by a conviction that its author is a self-proclaimed lesbian whose narrator must therefore be a disguised lesbian.

Even if one disregards the critics' tendency to read *Written on the Body* as a *roman à clef* in which her past affair with a married Pat Kavannah and her concurrent one with a red-headed Peggy Reynolds are waiting to be revealed by the critic skilled in literary gossip, this novel is still largely discussed in terms of Winterson's known sexual orientation.[1] On the one hand some offended British male reviewers have discerned in her work, this novel in particular, a "propensity for scrawling the graffiti of gender-spite across her pages" while privileging passages of "lesbian lyricism" (Kemp "Writing" 2). On the other hand, numerous feminist and lesbian critics have charged her with abandoning the identity politics that they consider obligatory for the lesbian writer by disguising the gender of a narrator whom they all assume to be female.[2] Either they criticize the novel on the grounds, as Sarah Schulman writes, that the narrator is "a confused, insecure lesbian who can't fully love the woman of her dreams" (20). Or they consider the novel a fail-ure because "Winterson refuses to write an 'out' lesbian novel" (Duncker 85). Or, most commonly, lesbian-feminist critics cite those passages where the narrator is most feminine to "prove" that the narrator must really be a woman so as to be able to read the entire book as a lesbian work of fiction. Some of these lesbian readings are extremely sophisticated and sensitively interpret selective aspects of the novel. But they inevitably distort its overall impact. Cath Stowers, for instance, sees Winterson as giving fictional life to Monique Wittig's definition of lesbianism as not just "a refusal of the role 'woman'," but "the refusal of the economic, ideological, and political power of a man" (13). Thus the lesbian school of criticism can only salvage Winterson's work by demonstrating how, despite appearances to the contrary, she actually conforms to lesbian politics. Ultimately, as Louise Horskjaer Humphries has suggested, in the readings of most lesbian critics "the work is being judged by the writer (in particular her sexuality) . . . rather than the writer being judged by the work" (15). Yet Winterson repeatedly insists: "I am a writer who happens to love women. I am not a lesbian who happens to write" (*Art Objects* 104).

In *Written on the Body* Winterson creates a fictive world in which the bina-ries of gender and sexual orientation no longer control the construction of identity. This is a world of polymorphous desire in which no gender pre-dominates and no sexual orientation is privileged. Marriage, that bastion of heterosexuality is comically savaged: "Marriage is the flimsiest weapon against desire. You may as well take a pop-gun to a python" (78). The only ungendered character in the novel is the narrator. But the narrator has sexual affairs with a bewildering assortment of men and women who range over the entire spectrum of sexual behavior. Among the girlfriends are Jacqueline, a nurturer but without passion, Bathsheba, a promiscuous and adulterous dentist, Estelle who owns a scrap merchant business, and Inge, "a committed romantic and an anarcha-feminist" (21) who expresses her solidarity with the new matriarchy by blowing up some ugly urinals. Winterson is at her comic best describing the narrator's attempts to evacuate the men ("doubting John Thomases") from the urinals: "Why do men like doing everything together? I said (quoting Inge), 'This urinal is a symbol of patriarchy and must be destroyed'" (22). The entire feminist protest is rendered absurd and distanced by the narrator's use of parenthesis.

The narrator also makes a point of recording that the affair with Inge ended not for any ideological reason, but because Inge, on moving to Holland, insisted on communicating by pigeons (rather than by the postal service that "was run by despots who exploited non-union labour" [23]). When the pigeons refuse to fly beyond the English coast (one of them settling for Trafalgar Square, "another victory to Nelson" [24]), the narrator fills the vacuum with Jacqueline. Inge is simply one of a bewildering variety of women and her extreme feminist stance is satirized, not endorsed. At the same time Bathsheba's typically heterosexist behavior, combining marriage with adultery, mirrors identical behavior by the unnamed rich banker who is about to be married. "'After we're married,' he said, 'I can't imagine wanting another woman'" (78), at which point he admits a long-time girlfriend who has come to stay for the weekend with the comment, "'I'm not married yet" (79). The two differently gendered characters show identical sexual behavior.

The narrator's male lovers prove to be just as sexually varied as the narrator's female lovers. Crazy Frank, for instance, is typically untypical in being adopted by two midgets whom he carries around with him on his shoulders. Lacking parents, he evades the symbolic order. He has "the body of a bull, an image he intensified by wearing great gold hoops through his nipples." The hoops are joined by a gold link chain. "The effect should have been deeply butch but in fact it looked rather like the handle of a Chanel shopping bag" (93). Once again the absurdity of the combination of different sexual attributes resists any easy gender categorization. The same is true of the most developed male character, Elgin, Louise's husband. As a doctor he is associated with the masculinist discourse of medicine that the narrator spends a significant portion of the book deconstructing. At the same time he is small, passionless and weak, "one of many indications," writes Christy Stevens, "that the Law of the Father is not as strong and pervasive in the world of the text as it is in our contemporary society." Even Louise resists easy classification. She is in some ways quintessentially feminine. Yet in refusing to adopt the traditionally passive role with the narrator, she is what Winterson describes as "less caught in the arm-lock of gender" ("40 Years" 6). She is the active initiator of the romance with the narrator whom she pursues. But even this role is exposed for its artificiality when the narrator reflects: "I still wanted her to be the leader of our expedition. Why did I find it hard to accept that we were equally sunk? Sunk in each other?" (91). Typically Winterson employs a linguistic trope (drowning) to undermine the masculinist associations of leading an expedition. Sexual identity is shown to be merely an effect of representation by Winterson's creative use of language.

Although the narrator is the only ungendered character in the book, each of the other characters represents a unique sexual stance. "The implication is," according to Andrew Gibson, "that, in that world, there are no monolithic, generalised sexualities at all" (195). Each character acquires an identity from his or her personal story, not from the sex-gender system. This raises the question of what happens when a narrator tells the story of another character like Louise's? Is this not similar to the interpellation of women by a patriarchal culture? In both cases representation appropriates self-representation. The narrator can only tell the narrator's story authentically. But that story involves interaction with Louise, interaction which entails those power relations which govern the relations between the sexes in the modern world. In *The History of Sexuality* Foucault argues that "we must immerse the expanding production of discourses on sex in the field of multiple and mobile power relationships" (98). In Foucault's view individuals are not so much the recipients of power as the location where power is enacted and resisted. Sexuality is "an especially dense transfer point for relations of power: between men and women . . . " (*History* 103). As has been mentioned, Louise initiates the affair with the narrator and appears at first to control how it develops. She is the one to announce that it isn't working and takes three days in which to decide whether to continue with or abandon the relationship (91). After five months together Elgin tells the narrator that Louise is suffering from incurable cancer which only he might be able to arrest. The narrator arbitrarily decides to leave Louise without discussing this decision with her despite the fact that Louise "would not go back to Elgin, of that she was adamant" (104). Power has now transferred to the narrator. It turns out that Louise refused to submit to Elgin's medical care and unsuccessfully spent time searching for the narrator. But the narrator presumes to know better than Louise what she wants.

Six months later the narrator hears a voice: "You made a mistake." Significantly this occurs once the narrator has learned to "think of Louise in her own right" (153). Shortly after, the narrator asks, "What right had I to decide how she should live? What right had I to decide how she should die?" (157). Even Gail Right in her cups tells the narrator, "You shouldn't have run out on her," to which the narrator responds silently, "Run out on her? That doesn't sound like the heroics I'd had in mind. Hadn't I sacrificed myself for her?" (159). The narrator finally appreciates that in turning Louise into a child whom "I wanted to protect," that the narrator had unconsciously slipped into a masculine role, becoming a "Sir Launcelot" to a "Pre-Raphaelite" Louise (159). The ideology of the masculine hegemony is hard to evade. Sexuality itself is found to be subject to the patriarchal paradigm. And how does the paradigm capture the narrator? Through narration. As Gail tells the narrator, "The trouble with you . . . is that you want to live in a novel" (160). The problem is that the narrator has been narrated by the masculine symbolic order. "Time has exposed me to a certain sickness at the center," the narrator concludes—the sickness of being enveloped by another's narration (187). On the penultimate page comes the definitive exchange between the narrator and Gail Right:

> "It's as if Louise never existed, like a character in a book. Did I invent her?"
> "No, but you tried to," said Gail. "She wasn't yours for the making." (189)

This tension between the already narrated subject and the unique other provides the motor power for this novel. We can all reinvent by re-narrating ourselves. But the self does not exist in isolation. Love in particular intertwines our life with those of others. Because our unconscious desire for the other makes us aware of the lack within ourselves we attempt to hijack the loved object into the narration of our self. As Rimmon-Kenan explains, "you are what you say performatively about others" (25). In incorporating the other into our story we unintentionally attempt to fit the other into a sexualized, binary stereotype of the hegemonic order. And that can lead to the loss of the loved one.

Winterson has written in *Art Objects* that the refrain that runs through *Written on the Body* starting with the opening line, "Why is the measure of love loss?," is the image "from which the other lines are gradually taken, like Adam's rib" (170). Winterson's unusual word order in this repeated sentence ensures that love and loss are directly juxtaposed. Love, the novel implies, necessitates and is constituted by loss, just as desire, viewed from a Lacanian perspective, is defined paradigmatically by a sense of lack. Talking of the subject, Lacan claims that "it is in so far as his desire is unknown, it is in this point of lack, that the desire of the subject is constituted" (*Four* 218–19). Lack is what produces desire. Similarly in Winterson's novel desire is consistently linked to a sense of lack, absence or unobtainability. In narrative time no sooner does the narrator succeed in luring Louise away from her husband than the "I" chooses to leave the relationship. This has the immediate effect of raising the register of desire in both the narrator and Louise and sustaining it at a high level for the rest of the book. Winterson is careful to build this interdependency of love and lack into the texture of her narrative. For instance at one point the narrator is describing a moment of tenderness between Louise and "I":

> I put my arms around her, not sure whether I was a lover or a child. I wanted her to hide me beneath her skirts against all menace. Sharp points of desire were still there but there was too a sleepy safe rest like being in a boat I had as a child. She rocked me against her, sea-calm, sea under a clear sky, a glass-bottomed boat and nothing to fear.
> "The wind's getting up," she said. (80)

The paragraph associates "Louise" with "boat" with "safety." No sooner has the narrator reached a childish sense of being protected from the storms of nature rocked in Louise's maritime arms, than Louise warns of impending danger. No sooner has love manifested itself than it paradoxically generates the condition for its survival—the immediate threat of loss.

According to Winterson "the tragic paradigm of human life is lack, loss . . . " She continues, "The arts stand in the way of this doomsaying" (*Art Objects* 19). After the loss of Louise and love the narrator falls back on writing, narration to fill the lack that was nevertheless always present during the time spent with Louise. But writing or language is by definition a substitution and deferral of the referents to which linguistic signs point. Writing about love and loss, then, inevitably reproduces the lack that constitutes love and desire. *Written on the Body*, the title of the novel, gives powerful figurative expression to this way in which bodily sexuality and textuality are imbricated. Simultaneously the title evokes Foucault's *The History of Sexuality*, a reminder of how many of these contemporary novelists have been tangentially influenced by poststructuralist theory. Foucault concentrates on the body to avoid any assumption that identity is stable. Bodies are constituted, according to Foucault, by discursive formations including that of sexuality: "The body is the inscribed surface (traced by language and dissolved by ideas)," he writes using a similar metaphor to that Winterson employs for her title, "the locus of a dissociated Self (adopting the illusion of a substantial unity), and a volume in perpetual disintegration" (*Language* 148). We are constituted as subjects by what has been written on our bodies, including what has been written by the pervasive, modern discourse of sexuality, Foucault argues. Winterson uses the imaginative freedom of the artist to explore the implications of this central metaphor. Love inscribes its language on the body ("You have scored your name on my shoulders, referenced me with your mark" [89]). But equally writing has to assume a bodily corporeality. For Winterson, as for Woolf whom she so admires, "words are things, incantatory, substantial" (*Art Objects* 70). If the body is what precedes the inscriptions of desire, then is it possible that by corporealizing written narration one can avoid the normal way in which language situates the speaker in the symbolic order? Is this a way of evading the gendered and deferred nature of language and the sense of lack that accompanies it?

In *Written on the Body* Winterson attempts to elide the distinction between the body of desire and the body of the text which is itself a product of desire. Lovers inscribe their desire on each other's bodies as the narrator inscribes a story about the love and loss experienced by bodies. Characters write on and read one another's bodies in the language of the senses. Winterson both describes humans as textual artifacts and thinks of texts as living beings. "Art is metaphor," writes Winterson. "Metaphor is transformation" (*Art Objects* 66). Winterson's elision of body and text transforms both of them. The writing of and on the body is an attempt to escape from the polarization of gender that afflicts conventional acts of sexuality and textuality. Metaphor offers a way of defeating the clichés of love and language in the novel. Clichés place the speaking and spoken subjects in a hegemonic discourse where their subjectivity is pre-constructed in gendered and heterosexist terms: "She's a nice girl, he's a nice boy. It's the clichés that cause the trouble" (71). This last sentence is reiterated like a refrain five more times in the book (21, 26, 71, 155, 180). The narrator offers a steady stream of clichés on the second page of the novel to alert the reader from the start to the pervasiveness and problematical nature of stereotypical language ("Love makes the world go round. Love is blind. All you need is love . . . " etc. [10]).

Winterson consistently makes humorous use of clichéd scenarios to satirize the narrator's six-month stands with different sexual partners, such as that with an anonymous married woman:

> These are the confines of our life together, this room, this bed. This is the voluptuous exile freely chosen. We daren't eat out, who knows whom we may meet? We must buy food in advance with the canniness of a Russian peasant. We must store it unto the day, chilled in the fridge, baked in the oven. Temperatures of hot and cold, fire and ice, the extremes under which we live. (72)

Yet the language and images employed simultaneously serve to undercut the clichéd situation, to place it within a wider moral frame that depends intertextually on references to, for instance, the extremities of ice and fire that afflict the damned in Dante's *Inferno*, and to Christ's sermon on the mount in which he counseled, "Sufficient *unto the day* is the evil thereof" (Matt. 6:34, my italics). After Louise has entered the scene the narrator has to be constantly on the lookout for a relapse into the world of clichés, especially in exchanges with Louise:

> "Hello Louise. I was passing so I thought I might pop in."
> Pop in. What a ridiculous phrase. What am I, a cuckoo clock?
> We went down the hall together. Elgin shot his head out of the study door. "Hello there. Hello, hello, very nice." (30)

Not content with mocking the narrator's temporary aberration, Winterson extends her comic image to ridicule Elgin, that representative of the clichéd heterosexual world, who pops out (rather than in) and sounds like the cuckoo in a cuckoo clock.

An antidote is offered to the world of cliché: "A precise emotion seeks a precise expression" (10). Precision of emotion and precision of language can shape the self-narration that helps defeat one's interpellation by gendered stereotypes. The narrator is always critical of language use ("Why do I collude in this mis-use of language?" [56–57]), and in using language with precision simultaneously establishes ethical standards. Consider the narrator's decision to settle for a comfortable passionless life with Jacqueline: "I became an apostle of ordinariness. I lectured my friends on the virtues of the humdrum, praised the gentle bands of my existence [. . .]" (27). The triple use of oxymoron underlines the folly of such conduct. In Greek oxymoron means "pointedly foolish," which accurately describes the narrator's self-deception at this point. Lurking within this passage are echoes of biblical language ("apostle," "virtues," "bands"). However precisely the narrator uses language there is no avoiding quotation. As the narrator ruefully admits on the first page, "'I love you' is always a quotation" (9). This book abounds in references to other books, especially ones concerned with love—*Madame Bovary, Jane Eyre, House of Fame, Anna Karenina, Romeo and Juliet, Hamlet, A Midsummer Night's Dream, Song of Solomon,* not to mention writers like D. H. Lawrence and Mark Twain, paintings such as Burne-Jones's "Love and the Pilgrim," songs such as "Lady Sings the Blues," and movies such as *Jules et Jim* and *King Kong.* Even Louise's ploy for forcing herself on the narrator's attention is borrowed from the narrative of history: she turns up at the narrator's door soaking wet, just as Lady Hamilton had done so successfully at Nelson's door. Neither words nor actions can avoid being derivative in the field of love. This incidentally is an example of how the national archive contributes to (but does not determine) the narrative that constructs Louise.

Intertextuality may be unavoidable, but it can be employed creatively. Because "[a]rt's counterculture . . . holds in plain sight what the material world denies—love and imagination" (Winterson, "Secret Life" 10), quotation from the linguistic art of her predecessors offers Winterson another means of escaping from the prison-house of the clichés of gender. Winterson evokes the different languages of a wide range of discourses—meteorology, biology, anatomy, chronobiology, physics, astrophysics, zoology, not to mention the Bible—and appropriates them to rejuvenate the jaded language of love. She uses tropes of travel and anatomy to pursue her textual exploration of the corporeality of love. She has written that travel is a simple trope for conveying "an inner journey and an outer journey at the same time" (101). The lover's exploration of the total person constituting the loved one (not just her body) is given substance by analogy to earlier explorers of new-found lands:

> Louise, in this single bed, between these garish sheets, I will find a map as likely as any treasure hunt. I will explore you and mine you and you will redraw me according to your will. We shall cross one another's boundaries and make ourselves one nation. (20)

Where the trope differs from the explorations of early travelers is in the lack of exploitation. This form of love is not a form of colonial conquest but mutual discovery. "I was lost in my own navigation," says the narrator (17). Winterson seems to want to differentiate this love from the stereotypical heterosexual version where penetration of the interior and possession of the gold mined there is the norm. The indirectness of these allusions to the lovers' bodies only adds to the erotic charge and demand on the reader's imagination: "Eyes closed I began a voyage down her spine, the cobbled road of hers that brought me to a cleft and a damp valley then a deep pit to drown in." The next sentence makes us realize that Winterson has used this trope to turn the little world of the lovers into an everywhere: "What other places are there in the world than those discovered on a lover's body?" (82). This is not the only occasion in the book when Winterson draws on Donne's comparison of love to territorial exploration, but with a difference. Where Donne turns the loved one into a conquest ("O my America, my new found land,/My kingdom, safeliest when with one man manned." "Elegy 19"), Winterson celebrates reciprocity: "I had no dreams to possess you [. . .]" (52).

The most extensive intertextual use of a different discourse in the novel is the long segment in the second half of the book in which the narrator explores Louise's cancer-ridden body by quoting from an anatomical textbook at the beginning of each section. If the measure of love is loss, then death, being the ultimate loss, must form the measure of the highest form of love. This long meditation has been frequently misunderstood, For instance Andrea Harris detects "a kind of violence" in the narrator's "desire to have Louise as a collection of body parts" (136). What needs to be borne in mind is that the medical discourse which the narrator is intertextually incorporating is masculine to the core. Like patriarchal ideology it employs a masculine perspective to represent both men and women. Within the novel medical discourse is closely associated with Louise's husband, Elvin, an oncologist. Elvin uses his expertise in this area to attempt to force Louise back into the heterosexual fold (in hopes of being named on the Civil List honors, it turns out). Moreover, as Gregory Rubinson suggests, the "clinical language" of medical discourse "assumes an implicit authority over its subject matter while obscuring any sense of a speaker." Its main characteristic "is that there is no place for the personal" (224). The narrator quotes from this impersonal medical discourse in order to rediscover the lost sense of the personal within the gendered text.

This entire section (115–39) constitutes an extended conceit centering on the paradox that love is so frequently thought of as a disease—lovesickness. The narrator, for whom love previously has usually lasted six months, cannot help seeing analogies between a vision of love by definition dependent for its power on its potential undoing or death and a terminal disease like cancer. Both love and cancer end in death (yes, death too in the sense that the Elizabethans loved to play on so exhaustively). Marianne Børch has succinctly summarized the extent of the parallels between love and cancer established in the text:

> no one knows why love or cancer strikes or how to cure it (pp. 67/96); neither can be controlled, but only known from its effect (pp. 53/105); normal rules of existence are suspended (pp. 115/10); the sick body hurts easily, even as intense love-making leaves the heedlessly passionate lover bruised (pp. 39/124); even as the sick body enters a recession of deceptive health (p. 175), so seemingly healthy love may mark a withdrawal into narcissism; cancer invades the body, an intrusion similar to the lover's exploration (pp. 115/123); the cancerous body dances with itself, self intimate with self in the way of dancing lovers (pp. 175/73). (47)

Winterson uses these variations on an anatomical theme to give poetic expression to the underlying duality of love and of the language of love that is the obsessive theme of this narration. As the narrator acknowledges, Louise "opened up the dark places as well as the light" (174). Not just love but language, words, can "poison you" (*Gut Symmetries* 119). In one interview Winterson agreed that disease is "one of those useful metaphors that everyone understands." She continues: "Even the dimmest people can see that this is not only to do with their own bodies but a kind of metaphor for the state crumbling away" ("Jeanette Winterson" 108). Louise's cancer, like the narrator's failures in love, can be seen as part of the wider failure of English society to liberate sexuality from gender and the heterosexist imperative in the narrator's country.

But if love has its death written into its genetic code, the process can be reversed by the language of love. Returning home from the library with an anatomy book, the narrator sets out to defy the quotidian world of decay and disease: "Within the clinical language, through the dispassionate view of the sucking, sweating, greedy, defecating self, I found a love-poem to Louise. I would go on knowing her, more intimately than the skin, hair and voice that I craved" (111). In writing a love poem about Louise, the narrator is simultaneously reinserting the personal into the impersonal discourse of medicine, and substituting a textual for a sexual and physical evocation of her. So in the section dealing with the clavicle or collar bone, the narrator opens his/her meditation with: "I cannot think of the double curve lithe and flowing with movement as a bony ridge, I think of it as the musical instrument that bears the same root. Clavis. Key. Clavichord" (129). This inventive use of language converts the negative and objective diagnosis of Louise into the musical and poetic evocation of the lover the narrator remembers. These prose poems resuscitate the dying Louise with the magic of language, the signifiers of which indefinitely defer, while kindling, desire. Where once the Word was made flesh (John 1:14), Winterson in godlike fashion seeks to turn flesh back into the word. "Let me leaf through you," Sappho says in "The Poetics of Sex," "before I read you out loud" (*The World* 46).

Winterson wages her war on cliché at the macro as well as the micro level by placing the entire novel within the well-worn genre of romance. Romance fiction reifies the sexual division of humans into men and women who relate to one another in exclusively heterosexual terms. Further the heterosexual relationship is primarily represented as sado-masochistic—sadist on the man's part and masochist on the woman's. The authors of *Rewriting English* offer a succinct summary of the codes and conventions of romantic fiction: "its concentration on the private sphere and personal emotion; its marginalization of history and public affairs; its subordination of themes of class and race to those of sex and gender; its spiritualization of sexuality; its sexual masochism; and its repeated promotion of a sexual double standard" (Batsleer 102). Winterson evokes the romance genre while undermining it from within. Prior to meeting Louise, the narrator appears to conform to the stereotypical hero of romance fiction by combining sexual arrogance with promiscuity. Like so many earlier romantic heroes, the narrator despises marriage for its drab and clichéd conventions. The narrator tries to avoid falling into the marriage trap by "playing the Lothario" (20), only to realize that the life of the libertine is equally subject to cliché:

> I suppose I couldn't admit that I was trapped in a cliché every bit as redundant as my parents' roses round the door. I was looking for the perfect coupling; the never-sleep non-stop mighty orgasm. Ecstasy without end. I was deep in the slop-bucket of romance. (21)

The narrator is conforming to generic type—except that we know nothing of the narrator's gender. Further, Louise, who fills the role of traditional heroine in the genre, upsets the traditional sado-masochistic balance between hero and heroine by initiating the central affair of the book. A habitué of romance fiction would find herself hopelessly adrift in this version of romance which lacks so many of the signifiers that hold the players in place in a patriarchal order and genre.

The second part of the novel totally reverses the conventional pattern of romance fiction in which "a powerful ideology . . . speaks to and resolves in imaginary form many of the most significant and fundamental aspects of women's subordination" (Batsleer 104). Louise refuses to submit to the decisions that both Elgin and the narrator make for her, leaving both competing lovers vainly searching for her. She has literally become the signifier of lack that drives the desire of both suitors and the narration of the narrator occupying the subject position of the hero. So the plot reverses the ideological premises underlying the romance genre and returns the characters to a world of polymorphous sexuality. How then are we to understand the enigmatic ending of the book? Consoled by a friend who says, "At least your relationship with Louise didn't fail. It was the perfect romance," the narrator comments, "Was it? . . . happy endings are compromises" (187). Next the narrator wonders, "Did I invent her?" (189). Finally in the penultimate paragraph Louise appears at the kitchen door, paler, thinner but warm. The effect on the narrator of this appearance is to turn her little room into an everywhere (*pace* Donne): "The world is bundled up in this room" (190). Yet in the final sentence the narrator admits, "I don't know if this is a happy ending" (190).

The clichéd conclusion of romance has been problematized. Is this because the reader is not meant to see this ending in realist terms at all? As Jordan reflects in *Sexing the Cherry*, "very rarely is the beloved more than a shaping spirit for the lover's dreams . . . To be a muse may be enough" (79–80). The conclusion of *Written on the Body* celebrates the transformative effects of self-narration. The ending is neither factual nor explainable simply as a character's fantasy. It celebrates the triumph of a textual recreation of a lover already dead ("I knew she would die," [154]), of a love renewed by a renewed use of language. "What have I said in *Written on the Body*?" Winterson asks in *Art Objects.* "That it is possible to have done with the bricks and mortar of conventional narrative, not as monkey-business or magic, but by building a structure that is bonded by language" (189–90). The linguistic structure is one of love freed from gender stereotypes, brought into focus through loss. It is also a structure bonded by language the symbolic meaning of which is reached only at the cost of lack of being—hence the enigmatic status of the ending, the realization that in an England of the 1990s ungendered sexuality can only live in the privileged, imagined world of textuality. We are left with the consolation of language.

Lists of Books Published

Fiction

Boating for Beginners, 1985.
Oranges Are Not The Only Fruit, 1985.
The Passion, 1987.
Sexing the Cherry, 1989.
Written on the Body, 1992.
Art and Lies, 1984.
Gut Symmetries, 1997.

The World and Other Places [short stories], 1998.
The.Powerbook, 2001.
Lighthousekeeping, 2004.

Non-Fiction

Art Objects: Essays on Ecstasy and Effrontery, 1995.
Weight: The Myth of Atlas and Heracles, 2005.

11
Graham Swift: *Last Orders* (1996)

In *Nights at the Circus* gender politics are complicated and critiqued by socialist politics. In *Last Orders* the politics of social class are imbricated with those of gender. "It aint like your regular sort of day" (1). *Last Orders,* Graham Swift's sixth Booker prize-winning novel, plunges the reader from its opening sentence into the lower-class demotic speech patterns and accompanying modes of thinking and behaving that constitute the world of this novel. That world is confined to the lives of working-class characters who, even when they leave Bermondsey, a borough in South London, manage to take its ethos with them. Despite the wide attention that has been paid to this novel, which a number of critics and reviewers consider to be equal to or better than his third novel, *Waterland* (1983), relatively little attention has been paid to ways in which all its characters have been interpellated by the behavioral norms of their working-class identity. To what extent are all the characters in *Last Orders* circumscribed by the class to which they belong? And how is the formation of their identity by their membership of a particular class modified by their gender, age, nationality, and other such potentially determining factors? Alternatively, to what extent do the characters escape from the limitations of income, vocabulary, and outlook that is traditionally associated with South London's working-class population? While poststructuralism has stressed the extent to which the subject is commanded and constructed by language, discourse, and ideology, it has failed to adequately explain how humans nevertheless acquire and exercise agency, how they cease being solely objects acted upon and become also subjects making genuinely individual choices.

To refer to the English working class of the post-Second World War period is fraught with problems of definition. The strict Marxist definition of social class is based on how money is earned. So under modern capitalism the working class consists of those individuals who sell their labor and do not own the means of production. If this definition were used for the characters in *Last Orders*, only Ray, the wage earner, would fully qualify as a member of the working class, as all the other men are what Marx would call *petits bourgeois*, because they own their own shops or businesses, even if these consist of nothing more than Lenny's fruit and vegetable stall in Borough Market. But most Marxists today accept the idea that, as E.P. Thompson expresses it, class is "something which in fact happens . . . in human relationships" and "entails the notion of historical relationship" (*Making* 9). As early as 1958 Stuart Hall was arguing that the earlier cohesive sense of class among workers had been changed by the movement of workers from unskilled jobs to jobs requiring more differentiated skills: "The worker knows himself much more as a consumer than as a producer" ("Sense" 28). Hall's emphasis on the changing composition of the working class is indebted to Gramsci's notion of "historical blocs," a term he employed to emphasize how social groups are formed in specific historical moments to promote common social interests. Hall insists that class struggles are equally cultural struggles the representation of which is as real as the political struggle being represented. Pierre Bourdieu even claims that side by side with the economic definition of class exists a cultural classification which allots status according to how much "cultural capital" one possesses. These much wider frames of cultural and representational reference would allow one to group all the older generation in *Last Orders* (Jack, Amy, Ray, Vic, and Lenny) as members of the same historical bloc, differentiated to some extent from the next generation (Vince, Mandy, Sue, and Sally) who have been affected by the cultural revolution of the 1960s in their teens. Certainly there is a hostility apparent in the book between these two generations of lower-class characters that is different in kind from any differences dividing members of the older generation.

The English have added to the economic and cultural definitions of class those of language. A self-made millionaire who still speaks in a working-class dialect will continue to be considered a member of the working class in England, unlike in America. Language of course entails representation. In a work of fiction representation takes on a special status as it is as much the invention as it is the reproduction of the patterns of speech and behavior of the working class. In Swift's case his representation of working-class identity and behavior relies heavily on investigating his characters' relationships to the past. As Marx and Engels wrote in *The Communist Manifesto*, "In bourgeois society . . . the past dominates the present" (Solomon 53). Lukács explains this: "the real motor forces of history are independent of man's (psychological) consciousness of them" (107). Swift's characters are certainly heavily imprinted by the past, especially by their parents and World War II. Yet each generation is also fighting with that past, resisting its predetermination of their identity. Swift uses his characters' ambivalent attitudes to the past as one way of constructing their working-class subjectivity. They are both victims of a past they seemingly cannot alter and individuals in search of a way of escaping the fate of their class, that is, the fate to which Swift's narrative construction of class subjects them.

Swift shares with Martin Amis a conviction that history since the Second World War has taken civilization into a new and frightening era. Born in 1949, Swift has said that "[g]rowing up in the 1950s, there was all the physical evidence of war . . . So the second world war," he concludes," has been my great history lesson" (O'Mahoney). It is referred to in all his novels. It is the historical marker for the start of a brutal modern era in which individuals are figuratively wounded by it, limping their way through life as Tom Crick's father does literally (but also symbolically) in *Waterland.* Bill Unwin, the protagonist of his fifth novel, *Ever After* (1992), is representative in thinking that "the world is falling apart; its social fabric is in tatters, its ecosystem is near collapse . . . that is, flimsy, perishing, stricken, doomed" (4). The same doomsday scenario haunts the imagination of Price, the star pupil of Tom Crick, the history teacher/narrator of *Waterland.* Price vividly conjures up the imagined last moments before a nuclear blast occurs: " . . . all the buildings go red-hot and then they go white and all the people go red too and white" (297). His teacher "too had a vision of the world in ruins" (240), but he is thinking of the leveled German towns he saw at the end of World War II. So Swift appears to share his history teacher's conviction that modern history is not progressive but a continuous reclamation of a past that recently has shown an inclination to accelerate in a destructive direction. The modern period is a record of decline characterized by loss, particularly the losses initiated by the Second World War. In the case of *Last Orders* the war was responsible for killing Vince's entire family, for killing Lenny's dad and forcing Lenny to settle for stepping into his dad's shoes selling fruit and vegetables, not to mention "all the dead 'uns . . . left behind in the war" (77). Its after effect haunts the thoughts of all the characters who live in a time, according to Amy, "when a good half of the world, when you think about it, when you think of all the misery, must be wishing for a good half of the time it'd never been born" (276). But the repetition of "half" warns the reader that this is not the complete picture.

All five principal male characters in *Last Orders* have served in the armed services: Jack, Ray, and Lenny in the army in North Africa, Vic in the navy during the war, and Vince as an enlisted soldier in Aden in the mid-sixties.[1] War and armed conflict have constituted these characters' main personal experience of modern history. The women of this generation left at home have also been affected by the war. On Lenny's return from the war he found that "there were more bomb-holes in Bermondsey than there was at Benghazi, [Libya]" (176). Serving in the ranks, all of the men have been trained to "settle for being commanded" (182). War, history, seems a monolithic force. Under its grip, each of them felt like a "small man at big history," as Ray puts it (90). Yet there is a difference between duty and orders, as Lenny says. As opposed to obeying orders in the services, "Doing your duty in the ordinary course of life is another thing, it's harder" (132). During the war, when his lieutenant is wounded, Jack tells his panicking next-in-line to assume command or he will. Observing Jack in bed in the hospital just before he asks Ray to bet a thousand pounds for Amy's future security, Ray reflects, "I suppose that's what he's doing now, assuming command, taking charge of himself" (182). Jack is the one who said to Ray in the desert, "we're all the same underneath, officers and ranks, all the same material" (27–28). Yet Lenny observes that on Jack's return to civilian life he mindlessly stuck "like glue to what he knew, like there was an order sent down from High Command that he couldn't ever be nothing else but a butcher" (132). The challenge for these working-class characters from the ranks is to move from a position of taking orders to assuming command of their lives, from being commanded by their superiors to transcending the conditioning of social class.

Yet the past cannot simply be left behind, because we internalize it and make it part of our present. Swift has said that his cast of older characters comprise "layers of time . . . They have a historical dimension which is nonetheless written intimately into their personal life" ("Glowing"). It is difficult to resist the inimical forces of modern history, according to Swift, when "[w]e contain our former selves, even when we may think we have shed them" ("I Hope"). A few critics have charged that Swift reifies history. Kate Flint, for instance, argues that " . . . the ritual that is performed by the narrative in *Last Orders* involves the affirmation of a certain view of England, both tacitly, between the men, and more generally, in its incorporation of the reader into a certain form of nostalgia for a fading way of life" (40). Catherine Bernard makes a similar assumption when she claims in the introduction to her interview with Swift that the characters of *Last Orders* "seem to be left stranded on the wayside of history . . . with haunting memories of betrayal and failure" ("An Interview" 217).

But Swift rarely takes such a unitary position in his fiction. His vision of the ways in which history affects the lives of his characters is complex and ambivalent. He has said: "you have the personal history of a character and then you have the history of the world through which they have lived . . . We're not just the individual person that we recognize as us, but we are formed, we're made, we belong to this bigger collective thing. We call it history . . . " ("Graham Swift in Interview" 159). Hartung-Brückner suggests the way in which Swift's ambivalence works in *Last Orders*: "The search for identity and continuity is presented as a fragile and contested process in which history appears both in its deadening and fossilizing aspects and in its therapeutic or constructive uses for a re-entry into the present." On the one hand even when characters like Vince think they are escaping the deadening hold of the past by enlisting to avoid becoming a butcher, they find themselves unconsciously repeating it in another form, as Lenny points out to Jack: "you can't say he aint following in your footsteps. You were a soldier once . . . " (45). Lenny himself comes to see that his instinctive reaction to his daughter's unmarried pregnancy—that she should abort (kill) the foetus—is an outcome of those years in the war when he spent his time "loading and firing,

loading and firing . . . and not thinking twice about it . . . because it's
. . . what you're trained for" (204). On the other hand Vince can learn finally to pay Jack the respect he never showed him while he was alive, just as
Lenny can decide to visit Sally and try to repair the rift that his insistence on
her abortion caused (209).

So personal and national history has placed these characters in a working-
class mold, which limits their options but cannot stop them from exercising
choices within the limits that class has imposed. When it comes to characterizing those traits that belong to the working class, there is always the danger
of offering essentialist definitions such as that which Engels gave in *The
Condition of the Working Class in England* (1845): "The failings of the workers
in general may be traced to an unbridled thirst for pleasure, to want of prov-
idence, and of flexibility in fitting into the social order." Recent Marxists have
stressed the diversity and the competing groupings within the postwar
English working class. In what Stuart Hall and others have dubbed the "New
Times" of the 1980s and beyond (the present of the novel is dated April 2,
1990), there has been an enormous "diversification of social worlds. At present most people only relate to these worlds through the medium of con-
sumption" ("Meaning" 234). What Hall calls this "'pluralization' of social life"
expands the identities available to working-class people (234). But the number of positions is still limited even while members of this class are offered a
wider choice. It may still be the case, as Andrew Tolson claimed, that men in
capitalist societies see work as central to their conception of masculinity and
sense of dignity (12, 27). It is interesting to note how some critics have chosen to emphasize either characters' confinement or their exercise of choice in
Last Orders. Representative of the former camp is Gary Davenport who gener-
alizes: "Life as the characters have experienced it is without exception hard,
cruel, deterministic" (443). Others such as Jakob Winnberg ricochet in the
opposite direction and call *Last Orders* "breathtakingly affirmative" (169).

Swift refuses to choose between these two axes. He prefers to show the
clash between the rival claims of fate and choice, class determination of
identity and characters' ability to choose between competing roles and identities. All the male characters find the low-income jobs they end up in a
major constraint on their range of life choices. Even Vic, thought by everyone to have "got it all sorted out" (284), reflects that his choice to join his
father's funeral business meant "Your life cut out for you, your chances
altered" (126). Jack has stepped willingly into his butcher father's shoes, but
the 1980s witnessed the arrival of a supermarket that forced him to take out
a loan just to stay in business. When asked by Ray why he didn't sell up
rather than incur increasing debt, his reply shows his fatalistic identification
with his job: "I'm a butcher, Raysy. That's what I am" (221). Lenny is the
least well-off and seemingly as a consequence the most embittered. He
wanted to become a boxer (hardly a lifelong career) but was forced by his
father's death and his mediocre skills as a boxer to take over his dad's fruit

and vegetable stall in the market: "You'd think that five years of shooting and being shot at and picking up the pieces of your dead mates would teach you a better way to make a living than trying to knock another man off his feet, but it was that or pushing a fruit-and-vegetable cart and that aint got no glory to it, nor quick readies either" (176). Yes, Lenny has choices, but neither offers him a way of earning a living that he respects. And the one he prefers (boxing) is the one he cannot have.

This is true of most of these working-class characters: they wanted to be something else. Ray wanted to be a jockey but his father insisted on raising (supposedly) his social standing by qualifying him for a job as a desk clerk. Lenny wanted to be a boxer and Jack wanted to be a doctor. That is what they would have been, according to Jack, "if there was anything other than the rule of blind chance in this world, if we could all see and choose in the first place" (283). Hauled up before his headmaster, Vince thinks, "I'd like to be Gary Cooper but I can't" (96). The lack of punctuation makes the "can't" part of "I'd like." The same is true of the women. Mainly their choice is limited to that of a husband or lover and the life attached to that choice. Amy desires Romany Jim, the gypsy and his freewheeling lifestyle, but chooses Jack and is tied to him and his shop in Bermondsey for fifty years. She explains to herself that the reason why she "was saddled with him and not a thousand others" was "luck of a summer's night," to which Jack adds, "All a gamble, aint it?" (268). Women make their choices before they can realize to what extent their choice will determine their lifestyles. Mandy falls for Vince: "It's never how you picture it," she reflects. "A butcher's van, an ex-soldier with oil under his finger-nails. Meeting a man from the motor trade" (159). Even Ray's wife, Carol, when she leaves him, fails to better her lot when she chooses "the sub-manager at the domestic-appliance centre where she worked part-time" (100). Vince's range of choices are wider by his day. Yet when his headmaster asks him what job he wants to do (a question that runs like a refrain through the book), Vince reflects:

And I see them all hanging up before me, like clothes on a rack, all the jobs, tinker, tailor, soldier, and you have to pick one and then you have to pretend for the rest of your life that that's what you *are*. So they aint no different really from accidents of birth. (96–97)

Vince is suggesting that it is not just the quality and earning capacity of the jobs available that is circumscribing, it is the necessity of choosing a job, any job, that will then define who you are. Vince offers a more radical critique of identity when he reflects: "He aint Jack Dodds, no more than I'm Vince Dodds. Because nobody aint nobody" (199). As David Malcolm observes, the "characters of *Last Orders* are deeply aware of their roles as roles—as identities assumed and maintained—although others might have been possible" (176–77).

If anything this realization that subjectivity is something selected from an available though limited repertoire of subject positions has an embittering effect on the characters. Amy thinks that it was her fault, for refusing to give up visiting June, their brain-dead daughter, in her nursing home, that Jack determined to "work till he dropped" (15). Lenny, the poorest-off, resents the fact that he cannot afford to take his daughter Sally to the seaside and imagines that Amy is "getting above herself" because she lived in bricks and mortar and he lived in a prefab (40). Vince is perhaps the clearest example of someone who finds himself confined by the job he chose of his own volition. To succeed he has had to virtually prostitute his daughter Kath to attract the custom of rich Mr Hussein. "There goes Vince Dodds," he tells himself, "who sold his daughter to an Ayrab" (166). His racist attitude to Hussein ("we used to shoot your lot when we were in Aden" [165]) is itself partly the product of his resentment at Hussein's wealth and privileged status: "he knows I've got to smile and lay it on thick and act like his humble servant" (165). All the characters champ against the constraints of the roles that initially they chose for themselves. All of them also show the way the working-class roles they chose are the result of early conditioning and have conditioned their later reactions to life. Faced with Jack's imminent death, Amy behaves as if she had been summoned by her headmaster (186), and Ray has "to look straight ahead, like when you're up on a charge, before they march you into the cooler" (187). They have been acclimatized to being dominated by more powerful figures of bourgeois authority from their youth.

But, restricted by social conditions as they are, they refuse to believe that they are in any way inferior to members of a higher class or a better-paid profession. When the four men set out in the car with Jack's ashes and are told by Vic that they make a good guard of honor, "We all sat up, as if we've got to be different people, as if we're royalty and the people on the pavement ought to stop and wave" (22). When Jack is lying in his hospital bed being given a pre-operation visit by the surgeon and puzzles the surgeon by asking him where he will make the cut in his stomach, he explains his question: "Professional interest," by which the surgeon realizes from his chart that he means his profession as a butcher. Apart from the implied joke (that a surgeon butchers his patients), Jack is instinctually assuming an equality between their two occupations. As Jack says to Vic when he is making his mind up to retire, "There's more to life than bacon [i.e. a butcher's life], aint there?" (82), but it is still framed as a question. Ray takes the argument a stage further when he insists that "what a man does and how he lives in his head are two different things" (38). All these characters may be severely restricted in their choices of occupation and income, but they have the same imaginative capacity as everyone else. Seeing that much of the novel consists of their inner thoughts and flights of imagination, the narrative has no trouble demonstrating this important aspect of their subjectivity to the reader.

One of the dangers of focusing on a single subject position such as class is that there is a distinct possibility of oversimplifying the way subjects are actually constructed by a number of different interacting ideologies. For instance class and gender mutually influence one another, but they also produce some of the principal dilemmas for both the male and female characters of this book. Communication and understanding between the two sexes is hampered by a lack of just that imagination which they all share in other areas of their life. Like Ian McEwan, Swift believes that, "[i]magination is the basis of morality" ("An Interview" 224). This is as true of life as it is of fiction. Fiction, he has said, "is all about imagining what it's like to be somebody else . . . If we didn't strive at least to imagine what other people's lives are like, then we would fail. We would fail as human beings, we would fail as societies" ("Graham Swift in Interview" 155). The leading instance of this failure to project into the feelings of the other is the relationship between Jack and Amy. Jack cannot understand why Amy cannot face up to the fact that their only daughter, June, is brain-dead, which makes Amy's twice weekly visits to her pointless in his eyes. Equally Amy cannot understand how Jack can simply turn his back on their only true offspring. Fatherhood, Richard Pedot points out, " is more than simply being a begetter" (62). During her last visit to June by bus, Amy reflects on the way this failure to imagine what the other feels left both of them rooted in fixed positions: "I watched him set solid into Jack Dodds the butcher, . . . because he couldn't choose June too, couldn't choose what was his . . . But when he looked at me then, like he was looking at someone I wasn't, I knew I was stuck in a mould of my own" (229). Amy did at least try to break out of this mutual quagmire early in their marriage by arranging a belated honeymoon in Margate. But after winning the teddy bear for her Jack throws this obvious stand-in for June into the ocean from the end of the jetty. Amy's reaction is "Goodbye Jack" (255). It takes the shock of Jack's sudden death for Amy to revert to her younger self when she still had the power to choose her future. As the protagonist of *The Light of Day* (2003) reflects, "Your life comes off its hinges, so you go back to where you were" (90).

Apart from Vic and Pam, the relations between the sexes, whether between husbands and wives or fathers and daughters, is messy, the outcome of repeated misunderstandings. Lenny and Joan quarrel over their unmarried daughter's pregnancy, just as Ray and Carol fight and separate over Sue's marriage to Andy leading to her emigration to Australia. "Daughters, eh Raysy? Nothing but trouble" Lenny remarks (48). But is the real trouble the working-class construction of masculinity? Most of the men have a similar attitude toward women. Ray offers a humorous insight into this when he describes his sexual awakening as a teenager allowed for the first time to take the reigns of the family business cart hauled by a horse named Duke: "I expect it was sitting there beside him, looking at Duke's backside, that I had my first dirty thoughts about women. It was what I had

to go on. I suppose women might as well have been another kind of animal
. . . " (38). A page later, when Ray first sees Carol, the woman he will marry,
he remarks as she bends over the gas fire, "She's got a good arse on her" (39).
These Bermondsey men tend to see and relate to women primarily at an animal level. The second chapter in which the men meet in the Coach and
Horses (appropriately titled) has them all focusing on the new mini-skirted
barmaid whose name (or identity) they don't even know for sure:

> Jack said, "Vince, your eyes'll pop out."
> Vince said, "So will her arse." (6)

These men largely see women in animalistic terms as sexual beings. Lenny's
assessment of Vince's daughter, Kath, is that "she pulled in the punters,"
punters meaning both gamblers, and clients of either Vince's car business or
of prostitutes (49). The only way their daughters can break free of their parents is to marry or trade on their sexual favors. When Sally's husband is sent
to jail, she is forced to go on the streets. Lenny sums up the two daughters'
situation: "Same old game now, it seems, for Kathy as for Sally anyhow. Just
better luck at it" — that is, Kathy has better luck because she is being kept
by rich Mr Hussein (205).

Some critics have accused Swift of marginalizing his female characters.
Peter Widdowson claims that either "the women characters are largely unde-
veloped [he instances Amy] . . . or are sexually promiscuous and responsible
for harm being done—or both" (220). Pamela Cooper also faults Swift's portrayal of women, but accuses him of idealizing them: "Swift's heroines are,
in a sense, goddesses. They suggest an archetypal femininity: 'woman' as a
kind of eternal principle" (29). Swift repudiates such charges. Asked why
women don't have much to say in *Last Orders*, he insists that Amy "is actually the strongest character" with the strongest voice and "the greatest
power of decision in the book" ("Graham Swift in Interview" 155–56). But
it is a mistake to assume, as Emma Parker does, that Swift is therefore
"debunk[ing] the very category 'man',," by creating " a world in which last
orders have metaphorically been called for masculinity" (89). Parker concentrates exclusively on gender and ignores class. Arguing that *Last Orders*
presents patriarchy as a lost order, Parker identifies Jack as a "real man"
working in Smithfield Market where, he tells Ray, he can see "how real men
make a living" (26). Because Parker sees Jack as "the novel's grand patriarch"
(90), his death, she argues, "symbolizes the demise of the model of masculinity he represents," precipitating "a crisis in the patriarchal order" (91),
which leads to an ending in which the four men undergo "a distinct change
of heart" (98). Swift is never politically correct in this manner, which has led
to the opposing accusations of male chauvinism.

His working-class characters fall back on a sexist attitude to women when
they fail to understand them or before they know them as individuals. Ray

first sees Amy as a desirable woman when Jack shows him a snapshot of her during the war. But they become lovers only after his own marriage has broken up and he has got to know her and all the unhappiness she carries around with her on their journeys to the nursing home. The men are also conditioned by their experience in the armed forces: "it keeps men together, . . . fighting" (240). So when Sally tells Vince that she knows he's an adopted child and it doesn't matter, he seemingly for no reason, "goes and knocks her down" (43). His learned physical response conceals from him the fact that he likes her enough to get her pregnant. In the same way Lenny's conditioning in the army makes him force his daughter to have an abortion as if there were no alternative, even though she is convinced that Vince would have returned to her after his service was up. Despite their conditioning, some of the male characters do come to make the imaginative leap necessary to enter into the minds of the women and make amends for their class- and gender-inherited instinctual responses. In particular Jack and Ray both atone for earlier mistakes in their treatment of women by the end of the book. In effect Jack gives Amy and Ray a second choice, a chance to exchange stasis for movement, or for Amy to exchange stagnant oscillation on the bus for a continuation of life's journey. Ray foresees the moment when he will give Amy the thirty thousand pounds he has won with Jack's "gift" of a thousand. He would explain that "it was sort of meant like a sign, like a permit [from Jack], like a blessing on the two of us, to carry on where we left off" (283).

The journey which acts as the principal movement of the plot in the present assumes strong figurative significance. Jack's last orders have sent all four men on a journey of discovery or rediscovery of life's potentialities. Their narrative journey takes them simultaneously on a journey into their past and the collective past of history. Fittingly the four set out on a journey in which initially pubs (with their own form of last orders) signal their progress (17–18), which makes it feel like they are "travelling but it's all the same place" (47). Traveling, it turns out, is not a matter of progressing in a straight line. It involves detours—to Chatham, Wick's Farm, and Canterbury. But these detours are equally ends in themselves, returns to respectively the war, to the hop fields where Jack met Amy, and to the death which has overtaken Jack and awaits them all. As Vince says before the first detour, "We can do detours," which parallels the way the narrative moves, continually spiraling back to earlier times in order to return to the present with better understanding. "That's why we're here, aint we?" Vince says to explain why detours are part of their journey. "To remember the dead" (115). Swift has explained that he employs digressions and "moving around in time" because "it's more truthful to the way our minds actually deal with time." For him such non-linear form "is governed by feeling, by the shaping and timing of emotion" ("I Hope").

At the start of their journey all the characters appear to be geographically and emotionally immobilized from the moment they chose their partners and occupations. Ray reflects on the ease with which his daughter took off for Sydney while he was "still living in Bermondsey, still sitting on the old man's yard to keep Charley Dixon happy." His life has reduced its parameters to "[t]he boozer, the betting shop, the bus to Blackfriars" (54). The armed services had provided all the men with their only experience of the glamor of foreign travel. Travel offers the excitement of escape from one's present situation, the possibility of change. Ray buys his camper-van to reintroduce some movement into his calcified marriage only for Carol, threatened by the possibility of such movement, to leave him. This is the van in which he and Amy have their short-lived affair, and it is the same van that Vince takes Mandy in to escape their adopted, loveless home and discover love for themselves. As Peter Childs points out, Mandy compares herself and Vince in the van to "a pair of gypsies" (157) who are associated by Amy with the glamor of being constantly on the move. Vince makes cars and the movement they offer not just his occupation but his credo in life: "I'll tell you what the big change is, the change underneath all the change . . . It's mobility, it's being mobile" (105). Jack's last orders ensure that all four men take this journey back to their joint pasts in order to release them to move forward again into the future. Amy is set on her own journey: "Neither here nor there, just traveling in between" (228). Amy's bi-weekly trips might be seen to have been, as Richard Pedot acutely observes, "one long journey, one long work of mourning—for Jack, long since dead to her as June was to him: to be eventually free of Jack and June's deaths" (68). Likewise, by the time the four men take the last of their three detours Ray comes to the realization that the journey has fundamentally altered their sense of what traveling is about: "It's like we aren't the same people who left Bermondsey this morning, four blokes on a special delivery. It's like somewhere along the line we just became travelers" (193–94). Journeying, like life and like narrative, is "Not the place from or the place to but the road" (153).

The journey is primarily a narrative journey. It is recounted by the main five male and two female characters.[2] The interiority and partiality of each character's monologue compels the reader to construct the underlying narrative journey which the characters take not just from Bermondsey to Margate but from the present back into their individual and collective pasts. The narrative each character tells is their journey in search of a meaning to their individual and communal life. If this narrative method is confusing, Swift says that he is confused because life is confusing. So he offers "the confusion of [his] characters who are nonetheless trying to steer some kind of sustainable and hopeful course through their confusion. That course is story-telling" ("I Hope"). Swift's narrative is patched together from the interior narratives that each character utters. Like the dramatic monologue of the nineteenth century, the interior monologue that Swift uses, as John Mullan writes, demands "that we infer actions and motivations that we are never directly told," which carries its own risk of being misunderstood (32).

Swift's most immediate model for his use of interior monologue is, as he acknowledges, William Faulkner's *As I Lay Dying* (1930), in which the characters deliver their narratives as they accompany a woman's dying request to have her body taken for burial to her home town in the deep South.[3] David Malcolm convincingly argues that Swift's use of intertextuality in *Last Orders* (there are also obvious allusions to T.S. Eliot's *The Waste Land* and Chaucer's *Canterbury Tales*[4]) works to "dignify the lower-class milieu and characters," as well as suggesting "that there is, at some level, a culture that is shared between past and present, between the poorly educated and high art" (173). Swift has offered evidence for this interpretation when he said in interview, "I believe there is no such thing as an ordinary person, but everyone is extraordinary, everyone is unique, everyone has something special inside him, and so the challenge of writing about ordinary and common things is to show that" ("Graham Swift in Interview" 155).

Malcolm proceeds to argue that both Swift's use of monologues and intertextuality act metafictionally by drawing attention to the artifice Swift has employed in *Last Orders*. The novel is not intended to offer a realist or mimetic picture of working-class Bermondsey life in the second half of the twentieth century. Swift has created his own fictional world in which the absence of his usual self-conscious narrator is compensated for by his use of a distinctive set of voices that gesture toward but avoid direct imitation of working-class South London vernacular speech. Both his use of voice and of the literary convention of the interior monologue point to the controlling presence of the unseen narrator of these narrative voices. Swift has said that while the language used is that of South London he wasn't "interested in just transcribing that language." Rather than use lots of apostrophes and missing 'H's, the language he chose to use is "very selective" ("Glowing"). Among its distinctive features are repetition, cliché, and incomplete sentences. Swift says he uses repetition "to create a kind of language which is specific to the novel" ("An Interview" 221). His use of cliché and incomplete sentences illustrate how this operates. When Ray is attempting to repair his relations with Carol after Sue has left them they hear that her father has died suddenly: "Never rains but," Ray remarks (59). The use of the proverb offers Ray the consolation that he is not alone in feeling that disaster is pouring (the omitted word) on him. When Amy is saying her last farewell to June by telling her that she won't ever be returning and that June's father is dead, her last word to June is an incomplete sentence. The fact that she cannot complete this last piece of news gives powerful narrative expression to the extent to which she is upset beneath the surface at Jack's death:

> It won't mean anything to you but someone's got to tell you, no one else is going to. That your daddy, who never came to see you, who you never knew because he never wanted to know you, that your daddy (278).

Repetition ("your daddy," "never") and incompletion combine forces with great economy and force. The broken-off last sentence ends her speech as abruptly as his death ended Jack's life. Swift uses the same combination of repetition and an incomplete sentence to end the section in which Vince rushes off to Wick's Field where his parents met and scatters some of Jack's ashes there. His failure to explain his action to the others gives added impact to the effect of his words on the reader: "'This is where,' he says, wiping his face. 'This is where'" (151).

Swift has also pointed out to interviewers that he has allowed "the characters the opportunity to express thoughts that they would certainly have, but perhaps would not be able to put into words" ("Glowing"). This non-realist literary device (already employed in *Money* by Amis who himself borrowed it from Bellow in *Henderson the Rain King*) has the realist effect of revealing the inner feelings of people that are not necessarily ever expressed in words. Swift is referring to a much broader expression of inarticulate consciousness than what Lukács called "ascribed class consciousness," by which he meant "the ideas, sentiments, etc., which men . . . would have, if they were able to grasp in its entirety [their] situation . . . " (Lukács, qtd. in Hobsbawm 127). Beneath the language of class lies the inarticulate language of universal human feelings. Swift is stripping language bare in order to strip bare the inner being of his characters whose class otherwise confines their vocabulary to the colloquial and everyday. As he points out "articulate language, sophisticated language" is "a system of protection" ("Glowing"). In *Last Orders*, he has said, "I want to do less to achieve more" ("An Interview" 221). In creating a world in which all the characters share a similar pared down language pattern, Swift is offering a linguistic community which communicates just as effectively and meaningfully as does the intellectual and articulate community presented in *Ever After.* Winnberg may have a point when he claims that *Last Orders*, seen in this perspective, is "a reaffirmation of the communal and intersubjective over and against the individual and subjective" (162).

"Stories," Swift has said, "are on the side of life . . . even when they're about death." In fact, he explains, *Last Orders* is "about death in order to be about life" ("I Hope"). I would argue that the novel takes the reader on a journey from seeing a group of individuals whose conditioning by class and gender is partly responsible for their isolation and mutual misunderstanding to a finale in which they lose their sense of separateness to merge into a common identity, one which shares a common feeling of living life in the midst of death, of death being a part of life. They narrate stories to themselves as a way of countering the entropy of life. Each of their monologues is, Swift says, "a defence against time, a glow against dark" ("I Hope"). Jack's death finally compensates for his failure to meet his obligations to others, especially his family, in life, while it simultaneously pressures the living to change. The journey which constitutes the four men's act of mourning compels them to mourn their own denials of life in the past, to recognize the deadly nature of the stasis they have settled for, even if much of it has been the consequence of the age they have lived through and the restrictions of England's class culture. The destination of their journey is both tawdry and elemental: "One way there's Margate and Dreamland, the other there's the open sea" (292). The destination evokes a potential beginning which fifty years before Jack turned into an ending. So he sends his friends back in order to have the choice of going forward. In the last long sentence of the book when the four men scatter Jack's ashes in the wind off the pier and Jack becomes one with the wind, the four of them who are "made of" Jack are reminded that they too are part of the elements and part of the continuum between the living and the dead.

Lists of Books Published

Fiction

The Sweet-Shop Owner, 1980.
Shuttlecock, 1981.
Learning to Swim and Other Stories, 1982.
Waterland, 1983.
Out of this World, 1988.
Ever After, 1992.
Last Orders, 1996.
The Light of Day, 2003.

Non-Fiction

The Magic Wheel: An Anthology of Fishing in Literature, co-ed. with David Profumo, 1985.

Notes

Introduction

1. Since 1820 Argentina had claimed the Falkland Islands which lay some 300 miles east of the Argentine coast in the Atlantic. They became a British dependency after being seized by Britain in 1833. In April 1982 the Argentine military junta under General Galtieri invaded and occupied the islands. Margaret Thatcher sent a British task force to recapture the islands. By June the British force had retaken the islands. A thousand British and Argentine troops died fighting over the right of eighteen hundred inhabitants to continue living there under British protection. The outcome ensured the reelection of Mrs Thatcher and her Conservative party in 1983 and the resignation of General Galtieri followed by the restoration of democracy to Argentina.

2. Jean-François Lyotard published *La condition postmoderne* in 1979, translated by Geoff Bennington and Brian Massumi as *The Postmodern Condition: A Report on Knowledge* (U of Minnesota P, 1984). In it he argued that "general human emancipation" could not be achieved through the grand narratives originating with the Enlightenment. They had been invoked to justify the Soviet gulags and the Holocaust. Allegiance to a universal narrative or standard entails hostility to and violence against those who differ from it. Lyotard therefore championed a respect for diversity, for local differences, and for *petits* rather than for *grands récits* (small rather than grand narratives).

3. Had I had more space, I would have included in this book three more chapters on *Renegade or Halo²* (1999) by Timothy Mo and *White Teeth* by Zadie Smith in the second section, and on *Great Apes* (1997) by Will Self in the third section. I will make available the essays on Self and Mo on my web site at: http://www.csulb.edu/ ~bhfinney, and intend to publish an essay on Smith in a scholarly journal.

4. Émile Henriot coined the term *nouveau roman* (meaning literally new novel) in an article in *Le Monde* on May 22, 1957 to describe a group of French writers who surfaced in the 1950s and who experimented with a new style in each new novel. The authors included Michel Butor, Marguerite Duras, Robert Pinget, Alain Robbe-Grillet, Nathalie Sarraute, Claude Simon, and Phillipe Sollers. In *Pour un nouveau roman* [For a New Novel] (1963) Robbe-Grillet argues that the traditional novel creates an illusion of order and significance which fails to correspond to the radically discontinuous nature of modern experience. The aim of the *nouveau roman* is to avoid offering any determinate meaning, placing the reader as the arbiter of meaning and significance.

Part I   Preface

1. Scanlan is quoting here from Hans Vilmar Geppert, *Der "andere" historische Roman: Theorie und Strukturen einer diskontinuierlichen Gattung* (Tübingen: Max Niemeyer, 1976): 1.

1   Peter Ackroyd: *Chatterton* (1987)

1. In his book of that name, Bloom claims that among poets "the anxiety of influence is strongest where poetry is most lyrical, most subjective, and stemming directly from the personality" (62). Bloom sees the strong poet in precisely the terms that Ackroyd condemned in *Notes*. The strong poet's "Word, his imaginative identity, his whole being," according to Bloom, "*must* be unique to him, and remain unique, or he will perish as a poet" (71). To create a space for his or her own uniqueness, Bloom argues, each new writer is forced to misread his literary forbears, to deny his or her indebtedness to the past. See Harold Bloom, *The Anxiety of Influence: A Theory of Poetry* (New York: Oxford UP, 1973).
2. Susana Onega comments in a footnote that Chapter 8 of *Betrayals* narrates "a complex game of appropriations . . . that is strongly reminiscent of Harriet Scrope's and Harrison Bentley's appropriation of Ackroyd's plots and titles." See also Susana Onega, "Textual Selves/Worlds and the Treacherous Nature of Writing: A Misreading of Charles Palliser's *Betrayals*," *Alfinge* 9: 317–32.
3. See Patrick McGrath, "Peter Ackroyd," interview with Patrick McGrath, *Bomb* 26 (1988–89): 45. In the same interview Ackroyd claims to have pillaged Dyer's voice in *Hawksmoor* from some three hundred books from the eighteenth century that he had read in the British Museum: "He doesn't really exist as a character—he's just a little patchwork figure, like his author" (44).
4. I am partly indebted to a passage in Gibson and Worsley's *Peter Ackroyd: The Ludic and Labyrinthine Text* (2000), pp. 132–34 for the discussion of the role death plays in *Chatterton* and for Derrida's connection of the trace with absence and death.

2   Julian Barnes: *A History of the World in 10 1/2 Chapters* (1989)

1. The Whig version of history is epitomized by Thomas Macaulay's *History of England from the Accession of James II* (1849, 1855, 1861). He interprets British history as the gradual and inevitable triumph of the Whig party's views on the supremacy of parliamentary power over the Crown's desire for autocratic rule. The phrase was coined by the British historian Herbert Butterfield in *The Whig Interpretation of History* (1931).
2. Leopold von Ranke (1795–1886) His first book, *History of the Latin and Teutonic Nations, 1494–1514* (1824), included an appended section, "Critique of Modern Historical Writing," in which he proposed to reconstruct the past as it actually was and to avoid interpreting the history of former times in the light of the present. This form of historiography is called historicism. As a historian, Ranke attempted to discount the bias of contemporary theories and by strictly adhering to primary sources to give a straight account of the facts. Because he considered that political power was the principal agent in history, he produced political histories that focused on the deeds of kings and leaders.
3. In an "Author's Note" at the end of the novel Barnes states that this chapter "is based on legal procedures and actual cases described in *The Criminal Prosecution and Capital Punishment of Animals* by E. P. Evans (1906)." Published by William Heinemann in London, Evans's book on inspection contains no reference to a case at Besançon. It does describe the legal career of one of the most successful defenders of animals in sixteenth century France, Bartholomew Chassenée, who made his reputation as a jurist defending rats in the ecclesiastical court of Autun. Chassenée is the only participant in Barnes's fictional court case to be named. Evans's book

also cites a case from the seventeenth century in which Franciscan friars in Brazil prosecuted termites in ecclesiastical court and threatened them with excommunication. The book also contains a large number of appendices reproducing original documents in Latin and French from legal proceedings against animals.

4. I assume that Michael Dirda has in mind the episode, "A Nice Place to Visit" (originally aired 4/15/1960), in which, while committing a crime, Valentine, a cheap hood played by Larry Blyden, gets killed and finds himself in an afterlife in which all wishes are granted. He is attended by Pip, a helper played by Sebastion Cabot. But heaven turns out to be the other place.

5. Michiko Kakutani called it "a 'novel' that reads like a hodgepodge of non sequiturs." ("A Cast of Characters Afloat on History's Indifferent Sea," *New York Times* 29 Sep. 1989, late ed.: C 33). Joyce Carol Oates called it "a collection of prose pieces." ("But Noah Was Not a Nice Man," *New York Times Book Review* 1 Oct. 1989: 12) Mark Lawson calls the author of *A History* "a brilliant essayist." ("A Short History of Julian Barnes," *Independent Magazine* 13 July 1991: 36) On the other hand Robert Adams sees it as "a novel in deep disguise" (*New York Review of Books* 26 Oct. 1989: 7), and Michael Wood declared, "Barnes is not an essayist who writes novels, but a novelist who uses his imagination as an instrument of thought" (*Times Literary Supplement* 30 June–6 July 1989: 713).

3 Martin Amis: *Time's Arrow or, the Nature of the Offense* (1991)

1. In an interview in 2002 Amis said of postmodernism, "I always thought it was kind of a dead end, as it's proved to be, but I thought there were comic possibilities in postmodernism that I hadn't exploited much." He adds that postmodernism is now played out, although it is "a theory or an idea with tremendous predictive power, because life became very postmodern, politics became postmodern" (Reynolds and Noakes 16–17).

2. As has been frequently pointed out, there are other precedents for narratives that have been told backwards. James Diedrick lists the following: Lewis Carrol's *Sylvie and Bruno* and the White Queen's claim to live backwards in *Alice's Adventures in Wonderland*; Jean Cocteau's *Le Testament d'Orphée*; Brian Aldiss's *An Age*; Philip K. Dick's *Counter-Clock World*; F. Scott Fitzgerald's "The Curious Case of Benjamin Button"; and J. G. Ballard's "Mr F is Mr F" (264–65). There are also Alejo Carpentier's *Viaje a la Semilla*, Carlos Fuentes' *Aura*, and Harold Pinter's play, *Betrayal*.
   In the Afterword Amis also refers to "Jachid and Jechidah," a story by Isaac Bashevis Singer in which an angel is sentenced to death and begins with her descent "to that cemetery called Earth." *Short Friday and Other Stories* (New York: Farrar, Straus and Giroux, 1964): 82.

3. The novel perversely reverses A.S. Eddington's image of the second law of thermodynamics (imaged as time's arrow) thereby seemingly defeating the force of entropy that characterizes the movement of history. See Richard Menke's fine essay, "Narrative Reversals and the Thermodynamics of History in Martin Amis's *Time's Arrow*" listed in Works Cited.

4. Instance the case of Prince Harry of England who attended a birthday party in January 2005 wearing a Nazi uniform and swastika. "'The whole event, the prince's choice of costume included, indicates a worrying trend of ignorance about the Holocaust that is reinforced by the results of a recent survey that 45percent of UK. residents have never heard of Auschwitz,' said a spokesman for the Board of Deputies of British Jews." John Daniszewski, "Critics Say the Prince Wore His

Ignorance on His Sleeve" (*Los Angeles Times* 14 Jan. 2005: A8). Cf. Amis's visit to Auschwitz in 1995 where his guide told him that "We now have people coming here . . . who think that all this has been constructed to deceive them. Not just from Germany. From Holland, from Scandinavia. They believe that nothing happened here and the Holocaust is a myth" (*Experience* 369).

4   A. S. Byatt: *Angels and Insects* (1992)

1. The term "retro-Victorian novel" was first coined by Sally Shuttleworth in "Natural History: The Retro-Victorian Novel" in *The Third Culture: Literature and Science*, ed. Elinor S. Shaffer (Berlin: Walter de Gruyter, 1997).
2. June Sturrock makes a similar observation as part of an argument about the nature of analogy in "Morpho Eugenia." See June Sturrock, "Angels, Insects and Analogy: A. S. Byatt's 'Morpho Eugenia'" (*Connotations* 12.1 (2003): 99).
3. The Glossary to Bakhtin's *The Dialogic Imagination*, ed. Michael Holquist (Austin: U of Texas P, 1981) defines "dialogism" as "the characteristic epistemological mode of a world dominated by heteroglossia. Everything means, is understood, as a part of the greater whole—there is a constant interaction between meanings, all of which have the potential of conditioning others" (426).

5   Ian McEwan: *Atonement* (2001)

1. Henry Perowne reads this sentence in Fred Halliday's *Two Hours That Shook the World* (2002).
2. Intertextuality is a term Julia Kristeva coined from her reading of Mikhail Bakhtin. As she argues in *Revolution in Poetic Language*, "If one grants that every signifying practice is a field of transpositions of various signifying systems (an intertextuality), one then understands that its 'place' of enunciation and its denoted 'object' are never single, complete and identical to themselves, but always plural, shattered . . ." (111). Kristeva claims that all texts are composites of other signifying systems, not the end product of a number of discernible sources. In "From Work to Text" Roland Barthes explains: "to try to find the 'sources', the 'influences' of a work is to fall in with the myth of filiation; the citations which go to make up a text are anonymous, untraceable, and yet *already read:* they are quotations without inverted commas" (*Image – Music – Text* 160). Derrida argues: "To write is to produce a mark that will constitute a sort of machine which is productive in turn" Signature Event Context. Trans. Samuel Webber and Jeffrey Mehlman. *Glyph* 1 (1997): 180.
3. In his ground-breaking "Discours du récit" (in *Figures III*, Paris: Seuil, 1972, *Narrative Discourse*, trans. Jane E Lewin, Ithaca: Cornell UP, 1980) Gérard Genette distinguishes three major categories for the study of narrative—tense, mood, and voice. By distinguishing between narrative perspective or focalization (who sees the story) and narrative voice (who recounts the story), he was able to expose the way the previous use of "point of view" was confusing because it failed to distinguish between focus and voice. He goes on (189–90) to differentiate narrative with zero focalization (cf. the omniscient narrator), from narrative with internal focalization which itself can be fixed (one focal character), variable (more than one focal character taking turns), multiple (the same event focalized from successive characters' perspectives), and from external focalization (where no character is permitted to know his or her own thoughts).

4. To distinguish the narrating subject from the subject of narration, Emile Benveniste posited in *Problems in General Linguistics* that narration falls along "two different planes of utterance." When narration calls attention to its act of narration as an "utterance assuming a speaker and a hearer," with the speaker attempting to influence the hearer in some fashion, it functions as *discourse*. When, however, "events that took place at a certain moment of time are presented without any intervention of the speaker," the narration functions as *histoire*. Benveniste 206–209.

5. In his interview with Adam Begley for *The Paris Review* 162 (2002): 31–60, McEwan said that in an earlier draft he wrote a biographical note for inclusion at the end of the book, which read as follows: "About the author: Briony Tallis was born in Surrey in 1922, the daughter of a senior civil servant. She attended Roedean School, and in 1940 trained to become a nurse. Her wartime nursing experience provided the material for her first novel, *Alice Riding*, published in 1948 and winner of that year's Fitzrovia Prize for fiction. Her second novel, *Soho Solstice*, was praised by Elizabeth Bowen as "a dark gem of psychological acuity," while Graham Greene described her as "one of the more interesting talents to have emerged since the war." Other novels and short-story collections consolidated her reputation during the fifties. In 1962 she published *A Barn in Steventon*, a study of domestic theatricals in Jane Austen's childhood. Tallis's sixth novel, *The Ducking Stool*, was a best-seller in 1965 and was made into a successful film starring Julie Christie. Thereafter, Briony Tallis's reputation went into a decline, until the Virago imprint made her work available to a younger generation in the late seventies. She died in July 2001."

6. See Sigmund Freud, "Creative Writers and Daydreaming," 1908, (*The Standard Edition of the Complete Psychological Works*, London: Hogarth, 1940–68, Vol. 9) where he claims to recognize in every hero in the fictional work of imaginative writers "His Majesty the Ego, the hero alike of every day-dream and every story" (143).

Part II   Preface

1. See Pierre Nora, "Between memory and History: Les Lieux de Memoire," trans. Marc Roudebush, *Representations* 26 (1989): 7–25.

6   Salman Rushdie: *The Satanic Verses* (1988)

1. "Iblis" comes from the Greek *diabolos*, "the slanderer," the name of the rebel angel/devil in the Qur'an. "Shaitan" is the Muslim (Arabic) name for the Jewish/Christian Satan ("Notes for Salman Rushdie: *The Satanic Verses*," by Paul Brians (<http://www.wsu.edu/~brians/anglophone/satanic_verses/contents.html>).

2. The Lawrence Inquiry by Sir William Macpherson reported on February 24, 1999 on the failure of the police to successfully prosecute the known white murderers of Stephen Lawrence, a black youth, in April 1993. The inquiry found that institutional racism was partly responsible for the bungled murder investigation by the Metropolitan Police Service and accepted the submission by the Commission for Racial Equality that institutional racism existed in other police services and other institutions.

3. The Bharatiya Janata party (Hindi for Indian People's party) or BJP drew its philosophy from the Rashtriya Swayamsevak Sangh, a group dedicated to the spread of orthodox Hindu religion and opposed to Mohandas Gandhi's secular philosophy. The BJP was formed in 1980 and first made its mark in 1909 when it won 85 seats in the Indian parliament. In the 1996 general elections it won 161 of the 545

parliamentary seats but fell short of a majority. The BJP again obtained the largest number of parliamentary seats in the 1998 and 1999 elections and successfully formed governments with Atal Bihari Vajpayee as prime minister. The party lost the 2004 elections to the Congress party coalition.

7   Hanif Kureishi: *The Buddha of Suburbia* (1990)

1. In "DissemiNation" Homi Bhabha argues that national identity is produced "within a range of discourses as a double narrative movement." The nation's people "are the historical 'objects' of a nationalist pedagogy, giving the discourse an authority that is based on the pre-given or constituted historical origin *in the past*; the people are also the 'subjects' of a process that must erase any prior or originary presence of the nation-people to demonstrate the prodigious, living principles of the people as contemporaneity" (*The Location of Culture* 145).
2. Is Shadwell intended to be an ironic allusion to Thomas Shadwell (ca. 1642–92), Restoration dramatist and poetaster? John Dryden in his poetic lampoon, *MacFlecknoe* (1682), made Shadwell the new Prince of the Realms of Nonsense, the "last great Prophet of Tautology," destined to "wage immortal War with Wit."
3. As Mooore-Gilbert suggests in a footnote, this charge of conflating race within the over-arching category of class is first leveled by Fanon in *Black Skin, White Masks*. It is subsequently taken up by Stuart Hall who in "Race, Articulation, and Societies Structured in Dominance" (1980) argues that Marxist reduction of the relations of dominance and subordination to the mode of production and class conflict failed to account for the way race entered into and complicated such relations. Homi Bhabha and Paul Gilroy further developed this critique of Marxist reductionism.

8   Kazuo Ishiguro: *When We Were Orphans* (2000)

1. Following the Sino-British Opium War of 1842 China was forced to open certain "treaty ports" including Shanghai to Western trade. In 1848 the United States set up its concession, followed by France in 1849. In 1863 the British and American concessions were amalgamated to become the International Settlement. On August 13, 1937 Japanese troops attacked the Chinese part of Shanghai and after three months' fighting occupied it at the cost of some 300,000 Chinese lives. After Pearl Harbor (December 7, 1941) the foreign zones were occupied by the Japanese. At the end of World War II the entire city was restored to the Chinese. In 1949 it fell to the Communist forces.
2. In 1923 Freud renamed what he had called the "ego-ideal" the superego, which he held responsible for secondary repression. The superego arises as the last of the great primal repressions which makes secondary or psychological repression possible. See pages 3–59 of Freud's "The Ego and the Id." Vol. 19 of *The Standard Edition of the Complete Psychological Works of Sigmund Freud.* 24 vols. Trans. James Strachey. London: Hogarth, 1953–74.

Part III   Preface.

1. In fact the term "subject" takes on a wide range of meanings. Agnes Heller lists an entire paragraph of them in "Death of the Subject?" *Constructions of the Self* (1992): 269–84.

9   Angela Carter: *Nights at the Circus* (1984)

1. See for instance, Rachel Billington, "Beware Women," *Financial Times*, 31 March 1979; Ann Oakley (in Works Cited); Julia O'Faolain, "Chamber Music," *London Magazine*, Aug./Sep. 1979; Sara Maitland, Review of *The Sadeian Woman*, *Time Out*, 4 May 1979.
2. Algirdas Julien Greimas, a narratologist, first employed the term *actant* in *Sémantique structurale* (1966). Following the precedent established by Vladimir Propp in *Morphology of the Folktale* (originally published in Russian 1928), Greimas adopted the term *actant* to emphasize the subordination of characters to action. Greimas posited the possibility of only six *actants* or narrative categories (such as sender, receiver) which can be occupied by any number of *acteurs*.
3. The Panopticon was proposed as a model prison by Jeremy Bentham (1748–1832), a Utilitarian philosopher and theorist of British legal reform, in *The Panopticon Writings* (1791), ed. Miran Bozovic (London: Verso, 1995) pp. 29–95. The Panopticon ("all-seeing") functioned as a non-stop surveillance device. Its design ensured that no prisoner could ever see the "inspector" who conducted surveillance from the privileged central location within the radial configuration. The prisoner could never know when (s)he was being observed—mental uncertainty that constituted a crucial instrument of discipline. According to Foucault, the new visibility or surveillance afforded by the Panopticon was of two types: the synoptic and the analytic. The Panopticon, in other words, was designed to ensure a "surveillance which would be both global and individualizing" (*Power/Knowledge*, ed. C Gordon, Brighton: Harvester, 1980, p. 148).

10   Jeanette Winterson: *Written on the Body* (1993)

1. Only one reviewer, Walter Kendrick, has chosen to identify the narrator as male. He argues unconvincingly that "he [the narrator] broadcasts his current affairs without hesitation, even to near-strangers; it's difficult to imagine that such love is not heterosexual" (131). See Walter Kendrick, "Fiction in Review," *Yale Review* 81 (1993): 131–33.
2. See, for example, Carolyn Allen, *Following Djuna: Women Lovers and the Erotics of Loss* (Bloomington: Indiana UP, 1996). Alison Booth, "The Scent of a Narrative: Rank Discourse in *Flush* and *Written on the Body*," *Narrative* 8.1 (2000): 18. Patricia Duncker, "Jeanette Winterson and the Aftermath of Feminism," *"I'm telling you stories": Jeanette Winterson and the Politics of Reading*, ed. Helena Grice and Tim Woods (Atlanta, GA: Rodopi, 1998): 77–88. Leigh Gilmore, "An Anatomy of Absence," *The Gay 90's*, ed. Thomas Foster et al. (New York: New York UP, 1997): 224–51. Michael Hardin, "Dissolving the Reader/Author Binary: Sylvia Molloy's *Certificate of Absence*, Helena Parente Cunha's *Woman Between Mirrors*, and Jeanette Winterson's *Written on the Body*," *International Fiction Review* 29 (2002): 88. Andrea Harris, *Other Sexes: Rewriting Difference from Woolf to Winterson* (Albany, New York: State U of New York P, 2000). Heather Nunn, "*Written on the Body*: An Anatomy of Horror, Melancholy and Love," *Women* 70 (1996): 16–27. Ute Kauer, "Narration and Gender: The Role of the First-Person Narrator in Jeanette Winterson's *Written on the Body*," Grice and Woods 40–51. Sarah Schulman, "Guilty with Explanation: Jeanette Winterson's Endearing Book of Love," *Lambda Book Review* 3.9 (1993): 20. Celia Shiffer, "'You see, I am no stranger to love': Jeanette Winterson and the Ecstasy of the Word," *Critique: Studies in Contemporary Fiction* 46.1 (2004): 50. Christy R. Stevens, "Imagining

Deregulated Desire," 27 July 2000 <http://www.ags.uci.edu/~clowegsa/evolutions/
Stevens.htm>. Cath Stowers, "Journeying with Jeanette," *(Hetero)sexual Politics*, ed.
Mary Maynard and June Purvis (London: Taylor & Francis, 1995): 139–58.

11   Graham Swift: *Last Orders* (1996)

1. National service in the British armed forces began in 1939 and ended in 1963.
   Vince signed up for 5 years "just when every kid his age was thanking sweet Jesus
   there wasn't no call-up no more" (44). He was also "one of the last troops to clear
   out of Aden" (69). This makes it hard to date his five years of service as Aden ceased
   to be a British colony in 1967.
2. *Last Orders* consists of 75 monologues divided between 7 characters. Ray narrates
   all 17 sections headed with place names as well as 22 under his own name. Vince
   narrates 12, Lenny and Vic 8 each, Amy 5, and Mandy and Jack 1 each.
3. The *Independent on Sunday* raised a storm in a teacup on March 9, 1997 when it pub-
   licized the absurd accusation leveled against *Last Orders* by an Australian literature
   professor, John Frow, that it was a "direct and unacknowledged imitation" of
   Faulkner's *As I Lay Dying*. A week later he modified his charge to one of "inert borrowing" (*Independent* 16 March 1997). A. N. Wilson, one of the judges awarding *Last
   Orders* the Booker Prize that year wrote to the *Independent* that had the judges been
   aware of "the Australian's devastating critique of *Last Orders*" the prize would have
   been awarded to Margaret Atwood, the runner-up (16 March 1997). Swift wrote in
   the same issue of the *Independent* expressing bemusement with the furor following
   such absurd charges, and Kazuo Ishiguro also wrote in defense of Swift's right to
   write a book about death without being accused of virtual plagiarism by "a reader
   devoid of sophistication." Salman Rushdie also repudiated the charges in a letter to
   the *Guardian* on March 14, 1997, as did virtually every other commentator including Jan Dalley, literary editor of the *Independent on Sunday*.
4. Allusions to T.S. Eliot's *The Waste Land* include the title, *Last Orders*, which anticipates
   the final call of publicans, "HURRY UP PLEASE ITS TIME" which occurs five times in
   the final stanza of "I. A Game of Chess"; Margate's Dreamland which parallels Eliot's
   Waste Land; and the novel's finale in Margate which both evokes the song of the
   third Thames daughter in "III. The Fire Sermon": "On Margate Sands./I can con-
   nect/Nothing with nothing" (lines 300–302), and which ends with the four men casting Jack's ashes to the wind in handfuls which is reminiscent of Eliot's "handful of
   dust" in line 30 of "I. The Burial of the Dead." Like Chaucer's *Canterbury Tales*, *Last
   Orders* has its modern pilgrims journeying to Canterbury Cathedral (and beyond) in
   April and telling stories along the way (though to themselves).

Bibliography

Ackroyd, Peter. *Albion: Origins of the English Imagination*. New York: Nan A. Talese/ Doubleday, 2003.

———. *Chatterton*. New York: Random House, 1989.

———. *The Collection*. Ed. Thomas Wright. London: Chatto & Windus, 2001.

———. *English Music*. New York: Knopf, 1992.

———. "Imagining the Labyrinth: A Conversation with Peter Ackroyd." Interview with Julian Wolfreys. *Interdisciplinary Literary Studies* 1.1 (1999): 97–114.

———. Interview. *Contemporary Authors* 127 (1989): 3–5.

———. Interview with Susana Onega. *Twentieth Century Literature* 42.2 (1996): 208–20.

———. *The Last Testament of Oscar Wilde*. New York: Harper & Row, 1983.

———. *London: The Biography*. New York: Nan A. Talese/Doubleday, 2001.

———. *Notes for a New Culture. An Essay on Modernism*. London: Vision P, 1976. Rev. ed. London: Alkin Books, 1993.

———. "Peter Ackroyd." Interview with Patrick McGrath. *BOMB* 26 (1988–89): 44–47.

———. "Peter Ackroyd." Interview with Amanda Smith. *Publishers Weekly* 1987: 59–60.

Acocella, Joan. "The Third Way." Rev. of *When We Were Orphans*, by Kazuo Ishiguro. *New Yorker* 11 Sep. 2000: 95.

Adorno, Theodor. "Cultural Criticism and Society." *Prisms*. Trans. Samuel and Shierry Weber. Cambridge, MA: MIT P, 1981.

Ali, Omer. "The Ages of Sin." Rev. of *Atonement*, by Ian McEwan, and Interview. *Time Out* 26 Sep. 2001: 59.

Althusser, Louis. *Lenin and Philosophy and Other Essays*. Trans. Ben Brewster. New York: Pantheon, 1969.

Amis, Martin. "Down London's Mean Streets." Interview with Mira Stout. *New York Times Magazine* 4 Feb. 1990: 32–36, 48.

———. *Einstein's Monsters*. New York: Vintage/Random, 1987.

———. *Experience: A Memoir*. New York: Talk Miramax/Hyperion, 2000.

———. Interview with Melvyn Bragg. *The South Bank Show*. London Weekend Television. 1989.

———. Interview with Patrick McGrath. *BOMB* 18 (Winter 1987): 26–29. Rpt. In *BOMB Interviews*. Ed. Betsy Sussler. San Francisco: City Light Books, 1992. 187–97.

———. "Jane's World." *New Yorker* 8 Jan. 1996: 31–35.

———. *Koba the Dread: Laughter and the Twenty Million*. New York: Vintage/Random, 2002.

——. "Martin Amis." Interview with Amanda Smith. *Publishers Weekly* 8 Feb. 1985: 79.

——. "The Sublime and the Ridiculous: Nabokov's Black Farces." *Vladimir Nabokov: His Life, His Work, His World: A Tribute.* Ed. Peter Quennell. New York: Morrow, 1980.

——. *Time's Arrow, or, The Nature of the Offense.* New York: Harmony, 1991.

——. "Unlike Father, Like Son. An Interview with Martin Amis." Interview with Carl and John Bellante. *The Bloomsbury Review* 12.2 (1992): 4–5, 16.

——. *The War Against Cliché: Essays and Reviews 1971–2000.* New York: Vintage, 2001.

——. "Window on a Changed World." *Daily Telegraph* 11 Sep. 2002: 17.

——. "The Wit and the Fury of Martin Amis." Interview with Susan Morrison. *Rolling Stone* 17 May 1990: 95–102.

Anderson, Benedict. *Imagined Communities: Reflections on the Origin and Spread of Nationalism.* Rev. ed. London, New York: Verso, 1991.

Auden, W. H. *The Dyer's Hand and Other Essays.* New York: Random House, 1962.

Ball, John Clement. "'A City Visible But Unseen': The (Un)Realities of London in South Asian Fiction." *Journal of Comparative Literature and Aesthetics* 21.1–2 (1998): 67–82.

——. *Imagining London: Postcolonial Fiction and the Transnational Metropolis.* Toronto: U of Toronto P, 2004.

Barnes, Julian. *Arthur and George.* London: Cape, 2005.

——. *Cross Channel.* New York: Vintage, 1996.

——. *Flaubert's Parrot.* New York: McGraw-Hill, 1985.

——. "From Flaubert's Parrot to Noah's Woodworm." Interview with Kate Saunders. *Sunday Times* (London) 18 June 1989: G8–9.

——. *A History of the World in 10 1/2 Chapters.* New York: Vintage/Random House, 1989.

——. Interview with Patrick McGrath. *BOMB* 18–21 (1987): 20–23.

——. "Julian Barnes," Interview with Amanda Smith. *Publishers Weekly* 3 November 1989: 73–74.

——. *The Lemon Table: Stories.* New York: Knopf, 2004.

——. *Letters from London.* New York: Vintage, 1995.

——. "A Talk With Julian Barnes." Interview with Alexander Stuart. *Los Angeles Times Book Review* 15 Oct 1989: 15.

——. "The World According to Julian Barnes." Interview with Gayle Kidder. *San Diego Union-Tribune* 5 Nov. 1989: E-1.

Barthes, Roland. *Critical Essays.* Trans. Richard Howard. Evanston: Northwestern UP, 1972.

——. "The Discourse of History." Trans. Stephen Bann. *Comparative Criticism: A Yearbook.* Vol. 3. Ed. E. S. Shaffer. Cambridge UP, 1981. 7–20.

——. "From Work to Text." *Image – Music – Text.* Trans. Stephen Heath. New York: Hill, 1977. 155–64.

——."Ant Heaps and Novelists." *Salon Interview.* 20 Aug. 2005<http://www.Salon.com/08/departments/litchat.html>.

Batsleer, Janet, Tony Davies, Rebecca O'Rourke, and Chris Weedon. *Rewriting English: Cultural Politics of Gender and Class.* London: Methuen, 1985.

Baucom, Ian. *Out of Place: Englishness, Empire and the Locations of Identity.* Princeton, NJ: Princeton UP, 1999.

Bauman, Zygmunt, *Modernity and the Holocaust.* Oxford: Polity P, 1989.

BBC News. 18 May 2004. 4 Aug. 2004 <http://news.bbc.co.uk/1/hi/uk/3725801.stm>.

Bell, Ian, ed. *Peripheral Visions: Images of Nationhood in Contemporary British Fiction.* Cardiff: U of Wales P, 1995.

Belsey, Catherine. *Critical Practice*. London and New York: Methuen, 1980.

Benjamin, Walter. *Illuminations*. Ed. Hannah Arendt. Trans. Harry Zohn. New York: Schocken, 1969.

———. "N [Re the Theory of Knowledge, Theory of Progress]." Trans. Leigh Hafrey and Richard Sieburth, *Benjamin: Philosophy, History, Aesthetics*. Ed. Gary Smith. Chicago: U of Chicago P, 1989. 43–83.

Benveniste, Emile. *Problems in General Linguistics*. Trans. Elizabeth Meek. Coral Gables: U of Miami P, 1971.

Bertens, Hans. *The Idea of the Postmodern: A History*. London and New York: Routledge, 1995.

Bevan, David. "Images of Indian Exile in Rushdie's *The Satanic Verses* and Ruth Prawer Jhabvala's *Three Continents*." *Literature and Exile*. Ed. David Bevan. Amsterdam/ Atlanta: Rodopi, 1990. 7–21.

Bhabha, Homi. "Culture's In-Between." *Questions of Cultural Identity*. Ed. Stuart Hall and Paul de Gay. London: Sage, 1996. 53–60.

———. *The Location of Culture*. London, New York: Routledge, 1994.

Bigsby, Christopher. "The Uneasy Middleground of English Fiction." *Granta* 3 (1980): 137–49.

Blair, Tony. *New Britain: My Vision of a Young Country*. Boulder, CO: Westview P, 1997.

Helene Bengtson, Marianne Børch, and Cindie Maagaard, eds. *Sponsored by Demons: The Art of Jeanette Winterson*. Agedrup, Denmark: Scholars' P, 1999. 41–54.

Börner, Klaus H. "Salman Rushdie, *The Satanic Verses*: Observations on Cultural Hybridity." *Anglistentag* (1994): 150–62.

Bourne, Bill, Udi Eichler, and David Herman, eds. *Voices: Writers and Politics*. Nottingham: Spokesman, 1987.

Bowers, Frederick. "An Irrelevant Parochialism." *Granta* 3 (1980): 150–54.

Brooke-Rose, Christine. *Between*. London: Michael Joseph, 1968.

———. "Ill Wit and Good Humour. Women's Comedy and the Canon." *Comparative Criticism* 10 (1988): 121–38.

Buford, Bill. "Introduction." *Granta* 1 (1979): 3–10.

———. "Introduction." *Granta* 3 (1980): 7–16.

Butler, Judith. *Bodies That Matter*. London and New York: Routledge, 1993.

———. *Gender Trouble: Feminism and the Subversion of Identity*. London and New York: Routledge, 1990.

Buxton, Jackie. "Julian Barnes' Theses on History (in 10 1/2 Chapters)." *Contemporary Literature* 41.1 (2000): 56–86.

Byatt, A. S. *Angels and Insects: Two Novellas*. New York: Vintage, 1992.

———. *Essays and Articles*. A. S. Byatt Web site. 9 Aug. 2004 <http://www.asbyatt.com/essays.html>.

———. Interview with Clive Collins. *Eigo seinen: The Rising Generation* 1 July 1999: 182–95.

———. Interview with Laura Miller. *Salon Interview*. 5 Aug. 2004 <http://www.salon.com/weekly/interview960617.html>.

———. "The Magic Brew of A.S. Byatt." Interview with Sarah Booth Conroy. *Washington Post* 29 Nov. 1991: D1.

———. *On Histories and Stories: Selected Essays*. New York: Vintage, 2001.

———. *Passions of the Mind: Selected Writings*. New York: Vintage, 1991.

———. *Possession: A Romance*. New York: Vintage, 1990.

———. "What Possessed A. S. Byatt?' Interview with Mira Stout. *New York Times Magazine* 26 May 1991: 12–15.

Calvino, Italo. *If on a winter's night a traveler*. New York: Harcourt Brace, 1979.

Cantle Report. Qtd. In *New York Times* 12 Dec. 2001: A3.

Carey, John. "Few Novels Extend the Possibilities of Fiction." Rev. of *When We Were Orphans*, by Kazuo Ishiguro. *Sunday Times* (London) 2 Apr. 2000, sec. 9: 45.

Carter, Angela. "Angela Carter." Interview with Helen Cagney Watts. *Bête Noire* Aug. 1985: 161–76.

———. "An Interview with Angela Carter." Interview with Anna Katsavos. *Review of Contemporary Fiction* 14.3 (1994): 11–17.

———. "I'm a Socialist, Damn It." Interview with Mary Harron. *Guardian* 25 Sep. 1984: 10.

———. *The Infernal Desire Machines of Doctor Hoffman*. Harmondsworth and New York: Penguin, 1982.

———. *Nights at the Circus*. London and New York: Penguin, 1986.

———. *The Sadeian Woman and the Ideology of Pornography*. New York: Pantheon, 1979.

———. *Shaking a Leg: Collected Journalism and Writings*. Ed. Jenny Uglow. London: Chatto & Windus, 1997.

———. "Sweet Smell of Excess." Interview with Ian McEwan. *Sunday Times Magazine* (London) 9 Sep. 1984: 42–44.

Childs, Peter. *Contemporary Novelists: British Fiction Since 1970*. Houndmills, Basingstoke, and New York: Palgrave Macmillan, 2005.

Clingham, Greg. "Chatterton, Ackroyd, and the Fiction of Eighteenth-Century Historiography." *Bucknell Review* 42.1 (1998): 35–58.

Connor, Steven. *The English Novel in History 1950–1995*. London and New York: Routledge, 1996.

Cooper, Pamela. *Graham Swift's Last Orders: A Reader's Guide*. New York: Continuum, 2002.

Cowley, Jason. "Telling Tale." Rev. of *Atonement*, by Ian McEwan. *Times* (London) 22 Sep. 2001, Play: 17.

Davenport, Gary. "The Novel of Despair." Rev. of *Last Orders*, by Graham Swift. *Sewanee Review* 105.3 (1997): 440–47.

DeCurtis, Anthony. "Britain's Mavericks." *Harper's Bazaar* Nov. 1991: 146–47.

Derrida, Jacques. "Afterword: Toward an Ethic of Discussion." Trans. Samuel Weber. *Limited Inc*. Evanston, IL: Northwestern UP, 1988. 111–60.

———. *Dissemination*. Trans. Barbara Johnson. Chicago: U of Chicago P, 1981.

———. *Of Grammatology*. Trans. Gayatri Chakravorty Spivak. Baltimore: Johns Hopkins UP, 1976.

———. "Signature Event Context.' Trans. Samuel Webber and Jeffrey Mehlman. *Glyph* 1 (1977): 172–97.

Diedrick, James. *Understanding Martin Amis*. 2nd ed. Columbia: U of South Carolina P, 2004.

Dirda, Michael. "Voyages on a Sea of Troubles." Rev. of *A History of the World in 10 1/2 Chapters*, by Julian Barnes. *Washington Post* 22 Oct 1989: X4.

Donne, John. *The Complete Poetry and Selected Prose of John Donne*. Ed. Charles M. Coffin. New York: Random House. 1994.

Duncker, Patricia. "Jeanette Winterson and the Aftermath of Feminism." Grice and Woods 77–88.

Dunn, Adam. "In the Land of Memory." *cnn.com Book News*. 27 Oct. 2000. 2 June 2001 <http://www.cnn.com/2000/books/news/10/27/kazuo.ishiguro>.

Dutheil, Martine Hennard. "The Epigraph to *The Satanic Verses*: Defoe's Devil and Rushdie's Migrant." *Southern Review* 30.1 (1997): 51–69.

Dworkin, Andrea. *Pornography: Men Possessing Women*. London: Women's P, 1981.

Eagleton, Terry. "A Beautiful and Elusive Tale." Rev. of *Atonement*, by Ian McEwan. *Lancet* 358.9299 (22–29 Dec. 2001): 2177.

———. *Figures of Dissent: Critical Essays on Fish, Spivak, Zizek and Others*. London and New York: Verso, 2003.

———. *Literary Theory: An Introduction*. 2nd ed. Minneapolis: U of Minnesota P, 1996.

Easterbrook, Neil. "'I know that it is to do with trash and shit, and that it is wrong in time': Narrative Reversal in Martin Amis' *Time's Arrow*." *Conference of College Teachers of Studies* 55 (1995): 52–61.

Easthope, Antony. *Englishness and National Culture*. London and New York: Routledge, 1999.

Ellmann, Richard. *Oscar Wilde*. New York: Alfred A. Knopf, 1988.

Engels, Friedrich. *The Condition of the Working Class in England*. 1845. 20 July 2005 <http://www.mdx.ac.uk/www/study/xeng1845.html>.

Fernihough, Anne. "'Is she fact or is she fiction?': Angela Carter and the Enigma of Woman." *Textual Practice* 11.1 (1997): 89–107.

Finney, Brian. "Demonizing Discourse in Salman Rushdie's *The Satanic Verses*." *ARIEL: A Review of International English Literature* 29.3 (1998): 67–93. Rpt. in *Salman Rushdie*. Ed. Harold Bloom. New York: Chelsea House, 2003. 185–208.

Fletcher, Judith. "The *Odyssey* Rewoven: A. S. Byatt's *Angels and Insects*." *Classical and Modern Literature* 19.3 (1999): 217–31.

Flint, Kate. "Looking Backwards? The Relevance of Britishness." *Unity in Diversity Revisited. British Literature and Culture in the 1990s*. Ed. Barbara Korte and Klaus Peter Müller. Tübingen: Gunter Narr Verlag, 1998. 35–50.

Foucault, Michel *The Archaeology of Knowledge*. Trans. A. M. Sheridan Smith. London: Tavistock, 1972.

———. *Discipline and Punish: The Birth of the Prison*. Trans. Alan Sheridan. New York: Vintage, 1979.

———. *The History of Sexuality*. Vol. 1. *An Introduction*. Trans. Robert Hurley. Harmondsworth, Middlesex: Penguin, 1984.

———. *Language, Counter-Memory, Practice: Selected Essays and Interviews*. Trans. Donald F. Bouchard and Sherry Simon. Ithaca, New York: Cornell UP, 1977.

———. *The Use of Pleasure. The History of Sexuality*. Vol. 2. Trans. Robert Hurley. New York, Vintage, 1990.

Fowles, John. *The French Lieutenant's Woman*. Boston: Little, Brown, 1969.

———. *Wormholes: Essays and Occasional Writings*. New York: Henry Holt, 1998.

Freud, Sigmund. *Beyond the Pleasure Principle*. Trans. James Strachey. New York: Norton, 1961.

Frye, Northrop. *Anatomy of Criticism: Four Essays*. Princeton: Princeton UP, 1971.

———. "Group Psychology and the Analysis of the Ego." *Civilization, Society and Religion*. Selected Works. Vol. 12. Harmondsworth, England: Penguin, 1991. 93–178.

———. "The Uncanny." *The Standard Edition of the Complete Psychological Works of Sigmund Freud*. Vol. 7. Trans. James Strachey. London: Hogarth, 1953–74. 219–56.

Gamble, Sarah. *Angela Carter: Writing From the Front Line*. Edinburgh: Edinburgh UP, 1997.

Gane, Gillian. "Migrancy, The Cosmopolitan Intellectual, and the Global City in *The Satanic Verses*." *Modern Fiction Studies* 48.1 (2002): 18–49.

Gasiorek, Andrzej. *Post-War British Fiction: Realism and After*. London: Edward Arnold, 1995.

Genette, Gérard *Narrative Discourse. An Essay on Method*. Trans. Jane E. Lewin. Ithaca, New York: Cornell UP, 1980.

Gibson, Andrew. "Crossing the Present: Narrative, Alterity and Gender in Postmodern Fiction." *Literature and the Contemporary: Fictions and Theories of the Present*. Ed. Roger Luckhurst and Peter Marks. Harlow, Essex: Pearson Education, 1999. 179–98.

Gibson, Jeremy, and Julian Wolfreys. *Peter Ackroyd: The Ludic and Labyrinthine Text*. New York: St. Martin's, 2000.

Gilroy, Paul. *The Black Atlantic: Modernity and Double-Consciousness*. London: Verso, 1993.

———. *"There Ain't No Black in the Union Jack": The Cultural Politics of Race and Nation*. London: Hutchinson, 1987.

Grice, Helena, and Tim Woods, eds. *I'm Telling You Stories: Jeanette Winterson and the Politics of Reading*. Amsterdam and Atlanta: Rodopi, 1998.

Haffenden, John. *Novelists in Interview*. London and New York: Methuen, 1985.

Hall, Stuart. "The Great Moving Right Show." *The Politics of Thatcherism*. Ed. Stuart Hall and Jacques Martin. London: Lawrence & Wishart, 1983. 19–39.

———. "Introduction: Who Needs Identity?" *Questions of Cultural Identity*. Ed. Stuart Hall and Paul de Gay. London: Sage, 1996. 1–17.

———. "The Meaning of New Times." Morley and Chen 223–37.

———. "Old and New Identities, Old and New Ethnicities." *Culture, Globalization and the World-System: Contemporary Conditions for the Representation of Identity*. Ed. Anthony D. King. Minneapolis: U of Minnesota P, 1997. 41–68.

———. "A Sense of Classlessness." *Universities and Left Review* 1.5 (1958): 26–32.

———. "The Toad in the Garden: Thatcherism among the Theorists." *Marxism and the Interpretation of Culture*. Ed. Cary Nelson and Lawrence Grossberg. Urbana & Chicago: U of Illinois P, 1988. 35–57.

———. "What is This 'Black' in Black Popular Culture?" Morley and Chen 465–75.

Hansson, Heidi. "The Double Voice of Metaphor: A. S. Byatt's 'Morpho Eugenia.'" *Twentieth Century Literature* 45.4 (1999): 452–66.

Harris, Andrea L. *Other Sexes: Rewriting Difference from Woolf to Winterson*. Albany, New York: State U of New York P, 2000.

Hartung-Brückner, Heike. "History and 'Englishness' in Graham Swift's *Last Orders*." *Postimperial and Postcolonial Literature in English*. 20 July 2005 <http://www.postcolonialweb.org/uk/gswift/lastorders/hhb1.html>.

Hawthorne, Mary. "Winged Victoriana." Rev. of *Angels and Insects*, by A.S. Byatt. *New Yorker* 21 June 1993: 98–100.

Head, Dominic. *The Cambridge Introduction to Modern British Fiction, 1950–2000*. Cambridge, England: Cambridge UP, 2002.

Hitchings, Henry. "Once Upon a Time Before the War." Rev. of *Atonement*, by Ian McEwan. *Financial Times* 15 Sep. 2001, Books: 4.

Hobsbawm, E. J. "Class Consciousness in History." *Identities: Race, Class, Gender, and Nationality*. Ed. Linda Martin Alcoff and Eduordo Mendieta. Oxford, England: Blackwell, 2003. 126–35.

Howard, Philip. "Swardback shafts novel trendy the." Rev. of *Time's Arrow* by Martin Amis. *Times* (London) 19 Sep. 1991: 14.

Hubbard, Kim. "Novelist Martin Amis Carries on a Family Tradition." *People Weekly* 33. 16 (23 April 1990): 117–18.

Humphries, Louise Horskjaer. "Listening for the Author's Voice: 'Un-Sexing' the Wintersonian Oevre." Bengtson, Børch, and Maagaard 3–16.

Hutcheon, Linda. *A Poetics of Postmodernism: History, Theory, Fiction*. London and New York: Routledge, 1988.

————. *The Politics of Postmodernism*. London and New York: Routledge, 1989.

Ilona, Anthony. "Hanif Kureishi's *The Buddha of Suburbia*: 'A New Way of Being British.'" *Contemporary British Fiction*. Ed. Richard J. Lane, Rod Mengham, and Philip Tew. Cambridge, England: Polity, 2003. 87–105.

Ingersoll, Earl G. "Intertextuality in L. P. Hartley's *The Go-Between* and Ian McEwan's *Atonement*." *Forum of Modern Language Studies* 40.3 (2004): 241–58.

Ishiguro, Kazuo. "Artist of his Floating World." Interview with Boyd Tonkin. *Independent* (London) 1 Apr. 2000, Features: 9.

————. "Artist in a Dirty World." Interview with Rosemary Goring. *Scotland on Sunday* 7 May 1995: 58.

————. "Between Two Worlds." Interview with Bill Bryson. *New York Times* 29 Apr. 1990, late ed., sec. 6: 38.

————. "Chartered Course." Profile/Interview with John Coldstream. *Chicago Sun-Times* 11 Oct. 2000, Features: 62.

————. "An Interview with Kazuo Ishiguro." Interview with Christopher Bigsby. *The European English Messenger* Autumn 1990: 26–29.

————. "An Interview with Kazuo Ishiguro." Interview with Gregory Mason. *Contemporary Literature* 30.3 (1989): 335–47.

————. "An Interview with Kazuo Ishiguro." Interview with Allan Vorda and Kim Herzinger. *Mississippi Review* 20.1–2 (1991): 131–54.

————. Interview with Tim Adams. *Observer Review* 20 Feb. 2005: 17.

————. "Interview with Kazuo Ishiguro." Interview with Linda Richards. *January Magazine* 2 June 2000 <http://www.januarymagazine.com/profiles/ishiguro.html>.

————. "In the Land of Memory." Interview with Adam Dunn. *cnn.com Book News*. 27 Oct. 2000. 2 June 2001 <http://www.cnn.com/2000/books/news/10/27/kazuo.ishiguro>.

————. "Ishiguro in Toronto." Interview with Suanne Kelman. *The Brick Reader*. Ed. Linda Spalding and Michael Ondaatje. Toronto: Coach House, 1991. 71–77.

————. "Ishiguro Takes a Literary Approach to the Detective Novel." Interview with Alden Mudge. *First Person Book Page*. Sep. 2000. 2 June 2001 <http://www.bookpage.com/0009bp/kazuo.ishiguro.html>.

————. "Kazuo Ishiguro Talks to Maya Jaggi." *Wasafari* 22 (1995): 20–24.

————. "Memories of Shanghai Fuel Intriguing Mystery." Interview/review with Philip Marchand. *Toronto Star* 20 May 2000, Entertainment: 1.

————. "Memory is the Terribly Treacherous Terrain." Interview with Graham Swift. *BOMB* 29 (1989): 22–23.

————. *Never Let Me Go*. New York: Knopf, 2005.

————. "Rooted in a Small Space." Interview with Dylan Otto Krider. *Kenyon Review* 20.2 (1998): 146–54.

————. "Stung by Critics, 'Remains' Author Rethinks his Style." Interview with Michael Kenney. *Boston Globe* 18 Oct. 1995, Living: 47.

————. *When We Were Orphans*. New York: Knopf, 2000.

Jaggi, Maya. "In Search of Lost Crimes." Rev. of *When We Were Orphans*, by Kazuo Ishiguro. *Guardian* 8 May 2001, Saturday Pages: 8.

Jefferson, Anne. *The Nouveau Roman and the Poetics of Fiction*. Cambridge: Cambridge UP, 1980.

Kaleta, Kenneth C. *Hanif Kureishi: Postcolonial Storyteller*. Austin: U of Texas P, 1998.

Kalliney, Peter. "Globalization, Postcoloniality, and the Problem of Literary Studies in *The Satanic Verses*." *Modern Fiction Studies* 48.1 (2002): 50–82.

Kappeler, Susanne. *The Pornography of Representation*. Cambridge: Polity, 1986.

Keenean, Sally. "Angela Carter's *The Sadeian Woman*: Feminism as Treason." *Angela Carter*. Ed. Alison Easton. London: Macmillan; New York: St. Martin's, 2000. 37–57.

Kelly, Kathleen Coyne. *A. S. Byatt*. New York: Twayne, 1996.

Kemp. Peter. "From tomb to womb." Rev. of *Time's Arrow*, by Martin Amis. *Sunday Times* (London) 22 Sep. 1991, Books: 5.

———. "Magical History Tour." "Talk with Carter". *Sunday Times* (London) 9 June 1991: sec. 6: 6–7.

———. "A Masterly Achievement." Rev. of *Atonement*, by Ian McEwan. *Sunday Times* (London) 16 Sep. 2001, sec. 9: 46.

———. "Writing for a Fall." Rev. of *Written on the Body*, by Zadie Smith. *Sunday Times* (London) 26 June 1994, sec. 7: 1–2.

Kenney, Michael. "Stung by Critics, 'Remains' Author Rethinks his Style." *Boston Globe* 18 Oct. 1995, Living: 47.

Kermode, Frank. *The Genesis of Secrecy: On the Interpretation of Narrative*. Cambridge, MA: Harvard UP, 1979.

———. "Retripotent." Rev. of *Like a Fiery Elephant: The Story of B.S. Johnson*, by Jonathan Coe. *London Review of Books* 5 Aug 2004: 11–13.

———. *The Sense of an Ending: Studies in the Theory of Fiction*. Oxford: Oxford UP, 1967.

Kiely, Robert. *Reverse Tradition: Postmodern Fictions and the Nineteenth Century Novel*. Cambridge, MA: Harvard UP, 1993.

King, Bruce. *The Internationalization of English Literature*. Oxford and New York: Oxford UP, 2004.

Kristeva, Julia. *The Kristeva Reader*. Ed. Toril Moi. New York: Columbia UP, 1986.

———. "Problèmes de la structuration du texte." *Théorie d'ensemble*. Ed. Phillipe Sollers. Paris: Seuil, 1968. 297–316.

———. *Revolution in Poetic Language*. Trans. Margaret Waller. New York: Columbia UP, 1984.

Kureishi, Hanif. *The Black Album*. New York: Scribner, 1995.

———. *The Buddha of Surburbia*. London and New York: Penguin, 1991.

———. "Hanif Kureishi on London." Interview with Colin McCabe. *Critical Quarterly* 41.3 (1999): 37–56.

———. *Intimacy*. New York: Scribner, 1999.

———. *My Beautiful Laundrette and Other Writings*. London: Faber, 1996.

———. *Sammy and Rosie Get Laid: The Script and the Diary*. London: Faber, 1988.

———. "Something Given: Reflections on Writing." Hanif Kureishi Web Site. 24 June 2005 < http://www.hanifkureishi.com/something_given.html>.

Lacan, Jacques. *Écrits: A Selection*. Trans. Alan Sheridan. New York: Norton, 1977.

———. *The Four Fundamental Concepts of Psychoanalysis*. Trans. Alan Sheridan. London and New York: Penguin, 1979.

Lane, Richard J., Rod Mengham, and Philip Tew, eds. *Contemporary British Fiction*. Cambridge, England: Polity, 2003.

Lawrence, D. H. *Kangaroo*. Harmondsworth: Penguin, 1968.

Lawson, Mark. "Against the Flow." Rev of *Saturday*, by Ian McEwan. *Guardian* 22 Jan. 2005, Guardian Saturday: 9.

Levenson, Michael. "*Angels and Insects*: Theory, Analogy, Metamorphosis." *Essays on the Fiction of A. S. Byatt*. Ed. Alexa Alfer and Michael J. Noble. Westport, CT: Greenwood P, 2001.161–74.

Lévi-Strauss, Claude. Interview. Canadian Broadcast Company. 28 July 2005 <http://www.dur.ac.uk/modern.languages/conferences/levistrauss.html>.

Lewis, Barry. *Kazuo Ishiguro.* Contemporary World Writers. Manchester, England, and New York: Manchester UP, 2000.

Lifton, Robert Jay. *The Nazi Doctors: Medical Killing and the Psychology of Genocide.* New York: Basic Books, 1986, 2000.

Lozano, María. "'How You Cuddle in the Dark Governs How You See the History of the World': A Note on Some Obsessions in Recent British Fiction." *Telling Histories: Narratizing History, Historicizing Literature.* Ed. Susana Onega. Amsterdam-Atlanta, GA: Rodopi, 1995. 117–34.

Lukács, Georg. "Class Consciousness." *Identities: Race, Class, Gender, and Nationality.* Ed. Linda Martin Alcoff and Eduordo Mendieta. Oxford, England: Blackwell, 2003. 107–25.

Luo, Shao-Pin. "'Living the Wrong Life': Kazuo Ishiguro's Unconsoled Orphans." *Dalhousie Review* 83.1 (2003): 51–80.

Lyotard, Jean-François. *The Differend: Phrases in Dispute.* Trans. Georgs van den Abbeele. Minneapolis: U of Minnesota P, 1991.

———. *Heidegger and 'the Jews'.* Trans. Andreas Michele and Mark S. Roberts. Minneapolis: U of Minnesota P, 1990.

———. *The Postmodern Condition: A Report on Knowledge.* Trans. Geoff Bennington and Brian Massumi. Minneapolis: U of Minnesota P, 1984.

Malcolm, David. *Understanding Graham Swift.* Columbia: U of South Carolina P, 2003.

Malina, Debra. *Breaking the Frame: Metalepsis and the Construction of the Subject.* Columbus, OH: Ohio State UP, 2002.

Martelle, Scott. "Exploring Typecast Writers." *Los Angeles Times* 27 July 2005: E1, 8. 47.

Martin, Richard. "'Just Words on a Page': The Novels of Christine Brooke-Rose." *Review of Contemporary Fiction* 9 (1989): 110–23.

McCarthy, Dermot. "The Limits of Irony: The Chronillogical World of Martin Amis's *Time's Arrow.*" *War, Literature and the Arts: An International Journal of the Humanities* 11.1 (1999): 294–320.

McCrone, David. *Understanding Scotland: The Sociology of a Nation.* London, New York: Routledge, 2001.

McEwan, Ian. "Adolescence and After." Interview with Christopher Ricks. *Listener* 12 Apr. 1979: 526–7.

———. "The Art of Fiction CLXXIII." Interview with Adam Begley. *Paris Review* 162 (2002): 31–60.

———. *Atonement.* New York: Doubleday, 2002.

———. "Blood and Aphorisms." Interview with Adam Hunt. *Ariel* 21 (1996): 47–50.

———. *The Cement Garden.* Harmondsworth, Middlesex and New York: Penguin, 1988.

———. "Frozen Moments." Interview with Bron Sibree. *South China Morning Post* 20 Feb. 2005: 12.

———. "He Triumphed Outside of the Mainstream." Interview with Ambrose Clancy. *Los Angeles Times* 17 May 1999: E1.

———. "Ian McEwan." Interview with Amanda Smith. *Publishers Weekly* 232. 11 (1987): 68–69.

———. "Ian McEwan Hints at a Coming Novel." Report by Alan Cowell. *New York Times,* 6 Dec. 2004, late ed.: E3.

———. "Ian McEwan Still a Virtuoso in Playing on Readers' Fears." Interview with Lewis Beale. *Los Angeles Times* 1 Apr. 2005: E1.

———. "Ian McEwan's War Zone." Interview with Holly Brubach. *Vanity Fair* Apr. 2005: 176–82.

———. Interview with Michael Silverblatt. *Bookworm*. KCRW, Santa Monica, California. 11 Jul. 2002.

———. "The Master of Literary Menace." Interview with Penelope Dening. *Irish Times* 5 Feb. 2005: Weekend, Book Reviews: 11

———. "Only Love and then Oblivion." *Guardian* 15 Sep. 2001. 23 Aug. 2005 <http://www.guardian.co.uk/wtccrash/story/0,1300,552408,00.html>.

———. *The Ploughman's Lunch*. London: Methuen, 1985.

———. "Points of Departure." Interview with Ian Hamilton. *New Review* 5.2 (1978): 9–21.

———. "Review: Interview: At Home with his Worries." Interview with Kate Kellaway. *Observer* 16 Sep. 2001, Review: 3.

———. *Saturday*. New York: Nan A. Talese/Doubleday, 2005.

Menke, Richard. "Narrative Reversals and the Thermodynamics of History in Martin Amis's *Time's Arrow*." *Modern Fiction Studies* 44.4 (1998): 959–80.

Michael, Magali Cornier. "Angela Carter's Nights at the Circus: An Engaged Feminism via Subversive Postmodern Strategies." *Contemporary Literature* (1995): 492–521.

Middleton, Peter, and Tim Woods. *Literatures of Memory: History, Time and Space in Postwar Writing*. Manchester and New York: Manchester UP, 2000.

Monterrey, Tomás. "Julian Barnes' 'Shipwreck' or Recycling Chaos into Art." *CLIO: A Journal of Literature, History and the Philosophy of History* 33.4 (2004): 415–26.

Moore-Gilbert, Bart. *Hanif Kureishi*. Contemporary World Writers. Manchester and New York: Manchester UP, 2001.

Morley, David, and Kuan-Hsing Chen, eds. *Stuart Hall: Critical Dialogues in Cultural Studies*. London and New York: Routledge, 1996.

Morrison, Jago. *Contemporary Fiction*. London and New York: Routledge, 2003.

Moseley, Merritt. *Understanding Julian Barnes*. Columbia: U of South Carolina P, 1997.

Mullan, John. "A Word in your Shell-like." Rev. of *Last Orders*, by Graham Swift. *Guardian* 19 Apr. 2003: 32.

Oakley, Ann. Review of *The Sadeian Woman*, by Angela Carter. *British Book News* Aug. 1979: 644.

Oates, Joyce Carol. "But Noah Was Not a Nice Man." Rev. of *A History of the World in 10 1/2 Chapters*, by Julian Barnes. *New York Times Book Review* 1 Oct.1989: 12–13.

Oertel, Daniel. "Effects of Garden-Pathing in Martin Amis's Novels *Time's Arrow* and *Night Train*." *Miscelánea: A Journal of English and American Studies* 22 (2001): 123–40.

O'Mahoney, John. "Triumph of the Common Man." Profile of Graham Swift. *Guardian* 1 Mar. 2003, Saturday Review: 20.

Onega, Susana. *Metafiction and Myth in the Novels of Peter Ackroyd*. Columbia, SC: Camden House, 1999.

Palmer, Paulina. "From 'Coded Mannequin' to Bird Woman: Angela Carter's Magic Flight." *Women Reading Women's Reading*. Ed. Sue Roe. New York: St. Martins, 1987. 179–205.

Parekh Report: The Future of Multi-Ethnic Britain. London: Profile Books, 2000.

Parker, Emma. "No Man's Land: Masculinity and Englishness in Graham Swift's *Last Orders*." *Posting the Male: Masculinities in Post-War and Contemporary British Literature*. Ed. Daniel Lea and Berthold Schoene. Amsterdam: Rodopi, 2003. 89–104.

Pateman, Matthew. *Julian Barnes*. Writers and their Work. Tavistock, Devon: Northcote House, 2002.

Paton, Maureen. "Sound of the Culture Clash." *Daily Express* 4 Nov. 1993.

Paxman. Jeremy. *The English: A Portrait of a People*. Woodstock and New York: Overlook P, 2001.

Peach, Linden. *Angela Carter*. New York: St. Martin's, 1998.

Pedot, Richard. "Dead Lines in Graham Swift's *Last Orders.*" *Critique: Studies in Contemporary Fiction* 44.1 (2002): 60–71.

Powell Enoch. *Freedom and Reality.* Ed. John Wood. Kingswood: Paperfront, 1969.

Raucq-Hoorickx, Isabelle. "Julian Barnes' History of the World in 10 1/2 Chapters: A Levinasian Deconstructionist Point of View." *Le Langage et L'Homme* 26.1 (1991): 47–54.

Reynolds, Margaret, and Jonathan Noakes. *Martin Amis: The Essential Guide to Contemporary Literature.* New York: Vintage, 2003.

Rimmon-Kenan, Shlomith. *A Glance Beyond Doubt: Narration, Representation, Subjectivity.* Columbus: Ohio State UP, 1996.

Robbe-Grillet, Alain. *Snapshots and Towards a New Novel.* Trans. Barbara Wright. London: Calder and Boyars, 1965.

Rosenfeld, Alvin. *A Double Dying: Reflections of Holocaust Literature.* Bloomington: Indiana UP, 1980.

Rubinson, Gregory J. "Body Languages: Scientific and Aesthetic Discourses in Jeanette Winterson's *Written on the Body.*" *Critique* 42.2 (2001): 218–32.

——. "History's Genres: Julian Barnes' *A History of the World in 10 1/2 Chapters.*" *Modern Language Studies* 30.2 (2000): 159–79.

Rushdie, Salman. *Conversations with Salman Rushdie.* Ed. Michael R. Reder. Jackson, MI: UP of Mississippi, 2000.

——. *Imaginary Homelands: Essays and Criticism 1981–1991.* London and New York: Penguin, 1992.

——. "An Interview with Salman Rushdie." Interview with John Banville. *New York Review of Books* 4 Mar. 1993: 34–36.

——. "Keeping Up with Salman Rushdie." Interview with James Fenton. *New York Review of Books* 28 Mar. 1991: 26–34.

——. *Midnight's Children.* London and New York: Penguin, 1991.

——. "Salman Rushdie Interviewed by Roger Burford Mason." *PN Review* 15.4 (1989): 15–19.

——. "Salman Rushdie Talks about *The Satanic Verses* to the London Consortium." Interview with Colin MacCabe et al. *Critical Quarterly* 38.2 (1996): 51–70.

——. *The Satanic Verses.* New York: Holt/Picador, 1997.

——. *Shalimar the Clown.* New York: Random, 2005.

——. *Shame.* New York: Random, 1984.

——. *Step Across This Line: Collected Nonfiction 1992–2002.* New York: Modern Library, 2002.

——. "What the Butler Didn't See." Rev. of *The Remains of the Day,* by Kazuo Ishiguro. *Observer* 1 May 1989: 53.

Sage, Lorna. *Angela Carter.* Writers and Their Work. Plymouth, England: Northcote House, 1994.

Salyer, Gregory. "One Good Story Leads to Another: Julian Barnes' A History of the World in 10 1/2 Chapters." Review Article. *Journal of Literature and Theology* 5.2 (1991): 220–33.

Sandhu, Sukhdev. "Pop Goes the Centre: Hanif Kureishi's London." *Postcolonial Theory and Criticism.* Ed. Laura Chrisman and Benita Parry. Cambridge: D. S. Brewer, 2000. 133–54.

Sassen, Sakia. *Globalization and its Discontents: Essays on the New Mobility of People and Money.* New York: New, 1998.

Scanlan, Margaret. *Traces of Another Time: History and Politics in Postwar British Fiction.* Princeton, NJ: Princeton UP, 1990.

Schor, Hilary M. "Sorting, Morphing, and Mourning: A. S. Byatt Ghostwrites Victorian Fiction." *Victorian Afterlife: Postmodern Culture Rewrites the Nineteenth Century.* Ed. John Kucich and Dianne F. Sadoff. Minneapolis: U of Minnesota P, 2000. 234–51.

Schulman, Sarah. "Guilty with Explanation: Jeanette Winterson's Endearing Book of Love." *Lambda Book Report* 30 Apr. 1993: 20.

Self, Will. *How the Dead Live.* New York: Grove, 2000.

Shaffer, Brian W. *Understanding Kazuo Ishiguro.* Columbia, SC: U of South Carolina P, 1998.

Shuttleworth, Sally. "Writing Natural History: Morpho Eugenia." *Essays on the Fiction of A. S. Byatt.* Ed Alexa Alfer and Michael J. Noble. Westport, CT: Greenwood P, 2001. 147–60.

Simon, Julia. *Rewriting the Body: Desire, Gender and Power in Selected Novels by Angela Carter.* Frankfurt: Peter Lang, 2004.

Solomon, Maynard, ed. *Marxism and Art: Essays Classic and Contemporary.* Detroit: Wayne State UP, 1986.

Spivak, Gayatri Chakravorty. "The Burden of English." *Orientalism and the Postcolonial Predicament.* Ed. Carol A. Breckenridge and Peter van der Veer. Philadelphia: U of Pennsylvania P, 1993. 134–57.

———. *Outside the Teaching Machine.* London, New York: Routledge, 1993.

Stevens, Christy R. "Imagining Deregulated Desire: *Written on the Body's* Revolutionary Reconstruction of Gender and Sexuality." 13 Feb. 2005 <http://www.ags.uci.edu/~clcwegsa/revolutions/Stevens.html>.

Stowers, Cath. "The Erupting Lesbian Body: Reading *Written on the Body* as a Lesbian Text." Grice and Woods 89–101.

Sutcliffe, William. "History Happens Elsewhere." Rev. of *When We Were Orphans*, by Kazuo Ishiguro. *Independent* (London) 2 Apr. 2000, Features: 49.

Swift, Graham. *Ever After.* New York: Vintage, 1993.

———. "Glowing in the Ashes." Interview with Scott Rosenberg. *Salon.* 19 July 2005 <http://archive.salon.com/weekly/swift960506.html>.

———. "Graham Swift in Interview on *Last Orders.*" Interview with Bettina Gossmann, Roman Haak, Melanie Romberg and Saskia Spindler. *Anglistik* 8.2 (1997): 155–60.

———. "I Hope I Write with my Soul First and My Mind Second." Interview with Lidia Vianu. *România Literară* 21–27 Feb. 2001. 19 July 2005 <http://www.lidiavianu.go.ro/graham_swift.html>.

———. "An Interview with Graham Swift." Interview with Catherine Bernard. *Contemporary Literature* 38.2 (1997): 217–31.

———. *Last Orders.* New York: Vintage, 1993.

———. *The Light of Day.* London and New York: Penguin, 2004.

———. *Waterland.* New York: Vintage, 1992.

Taylor, D. J. "A Newfangled and Funny Romp." Rev. of *A History of the World in 10 1/2 Chapters*, by Julian Barnes. *Spectator* 24 June 1989: 40–41.

Tew, Phillip. *The Contemporary British Novel.* London and New York: Continuum, 2004.

Thatcher, Margaret. The Resolute Approach Interview with Brian Walden. *London Weekend Television.* 16 Jan. 1983. 26 July 2004. <http://www.margaretthatcher.org/speeches/displaydocument .asp?docid=105087>.

Thompson, E. P. *The Making of the English Working Class.* New York: Vintage 1966.

Todd, Richard. *A. S. Byatt.* Writers and Their Work. Plymouth, UK: Northcote House, 1997.

Tolson, Andrew. *The Limits of Masculinity*. London: Tavistock, 1977.

Tredell, Nicolas. "Christine Brooke-Rose in Conversation." *P-N Review* Sep./Oct. 1990: 29–35.

Trueheart, Charles. "Through a Mirror, Darkly." *Washington Post* 26 Nov. 1991: B1–2.

Trussler, Michael. "Spectral Witnesses: Doubled Voice in Martin Amis's *Time's Arrow*, Toni Morrison's *Beloved* and Wim Wenders' *Wings of Desire*." *Journal of the Fantastic in the Arts* 14.1 (2002): 28–50.

Vonnegut, Kurt. *Slaughterhouse Five*. London: Panther, 1970.

Waugh, Patricia. *Metafiction: The Theory and Practice of Self-Conscious Fiction*. London and New York: Routledge, 1985.

West, Cornel. "The New Cultural Politics of Difference." *Out There: Marginalization and Contemporary Culture*. New York: The New Museum of Contemporary Art; Cambridge, MA: MIT P, 1990. 19–36.

White, Hayden. *The Content of the Form: Narrative Discourse and Historical Representation*. Baltimore: Johns Hopkins UP, 1987.

———. *Metahistory: The Historical Imagination in Nineteenth Century Europe*. Baltimore: Johns Hopkins UP, 1973.

———. *Tropics of Discourse: Essays in Cultural Criticism*. Baltimore: Johns Hopkins UP, 1978.

Widdowson, Peter. "The Novels of Graham Swift." *Literature in Context*. Ed. Rick Rylance and Judy Simons. New York: Palgrave, 2001. 209–24.

Williams, Raymond. *Key Words: A Vocabulary of Culture and Society*. Rev. ed. New York: Oxford UP, 1983.

Winnberg, Jakob. *An Aesthetics of Vulnerability: The Sentimentum and the Novels of Graham Swift*. Göteborg, Sweden: Acta Universitatis Gothoburgensis, 2003.

Winterson, Jeanette. *Art Objects: Essays on Ecstasy and Effrontery*. New York: Vintage, 1995.

———. "Experiment! It's the Only Way to be Free." *Independent on Sunday* 12 May 2002, Arts: 7.

———. "40 Years of Bond." *Guardian* 13 Sep. 2002, Guardian Friday Pages: 56.

———. *Gut Symmetries*. New York: Random House, 1998.

———. "Jeanette Winterson: The Art of Fiction CL." Interview with Audrey Bilger. *The Paris Review* 145 (1997–98): 68–112.

———. *Lighthousekeeping*. London: Fourth Estate, 2004.

———. "No, No, Jeanette." Interview with Lucretia Stewart. *Harper's Bazaar* Feb. 1993: 74–76.

———. *Oranges Are Not the Only Fruit*. London: Unwin, 1990.

———. "The Secret Life of Us." *Guardian* 25 Nov. 2002, Features: 10.

———. *Sexing the Cherry*. New York: Grove, 1989.

———. *The World and Other Places*. New York: Knopf, 1998.

———. *Written on the Body*. New York: Knopf, 1993.

Wittig, Monique. *The Lesbian Body*. Trans. David Le Vay. Boston: Beacon, 1986.

Worsthorne, Peregrine. "Race and the Pull of Patriotism." *Sunday Telegraph* 27 June 1982: 20.

Yousef, Nahem. *Hanif Kureishi's* The Buddha of Suburbia. New York and London: Continuum, 2002.

Index

Breinigsville, PA USA
09 October 2009
225552BV00003B/10/A

9 780230 008557